O9-BTO-522

HIS VAMPYRRHIC BRIDE

Recent Titles by Simon Clark from Severn House

LONDON UNDER MIDNIGHT
THE MIDNIGHT MAN
VENGEANCE CHILD
WHITBY VAMPYRRHIC

HIS VAMPYRRHIC BRIDE

Simon Clark

This first world edition published 2012
in Great Britain and in the USA by
SEVERN HOUSE PUBLISHERS LTD of
9–15 High Street, Sutton, Surrey, England, SM1 1DF.
Trade paperback edition first published
in Great Britain and the USA 2013 by
SEVERN HOUSE PUBLISHERS LTD

British Library Cataloguing in Publication Data

Clark, Simon, 1958-
  His vampyrrhic bride.
  1. Horror tales.
  I. Title
  823.9'2-dc23

ISBN-13: 978-0-7278-8184-7 (cased)
ISBN-13: 978-1-84751-445-5 (trade paper)

All Severn House titles are printed on acid-free paper.

Severn House Publishers support The Forest Stewardship Council [FSC],
the leading international forest certification organisation. All our titles that
are printed on Greenpeace-approved FSC-certified paper carry the FSC logo.

MIX
Paper from
responsible sources
FSC
www.fsc.org   FSC® C018575

Typeset by Palimpsest Book Production Ltd.,
Falkirk, Stirlingshire, Scotland.
Printed and bound in Great Britain by
MPG Books Ltd., Bodmin, Cornwall.

ONE

He sees her . . .

Tom Westonby's life changed the moment he saw the woman. She shouldn't have been there. Certainly not at this time of night.

But there she was. Tom looked out of the window and watched the stranger walk across the lawn. Moonlight flooded the valley. That other-worldly radiance gave the white cotton dress she wore a spectral glow. While her pale, yellow hair had the appearance of a luminous mist that cascaded down around her shoulders.

She was beautiful. Uncannily beautiful. Somehow dangerously beautiful. As well as tingles of physical attraction, he felt the cold, tingling sensation of an inexplicable fear trickling down his spine.

So, what was this striking, yet ghostly figure doing gliding across his lawn at midnight? The question made him wonder if he'd fallen asleep on the sofa again. These fourteen-hour working days were exhausting. Maybe he was busily dreaming about the remarkable, luminous vision dressed in white?

'My God,' he breathed, 'what on earth is she doing?'

The stranger lifted the skirts of her dress before stepping into the little pool in the garden that was fed by a natural spring. She took a deep breath as her bare feet entered the cool water. At the same time she raised her face to the moonlight, an expression of sheer bliss spread across her face. She closed her eyes, a smile touched her lips. Even from this distance, Tom could tell she loved the sensation of chilled liquid stroking her skin.

The expression on her face sang out: *this is ecstasy!*

He had two choices. Either turn away, forget he'd seen the woman, or go out there and find out what the hell she was doing on his lawn. Tom Westonby wasn't one to back down from a challenge. He decided to learn more about the mysterious beauty dipping her bare toes in the spring pool.

The possibility that this was a dream vanished when his hip smacked into the table as he strode across the room to the patio door. The blow hurt. So maybe it was the pain that made him act out of character, because a dangerous, reckless spirit seized control. He decided to confront the woman. No, he'd do more than that. This was going to get physical. His heart pounded, his breath vented in gusts through gritted teeth. A wild excitement ignited his blood.

The moment he opened the patio door and stepped out into the night air he passed the point of no return. Something significant would happen tonight. No . . . More than significant. *Tonight will be momentous.*

He follows her . . .

Tom Westonby knew that in the next few minutes life as he'd lived it would die. Nothing would ever be the same again.

The sound of his feet on the patio immediately warned the woman that she wasn't alone.

His midnight visitor turned towards him. Her eyes locked on his. There wasn't any sense of fear, or even surprise. It was as if she'd expected all along that he'd come out of the house. If she'd stayed there, then what happened next would never have happened at all.

But even though she'd held his gaze for a moment without any sign of being frightened of him, she suddenly ran. Her bare feet splashed through the shallow pool. Moonlight caught the drops of water, turning them into glittering gems that flew up to speckle her white cotton dress. By the time she left the pool those sparkling drops of water were caught in her fair hair. Twinkling diamonds flung outwards as she quickly twisted her head to watch what he'd do next.

He followed.

No. Not followed.

Chased.

With a mixture of dread and excitement, Tom realized this was more than a chase. *I'm hunting her*, he thought. *I'm actually hunting her, like she's prey.*

A small voice inside his head told him to stop. But it was the massive, roaring voice that erupted from some primeval hunting instinct that issued the orders now: CATCH HER. FORCE HER TO TELL YOU WHAT SHE WAS DOING IN THE WATER.

Sheer hunt-lust had its teeth in Tom Westonby. He focused hearing and sight on to the woman. He heard her bare feet whisper across the grass. He saw the searing white flash of her dress. Even when she'd darted out of the moonlight and into the deep, dark shadow of Thornwood Vale he still kept his eyes nailed on her. He was a wolf pursuing the vulnerable fawn. Instinct ruled his movements. Nothing else mattered. He was determined to catch the woman – seize her tightly by the arms, and . . .

. . . and then what? Rationally, he didn't know what he'd do when he caught her.

Irrationally, though? Oh, the irrational side of his brain supplied him with vivid images. That ancient beast segment of brain told him EXACTLY what he must do to her, once he'd got his hands on her.

The chase took them deeper into the forest. Mull-Rigg Hall, the house he'd just raced from, was the only property for miles. Nobody else ventured into this remote English valley at midnight.

He and the woman were alone. Just the two of them. Nobody would see. No witnesses. No one to stop the madness of what would happen next.

His dangerous thoughts . . .

The chase took them by the river. These turbulent rapids gushed down from the surrounding hills. At this time of night the water was black. Tom Westonby caught a glimpse of an eager figure that seemed to be on a vital mission. To Tom's surprise he realized that the eager figure, with the wide, staring eyes, was him. He'd seen his own reflection there in the dark waters.

What had come over him? Why was he driven to catch the woman that he'd watched dipping her bare toes into the spring pool?

As he ran through the forest he kept that blazing stare of his on the slender feminine shape. Yet other thoughts, which seemed strangely disconnected from the present, floated through his head. He remembered working long, fourteen-hour days to empty the big house of accumulated rubbish. All those heavy brown wood chairs that filled every room. His aunt must have been obsessed with them. Who knows? Maybe before she'd died she'd been planning to seize the world record for having the greatest number of uncomfortable, straight-backed chairs crammed into one house.

Yesterday, Chris Markham had phoned. Chris was his business partner – at least, he would be once they raised enough capital to open the scuba-diving school in Greece: something they'd been planning ever since they were at college together. After devoting weeks searching for suitable premises, Chris had discovered the perfect place just yards from the beach.

The big problem was this: the building's owner had demanded seventeen thousand dollars in cash. Five thousand dollars bond, twelve thousand for a year's rental in advance.

'I don't know why he wants dollars not euros,' Chris had said over the phone. 'He just does.'

'Where are we going to get that kind of money?' Tom had asked. 'We don't have anything like seventeen thousand dollars.'

'Tom, we've got to have this place. It's next to a whole bunch of hotels; think of the passing trade. It's perfect.'

'It'd be easier for us to raise the Titanic than raise seventeen thousand!'

Chris had begged Tom to somehow find the cash. What's more, he must have it by the end of the week, otherwise the landlord would find other tenants. 'Get that seventeen thou, Tom. We'll never find another place as good as this.'

Before ending the call, Chris had reminded Tom that serious girl-friends were forbidden until they'd got the dive school up and running. DIVE SCHOOL FIRST. MARRY THE GIRL OF YOUR DREAMS LATER. That's the rule they'd agreed upon back in their college days. Not that they'd taken a monastic vow of celibacy. Both had enjoyed casual dating; quite a few girls had featured in their lives.

Tom murmured the words, 'Seventeen thousand,' as he pursued the stranger . . . or was it his intended victim . . . down the forest path.

Seventeen thousand dollars. Where am I going to get seventeen grand by the end of the week? He'd thought about nothing else all day. Even tonight, when he'd been clearing the basement of yet more wooden chairs, he'd been so preoccupied with schemes for mustering the cash that he'd accidentally kicked over a big glass jar that contained a green spirit. Probably the kind of stuff used to clean paintbrushes, though there must have been half a gallon at least. In that confined place its stench had made him dizzy.

Come to think of it, he told himself, *I might still be high on the fumes. That's why I'm chasing some woman I saw in the garden pond.*

He realized that the intoxicating vapour might leave his body, if he took deep enough breaths. But it was far too late. Tom Westonby sped around the trunk of a huge oak and found himself face-to-face with the mysterious creature he was hunting.

A sudden violence . . .

'Are you following me?' the bewitching stranger asked in a surprisingly soft voice. The tone suggested mild curiosity rather than terror at being pursued by a menacing figure at midnight.

Tom Westonby stood there panting. Not for a moment had he expected her to stop running. He'd thought he'd have to grab hold of her to prevent her escape. For a moment all he could do was stare in astonishment. Her pale blue eyes were as striking as the incredibly light blonde hair. It seemed more like a luminous mist than individual hairs. He judged her to be close to his age. Twenty-three or thereabouts. *And she really is beautiful. Amazingly beautiful.*

'I asked if you were following me.' Her words seemed more like a pleasant invitation to agree, rather than an accusation. The woman in the white dress didn't even appear to be annoyed that she'd been pursued. 'You *were* following me, weren't you, Tom?'

'You were on my property.'

'Oh? Your property?'

'My parents' property. I'm clearing out the place before they move their stuff in. They're planning—' He stopped himself from saying more. The thing is, he wanted to say more. Her wide-eyed expression gently encouraged him to keep talking.

'So you're living there by yourself, Tom?'

'Wait a minute, how do you know my name?'

'Do you usually chase girls you've never met before in the dead of night?'

'You were trespassing.'

'And now you want to prove how tough you are?'

'No . . .' But he recalled the hot excitement pumping through his veins as he'd chased her. 'I just wanted to know what you were doing in my pond.'

'Your parents' pond,' she corrected.

'What's that supposed to mean?'

'Well . . .' Her eyes fixed on his. 'Owning that big house, they must be rich.'

'What's it to you?'

'Why don't you ask your parents to give you the seventeen thousand dollars?'

Tom stared at her in surprise. 'What seventeen thousand dollars?'

'You need the rent money, don't you?' She gave a knowing smile. 'And by the end of the week?'

'Hey.' His surprise ignited into anger. 'How do you know about that?'

'I just do.'

'I've never even met you before.'

'Well, you have now,' she said as she turned away. 'Goodnight, Tom.'

'Wait! How the hell do you know about the seventeen thousand dollars?'

She silently darted away into the forest shadows.

Tom shouted, 'I told you to wait!'

He became the hunter again – in furious pursuit of his prey. Dear God, he *would* put his hands on her this time. He imagined how her fragile arms would feel when he gripped them in his muscular fists. Even though the fumes from the green spirit still made him groggy, he ran faster. His heart pounded.

Just wait till I get my hands on you . . .

He'd only just lost sight of the woman when the branches crashed above his head. He heard twigs snapping. Then a heavy object slammed into his back. He yelled as he was flung upwards. For a moment, he flew through the air high above the ground. Pain tore through him.

I'm dying, he thought in surprise. *I'm actually dying . . .*

Moonlight pierced the leaves. Suddenly, there were faces. Dozens of faces. Eyes glared at him.

Then darkness fell. And nothing more.

TWO

Tom Westonby opened his eyes. The first words that entered his head were: *I've killed her.*

The sun blazed down from a clear blue sky. He was lying on the riverbank, and he was hurting all over.

'I murdered the stranger.' This time the horror of those words exploded inside his head. Tom lurched to his feet. The sudden movement ramped up the agony. But there were more important things to worry about than mere physical pain.

Because memories of the night before came hurtling back. The woman . . . He'd seen the woman on the lawn at midnight. Then, like a madman, he'd pursued her. He'd relentlessly chased her through the forest.

What was I thinking? His heart pounded as a growing sense of dread gripped him. *It's like I was determined to murder her.*

His eyes swept over the riverbank. He absolutely expected to see the fair-haired woman in the white cotton dress. His imagination conjured visions of her lying there dead, her arms flung out, eyes staring. There'd be blood . . . Oh, yes, there'd be blood – great crimson pools of it. Blood would smear the grass. Her white dress would be drenched with a violent, screaming red.

Tom Westonby frantically searched amongst the trees.

I've murdered her . . . What have I done with the body?

Behind every rock and beneath every bush he expected to see the corpse. Tom's chest heaved. Panic gripped him. As he hyperventilated, the forest leaves became a vivid green, like dazzling green fire. Desperately, he tried to make sense of the confusing memories of last night.

I caught the woman. We argued. When I realized she'd been spying on me and knew about the seventeen thousand dollars, I got angry, I grabbed hold of her. Then I murdered her.

Tom ran his fingers through his hair. 'No,' he hissed. 'She ran off . . . *then someone attacked me*.' This recollection brought a surge of relief. He sighed as his muscles began to relax. 'Someone hit me from behind.' The more he thought about what really did happen, the more he realized he'd been the victim. 'Maybe that's how they do muggings in this part of England.' He found himself so relieved that he hadn't slaughtered a stranger in cold blood, he started to smile. 'It's obvious. Muggers use a beautiful woman to lure the victim from the house – that's when the accomplices pounce.'

He scanned the riverbank again. The forest appeared tranquil. There wouldn't be a body to find. He'd murdered no one. No, he was the victim. A gang of rural muggers had made a fool of the city boy.

Tom's back hurt most from the blow. The force of the impact

had painfully wrenched the muscles. He didn't think he'd been
punched or kicked. Even so, he decided to check his reflection in
the river for black eyes and busted lips.

He made his way down the bank where he crouched at the water's
edge. The melody of the river pouring over the stones had a calming
effect. His usual sense of well-being returned. Once again he was
the twenty-three-year-old easy-going guy with a plan to open a
scuba-diving school in Greece – not a murderer facing prison.

Tom Westonby examined his reflection in the water. His dark
hair stuck up in tufts. What else can you expect from sleeping
outdoors? His brown eyes were clear. There were no signs of being
punched. What there was, in massive abundance, were red blotches.
Midges had made a meal of his face. Just the sight of them triggered
a tide of itchiness. A rash of insect bites covered his bare arms, too.
He scooped up handfuls of water to drench his skin. Its coldness
helped counteract that hot itch of the bites. The sooner he grabbed
a shower the better. Then get to work with the antiseptic
ointment.

As he sluiced his face he noticed that the gold chain was still
around his neck. He checked his watch. 'Still there,' he murmured
in surprise.

Quickly, he stood up to yell into the forest. 'You muggers are
crap! In fact, you've got to be the crappiest muggers ever! You
forgot to take this!' He pointed at the diver's watch on his wrist.
'You are absolutely crapping useless!'

Even as images blazed inside his head of a gang of thugs comically blaming one another for not stealing the expensive watch,
another explanation of last night's events occurred to him. A more
rational one.

The jar of green spirit he'd smashed in the basement? He'd been
working in those pungent fumes for more than an hour. When he'd
finally cleaned up the glass, and the pool of green stuff that reeked
so powerfully, it felt as if his tonsils had caught fire; he'd gone
upstairs to grab some fresh air at the window. That's when he'd
seen the beautiful barefoot stranger.

Or thought he'd seen her.

By the time Tom Westonby headed home along the woodland
path, he found himself grinning. *I haven't killed anyone. I haven't
been attacked. There never were any muggers. No . . . I was high
on fumes. I was like a glue-junkie after a monster sniffing-binge.*

As he pushed open the back gate that lead to Mull-Rigg Hall he realized what had really happened last night. He'd been intoxicated by the spirit vapour – high as a solvent-junkie. All this about seeing the woman in the pond had been a bizarre vision generated by inhaling the chemical. After that, he'd gone on a crazy rampage through the forest – all the time, hallucinating like mad.

I must have fallen over one of the boulders down by the river, he told himself, and the grin got even bigger. *Then I passed out. Just wait until Chris hears about this. He'll be laughing for a week.*

As Tom headed towards the house a stern, male voice rang out: 'Mr Westonby? I have reason to believe that you have just returned from the scene of a crime.'

THREE

Tom Westonby's heart nearly exploded when he heard those words: '. . . *you have just returned from the scene of a crime.*'

He spun round on the path to catch sight of a broad face grinning at him from over the fence.

'Chester! Are you trying to blow a heart valve or something?'

Chester jerked an oily thumb back over his shoulder. 'I brought the lawnmower that my dad said you're renting. The van's parked on the drive. When I couldn't get you to answer the door I was just about to give up, then . . .' He gave a knowing smile. 'I saw you sneaking back from the scene of the crime.'

'What scene of the crime?' Spasms of guilt clenched up his muscles. For one disturbing moment he wondered if he really had killed the woman in white. 'What the hell are you talking about, Chester?'

Chester vaulted over the fence; he couldn't keep that big smile off his face. 'You know what crime I'm talking about.'

'Oh?' Tom finally guessed what Chester was hinting.

'Coming home at nine in the morning? Looking like you've been mauled by a she-tiger? You've had a night on the tiles, haven't you?'

Tom smiled. 'Something like that.'

'Who is she?'

''Ah . . . that's just for me to know, Chester.'

'Enough said, Tom. Your love secrets are safe with me.'

Even though Chester's talk about 'scene of the crime' was just a leg-pull, Tom still found himself changing the subject. 'You say you brought the mower?'

'Don't worry, Tom. I won't bug you about your girlfriend. But you could always bring her to the pub. Tomorrow's quiz night.'

'Cheers.' Once more he changed the subject. 'Did you bring the chainsaw as well?'

Chester said that he had. They followed the path round the house to where Chester had parked the van.

Tom had known Chester Kenyon for the past two months, ever since Tom had moved into Mull-Rigg Hall. Chester – or Cheery Chester as he was popularly known, on account of his happy nature – stood six foot six, had a mop of curly, blonde hair, and always wore a nigh-on impossibly broad smile. The man was clumsily playful, endearing, and nobody could ever actually bring themselves to be angry with him. He was in his early twenties, and he worked with his father at the village tool-hire store. Come to that, you could get anything repaired at the Kenyons', from a computer to a combine harvester. The people in small, back-of-beyond communities like Danby-Mask tended to be versatile. Even to the point of being a little self-contained world all of their own.

Tom almost told Chester about accidentally getting high on fumes in the cellar and then hallucinating like crazy as he chased some non-existent woman through the woods. After a moment's thought, though, Tom decided against sharing the anecdote. Chester would tease him relentlessly for months to come. Chester was a great guy. Tom liked him. However, Chester believed his mission in life was to keep all his friends laughing. And sometimes that would mean endless micky-taking. Chester might be the warmest-hearted guy in the world, yet sometimes he had the sensitivity of a charging bull.

Chester opened the back doors of the van. Tom helped the big man lift the mower on to the drive. After that, he hauled out the chainsaw while Chester unloaded a fuel can.

The gentle giant chatted in that amiable way of his as he dealt with the paperwork. 'It's the first time I've been back to the house since your aunt died.'

'I'd never been here before, either,' Tom confessed. 'It amazed me how big the place is. It's a proper mansion.'

'Dad said your aunt was a good customer . . . always paid her bills early.' As Chester wrote on the clipboard he glanced round the garden. 'So you landed the job of getting the house ready for your parents to move in?'

'It's a full-time job, too. For some reason the house is full of chairs. You know, the straight-backed kind? I think my aunt must have been a bit nutty about them.'

'She was a nice lady, Tom. She'd set out the chairs on the back lawn and invite local people to cream teas.' He held out the clipboard for Tom to sign. The rental agreement was covered with Chester's big oily fingerprints. 'I'm glad somebody will be living here again. I'd hate to see the place fall apart.'

'Lately, I've been concentrating on moving all those chairs into the garage, so there'll be space for the new furniture.'

'And cutting the grass.' Chester nodded at the mower.

'My mother wanted the garden tidying so Owen will have some-where to play.'

'Owen?' Chester's eyebrows rose in surprise. 'Owen Gibson? Your aunt's son?'

'Yeah, my parents inherited a chunk of my aunt's money. They also inherited her kid.' Tom paused. 'That sounds a bit brutal. I didn't mean it to come out like that.'

Chester shrugged. 'I'm always saying stuff that comes out wrong. Last week I told Grace Harrap that she didn't look a day over forty.'

'Chester. She's twenty-six.'

'I know.' He gave a pained sigh. 'Grace took the ice out of her drink and rammed it down my shirt.'

'Maybe she's flirting?'

'Flirting? I fell over a chair and nearly smashed my head on the pub's fireplace trying to get that flipping ice out.'

Tom handed the clipboard back. 'Owen's only ten. I'm not sure how to talk to him. Sometimes he doesn't say a word for days.'

'It's going to be hard on him losing his mother at ten years old.' Suddenly, the man that Tom thought of as being the giant toddler sounded so mature and wise. 'Owen's going to need a lot of love and patience. He found the body, didn't he?'

'The coroner said she'd died of a heart attack out here on the drive.'

After a pause, Chester was the one to change the subject this time. 'How you doing with your diving school? Any sign of going to live in Greece yet, you lucky sod?'

'We're getting there. Chris found some premises next to the beach.' He didn't mention the worrying conundrum of how they'd claw together seventeen thousand dollars by the end of the week.

'Your own diving school? It'll be a dream come true, won't it?'

'Believe it or not, we started planning this three years ago. It's taken eighteen months to save up enough money to get the ball rolling.' *And we're still seventeen thou short.*

'You'll be taking her?'

'Taking who?'

'The new girlfriend. The one you were tangling with last night.'

Tom decided he would keep that particular girl a secret. Especially as she was a product of hallucination. So he just shrugged, winked, and said, 'Who knows?'

'OK.' Chester laughed. 'I'll keep my schnozz out of your biz. Right. I'll show you how to use the chainsaw.'

'I'm sure I can figure it out.'

'No. I'll give you a safety lesson. If you cut your legs off with that thing don't come running to me, complaining that I didn't teach you how to use it.'

'If I cut my legs off, I won't be running anywhere.'

'Just my little joke, Tom, to put you at ease.'

A low roar came from the direction of the forest.

Chester nodded towards the trees. 'Don't worry about the sound. It's only the local dragon clearing his throat.'

'The local what?'

'The dragon. Haven't you heard of it? A dragon's supposed to roam those woods.'

'Sounded like a bus to me.'

'When we were kids we were told a dragon lurked up here in the valley. A big, ugly monster that loves to suck out your blood.'

The sound of the bus grew closer.

'I haven't seen any dragons.' Tom played along with the joke.

'Neither did us kids. I reckon they made up the dragon story to keep us away from the river.' He picked up the chainsaw. 'See the D-ring? That's how you start the motor.'

Tom wasn't listening. He couldn't take his eyes from the bus passing by.

'Did you hear me, Tom? This starts the motor.'

Tom didn't hear. He wasn't thinking about the chainsaw. Or about the appetites of the neighbourhood dragon. He was watching the bus. Or, rather, a specific individual on the bus.

Because sitting in the middle of the vehicle was a woman dressed in a white blouse. The woman from the hallucination. The same woman he thought he'd chased through the forest last night.

She turned her head. He thought he saw her nod in his direction. Then the bus accelerated away into the distance.

FOUR

Cheery Chester drove away from Mull-Rigg Hall. He waved a happy goodbye from the van window and left Tom Westonby alone with the rented lawnmower, the chainsaw, and his thoughts.

Tom ate baked beans on toast for lunch. Nothing like beans, the boldly symphonic fruit, to inflate a wetsuit, or so the scuba fraternity insisted. The sense of humour shared by professional divers tended to be pretty unsophisticated at the best of times.

After he'd eaten his meal Tom prowled the grounds of Mull-Rigg Hall. He'd lived here alone for the past two months, ever since he'd agreed to get the place ready for his mother and father, and what amounted to a new brother. His late aunt's son, Owen, was likeable. Tom was sure he'd get on well with the ten-year-old once he got to know him better. In truth, though, they'd spent very little time together. Before Tom had accepted the role of janitor here, along with the post of general fixer-upper, he'd taken a whole string of jobs in different parts of the country in order to raise money for the new dive school.

Today, Tom found himself preoccupied with how he'd find the seventeen thousand dollars for the premises in Greece. It didn't help matters that he'd seemed to have a weird out-of-body experience last night after accidentally inhaling those fumes in the basement. By this morning he'd convinced himself he'd been in the grip of a bizarre hallucination: that he'd been chasing nothing more than a phantom of his own imagination through the forest.

However, just an hour ago there'd been another twist to that particular story. He'd actually seen the woman riding by on a bus. So who was she? The beautiful stranger with fair hair.

What really troubled Tom was that the woman must have been in the garden at midnight. Therefore, she really *had* been dipping her bare feet into the pond. So that meant he *must* have pursued her. Dear God, he'd been chasing her like he was going to attack her or something!

I don't stalk women. It's out of character for me to grab hold of a stranger like that. He kept telling himself this to avoid the guilty notion that he might have frightened someone who'd been innocently taking a midnight stroll. *Though that's a dangerous thing for a woman to do, even in the countryside.* He decided the intoxicating effect of the spirit had briefly sent him . . . what? Crazy? Psychotic? Murderous?

Shivers ran down his back. His imagination conjured up big, bright pictures of what he might have done after the woman made him angry by revealing that she'd been spying on him. As he paced about the lawn he found himself, to his horror, picturing how he might have grabbed hold of the stranger before strangling the life out of her. Then what? Frantically returning to the house for a spade so he could dig a grave out in the woods? Or dumping the corpse in the river?

Those gruesome scenarios unsettled him so much that he couldn't concentrate on any one job. He'd a long list of chores – rooms to be emptied of the army of chairs that his aunt had accumulated, walls to be painted, new curtain tracks to be fitted, fences to be repaired, lawns to be cut, dead wood to be lopped (the orchard was a spectacular jungle). Yet he couldn't settle on any one task.

He mooched from one of the mansion's ten bedrooms to the other. Started to remove plastic light-switch covers to replace them with the beautiful antique brass ones bought at auction, then found himself remembering – or was that obsessing? – about the woman in white. Eventually, he returned to the basement.

The fumes still caught at the back of his throat. Even after one lungful of vapour coming off the spirit that had soaked into the brick floor he felt light-headed. His lips started to tingle. Brick walls began to ripple strangely. It was a wonder he hadn't choked to death last night. Tom quickly opened the hatch that once allowed delivery men to pour coal down into the cellar. With the hatch open, the air should start to circulate and dispel the evaporated spirit. He decided not to return to the basement until the fumes had gone.

In order to get some fresh air himself, he strolled around the garden. It wasn't long before he found himself by the pond where *she* had walked barefoot.

Ponds tend to be slimy. At the bottom, there's usually a disgustingly noxious black layer of mud and rotting leaves, which would be vile to actually walk on.

However, this pond, fed by a natural spring, contained beautifully clear water. In bright sunlight, the liquid looked deliciously sweet. A sparkling Perrier effect. There was no foul, black mulch at the bottom. On the contrary, the pond-bed was covered with light grey sand, speckled with tiny blue pebbles. He found himself thinking that on a warm, summer's night, the pond would be pleasant to bathe hot, tired feet. Even a skinny-dip seemed a temptingly refreshing way to escape the heat.

Outdoors was definitely more attractive than cooping himself up inside and drilling holes in dusty plasterwork so he could install light switches. Now the chainsaw had arrived he could make a start on taming the orchard.

He headed back round the house towards the garage. At first sight, the mansion had seemed intimidating. Its size, its age, the imposing pillars at the front. The edifice had resembled a Victorian courthouse. The kind of place where hungry kids arrested for stealing bread would be sentenced to go to rat-infested jails.

However, he'd grown to like the building. The roof tiles were as red as sun-ripened tomatoes. The stonework had mellowed down to a soft, buttery yellow. A slate tablet over the front door boasted that Mull-Rigg Hall had been *Raised From Ruin In The Year Of Our Lord 1866*. That's when the pillars and imposingly posh frontage had been added.

Tom collected the chainsaw from the garage. When you're twenty-three, chopping down dead trees with a powerful, motor-driven saw is immensely appealing. Even Chester's jokey warning of 'if you cut your legs off with that thing, don't come running to me' did nothing to lessen his enthusiasm to start blasting tree trunks with the ferocious blade.

Tom Westonby had just returned to the driveway when he heard a familiar roar.

The bus was making its return journey. At that moment, he recalled a vivid image of the bus as it headed to the village a couple of hours ago. The stranger in white had been on board. The one he'd pursued through the forest at midnight.

Without a second's hesitation, he dashed to the end of the drive. He was just in time to see the bus pass by the gates. There were a dozen passengers: mainly adults with bags of groceries. His heart pounded as he searched the faces.

Where was the woman in white? He scanned face after face. Where was that flow of pale, almost luminous blonde hair?

Twin girls were in the seat that his midnight stranger had occupied earlier. They were about eight years old; simultaneously, both stuck their tongues out at him.

The bus roared away.

His heart went from pounding with excitement to a plunge of disappointment.

Maybe I really did imagine her, he told himself as he headed back to the garage. *Not that I want to see her again.* He tried to rationalize away his confused swirl of feelings. *After all, why on earth would I want to see her? If she's prowling around the forest at midnight she must be a nut-job.*

'Hello.'

Catching a lungful of air, he spun round.

There at the end of the drive stood the stranger. His gaze swept over her, taking in the blue eyes, the beautiful face, and the mist of pale, blonde hair.

She took a step towards the gate, her head tilting slightly to the side as she studied his face; it seemed as if she was reading the thoughts inside his head.

'I got off the bus around the corner.' Her voice possessed a pleasant, light quality. 'I wanted to pay you a visit.'

'Oh?' He knew his response was staggeringly inarticulate. Because at that moment he felt spectacularly inarticulate. What did you say to someone you'd hunted like a wild animal?

'You were planning to kill me last night, weren't you, Tom?'

All he could do at that moment was stare in shock. Once more he had a vision of being hauled away to jail. *Surely, the woman will complain to the police. She'll tell them that she's been assaulted by the savage madman of Mull-Rigg Hall.*

Her lips formed a ghost of a smile. 'Well, Tom, here I am. Your helpless victim. The one you attacked last night. So . . .' Her gaze turned to the chainsaw in his hand. 'Aren't you going to finish what you started?'

FIVE

Tom Westonby stood there on the drive and gawped at the stranger who had just had made that extraordinary suggestion: *aren't you going to finish what you started?* The way her eyes had fixed on the chainsaw suggested she really believed he would attack her.

Tom's patience vanished. He realized she was playing games with him, and that annoyed him so much that he put the chainsaw down, then rounded on the woman.

'Don't be so ridiculous!' he snapped.

'Ridiculous? I'm not the one who goes chasing after people they've never met before.' Her blue eyes registered genuine shock at the abrupt way he'd spoken.

'I've got every right to chase trespassers. You shouldn't have been on this property. Were you seeing what you could steal from the house? Because I know you weren't alone, were you? One of your friends clubbed me from behind.' As he snarled the words, he still couldn't prevent himself from giving her the kind of visual examination that many young males give females.

The part of his brain reserved for noting details about girls filed the following:

Breasts: Great breasts. Wonderful breasts.
Hair: Blonde.
Build: Slender. Delicate. Hands very delicate, too.
Breasts: Wait . . . breasts already noted. Don't have to check those again.
Nevertheless: Breasts. Great breasts. The white cotton blouse shows them off nicely. Wonderfully.
Eyes: Pale blue.
Mouth: Small. Lips with character. The way the bottom lip pushes out slightly.
Breasts: You've done breasts. They're already covered.
Can you imagine them uncovered?

He realized his eyes had moved down her calf-length white cotton skirt to make mental notes about her delicate bare toes, which were revealed by a pair of sandals.

'Listen. Whoever attacked me . . . whichever one of your friends . . . left me for dead by the river . . .' Several million years of nature's programming wouldn't quit. Male instinct demanded he note the way she pushed her hair back from her shoulders. 'I woke up this morning covered with insect bites. I ache so much I feel like I've been hit by a rhino.'

She didn't raise her voice. Even so, she spoke firmly. 'You attacked *me*, Tom. As for you being attacked, I haven't a clue what you're talking about.'

'Someone hit me from behind.' His voice wavered slightly. He'd been so high on those fumes he wasn't exactly sure of the details. Other than that he'd found himself flying through the air. Meanwhile, an important question needed answering: 'And how the hell do you know my name?'

'I also know that you're a nice person.'

'What's that supposed to mean?'

'You were acting out of character last night.'

'You know nothing about me.' He didn't want her thinking she'd surprised him with this statement – but she had.

'You feed the wild fox cubs in the orchard.'

'How do you know about that?'

'Their mother had died. You're keeping those cubs alive.'

'What's all this about? I don't even know your name.'

'Do you want to know it?'

'What I want to know is how you've found out private stuff about me.'

'Like the seventeen thousand dollars you're trying to raise?'

'You better leave now, Miss Whoever-you-are.' He felt his anger rising.

'I came here to apologize.'

'For what?'

She looked him in the eye. 'For frightening you last night.'

'Frightening me? Ha! You're crazy.'

'I'm also thirsty. It's such a hot day. I hoped you'd invite me into your garden for a cold drink.'

She couldn't have surprised him more if she'd suddenly clawed at his face.

'A drink?' he echoed. 'The last thing I'm going to do is offer you a drink. Now for the last time: go away. Keep walking down that road. And don't come back.'

SIX

Tom Westonby stopped dead. For a moment this seemed so unreal. *Why am I fetching the girl a drink?* he asked himself. *I've just told her to clear off, for goodness' sake. I must be going mad.* Then he shook his head before walking out of the house.

'Here's some lemonade.' Tom didn't want to seem like some pushover that she'd just taken control of so he added, 'There's no ice. You'll just have to make do with it as is.' He handed her the glass . . . and, yes, he absolutely felt every inch the pushover that the woman had just taken control of.

'It's fine.' She took the drink. 'Thanks.'

'You already know I'm called Tom.'

'Tom Westonby. Yes, I overheard people talking about you in the village.'

'Oh.'

'You're already famous. The girls there are excited about the handsome guy that inherited Mull-Rigg Hall.'

'My parents inherited it. Well, to be more accurate, my parents have it until my cousin takes full ownership when he's eighteen.'

'Village girls don't quibble over those kind of details.'

'And you are?'

'Nicola Bekk.' She held out her free hand.

Tom shook it. Her hand was small and delicate in his muscular paw. She seemed more like an artistic arrangement of deliciously light bones under that pale skin. Tom Westonby felt his earlier hostility melting away. *Yes, OK, she trespassed last night. She's got an odd sense of humour. She's outspoken. But she's extremely good to look at.*

She possessed another quality too, which he couldn't readily identify. Charisma? Self-confidence? No, more powerful than that. Almost a sense of being invincible. An aura of strength. Once, at school, a teacher had brought in a war hero to talk about his experiences. He'd survived being blown clean out of a building by an artillery shell. After that, a sniper shot him in the chest. The veteran had shrugged. 'I've been blown up and I've been shot,' he'd said. 'If that didn't kill me, then there must be a friendly saint taking care of me.'

Nicola Bekk had that same air about her. As if she had an all-powerful protector.

Even as they chatted she strode confidently into the garage.

'I noticed the van,' she said brightly, then read what was painted on its side out loud. 'Markham & Westonby – Scuba School.'

'I'm planning to drive that down to Greece later this year. Me and my business partner are starting a dive school.'

'The "Scuba School" on the van suggested that's the case.'

He saw from her expression that she was gently teasing him. Now the ice had been broken he didn't mind. In fact, he'd started to feel lonely up here all by himself at Mull-Rigg Hall. He wondered if there was a chance that he and Nicola might . . .

'And all this equipment.' She seemed impressed.

He patted a shelf on which were stacked a dozen aqualung tanks. 'We picked them up cheap at an auction. Most are in good condition.' He pulled a cylinder from the shelf. 'This one isn't. See the scratches and the gouges?'

'So, it's no good?'

'No good? It's lethal. It's a bomb waiting to go boom.' He enjoyed her interest. 'Just imagine, if you took all the air in a garage as big as this and squashed it down into a cylinder that's not much bigger than a family-size carton of milk. The pressures are enormous.'

'So that thing is likely to kill us?'

'It's empty. We're perfectly safe.' He put the cylinder back on the shelf. 'Though this tank's only fit for scrap metal.'

'All that equipment must have been expensive?'

'We've been saving for the last eighteen months.' He shot her a look. 'And you already know . . . somehow . . . that we need another seventeen thousand dollars.'

'And by the end of the week.'

That flicker of anger returned. 'How do you know so much about my private finances?'

'I happened to be walking along the path at the other side of your fence. You were in the orchard when you were talking on the phone.'

'And you eavesdropped?'

'I could hardly throw myself in the river to stop hearing, could I?'

To his surprise he found himself laughing. 'Point taken.' That teasing way of hers suggested that she wanted to engage with him. This was playful sparring.

So, do you want to play, Nicola?

Nicola turned her attention to the straight-backed chairs that occupied three-quarters of the garage space. 'I used to love your aunt's garden parties.'

'So you came, too?'

'Only after the other villagers had gone.'

'Oh?'

'Your aunt gave me and my mother big bowls full of strawberries and cream.' She smiled as she remembered happy times. 'When I was a little girl your aunt let me paddle in the pond.'

'You were paddling last night.'

'I just wanted to find out if walking barefoot in the water was as nice as I remembered.'

'And was it?'

She nodded. 'Lovely. Like angels kissing your feet.'

'Who attacked me last night, Nicola?'

'Have you heard about our dragon?'

'Coincidentally, Chester Kenyon was telling me about it this morning.'

'Let's say the dragon gave you a flick of his tail.'

That quirky sense of humour again – he liked it. 'Chester said that the dragon was an invention of the adults to keep children away from the river.'

'Don't let my mother hear you saying that. She's very particular about our dragon.'

Tom fixed her with a serious look. 'I don't believe in dragons, Nicola.'

'Suit yourself.'

'So who knocked me clean off my feet?'

'Thanks for the drink, Tom.' She handed him the glass, then walked smartly away.

'Wait!'

'I'm expected home.'

He followed her to the gate. When she started to run he ran, too. At that moment, he hated the idea of her slipping away.

'Nicola. There's a quiz at the George tomorrow. Do you want to come with me?'

'The village pub isn't for me.'

'Oh.' So there was the brush-off. He did what a twenty-three-year-old guy does with rejection. Tried to look cool about the snub. While feeling like crap inside.

Nicola ran along the road. Her white cotton skirt and blouse resembled a bright flame against the shade of the trees. At the entrance to the woodland path she stopped.

Then she sang out, 'You could always come over to my house tomorrow?'

'OK,' he called back, trying to be nonchalant. Yet a fiery excitement flared up in his veins. Already, the erotic possibilities of Nicola flooded his mind. 'How do I find your house?'

An intimate meal for two at Nicola's? Result!

'No, I'll pick you up at six. My mother wants to meet you.'

She waved before vanishing into the wood.

Her mother's going to be there? A chaperoned date wasn't what he was hoping for.

SEVEN

This would be an easy robbery. The cottage in the forest was so remote it was a joke. The two men passed the can of beer between themselves and laughed.

'Shit. That dump should be called The Last Place On Earth.'

'World's End.'

'Middle Of Bastard Nowhere.'

Zip Pearson lit a cigarette. This was going to be so bloody easy. They'd been staking out the cottage since early evening. The little crap-heap of stones that passed for a home was at the end of a path. There wasn't so much as a frigging road. Even if the two bitches in the house could make a phone call it would take an hour for the police to reach here.

He pulled on the cigarette. Runty, the rat-faced guy he was with, squinted at the burning tip of the cigarette in the darkness.

'Should you be smoking, Zip?' he wheezed. 'In a place like this you can spot a cigarette from miles away.'

'Who's out there to see, Runty? Who'd give a damn? This place is the end of the world, isn't it?'

'Yeah, but if someone saw . . .'

'Scared, Runty?'

'No.'

'Then stop whining.'

'I know I'll end up back inside. I just don't want it to be before my kid gets married.'

Zip pretended to play a violin. 'You're breaking my heart, Runty. Just look at these tears pouring down my face.'

'Yeah, it's OK for a psycho like you. You don't care whether you do time or not.'

Zip and Runty were at the bottom of crime's career ladder. They earned their cash by thieving copper cable from railway tracks or peeling lead off church roofs. The other easy picking for lowlifes like them was driving round the countryside, searching out remote farms and houses they could rob. What marked Zip out from the other rural burglary packs was that he liked to hit occupied houses. That way he could take the credit and debit cards. Of course, he had to get the pin numbers, too.

That's where the entertainment started. After he'd tied up the homeowners, he enjoyed making them give him the pin codes. Sometimes he'd even push them hard enough to reveal where they'd hidden their cash. It was surprising how many people kept large amounts of banknotes at home these days.

'OK, Runty.' He sucked on the cigarette. 'Let's get 'em done.'

'Go easy on the women.'

'You've got to get rough. Otherwise they don't give up the numbers.'

'Shit, Zip, you nearly killed that old bitch last time.'

'Stop whining and move your stinking backside.'

After Zip had lobbed the beer can into the bushes, he picked up the rucksack with his tools of the trade – hammers, screwdrivers, tough nylon string to tie up his victims, and gardeners' secateurs. If he threatened to cut off fingers with the secateurs, that generally had pin numbers spilling from people's lips in no time.

The two men headed through the dark.

Even Zip appreciated this was real darkness. Deep darkness. Total darkness. He had to switch on the flashlight otherwise they'd have both blundered into tree trunks.

'Think about it, Zip,' hissed Runty. 'Don't end up killing those women. I'm not going down for murder.'

'They're going to die one day, Runty.' He laughed. 'Didn't your mammy tell you that everyone dies one day?'

'Just threaten them, OK? No cutting off fingers.'

'Sensitive soul, aren't you?'

'What you did to that guy at the pig farm made me puke.'

'He wouldn't cough the numbers, would he?' Zip laughed again. He was getting excited about the thought of frightening the women in the cottage. 'After I'd finished with pig guy he'd got nothing left to pick his nose with, had he?'

'I'm not laughing, Zip. I'm not laughing.'

Zip shone the light in Runty's face. A fear sweat bled from his forehead. Strange, that. Zip loved breaking into houses. He got a kick out of tying up the occupants. Runty, on the other hand, got scared. The man looked as if he'd pass out from sheer fright.

They headed towards an old stone archway. This was the most impressive part of the property. Even Zip could tell it must have been here before the cottage. Medieval? Roman? Who the frick knew. On the massive keystone at the top of the arch some kind of animal had been carved, though the shape was well weathered now.

'See that, Runty? The carving might be worth something, if we could move it.'

Runty squinted up at the image. 'What is it? A dinosaur?'

'God knows. It'll weigh a ton though, so we'll have to forget it.'

'Suits me.'

'Come on, then. Let's say hello to the girls.'

'For God's sake, go easy. Don't kill anyone.'

'I'll do what it takes.' He grinned. 'After all, you'll want enough cash to buy something decent for your kid's wedding present, won't you?'

They approached the cottage. Zip could see through the kitchen window. A pair of women sat at a table buttering bread. Yum yum. Supper-time. He was feeling hungry.

He got even hungrier, although in a different way, when he eyeballed the younger of the two. She was in her early twenties and downright beautiful. She had fair hair that came down her back in sexy waves. Zip's heart beat faster. *This is going to get interesting.*

The older woman would be the one he'd squeeze the pin numbers out of. He'd tickle her toes with the secateurs.

The thought made him laugh out loud.

'What's that?' Runty froze.

'Laughter, Runty. What do you think?'

'No . . . over there – someone's stood by the door!'

Zip was borderline insane. Prison psychiatrists diagnosed acute behavioural disorder in his psychological make-up. Or so they insisted. *Bastards.* Their tests showed that he suffered from an over-inflated sense of his own importance. *The stupid bastards.* And sometimes, they insisted, he genuinely couldn't tell the difference between reality and daydreams.

But what he saw standing just five feet from the cottage door was real and most definitely not a figment of his imagination. For Christ's sake, Runty saw the thing, too; his eyes bulged as he stared at the strange creature. Zip's eyes darted to the kitchen window. The women were still making sandwiches. They'd heard nothing from outside yet.

But what was this spook outside the door?

Zip pushed Runty aside so he could approach the pale creature. He shone the light full in its face.

Dear God.

Runty made stupid groaning noises. The idiot was scared half to death.

Borderline-psychotic Zip Pearson wasn't scared. Once, when a skinhead had stabbed him in the neck he'd only laughed. Zip got ready to punch the monster.

That's what it is, isn't it? A bog-ugly monster. Zip wasn't afraid. He was excited.

A man stood there. Shreds of fabric passed for clothes. They hung in strips from his shoulders. His skin held a peculiar blue-white tint. The veins in his neck revealed themselves as black lines, almost as if a bizarre road map had been tattooed there.

There wasn't a single hair on the creature's bald scalp. Most striking were the eyes. They were white. The same white as the flesh of a boiled egg. In the centre of each eye, a black pupil. A tiny black dot like a punctuation mark against a white page.

The man didn't move. He simply stood there straight as a soldier, guarding the door. The pinpoint eyes did nothing but stare forwards.

'No . . . no . . .' Runty whimpered. He backed away along the path towards the stone archway. Runty wasn't sticking around.

'I like you,' Zip murmured to the creature. 'You look cool.' His psychotic condition suddenly erupted. Zip pushed the figure. The bare chest felt as cold as raw beef taken from the fridge. The skin was wet.

'You were born too beautiful.' Zip grinned. 'Want to take me on?'

There was no response from the stark, blue-white man. Zip pushed harder. The figure staggered backwards. Zip nearly whooped with excitement. He grabbed hold of the bony shoulders and threw the spook into the bushes.

'Runty. Come back. It can't hurt you.' He chuckled. 'The pasty bastard's weak as gnat jizz.'

'I'm not staying here,' hissed Runty from the archway. 'There's something wrong with the place.'

Zip turned round. Two more figures stood on the path between him and the house.

Spooky buggers. They'd just appeared there.

So what . . .? They're pushovers. Easy pushovers.

Zip approached the two figures, which were identical to one another. They *were* easy pushovers. He shoved them over into the bushes to prove it. There they lay like oversized Halloween dolls. Their white eyes, which were centred with the fierce black pupil, stared up at him.

'Runty,' he called, 'they can't hurt you.'

He shone the flashlight along the path, catching a glimpse of Runty's feet. They seemed to flicker he was running so fast. Chicken-shit coward.

Quickly, he shot a glance at the kitchen window. The beautiful blonde stared out through the glass. So strange . . . it was one of those sleepwalk stares. A trance state. She didn't move a muscle. The fact that there were intruders, and ghostly statue men, just outside her house didn't attract her attention at all.

Somewhere in the distance Runty screamed. A full-blooded scream of pain, terror, despair . . .

Death was in that scream. Death ran through it like an electric current runs through a wire. Runty was gone.

'Cool.' Zip smiled; this place was more interesting than he antici-pated. He walked purposefully towards the cottage. A plan took shape: kick in the door, tie up the women, and then let the good times rip.

Only, the path to the door had been blocked again. This time it wasn't a white dummy spook. What blocked the way couldn't be pushed over.

Zip shone the flashlight on the huge mound that rose out of the shadows.

A moving mound. A hissing mound.

And at that moment he wondered if the psychiatrists had been right all along. That he, Zip Pearson, couldn't tell the difference between reality and dreams.

Because this was a living nightmare.

The mound's surface undulated. There was a Mexican wave kind of ripple across the huge body.

Faces. Zip saw faces. Masses and masses and masses of faces. A wall of faces . . . an entire constellation of staring eyes . . .

'Cool . . .'

Zip never backed off from a fight; eagerly, he threw himself at the mound. Abruptly, there was a sense of being enclosed . . . being swallowed.

The robber was held in a crushing grip. Teeth from dozens of jaws bit deep into his skin. The CRACKLE he heard was the sound of his ribs breaking. The GASP he heard erupted from his own mouth.

Nothing less than a tidal wave of agony broke over him – that's when he really started to scream. This habitual torturer eventually understood what torture really felt like.

And the worst pain? That was still to come.

EIGHT

A t ten minutes to six, Tom Westonby locked the front door of Mull-Rigg Hall. He didn't want to stand waiting at the gate for Nicola as if he were some overeager teenager. Instead, he headed round the back of the house.

When she knocked, he could stroll round the corner in a nonchalant way. OK, maybe he was overdoing the relaxed nonchalance. The trouble was, he still hadn't figured out how he'd made that significant transition between telling the stranger in white to clear off and inviting her into the garden for that drink she'd asked for.

She was beautiful. He was twenty-three and had been without a girlfriend for months. So that might account for something. And he knew that sexual attraction played a large part in his motivation.

Tom also remembered a teacher from secondary school pointing out (when Tom was distracted by sixteen-year-old girls promenading by the class window) this important fact: 'Westonby. In the Middle Ages, if you said a girl had "glamour" it meant you were calling her a witch. Don't let those glamorous girls cast their spell on you. At least not until you've finished that essay on Dickens.'

Nicola had glamour. Without a shadow of doubt, she had glamour. The vital question was: *has she cast her spell on me?* He'd reached the back lawn when the phone in his pocket croaked, 'Tom! Your air tank's run out! You're gonna die!' Scuba-diver humour even extended to ringtones.

The name on the screen ID'd the caller.

'Chris,' he said, 'how's it going?'

'Any sign of that seventeen grand?'

'I've been doing some calculations. I converted what we've got in the equipment fund from pounds sterling. That comes to seven thousand dollars.'

'So where do we magic up the other ten thou?'

'My dad's paying me to get the house ready, so I'm going to ask if I can stay on here for another three months.'

'You mean at Money-Pit Hall?'

'Mull-Rigg Hall.'

'That's what I said, Money-Pit Hall. I didn't know your dad was loaded.'

'He isn't. But my aunt left some cash; they're spending it on the renovations.'

'Tom, I *need* the rent. We can't wait three months for you to make that money refurbing your parents' house.'

'The place out there is really that good?'

'It's perfect. Just seconds from the beach. We'll be right next to masses of hotels. There isn't a better location in the whole of Greece. I know one hundred per cent – shit, one million per cent – we've got the right place!'

'I planned to persuade my dad to give me an advance on my wages.'

'He'll give you the money upfront?' Chris sounded doubtful.

'That's what I'll be asking him.'

'Tom, there might be another way to solve our problem.'

'Oh?'

'Listen. I've got some important news, though I wish I could talk to you face-to-face.'

'Go on.' Tom had a sinking feeling.

'You're not going to like this . . .' Chris sounded like a man breaking bad news. 'Well, here goes: Carol's here.'

'I thought you broke up with her last year?'

'We did. The thing is, she's wanting to try again.' He finished the rest in a rush. 'And she's got the seventeen thousand dollars we need. She's keen to buy into the business. As a full partner.'

'Chris, that woman set fire to your car! You can't seriously be thinking about taking her back?'

'Carol has the money *right here.*'

'Are you insane?'

'Shh . . . I'm here on the beach with her.'

'No. Damn well no!'

'Tom—'

'That lunatic woman will ruin everything!' Tom looked up. Nicola stood no more than ten paces from him. He hadn't even noticed her appear.

When he lifted the phone from his ear so she could see that he was taking a call, she gave an *I see* gesture and pantomimed putting her fingers in her ears before backing away amongst the apple trees.

He turned his attention back to the call that threatened to ruin his and Chris's dive-school plans. 'Chris!' he bellowed, not caring whether Carol on the Greek beach, or Nicola in the orchard could hear. 'Chris. We promised each other not to get seriously involved with girlfriends until we'd got the business up and running. Don't agree anything with Carol. Nothing at all! I'll call you tomorrow after I've talked with my dad.'

He switched off the phone, savagely kicked the heads off a clutch of dandelions, then went to find Nicola.

'Trouble?' she asked.

'Seventeen thousand dollar trouble,' he growled.

'Sorry to hear it.' She smiled.

The smile made him feel better. What was it that his teacher had said about girls with glamour? Witchcraft? The power to cast spells? Her smile was one of the nice spells. His anger at the menacing reappearance of Chris's old flame evaporated.

Nicola's fair hair spilled down over a T-shirt that was the colour of burnt orange. With that, she wore a flowing white skirt. Once more he noticed the way her delicate toes peeked from under the straps of her sandals. There was something fetching about those toes. He imagined Nicola's bare feet slipping into cool pond water. The image quickened his heartbeat. Those bare toes were downright sexy.

'This way's the quickest.' She headed for the bottom of the garden.

'That's where you parked your car?'

'Car? We're walking.'

'We could go in mine.'

'Not to my house. No roads go there.' Smiling, she led the way.

'I didn't know there were any other houses nearby.'

'You probably didn't notice. What with living in that big mansion.'

'So, where are you taking me?'

'To a mysterious realm all of our own.' Her tone was light and somehow pleasantly enticing. 'We do things differently there. The normal laws of the universe don't apply.'

He politely laughed at her joke. 'OK, take me to fairyland.'

'Be warned, Tom Westonby. You'll pass the point of no return. Your world will never, ever be the same again.'

Nicola moved along the woodland path, almost skipping rather than walking.

Tom followed. He'd been amused by her playful banter about mysterious realms. In fact, this suddenly did seem a magical place. Birdsong filled the forest. The sun drove shafts of light down through the branches, so the place resembled a stage, complete with spotlights ready to illuminate glamorous actors the instant they appeared. Warm air enfolded him in a comforting embrace. Wild flowers scented the air. Above all, he was in the company of a beautiful woman, with bright, shining eyes.

What could be better than this?

Only, that's the precise moment Tom's world went wrong. There was that ominous feeling you get when forbidding storm-clouds kill a blue sky. The sunshine vanished. The forest path became so dark that he could barely see Nicola. The temperature plunged. A cold-ness emerged from the earth. Ice worked its way into his veins. There was an awful sensation, as if snow was being tightly packed around his heart.

Then the birdsong stopped.

In that silent wilderness, there was some *thing* present. A sense that a huge, malignant spirit was focusing all its hatred on him, Tom Westonby. Even though he could see nobody other than Nicola, he had an overwhelming feeling of being stared at.

Shivers swept over his body. As if thousands of vile insects had poured out of a tomb and then scurried up over his body and his face.

Once, a few years ago, his diver's instinct for survival had warned him not to venture into a shipwreck. A moment later he'd noticed a vicious conger eel lurking there. That monster of an eel could have bitten clean through flesh to the bone. If it had embedded its teeth in his arm it could have held him underwater until he'd drowned. That same survival instinct rose up inside of him now. The mechanism for self-preservation screamed at him to turn back. To run home. *Get out of here. Don't go with that woman. Glamour means witchcraft. Witchcraft means curses. Something bad is waiting in the forest . . .*

Then the inexplicable moment of dread was over. Whatever blocked the sun moved away. Birds sang again.

Nicola hadn't noticed the eerie change in the forest and called out, 'Catch up, Tom. Nearly there.'

Tom followed her into the heart of the wood. This had all the importance of crossing over a threshold from one world to another. His diver's instinct for survival still warned him to turn back.

Glamour's a powerful thing. Tom Westonby ignored the warning voice in his head. He caught up with Nicola, and both of them walked through a gap between two huge trees – and it felt like he was entering the mouth of a monstrous beast.

NINE

The path took them to the river.

'Do you know your way around the valley yet?' Nicola asked.

'I thought I did.' Tom skimmed a stone across the water. 'One, two, three, four . . .' The stone clattered over boulders on the far bank. 'Not bad; I reached the other side.' He shrugged. 'I didn't know that I had neighbours living so close.'

'Not so close. We live half a mile from you.'

'Been here long?' He picked up another stone.

'Just over a thousand years.'

He laughed. 'Sometimes it feels that long to me. There's no cinemas, no night clubs. And I only came here a couple of months ago.'

'No. Really.' She took the stone from Tom and skimmed it. 'Our family have lived here for more than a thousand years.'

He whistled. 'That's what I call commitment to location.'

After that, she told him about how she grew up in this remote valley. If anything, her memories weren't of school, or about the people she'd met. Instead, she pointed out trees that she'd seen struck by lightning, or reminisced about the time the river flooded and the flow of water was so powerful she could lie in bed at night listening to boulders rolling along the river bed. 'It sounded like angry men grumbling all night. When we woke in the morning the boulders had built up into a dam that threatened to flood the valley. The army had to blow it apart with explosives to let the water out.'

He liked the sound of her voice, so he was content to listen to her stories of rescuing wounded animals from traps, or the time archaeologists came looking for the Viking village that once stood at the bend in the river. 'My mother knew where the site of the village was.'

'So she showed the archaeologists where to dig?'

'No way.'

'Why?'

'Would you want archaeologists pawing through your house?'

'No, but surely—'

'Thorpe Lepping is where my ancestors lived. It's our land.'

Our land? He guessed that Nicola's family were claiming moral ownership, rather than legal possession. He decided not to quibble over such things. Because he realized this surprising fact: *Nicola's becoming more attractive by the moment.*

In his imagination, the old schoolteacher whispered into his ear, 'Tom Westonby. The woman has glamour – you know what that means? Witchcraft. The woman is casting a spell over you.'

When Tom picked up more stones, the teacher's voice in his head faded away. Nicola skimmed pebbles, too. She bettered his number of skips. He suspected that she'd grown up making those stones dance across the water. He admired the curve of her back as she threw; the swish of her white skirt, and the flick of her wrist that caused the stones to bounce across the stream to the far bank.

Kiss her.

Tom was twenty-three. At twenty-three you rush in where angels fear to even dip their toes.

Kiss her now.

'Nicola. We've only known each other for a couple of days. But I really like—'

'There's my mother!' She waved to a white-haired woman along the path. 'We'll be right there!'

The woman didn't answer. She simply retreated into the shadows as if the sunlight wasn't to her liking.

Nicola paused. 'What's that you were saying, Tom?'

'Uh . . . nothing much. Come on, we'd best not keep your mother waiting.'

Nice timing, Mrs Bekk.

They headed in the direction of where the woman had stood. Soon they were immersed in a deep lagoon of shadow beneath the trees. Meanwhile, Nicola's mother had already reached a cottage that seemed to bulge with the weight of red tiles on its roof. The place looked ancient.

Welcome to the Witch House . . .

Perhaps the most imposing part of the property was the stone archway set in the garden wall. The structure must have been ten feet tall.

Tom Westonby gazed up at the yellow stonework that arched over the path. An image had been engraved into one of the huge blocks. The thing was so old that the carving had been eroded to the point that whatever was depicted there consisted of seemingly random, curving lines. There were a dozen or so circles within the image. If anything, the carving resembled a whale (or some kind of bulky creature, anyway) with lots of legs – part whale, part crab? Strange.

'What's that?' he asked.

'The family dragon. You'll meet him later.'

Nicola took his arm and drew him under the archway as if afraid that he'd suddenly change his mind about entering the eerie house in the wood.

TEN

Nicola made the introduction. 'Tom, meet Helsvir. Helsvir, this is Tom.'

He looked in the direction she pointed. Above the front door of the ancient house, which seemed to be on the brink of ruin, was an oblong tablet of stone. This bore another engraving of the creature. The tablet must have been protected by the overhang of the roof, because this image hadn't been so badly weathered.

'Hello, Helsvir. How you doing?' He didn't mind Nicola's little bit of whimsy about meeting the family dragon. In fact, her subtle wit made her even more likeable.

Substitute 'likeable' with 'desirable'. He desired the curves of her body beneath that clingy orange T-shirt.

'Helsvir is an old Viking word,' she was saying. 'It means "eternally protecting the favourites of the gods".'

He smiled. 'Helsvir means all that?'

'And a heck of a lot more. Vikings were very good at cramming plenty of meaning into single words, or even into a carved symbol.'

'Your Helsvir looks pretty awesome.' He studied the carving. The vertical lines at the bottom of the bulky body were legs. The circles had pairs of dots inside. Some kind of wings? Or fins? 'I've never seen a dragon like this one. All those legs? It must have scuttled round like a crab or a beetle – or at least it would have done in your ancestors' imaginations.'

'Our family are very proud of our dragon.'

'And why not? All I had for a pet was a boring goldfish.'

She caught hold of his arm; her expression was serious. 'When you meet my mother, don't make fun of Helsvir. In fact, it's best not to even mention it.'

'Oh . . . kay,' he said thoughtfully. 'If that's what you want.'

Her grip tightened on his arm. Suddenly, she looked uneasy. 'Tom.' Her voice dropped to a whisper. 'My mother gets anxious when she meets strangers. Sometimes she comes across as being a bit, well . . . odd.' She sighed. 'My mother's crazy, really. Cuckoo.

Oddball. Sorry to be so blunt. It's better that you know she's nuts from the start.'

'OK.' He wasn't really sure how to respond to a statement like that. He glanced at the cottage, expecting to see the woman's face rammed up against the glass, her mad, staring eyes blazing at him. Of course, there was no one there. 'I'm sorry to hear that she's not well.' *Does that sound sympathetic, or crass? But what do you say in a situation like this, when the girl you really, really fancy has just confessed that her mother's a nut-job?*

Nicola gave his arm a friendly squeeze. 'Don't worry. Maybe I exaggerated the part about her being crazy. She doesn't swing from trees. And she's never chewed the table legs, or gargled with frog-spawn.' She gave a shy smile. 'I didn't want to say anything about my mother earlier because I was afraid you wouldn't come over tonight.'

'I'm sure it'll be fine.' *Being with you is fine,* he thought. 'I won't mention the dragon.' He drew his finger across his lips as if zipping them shut.

'Good. Anyway, now I've introduced you to the family dragon, it's time to meet my mother. There's no symbolic link, by the way.'

Nicola kept her arm linked with his. Instead of entering the house through the front door, she guided him to the back. The building was so old it had a magical quality. As if it had slowly grown out of the earth. The walls were of local stone, so the cottage resembled the craggy outcrops in the woods. The weathered roof tiles were an evocative mottling of reds and mossy greens. They had a striking, organic appearance: something like reptile scales. Tom found himself thinking that those tiles could have been the skin of the family's legendary dragon. Part house, part monster. A dwelling from a child's fairy tale.

The windows were small and very deep-set in the thick stone walls. Hardly any paint remained on window frames or doors: years of hard, driving rain had stripped everything down to bare wood. This cottage needed far more restoration than Mull-Rigg Hall. *The Bekk family might have one hell of a funky dragon,* he thought, *but they haven't got any money. They're living in a wreck.*

He glanced round the overgrown flower-beds. Some of the plants had been trampled flat. *The Mad Mother's doing?* He pictured her rolling about the garden, eyeballs bulging, while furiously chewing nettles. The image was a cruel one. Even so . . . he couldn't help but wonder if it might be accurate.

'Don't you get lonely out here in the forest?' he asked.

'We like living far away from other people,' she replied in a matter-of-fact voice. 'We're safe here.'

'Safe from what?'

Instead of replying, she opened the door to a rustic kitchen. 'I'll introduce you to my mother. If she says anything that seems strange, don't worry. It's just her way.'

Tom followed Nicola into the eerie old house. His gut feeling told him that things were about to get extremely interesting.

ELEVEN

They sat in the living room. This had the same rustic charm as the kitchen. All the walls were a pristine white. Tom noticed that not a single one of those walls was straight. The ancient stonework bulged outwards as if fists were being pushed into a soft material from the other side. Rather than being any sign of collapse, though, those bulges in the masonry appeared to be part of the construction. The massive thickness of stonework suggested that the place might have served as a fortified dwelling hundreds of years ago.

The kitchen and living room were scrupulously clean. There were bunches of yellow and blue flowers in vases on the window sills. Even better for Tom, a delicious aroma of freshly baked bread drifted on the air. He liked the homely feel of the place.

Nicola's mother sat in an armchair. Of slim build, with a pleasant face and white hair that fell about her shoulders, she didn't look like the demented crone that Tom's imagination had supplied. She wore a cream blouse and black skirt that wouldn't be out of place in any home or office. There was nothing obviously oddball about her.

Nicola pushed back a strand of her pale, blonde hair. 'Mother. This is Tom.'

'Oh?'

'Tom Westonby,' Tom added. 'From Mull-Rigg Hall. Pleased to meet you.' He held out his hand.

Mrs Bekk stiffened in the chair. Her features tightened as if she'd experienced a stab of pain. She didn't hold out her own hand. In fact, she pushed her fists down by her side against the chair cushion.

'Mother, this is Tom Westonby. You asked to meet him.'

Mrs Bekk hissed, 'There's no food. Your friend should go home now.' She shuddered as if Tom's presence in the room revolted her. 'Send him away.'

'Mother. There is food. You baked bread this afternoon. I got the cheese from the farmer's market, remember? The Wensleydale?'

'It's gone mouldy . . . There's green mould all over it.'

'There isn't any mould.' Nicola spoke with loving patience. 'It's a gorgeous piece of cheese.'

During this, Tom found his eye drawn to the fireplace. With it being a warm evening, there was no fire. What he did notice, engraved there in the stones at the back of the cavernous fireplace, was another picture of Helsvir. The Bekk family obviously loved their family dragon. There were pictures of the creature everywhere. Tom knew a diver who wouldn't go into the water if he didn't have his lucky shamrock with him. Tom guessed the dragon picture operated as a good luck charm for the family. He glanced round the old, worn out furniture. Pity the dragon's stash of magic had all been used up. Nicola must live with her mother out here in near poverty.

At this point Nicola crouched down to hold her mother's hand. She murmured reassurances.

At last, the older woman nodded. 'We don't get visitors, Mr Westonby.'

'Tom . . . Please call me Tom, Mrs Bekk.'

'Seeing a stranger in the house gets me het up.'

'Het means hot and bothered,' Nicola explained. 'In this part of Yorkshire we still use a lot of old Viking words.'

Mrs Bekk's shoulders drooped as she began to relax. Her daughter had managed to calm her. 'I baked bread,' the woman said. 'We have wild strawberries, too. Nicola picked them.' Without putting any knowing emphasis on the words, she added, 'Nicola was excited that you were coming tonight.'

'*Mother.*' Nicola pretended to gently scold her mother. 'Don't be giving Tom the wrong idea.'

'You were singing in the bathroom. You never sing in the bathroom.' Mrs Bekk turned to Tom. 'So you're Barbara Gibson's nephew.'

'That's right. My mother's her sister.'

'Owen? The boy Owen . . . Barbara's son?'

'Yes?'

'Is he still alive?'

Tom masked his surprise at the question. 'Yes. Owen lives with my parents, Mrs Bekk. It was his tenth birthday recently. Owen inherits Mull-Rigg Hall when he's an adult. Until then, my parents plan to live there. That way Owen grows up in a place he knows, and he can still go to school with his friends.'

'I find myself thinking about Barbara a lot. She died so young . . . and to leave a child without parents? Tragic . . .' Mrs Bekk's voice tailed off, and she lapsed into brooding silence.

Nicola gently steered the conversation away from bereavement to another topic. 'I was telling Tom that our family has lived here for over a thousand years.'

This must be a favourite subject of the mother's, Tom thought, because she started talking quite happily about the Bekk family history.

'The cottage is called Skanderberg. That's the name of the town in Denmark from where our family came. You've heard of the Viking Gods Odin and Thor?'

He nodded.

She patted the arm of the chair beside her, inviting him to sit. 'And so you should know them. Certain days of the week are named after Viking gods. Wednesday is Odin's Day. Thursday – Thor's Day. Well, Tom, twelve hundred years ago, Thor picked up my ancestor Guthrum Bekk and carried him through the sky all the way from Denmark to this valley in England. Thor showed him that the fertile land here would produce so much food that mortal children would never starve. So the god ordered Guthrum Bekk to bring his family to the Lepping Valley and build a farm.'

Tom nodded, listening politely. He wanted to please Nicola rather than the mother. He knew that seemed such a calculating action. But he found himself calculating how long it would be before he could plant his first kiss on Nicola's soft lips.

Mrs Bekk talked in a low, rhythmic voice. Despite him pretending to be polite at first, he found himself drawn into the family legend of Viking gods and warriors.

If anything, this reminded him of lessons when he learned about the history of the Vikings, or the Norse people as they were some-times described. He knew that the Vikings had terrorized England over a thousand years ago. That they'd stormed ashore from their longships. Legends also revealed them to be bloodthirsty pagans that plundered the monasteries and gruesomely slaughtered the monks, often inflicting something called the Blood Eagle; this involved hacking apart the ribcage so the ribs could then be pulled back to resemble blood-soaked wings. Not all the invaders returned to their homelands in Norway, Sweden and Denmark. Huge numbers settled in England. Plenty married local girls. 'So proving that love is the most formidable conqueror of all,' proclaimed the history teacher. Then she'd pointed out children with blonde hair and blue eyes, and made this surprising claim: 'What you probably didn't know is that there are still plenty of Vikings in England, or at least their descendants are here. As likely as not, you'll find Scandinavian DNA in these children.'

Meanwhile, Mrs Bekk plaited her fingers together as she continued her tale. 'Guthrum Bekk sailed with his wife, brothers, sisters, and their children to England. They weren't an invading army. They were a family intending to peacefully settle in this valley. When Guthrum arrived he was scorned by the Christians who lived in Danby-Mask. They sent their best fighters to challenge Guthrum to a duel. Guthrum had fought many battles in the past. He was a brave warrior, but now he dreamt only about living peacefully. So he made a bargain with the Christians. He explained he could dam one of the valley streams to make a deep pool that would never dry up in even the worst of droughts. He promised the villagers that they could take fish from the pool and use the water to irrigate their crops when the rains didn't come. The villagers agreed. But they were scheming behind my ancestor's back. They pretended to become friendly, and all the time they were planning to attack Guthrum Bekk's farm, steal his cattle, and murder his family.' She held up her finger. 'And every Bekk mother tells their children this blood history. It is so important that every generation of our family knows. Our survival depends on the secret of what happened next.'

'Mother. I'm not sure that Tom is interested in all the gory details.'

'That's OK, Nicola. I'd be interested to hear it.' Again he said this to please Nicola. *Yes, it's manipulative; yes, it's calculating. But my motives are good. In fact, my motives are romantic.* He tried to suppress the words LUST and SEX that were hotly circling his mind.

'On Midsummer's day Guthrum went to pick strawberries. He

planned to take baskets of fruit to the village as a gift. He'd make a gesture of friendship to his neighbours. Guthrum's five daughters went with him to help with the harvest. While he was away, the villagers struck. They killed everyone in the farm. Then they set fire to Skanderberg.' She pointed to the walls. 'You can still see the burn marks on those stones. Even if you paint over them they'll come through the new paint within the day. They're the black tear-stains of the house as it witnessed the death of Guthrum's wife and sons.'

'I'm sorry,' Tom said. 'That sounds like a terrible massacre.'

Mrs Bekk's voice rose, growing clearer. Harder. 'Guthrum swore revenge. Even as he dug the graves, Thor whispered into his ear. Thor told Guthrum not to bury the dead but to gather them up and heap them into a pile in the ruins of the house. Guthrum did so. And that night Thor breathed life into the bodies. Then he wove their limbs together to make a single living creature.'

'The dragon?' Tom made the deduction. 'Thor turned the bodies into Helsvir.'

Mrs Bekk fired out the words: 'Yes, the corpses of my ancestors became Helsvir. The dragon isn't like the fairy-tale dragons that blow fire out of their mouths. Helsvir is the Viking war-snake! A sacred weapon of vengeance!'

'Mother.' Nicola's voice held a warning note. 'Don't get yourself worked up.'

Mrs Bekk rose to her feet. 'Helsvir struck Danby-Mask. A whirl-wind of vengeance. He smashed down the doors, and he tore the murderers apart. Helsvir killed the betrayers. Then he became our protector. We tell our children these facts so they can sleep knowing that a dragon stands guard at this house.'

'That's an amazing story,' Tom said.

'*Story? Story! That is the sacred blood history of our family!*'

'Mother, please—'

'Without Helsvir those bastards from Danby-Mask would have destroyed our family years ago. The villagers are always plotting against us. They want us dead!'

'*Mother, stop this.*' Nicola took hold of her mother's arm. Once again she tried to calm her. By now, though, the woman's face had turned a fiery red with anger. Her eyes blazed.

'Tom Westonby. It's important you hear this. I'll tell you the rest of our history.'

'Mother, please!'

'Guthrum lived. So did his five daughters. They were all grown women when Danby-Mask butchered our family. Thor went into their beds at night. The god fathered their children.'

'That's *enough*, Mother.' Nicola's voice rose. 'You've got to stop saying these things.'

'But Mr Westonby hasn't heard the best part! The most vital, significant truth!' Her tone was gleeful; she laughed as she shouted the words: 'Do you know who Nicola's father is, Tom?'

Tom stared at her, not knowing what to say.

'Twenty-four years ago, Thor came into my bed, too. He made me pregnant with Nicola. That's why you will never get her into *your* bed, Tom Westonby. Yes! I've seen that hungry look in your eye.' Her laugh became a roar of pure joy. 'That's right, Tom! Nicola is the daughter of a living god! It's her destiny to wipe that Christian village from the face of the earth. Then Nicola will destroy you! *She'll feed you to the dragon, Tom Westonby. She'll feed you to his many heads!*'

TWELVE

'Get them dirty bones out of that pit!' The voice pierced Tom's dreams. One moment he lay fast asleep, dreaming he chased Nicola through a midnight forest – trees growing denser and denser until branches were clutching at his head – the next: 'Open the door or we'll break it down!'

Tom stumbled out of bed, half-awake. For a second he imagined that the Bekk family dragon – the wonderfully named Helsvir – had come to smash down the door. He looked out of the window. The figure making all the noise was ten years old, had a wild splash of black hair, and was hammering on the woodwork with his fists.

'Tom, you lazy chuff!' shouted the boy.

Tom pushed open the bedroom window. 'Owen, stop trying to murder the door. I'll be right down.'

He rubbed his eyes. His mother and father were lifting luggage out of the car. There came one of those mental blanks when he watched them hauling a coffee table from the back seat.

'They can't be moving in,' he grunted. 'I haven't got the house ready yet.' The bright sunlight made him squint. 'They're not even supposed to be here until next week.'

'Tom! You lousy, lazy basket,' Owen shouted good-naturedly. 'Open the freaking, wrenching door.'

'Hey, watch that freaking language,' Tom called down. 'Or I'll chuck you in the pond.'

Owen grinned up at Tom, and Tom found himself grinning down at the ten-year-old. The last time he'd seen his cousin the boy had been so withdrawn and so quiet; understandably, his mother's death had hit him hard. Now Owen seemed indestructibly cheerful – just as a ten-year-old should be.

'I'll put some clothes on,' Tom said.

'Gross.' Owen pantomimed a look of disgust and called back to Tom's mother, 'Hey, Auntie, Tom's strutting round the house naked.'

Tom's parents laughed. After an awkward start to the new living arrangements, when Owen moved in, they'd obviously grown fond of him. In fact, Tom realized the kid was rapidly becoming their new son. He wasn't resentful. Tom knew that his mother and father didn't love him any less because Owen had become part of the family. Owen's mother was dead. The boy had never known his own father – the Gibsons had divorced when he was a baby – and Owen was still a child: he needed Mr and Mrs Westonby to be his new parents.

An accumulation of T-shirts had formed a mountain on a chair. Somehow the need to put them in the washing machine had repeatedly slipped Tom's mind. He tipped the clothes on to the floor and kicked them under the bed out of sight. Stuff like that could be taken care of later. Besides, he felt his spirits rising. He wanted to see his parents and Owen. He and the boy could have fun mucking around with the air compressor he'd bought for the dive school. With one of those machines you could blow up a domestic rubber glove to something larger than a fridge. Then the rubber glove would explode with a tremendous bang. Boys loved that kind of thing. Heck, Tom Westonby loved that kind of thing.

Tom dragged on jeans and his last clean shirt then bounded downstairs. As soon as he opened the door Owen playfully punched his stomach.

'What kept you, lazybones!' Then Owen dashed upstairs. This was his first trip back to the house since his mother's sudden death.

'Let me help you with that.' Tom took the coffee table from his mother. Meanwhile, his father dragged two wheelie cases.

'The gravel's getting stuck in the wheels. Hello, Tom, great to see you.'

'Kiss for Mother.' His mother turned her face.

Tom kissed her cheek. 'You weren't coming until next week, were you?'

'So we're not welcome?'

'No . . . I mean yes, but the house isn't ready. Did you know there are seventy-seven straight-backed chairs in that place?'

'Have you got a girl in the house?'

'No.'

'If you have, we can get back in the car, drive round for ten minutes, then pretend we've just arrived.' His mother grinned. She was easy-going about him having girlfriends to stay. She didn't mind in the least.

'There's no girl.'

'Oh?'

'No.'

'When you look out of the corner of your eye like that I know you're fibbing. You've done it since you were five years old and used to hide cake in your socks.'

Tom laughed as he carried the table indoors. 'There's no girl. At least, not in the house.'

'Ah, so who is she?' Tom's mother could read her son as easily as text on a page.

What can I say that won't sound too strange? She's the girl I chased at midnight. Or: the mother believes they have a guardian dragon. No . . . best leave those unusual facts for later.

Instead, he shrugged like the girl didn't matter (she really did) and said, 'Oh, just someone I met locally. We're . . . you know . . .'

'Just friends?'

To avoid his mother scrutinizing his face to check where his eyes were headed when he answered her precisely targeted question, he asked, 'Where do you want the table?'

'By the wall's fine for now.'

'So, how come you're here today?'

'We're not welcome, Tom?' His father dragged in the wheelies.

'I've already asked that question, Russell. Apparently, there's some girl.'

'Ah-ha, the formidable Westonby males strike again.'

'This formidable Westonby male –' she playfully tweaked her husband's ear – 'can bring that frozen food in from the car before it melts.'

Tom knew his parents were only teasing him about not being welcome, but he repeated his answer: 'Of course I'm glad to see you, it's just that you weren't supposed to be coming until next week.'

'We've decided to bring the moving-in date forwards.' With that, his father hurried off to save the frozen food from thawing.

Tom's mother filled in the details. 'We're giving up the lease on our house a month early. So we've brought the coffee table today. It was the first present your father bought me. I don't want it getting broken when we do the big move.'

'There's still the painting to be done,' Tom explained. 'I haven't even begun to sand the floors.'

'What's this? Tom Westonby, king of the messy bedroom, being suddenly house-proud?'

'I just wanted to get the place ready.'

She smiled. His mother was touched by what he'd meant. 'You wanted everything right for us, didn't you? To make it homely?'

He nodded – once more her razor-sharp intuition saw the real meaning behind his words.

'That's why you're a lovely son. You're just like your dad; he always wants the best for other people.' She gave a sigh. 'Just don't let being a good person take over your life. Remember to live for yourself, too.'

'The ice cream's turned to milk.' His father strode in with bags crammed full of groceries. 'It's dripped through the bag into my shoe. I can feel it squelching.'

All of a sudden, Mull-Rigg Hall sprang into life. His dad rinsed vanilla ice cream from his shoes in the kitchen. Owen bounced a tennis ball on the patio. His mother started making BLTs for breakfast. Tom finished collecting luggage from the car.

As he lugged suitcases upstairs, he found himself thinking about the extraordinary visit to Nicola's house in the forest. He suspected they lived a solitary life there. Yet *solitary* didn't seem a strong enough word to describe their isolation in that remote part of the valley. Clearly, Nicola took care of her mother, who suffered from some mental condition. Mrs Bekk was obsessed with her family's

Viking ancestry. She also believed that the Bekks had been at war with the villagers of Danby-Mask for generations. Then there was all this about the dragon guarding their home. Topping it all: Mrs Bekk's claim that the Viking god Thor had impregnated her with Nicola. Wasn't Thor the warrior god? Tom remembered seeing pictures in history books of a towering, powerful man with ferocious eyes, red hair, and a flaming red beard, brandishing a huge hammer that he used to shatter his enemies' skulls.

If Mrs Bekk wasn't Nicola's mother, he'd have been thinking in terms of the woman being a nutty coot. What's more, he'd stay well clear of her. But there was Nicola . . .

Nicola was the magic ingredient in all this. The lynchpin.

Besides, he reasoned, *I like mythology and history. OK, so what if Mrs Bekk gets all wrapped up in ancient history, legends, massacres and the like? It's obsessions that make people interesting . . .*

Last summer he'd worked with archaeologists who were exploring a Roman town that had sunk under the Mediterranean Sea two thousand years ago. An earthquake had created a real-life Atlantis. Tom had provided the muscle. He'd make dives with the archaeologists, and they'd point out which rubble on the seabed had to be moved from the collapsed houses so experts could reach the precious artefacts and colourful mosaics. Tom had been so interested in the work that the archaeologists had invited him into their inner circle. Over glasses of Italian beer they'd talked about their investigations and the history of the submerged town. They'd been enthusiastic. They would piece together facts from what they uncovered on the seabed, then vividly describe to Tom what life was like in Portus Hesculum before the earthquake struck in the year that Christ was born.

Tom Westonby loved to sit beneath the stars with his cold beer and just listen. He pictured the Roman families in their houses. The laughter. The games they'd play. And even the taste Romans had for roast dormouse on a stick – a kind of savoury lollipop. 'Just imagine the crunch of those little bones between your teeth,' said an archaeologist with a laugh as Tom had bitten into a breadstick.

As Tom headed downstairs, his father appeared in the kitchen doorway. He carried a damp shoe in one hand. The other shoe was on his foot.

'The good news is –' his father spoke with the seriousness of a doctor making a diagnosis – 'I managed to save the shoe. Sadly, the bad news is there's no hope for the ice cream.'

Tom needed to talk to his father about the not so little matter of finding ten thousand dollars for the premises in Greece.

'The other good news is –' Tom playfully echoed his father's doctor-with-a-diagnosis tone – 'Chris has found the perfect place for the dive school.'

'That's great.'

'It's right next to the beach.'

'You already gave me the good news. So what's the bad?'

Tom explained about needing the rent money by the end of next week. Otherwise they'd lose the building.

'I'd love to be able to lend you the cash, Tom.' His father's tone was regretful.

'No, I wouldn't ask for a loan, Dad.'

'It's just that we've already spent such a lot of money on the house.'

Tom had a sinking feeling. 'I'd planned to ask you for an advance on my wages, if I promised to work through the summer.'

'The reason we're bringing the moving-in date forward is so I can do most of the renovation myself to save on cost.'

'I thought we'd agreed I'd be doing the work.'

'And so you will be through June, like we planned. It's just that the barn conversion, and the expense of getting Mull-Rigg Hall in shape, are going to take all the available cash. Sorry, Tom. I really wish I could help.'

'Don't worry, Dad, it's not your problem.' Tom winced when he saw the anguish on his father's face. 'I can shuffle some of the funding we'd put aside.'

'Don't humour me, Tom. You need that money, don't you?'

'Yes. Or we'll lose those premises. They're the best Chris has seen.'

'How much are you short?'

'Ten thousand dollars.'

'Dollars, not euros?'

'The landlord's asking for dollars.'

'No doubt to avoid declaring it to the Greek tax office.' Tom's father scratched his head. 'Ten thousand dollars . . .'

'It looks as if we'll have to find another property.'

'You know . . .' His father looked thoughtful. 'I was talking to one of my old colleagues. He was telling me he needs help restoring some industrial units.'

'I've promised to help out here, Dad.'

'We'll cope. You need to earn some money fast.'

'He won't pay me much for doing basic cleaning out and painting.'

His father shook his head. 'The units are steel construction. He needs a welder, and you're a first-rate welder. Jack will pay professional rates, so that should get you what you need.'

'We must have the money by the end of the week.'

'Give the landlord a ten per cent deposit. That should be enough to secure the lease.'

Tom felt his spirits rise. Problem solved. He'd phone Chris with the news. 'Thanks, Dad.' Tom hugged his father. 'I'll do just that.'

'So you'll commit to the work? Jack needs someone who'll finish the job.'

'Count me in.'

'Good. And it's in France. You'll get to see the sights, too.'

'France?' Tom hadn't expected that.

'Jack's starting work on the units after the weekend. He'll want you on site then.'

Tom Westonby had been expecting to spend the summer in this beautiful corner of Yorkshire.

More importantly: what about Nicola Bekk? He'd be leaving before he'd really got to know her.

THIRTEEN

When Tom Westonby strolled into Chester Kenyon's workshop, 'Cheery' Chester had some surprising news. So surprising, in fact, that Tom didn't think he'd heard right.

'Married?' Tom echoed. 'You're getting married?'

Chester grinned as he unscrewed bolts on an old lawnmower. 'Yes. Married. Joined in holy deadlock.'

'You'll find the word's *wedlock*.' Tom was smiling as much as Chester. 'When? Where? *Who*!'

'The last Saturday in August.' *Clack.* He dropped the bolts into a steel bowl. 'At Saint George's.' *Clack.* 'You're invited, Mr Westonby.'

Clack. He pointed an oily finger out through the workshop door. 'And that's who I'm marrying.'

'Grace Harrap? Isn't she the one who shoves ice inside your shirt?'

'Romantic, isn't it?' Chester wiped his fingers on a rag. 'We've had this on-off thing for years.'

Tom held out his hand. 'Congratulations. I'm pleased for you both.'

Chester whistled to Grace. Grace smiled back, though for some reason she shook her fist rather than waving. *Maybe in these little Yorkshire villages the gesture means something different*, Tom thought. *Fist shakes might be as good as blowing kisses.*

'She looks pleased to see you,' Tom said optimistically.

'Nah, she's mad at me. I'm not asking her brother to be best man.'

'Any ideas about a best man?'

'You.'

Tom thought he'd been asked a question. 'I don't know who should be your best man, Chester. That's for you to decide.'

'No, I mean: YOU.'

Tom blinked in surprise. 'I've only known you for a few weeks. Are you sure—?'

'I'll be blowing fanfares if you would. You're a good bloke, Tom. You see . . .' Chester was habitually cheerful. Yet revealing his true emotions came tougher. 'For one of those city wimps you can take your beer with the best of them.'

'Thank you, Chester. But . . .'

'But what?'

'Won't Grace still be angry at you? After all, if she wants her brother as best man.'

'Nah, Liam's a twit.'

'If you want me to be best man, Chester, then yes, sure. I mean, I'm honoured.'

'Great. I'll tell Grace.' He gave a big, beaming grin. 'Though I'll probably end up with a whole iceberg down my shirt when she hears.'

'I won't be offended if you change your mind. After all, I don't want to be the one to cause rows between you and your fiancée.'

'She'll come round. Will you grab the hammer? It's outside on the bench.'

Tom stepped out into the sunlight. On the other side of the village's main street was St George's. The church was in the typical Yorkshire style. Its walls were built of white stone that uncannily resembled the local white cheese. The main part of the church dated back a thousand years or so, while the square tower would be seventeenth century.

A notice board stood by the graveyard gate. At the top of the board, a painting depicted St George in golden armour driving a lance into an evil-looking green dragon. Tom hadn't realized its significance before, in relation to Danby-Mask. St George, the patron saint of England, was also the famous dragon-slayer. He began to wonder if dedicating the parish church to St George, the knight who killed the dragon, had any connection to Mrs Bekk's wild stories about her ancestors being guarded by such a creature, which had also rampaged through the village centuries ago.

'Any luck finding the hammer, Tom?'

'Sure. Right here.' As he headed back he heard a commotion along the street. Tom stopped dead, staring hard, his heart pounding. This was a day for surprises alright. He couldn't believe what he was seeing right now.

Nicola Bekk walked along the street. She had her back to Tom, so she didn't see him standing there outside the workshop. Three guys in their twenties walked with her. They took it in turns to put their arms round her shoulders. When she pushed one away that's when Tom realized they were doing this against her will. In fact, they were clearly goading her. Nicola walked faster. Maybe she hoped they'd tire of following.

They didn't. If anything, the horseplay ramped up towards intimidation. These bullies were enjoying scaring the woman. When she wriggled free of one of those rough hugs the men started pushing her.

Chester hadn't seen what was happening; he was inside the workshop. 'Need any help carrying that hammer?' he joked. 'My grandad always said that gravity's stronger here in Danby-Mask. He says that after eight pints of beer he can hardly lift his head off the table . . . Tom? What are you doing?'

Tom Westonby dropped the hammer and charged down the street. Neither the thugs nor Nicola had seen him yet.

The three guys were shoving her hard now. One push sent her stumbling against a fence. Another guy snatched the bag she was carrying. Nicola was slightly built; nevertheless, she hung on tight to stop the man taking it. Of course, the plastic ripped. Eggs, oranges and flour cascaded on to the ground.

Tom's feet pounded the pavement. Rage electrified him. *The bastards! What the hell are they doing?*

Before Nicola caught sight of Tom, she abandoned her groceries. The last he saw of her was a flash of blonde hair as she cut down a path away from the road.

The three thugs were laughing. They stamped on the eggs that had survived the fall. Once they'd done that they ran after her. The chase was on.

FOURTEEN

Tom knew the situation was becoming dangerous. After all, what were those three men planning to do to Nicola? Whatever it was, she wouldn't be able to defend herself. What's more, Tom noticed that even though some villagers had witnessed the attack, none had done anything to stop it. Come to that, several were laughing as if they'd witnessed a harmless prank. This was no harmless prank, though: those thugs had been brutally shoving her.

Tom took a short cut. He vaulted over a fence, sprinted across a lawn, then through a succession of private gardens. As a pro diver he kept himself fit. That, and heavy work at the house, had developed his physique. His biceps formed hard bulges under the skin.

So he wasn't even breathless when he vaulted a wall to drop down on to a public footpath. He'd judged it well. The three men were just appearing round the corner. Now he found himself between them and Nicola. He glanced behind him. He couldn't see her; she must have been moving fast. Probably scared half to death by these three goons.

He'd seen the guys before in the pub. If there was the sound of breaking glass, or drunken yelling, they were usually the ones behind the rumpus. He knew the one in the red cap was called Bolter. He didn't know the names of the other two.

Tom held up his hand. 'What do you think you're doing?'

'What's it to you?' said the smallest of the three. This was Bolter – a thin-faced runt with red blisters erupting from his face. Those blisters hinted strongly at amphetamine use.

'I don't know what you're playing at.' Tom kept in the path's centre to block the way. 'But leave her alone.'

The little one had the largest mouth – and was hell-bent on using it. 'What you bothered about Crazy Bekk for? Nobody wants her hanging about.'

The biggest of the three rumbled in a slow-witted way, 'We're getting her out.' He wore an expression of genuine outrage. 'She shouldn't even be coming into the village.'

'Not when there are little kids about,' added the one in the middle. He seemed to be trying to grow a beard. However, the tuft of mousy hair had given up trying to cover the entire jaw and contented itself, instead, with sprouting from the tip of his chin.

Tom spoke firmly: 'I'm telling you to leave her alone.'

'Shit. Are you one of these do-gooders?'

'If you don't turn back, I can be one of those do-badders, understand?'

The three weren't used to one person standing up to them; they looked at each other, hoping someone would come up with a tough response.

It was down to Bolter, the guy with the face blisters. 'What are you interested in Crazy Bekk for? Didn't you know she's a nut? She can't even read and write.'

The big one grunted. 'And she's been warned off for hanging round the village.'

'By you three, I suppose,' Tom said.

'I know what you're doing.' Bolter leered. 'You're sticking her with the love bone, aren't you? You dirty dog – shagging a mental case. You filthy little fecker.'

'Bastard pervert.' The big guy appeared genuinely offended. 'You need teaching a lesson.'

The threat of violence crackled on the air.

Tom knew what was happening. Big guy was the muscle of the gang. Bolter was trying to get his pal angry, so he'd be the one to punch first.

Tom decided to catch them off-guard. Before Bolter could say anything else, Tom pounced on the big guy. He pushed him hard enough to get him off balance. The big guy now had to hang on to Tom to stop himself falling back into a clump of stinging nettles.

'Hey, let him go,' shouted Bolter.

'Shut your mouth,' Tom snarled. 'And keep it shut.' He glanced at the one with the ridiculous tuft on his chin; he was bunching his fists. 'If you take a swing at me I'll rip your head off.'

The guy flinched back.

Tom used the moment to shove the big man hard enough at the other two to show he meant business.

Tom pointed back along the path. 'Start walking that way. Understand?'

'You're crazy taking Bekk's side,' shouted Bolter. 'She's not right in the head.'

'We'll remember your face.' Tufty was more confident about dishing out threats now his mates were between him and Tom. 'You live up at Mull-Rigg Hall. We'll show you that you don't cross us.'

'Just wait until you're in the pub,' the big one growled. 'We'll bloody well knock the shit out of you.'

Tom strode away in the direction Nicola must have headed. The three still hurled threats, though he noticed they were retreating towards the village. They weren't confident in tackling Tom head-on. Tom was savvy enough, however, to realize they'd wait for him down some alley one night and take him by surprise.

So be it. But he wasn't going to stand by and let them ill-treat Nicola.

Tom began to run along the path to the river. Soon he'd left the village behind. Now the trees arched over him to create a dark tunnel. When he ran round a clump of bushes he startled Nicola who'd stopped to brush spilt flour from her skirt.

'Leave me alone! If you touch me again, it'll be the last thing you do!'

He realized the shadows hid his face. 'Nicola. It's me – Tom.'

'What do you want?' She sounded suspicious.

'I saw what those men were doing.'

'Men? They're pathetic cowards.'

'Are you alright?'

'Fine.'

'I'll walk you back home.'

'There's no need.'

'Why did they do that? It's like the whole village hates you.'

'They hate our family.' She lowered her voice. 'They always have.'

He realized her eyes glittered with tears. 'Are you sure you're alright?'

'You don't know what's happened to me in that village.'

'What? Just now?'

'No. It's what they've done in the past.'

The implications were so ominous that shivers ran down his back. 'You should tell the police.'

'Police? Ha!'

He could hear the river falling over the stones. At that moment, however, his eyes were fully on Nicola's face. There was such an expression of pain there. It was heart-rending to see her like that. And he had news for her. *I'm leaving the valley. I'm going to work in France. Goodbye.*

That was the moment he knew he could never utter those words.

'We've got flour and eggs at home,' he told her. 'You can have those.'

'Keep your damn eggs.' She was still angry from the attack. 'Why should I want your charity?'

'So what *do* you want?'

Nicola stared at him. She didn't say anything. The shadows seemed to grow darker. In contrast, her eyes grew brighter. They were like lamps burning out of the gloom.

Some inbuilt resistance broke inside him. At that moment, he couldn't stop himself from doing what he did next. 'Do you want this?' His tone seemed brutal even to his own ears. Then he took hold of her shoulders. When she didn't react he kissed her on the mouth.

That's when she did react. She put her hand around the back of his head and pushed her face up to his. She was kissing him, her lips moved against his.

The sound of the river stopped. Or, at least, he stopped hearing it. The only sound now was the pounding of his heart.

This time he really did feel as if he'd crossed the point of no return. He'd started something important. And he wondered what the consequences would be.

FIFTEEN

Sunlight blazed down on the orchard at Mull-Rigg Hall. Tom Westonby had started chopping down a dead apple tree when his father gave him some startling news.

'Tom, I'm getting married.'

Tom stared at the man in shock. 'Married? Who are you marrying?'

He felt an unnerving sense of déjà vu. Just two hours ago, Chester Kenyon had told him that he was getting married to Grace and had asked Tom to be best man. Then came the confrontation with the village bullies led by Bolter, the man with a face full of scarlet blisters brought on by drug abuse. Following that, he'd caught up with Nicola on the river bank. And then the kiss. He could still feel Nicola's lips on his. For the last couple of hours he'd thought about nothing else.

'So, who . . .?' Tom felt mentally winded. He couldn't catch a sensible train of thought. He gave his father a hard look. 'Married?'

'I shouldn't have sprung the news like that.' Russell Westonby still wore a huge grin. 'I'll give you a clue who I'm marrying. You will be the son of the bride.'

'Uh, thank God.'

'You didn't think I was running off with the local milkmaid, did you?'

'Something like that.' Tom sighed with relief. His hands were actually shaking. 'But you're already married to Mum . . . aren't you?'

'We had a civil wedding when we worked in Uganda. Both of us were younger than you at the time. We married in a mad rush. The impetuousness of youth, eh?'

'So, why now?'

'Your mother and I are starting to regret that we didn't do the full family thing, inviting everyone to a traditional wedding.'

'Though you aren't getting remarried?'

'Technically, no. It's a renewal of our wedding vows.'

Tom held out his hand. 'Congratulations, Dad.'

Smiling, his father shook it. 'Thank you, son. Oh . . . by the way, I wondered if you'd be best man.'

'Really?'

'I couldn't think of a better man to ask.'

'Thanks . . . but that's weird.'

'Why weird?'

'You're the second person to ask me to be a best man today.'

'Oh?'

'Chester Kenyon asked me this morning.'

His father smiled. 'Maybe there's a wedding virus in the air.'

'Maybe.' Tom leaned the axe against a tree. He was pleased . . . of course he was pleased, on both counts of being asked to serve as best man. Only, he felt a chilling creep of unease. As if he'd just caught sight of a gravestone with his name on it. *No, that wasn't logical. You can't be alarmed if good things happen to you.* Suddenly, he remembered a veteran diver who used to worry when he found himself enjoying life too much. 'It's like I'm being given one last good time before I die,' the superstitious man would utter, full of doom-laden woe. 'One last party spree before they nail down my coffin lid.'

Tom shook off that inexplicable sense of mortal danger. 'Thanks, Dad. I'd be glad to.'

'That's great. I'm really pleased you said yes.' He slapped Tom on the back.

'When's the big day?'

'Mid-August. We're renewing the vows at St George's Church in the village. Then we're having a party back here.'

'I look forward to it.'

'We'll make sure you get the weekend off from that job in France.'

France? Tom realized that he'd forgotten all about going to work for his father's friend. That kiss on the riverbank with Nicola had wiped everything else from his mind.

'Dad, about this job in France . . .'

'Don't worry. I've sorted everything out with Jack. He's going to email the Eurostar tickets tonight. Stay here, I'll get us a cold drink.'

Tom went to pick up the axe. He couldn't even bring himself to face the man he loved when he said, 'Listen, I've decided not to go to France. I'm staying here.'

The breeze blew through the orchard, rustling the leaves. His

father had already hurried back towards the house and hadn't heard
what would be bad news . . . Hell, it would be bombshell news.
His father had worked hard to get Tom this high-paying job. He
may even have staked an old friendship on it.

Tom found himself tangled up in thoughts about France, about
the urgent need for money for the dive school, and about Nicola
Bekk. Especially Nicola Bekk. Absolutely about Nicola Bekk. He
rested his finger against his lips where she had pressed hers.

*What do I do? Go to France? That way I don't let Dad down.
What about Nicola? Do I just leave? As if she means nothing to
me?*

Under bushes by the fence were dry sticks. He started to pull
them out, intending to burn the dead wood in the orchard. These
thin twigs were ideal kindling.

When he saw the eyes glaring from the shadows he thought that
the thugs from the village had arrived to cause trouble.

Then he recognized the face.

'Mrs Bekk?'

'I warned you,' she hissed. 'I explained that Helsvir stands guard
at our door. You've chosen to ignore me. You think I'm insane.'

'No, I don't, Mrs Bekk.'

She waved her finger from side to side. 'Leave Nicola alone,
Tom Westonby. If you don't, you will be sorry.'

Tom resented orders – especially those kind of orders. 'Whether
we want to see each other is our decision, Mrs Bekk.'

'I'm warning you, boy. Don't lay a finger on her – *you know
what I mean by that!* Because if you do, you'll regret it for whatever's left of your life. Understand?'

'I like Nicola. I respect her. She's—'

'So be warned! If you continue this relationship, you'll be doing
more harm to my daughter than you can even begin to understand.
You must never see her again.'

'Tom?' His father's voice came from the orchard. 'Tom, where
are you?'

'Here, Dad.'

By the time he'd turned back, Nicola's mother had vanished. He
peered into the forest but couldn't see her. It was as if she'd been
transformed into one of the shadows before merging with the gloom.

'Here you go.' His father handed him a glass that clinked with
ice. 'Anything wrong?'

'No. Why?' He decided not to mention Mrs Bekk's strange visit.

'That shocked expression on your face. You look as if you've just seen your own funeral cortège.'

'Nicely morbid line, Dad. Cheers.' Mrs Bekk's words troubled him, but he pretended nothing had happened. 'Thanks for the drink.' They tapped glasses.

The breeze stirred the forest again, creating a huge *whooshing* that majestically rose and fell. For reasons that weren't entirely rational, the sound conjured images of a prehistoric beast that sucked in colossal breaths of air as it prowled its domain in search of human prey . . . and a taste of human blood.

Despite the sunlight, Tom shivered. Once more he recalled the doom-laden premonition of the old diver: '*It's like I'm being given one last good time before I die . . . one last party spree before they nail down my coffin lid.*'

SIXTEEN

They met by the river. Yesterday, Tom had kissed Nicola after he'd had that run-in with the village thugs. The pair had not arranged to meet this morning. In fact, everything seemed a bit hazy after the kiss. Tom couldn't remember anything except them smiling at each other as they went their separate ways.

Now here they were, perched on a big boulder at the water's edge. Birds swooped low, catching insects. There was a splash – the fish were jumping. Tom glanced at Nicola's profile as she gazed at the flowing stream. He found himself fascinated by her pale blue eyes and the fine blonde hair that rolled about her shoulders.

'How did we know we'd find each other here?' he asked.

'It's the exact halfway point between our two houses.' She shot him a glance. 'Coincidence?'

'Yep, coincidence.' *Though it feels more like inevitable destiny.* 'Your mother came to my house yesterday.'

'Oh?'

'She warned me not to see you again.'

'Did she say why?'

'That there'd be consequences. Something about you being harmed in some way.'

'So, has my mother frightened you off? You're going to tell me you don't want to see me again?'

Tom shook his head. 'No.'

'You can if you want.'

'Is that what *you* want?'

'What do *you* think?'

There was a sensation that their relationship – even though it was at the very beginning – hung in the balance. Tom knew that when they went their separate ways today it would either be for the last time, or it would be start of something deeper and more meaningful.

He picked up a stick, broke it in half, and handed her a piece. Neither spoke. Instinctively, they seemed to follow a program that had been burned deep inside their minds long ago. Nicola threw her stick into the water. Tom threw his.

Both watched with a quiet satisfaction as his piece of the stick fell close to hers and they floated together. He knew he was being sentimental when he saw the two sticks as loyal companions; they were setting off downriver on an adventure together. *Mr & Mrs Stick.*

Smiling, he glanced at Nicola as she watched the sticks float away into the distance. Was she thinking the same? Because he couldn't escape the notion that there was a powerful romantic symbolism about the sticks they'd thrown into the water. He wanted to kiss her again. Only, this wasn't the right moment. Nicola clearly had something on her mind.

'Has your mother said anything to you?' he asked.

'No.'

'Nothing about us?'

'That's just it. She hasn't said a word all day, which means she's brooding. That worries me.'

'I'm sorry.'

'It's not your fault.'

'Has this happened before?'

'You mean me taking a boy home? Look, Tom, I'll tell you the truth. I think my mother's worried about me being made a fool of . . . or even being made pregnant by some here-today-gone-tomorrow guy.'

'I'm not like that.' Even as he said the words he thought about the job in France. *I need the money for the dive school . . . Damn, this is getting awkward. I don't want to work abroad. Trouble is I can't afford not to. We'll lose the place in Greece if I don't go.* He took a deep breath. 'Parents aren't always the easiest people to get along with, are they?'

'You can say that again.' Nicola picked up a stick, snapped it in two; she handed Tom half.

'My parents used to work for a charity in Africa. They dug wells so people would have clean water.' He watched Nicola throw the stick. 'Believe it or not, dirty drinking water is one of the biggest killers in the world. One in eight of the world's population don't have access to safe supplies.'

'I wish I could do something worthwhile.'

'They're extremely dedicated.' He lobbed his stick and felt an intense dismay when it went wide. His half caught fast on a patch of mud, leaving Nicola's to drift away alone. The fate of his marooned stick appeared uncomfortably significant. He continued talking to mask his unease. 'My mother and father are so dedicated to *giving* that I keep being told by other people that they are saints. You wouldn't believe how much they do care. They're devoting themselves to renovating Mull-Rigg Hall for Owen to inherit when he's eighteen. My aunt's will provided cash for the work, but giving and doing good is a quest for my parents.'

The outburst surprised Nicola. 'You sound almost angry about it!'

'This is going to sound so selfish, but I remember when I was a kid. We lived in Uganda, on this arid plain with millions of weird thorn trees. My mother and father worked for weeks to sink wells for the local population. When this fresh, sparkling water gushed out of the ground the villagers surrounded our house. They hugged and kissed my parents. I saw all these shining, happy faces of parents whose children would now be spared from God-awful parasitic infections. And I was so damn ripped up inside. Because I felt so guilty that I wanted things for me . . . you know what I'm saying? Like any other child, I wanted birthday treats, toys, computer games.' The words spilled from his lips; his heart was pounding. He'd never revealed these feelings before. 'You know, when I was ten, I asked for a new bike, just like kids do. Yet I felt so guilty and mean-spirited for wanting something for myself when my parents were saving thousands of lives. There I was, Nicola, just a little boy, and I was lying awake at night, hating myself. It got so bad that when I did get the bike I was too ashamed to ride it. Whenever I touched the handlebars it felt like touching something dirty. A child shouldn't experience that level of guilt.'

'When I was seven my mother told me I was fathered by Thor, the Viking god of thunder.' She looked Tom in the eye. 'It's OK – laugh if you want to.'

'I'm not laughing, Nicola.'

'Everyone else does.'

'I'm the son of two saints,' he said with the ghost of a smile. 'You're the daughter of a god. I reckon we're a good match.'

They didn't speak for a while. Tom knew that the words they spoke to each other were gradually making their way deeper inside than was usual when people speak. As if there was some deep, sacred place of the heart for such an exchange of confidences to take root.

At last Nicola said, 'I should go now.'

'When shall we see each other again?'

Never. He could almost hear that awful word ringing in his ears. Instead, she patted the boulder. 'Here – tomorrow.'

Tomorrow's too far away, he thought. *In fact, as they say: tomorrow never comes.* Tom said, 'My parents are away until late. They're taking Owen to the cinema. You could come over for a drink.'

She nodded.

'Eight?'

'Eight sounds good. Thank you, Tom.'

He took her hand to help her down from the boulder.

'So . . .' she said, 'what're your plans for the rest of the day?'

Being with you would be nice . . . He resisted pitching the line; instead, he shrugged. 'Oh, clearing more chairs out of the house.'

'Those chairs are famous. I remember your aunt setting them out in rows on the lawn.'

'Well, they haunt me. I have dreams about chairs. About being mugged by chairs. Being chased by man-eating chairs.'

'Your aunt must have collected them for years.'

'They fill Mull-Rigg Hall. The place is bursting with chairs. I've been stacking them in the garage.'

'So you're keeping them?'

'Keeping them?' Flippantly, he said, 'I'm going to pile the things up then set fire to them.'

'You wouldn't do that!' Her eyes widened in shock.

'Try me. Ever since I started work on the house I've been plagued by those crap chairs.'

'Those chairs aren't crap.' Ice crept into her voice. 'I told you that Mrs Gibson held garden parties for the villagers, didn't I? We'd never dare go while they were there. After they'd gone, though, your aunt would open the gate that leads to the forest and call us in.' Her eyes became dreamy. 'I remember once, when I was eight years old, the sun had started to set. Your aunt was talking to my mother. There must have been fifty chairs on the lawn. I went from one to the other, sitting in each. I pretended to be a different person in the audience. In one chair, I was the rich lady who fanned her face all the time. Then I was a Duchess who glared at everyone. Then I sat in the back row and pretended to be a serving girl who'd secretly crept in to listen to that amazing music, and who knew she'd get a beating from her mistress if she was found out.' She smiled. 'The only person I didn't try to be was me.'

Tom Westonby returned to Mull-Rigg Hall and slotted a bottle of Greek wine into the fridge; he'd brought this back after visiting Chris a few weeks ago. Greek wine sometimes had a reputation for being as harsh as nail-varnish remover. This, however, was smooth as silk, with a bewitching taste of honey.

After that, he went to stare at the chairs in the garage. There were dozens of those brown wooden relics. He pictured himself piling the monstrosities up and setting them ablaze. All that old, volatile furniture would ignite in seconds. So, he set about moving those straight-backed chairs. He'd shifted so many of the things in the last few weeks he could easily carry four at a time out into the garden.

After he'd finished, he worked through his schedule of jobs, which included redecorating the ancient scullery. With the painting done, he showered, shaved, changed his clothes, and began setting the table for supper. As he prepared a spaghetti bolognese he switched on the television in the kitchen. The weather forecast warned there was a storm coming – an unusually ferocious one: 'Areas at risk must prepare for flooding. There will be storm damage . . .'

The sky was clear here. A storm might be on its way, though it wouldn't strike yet, that was a certainty.

Taking the wine from the fridge, he found himself thinking about Nicola. He pictured her as a child as she delighted in playing amongst the chairs on the lawn. All the villagers would have gone home by then. The little blonde girl would be alone in the garden. She'd happily sit in each chair in turn to pretend at being a grown-up: the stern duchess; the rich lady with the fan; the shy serving girl. After living alone with her mother in the isolated cottage, the sight of all those chairs set out as if for a concert must have been so exciting. And he remembered her comment about the evening she played on the lawn all those years ago: *'The only person I didn't try to be was me.'*

He went to greet Nicola as she walked up the drive. She wore a calf-length white dress and sandals. The blonde hair had been brushed into soft waves.

'Did you burn the chairs?' she asked.

'See for yourself.' He led her round to the back lawn.

The chairs were as he'd left them. Set out in neat rows, as if for a concert.

She stopped dead. The sight astonished her.

'Sit anywhere you want,' he told her with a smile. 'Only, promise me that you'll be nobody else tonight. I want you to be Nicola Bekk.'

SEVENTEEN

Moonlight fell through the open window. Tom Westonby lay in bed with his hands behind his head. He gazed at a bright silver moon floating above the treetops.

He felt good. He felt wonderful.

Three hours ago he'd sat out in the garden with Nicola. Seeing those chairs lined up on the lawn had evoked such happy memories from her childhood – back in that golden time when his aunt had held garden parties. Nicola had been in such a good mood that they'd spent the evening talking and laughing.

Two hours ago he'd walked her home. They'd spent a long time at the archway that led into the garden, the one engraved with the Viking dragon. That hadn't been a time for conversation, or for laughing; instead, he'd put his arms around her in the dark. The kisses were long ones. Only eventually, and reluctantly, had they stepped back from another.

Tom had watched Nicola walk to the cottage door. They'd waved to each other. Her smile had fixed itself so deeply inside of him he could see it now.

He cast a glance at his clock-radio. One a.m. He was too happy to sleep. Even as he recalled playing catch around the chairs on the lawn with Nicola, he found himself replaying those words of the superstitious diver: *'It's like I'm being given one last good time before I die . . . one last party spree before they nail down my coffin lid.'* Tom silenced the doom-laden thought by saying a name aloud that meant so much to him: 'Nicola . . . Nicola Bekk.'

What did kill his smile was the voice echoing up the stairs: 'Mum . . . where are you?'

Tom sat up in bed. His parents had returned from the cinema at ten thirty, just as he was ready to walk Nicola back home. He knew Owen had gone straight to bed.

'Mum, I can't find you.'

'That's Owen,' Tom murmured in surprise.

Quickly, Tom pulled on his jeans. As he padded out on to the landing a draught of air told him the front door had been opened.

'Owen,' he whispered. 'Are you OK?'

'Late for school.' The ten-year-old's voice sounded odd: a lifeless monotone.

Puzzled, Tom moved along the landing. His parents' door was ajar. He glimpsed heads on pillows; they were fast asleep.

'I'm late,' Owen intoned. 'Mum, where are you?'

Tom silently headed downstairs. Owen's mother had died of heart-failure months ago, and he wouldn't be starting school again until the new term; all of which suggested that the boy was both walking and talking in his sleep. Was there any wonder, considering the trauma he'd been through?

'Owen?' He kept his voice low; no point in waking his parents. 'Owen, come back inside.'

Owen didn't seem to be listening. Although, at that moment, Tom was confident he'd quickly catch up and bring him back to the house. He was halfway through the door when he realized he'd nothing on his feet. He quickly pulled on his shoes, which were just inside the hallway, then he ran lightly along the drive. The moon cast plenty of light, clearly revealing the gates, the road, and the edge of the forest.

No sign of the boy.

'Owen,' Tom called. 'Owen, come back.'

A rustle of branches suggested that Owen was heading along the path to the river. Tom ran across the road. A second later he plunged into the deep shadow of the trees. The rustling continued. Owen must be running, too, otherwise Tom would have caught up with him. He loped along the path, low branches catching his hair. Now he'd entered the forest he could barely see. The moonlight hardly penetrated the leaves at all.

'Owen,' he called. 'Come back. It's not safe out here at night.'

No reply. Tom ran faster. The roar of the rapids grew louder. He pictured steep banks. So easy for a boy to slip down: especially if he was walking in his sleep. There were deep channels in the river, and the water rushing round boulders created whirlpools. A ten-year-old would all too easily be sucked down.

Then another noise . . . a deep, throaty rumble. Tom tilted his head as the rumble came again. The weather forecast had predicted a storm. From the muttering of that thunder it was on its way.

Tom followed the line of the path the best he could. More than once he blundered off it in the gloom. Immediately, tree trunks closed in. They were like intimidating thugs trying to block his way.

'Owen! Where are you?'

Owen didn't answer. The thunder did, however. That rumble grew louder, like the sound of bombs falling on houses. He found himself off the path again. Nettles stung his bare hands as he brushed by. Suddenly, a noise.

'Owen?'

A heavy body surged through the bushes: certainly something too big to be even remotely Owen-like. In the deep shadow, he glimpsed a silhouette. What he heard above the crunch of sticks was a flurry of whispers, as if a dozen people were urgently hissing comments at one another.

The strangeness of those whispers sent cold shivers down his back. Instantly, his diver's instinct for self-preservation slammed through him. In moments, he'd managed to scramble back to the path. His breath came in spurts; his heart was smashing like crazy against his ribs.

No. Don't run away. His need to find Owen overrode the inner alarm that screamed DANGER!

Straightaway, he plunged into the trees again, heading in the direction of that object crashing through vegetation. What if Owen was in there with that thing? The boy might be hurt. But what *was* that thing? Surely, it must be big . . . damn big. Sticks snapped under its weight. The underbrush shook with surprising violence as a heavy body surged powerfully through.

Tom scanned his memory for big animals that were native to England. Maybe a stag? Or even a wild boar – those heavyweight brutes could be dangerous.

As he stumbled towards the beast that crashed its way through the forest, he forced his eyes to adjust to the lack of light, and he glimpsed the creamy flesh of a tree trunk that marked where a large branch had been ripped away above his head.

Hell, this was a big animal.

The thunder came again. This time a great, rolling roar: mimicking the bellow of a huge, hungry beast.

Then the scream. A boy's scream. High and thin, and full of terror.

Tom hurtled through the trees. The lumbering beast moved just ahead of him. He found himself knowing to the core of his being that he'd have to confront it.

Not just confront it. *Fight it!* The thing was attacking Owen.

He burst into a clearing. Moonlight poured down; a cascade of brilliant white.

Owen stood on open ground. His mouth hung open. His eyes were staring in shock. They looked like big glittering balls of glass in his head. Just the expression on the boy's face delivered a stab of fear into Tom's stomach.

Oh my God, what's happened to him?

He rushed forward. In the light of the moon, he saw the sandy soil had been gouged. There seemed to be a messy confusion of footprints, as if a group of people had gathered here. Near the ripped-up patch of soil there was a line of single footprints. He saw the shapely line of a bare foot. Individual toe prints were clearly visible.

Once again the thunder bellowed. Immediately after that, he

heard the rustle of branches; the animal seemed to be heading towards the river. Strangely, he made out what appeared to be people hissing words at each other. Though he couldn't decipher the actual words, the unusual quality of that hiss made his scalp prickle. The sound alone pushed a cold current of fear through his veins.

Being scared of something he could not see infuriated Tom. He charged towards the sound. Already, he heard a splashing, as if the animal had blundered into the river. Then a female voice . . . calling.

He stopped dead. *Damn it, that sounds like Nicola! What the hell's she doing out here?* He listened carefully as he padded towards the riverbank. Before he could hear the voice again, another crash of thunder barrelled along the river. When that faded he heard another voice – this, the rising cry from Owen.

There was no way he could leave the boy alone any longer while he chased shadows.

In seconds he'd reached Owen. He picked him up in his arms. 'It's alright, Owen, it's me, Tom. Everything's OK.' He spoke in soothing tones. 'We'll go home now. There's nothing to worry about.'

The boy, however, stared at the churned patch of earth.

He didn't blink. When he talked, it seemed to Tom that he did so in a trance. 'It's not like you see in films. It's not like that at all. It's all made from people. Lots of people. They're all mixed up in it. Stuck together . . .'

Tom carried the boy back home. Soothingly, he reassured Owen that everything was alright. The boy, however, continued to stare back over Tom's shoulder. He seemed to see something haunting the shadows.

'It's not like the one you see in the church window,' Owen said, still speaking in that trance-like way; a chilling monotone. 'It was going to hurt me . . . She called it away.'

'Who called it away, Owen?'

At that moment the thunder let loose a monstrous bellow. The sound could have come from gigantic jaws. There was fury in the sound. A threat of violence and death.

Owen sagged in Tom's arms and started sobbing. 'I want my mother. Take me to my mother.'

Tom couldn't do that. Owen's mother had been found dead at Mull-Rigg Hall. All he could do was murmur that everything would be alright.

But would it? Tom Westonby felt as if a huge, dark pit was opening beneath his feet. Something was badly wrong here in this remote corner of Yorkshire. Something was rotten. And dangerous. Incredibly dangerous.

Tom managed to get Owen back into bed without waking his own parents. Then he sat in the chair beside Owen's bed as the child bunched his fists in his sleep. All night long the boy muttered with a dark, fretful intensity about the monster that haunted his nightmares.

EIGHTEEN

The rain came. Thunder growled in such a way that it sounded as if an angry dinosaur prowled the valley. Lightning had struck a tree on the village green. The intense heat transformed the oak into an ugly black skeleton. Floodwaters engulfed potato fields by the river. The rain came even harder. Huge drops exploded against the road. In Chester Kenyon's workshop, the din of falling rain could have been angry fists beating against the roof.

That wasn't the worst of it. Chester Kenyon stared at Tom Westonby as if his friend has suddenly stabbed a knife into his stomach.

'Jesus, Tom, you are joking, aren't you?'

'No.'

'Nicola Bekk?'

'Yes.'

'You're seeing Nicola Bekk?'

'What's the problem?'

'Jesus Christ, Tom. You idiot!' Chester flung a hammer down on to the workbench, then ran his fingers through his hair. His eyes bulged as he stared at Tom. 'Nicola Bekk's retarded.'

'Hey, take that back. Nicola's a great girl.'

'Tom, she's got problems here.' He touched his forehead. 'Learning difficulties. Backward. Retarded. Do you understand?'

Tom kicked aside a chair. 'I thought we were friends. Truth is, I feel like punching you in your damn face.'

'Oh my God. You've not had sex with her?'

'None of your business.' After the incident last night, when Owen had wandered off into the forest – sleep walking, he guessed – his nerves felt raw. His parents had said they would keep a close watch on Owen after Tom had explained what happened. They wondered if Owen's grief over his mother's sudden death had triggered frightening nightmares.

Right now, Tom needed to see a friendly face. Yet for some crazy reason Chester was making these disgusting accusations. Good grief, they were bizarre accusations at that.

Chester grabbed Tom by the elbow. When he spoke it was in a caring voice, though; he seemed deeply troubled. 'Tell me you haven't had sex with Nicola Bekk.'

Tom didn't reply. The rain fell harder. The furious drumming on the roof became frenzied – it would be easy to imagine the weather itself was growing excited by the atmosphere of violence in the workshop. Thunder roared across the valley.

'Tom. This is important. Have you had sex with that woman?'

'Shit . . . I thought we were friends.'

'Spit it out, Tom. Have you screwed her?'

'No.'

Chester let out a yell of relief. 'Thank God for that!'

'You're just like the other people in the village, you bastard. You hate the Bekk family. You've got a grudge against them.' Tom stormed out into the rain.

Chester ran after him. 'Listen, we need to talk.'

'I never want to talk to you again.'

'Tom—'

'If you don't let go of my arm I'm going to break your jaw.'

Chester spoke gently: 'Go ahead, punch me. But I'm going to tell you something important.'

Tom said nothing.

Raindrops streamed down Chester's broad face as he continued speaking: 'You must have seen for yourself. Nicola doesn't talk.'

This statement flabbergasted Tom. 'Of course she talks.'

'OK, she says a word here and there.'

'No. I've had conversations with her.'

'We're talking about the same Nicola Bekk, aren't we?'

Tom looked him in the eye. 'What's all this about?'

'Come inside.' Chester's voice was friendly. 'There's something you should know . . . It might just save your neck.'

NINETEEN

The rain kept slamming at the roof. Once again thunder crashed from the clouds. Fury and anger were there. As if Mother Nature threatened to punish the population of Danby-Mask.

Chester Kenyon handed Tom a mug of coffee before pulling a book from a shelf on the workshop wall. That done, he sat down on a chair alongside Tom.

Chester thought for a moment before speaking. 'I'm going to show you something. I want you to know that I'm not doing this to insult you, or hurt you. But it's important that you know the truth, even if that means you knock my teeth out.'

'After what you've said about Nicola I might just do that.'

'OK, you say she's your girlfriend. You kissed her. But haven't had sex yet.'

'Chester?' Tom's voice held the same warning growl as the thunder.

'Listen. I'm twenty-three years old – the same age as Nicola. We went to the village school together. When she was twelve she stopped going. That was the end of her education.'

'So explain why you think Nicola has learning difficulties.'

'For seven years I was at school with Nicola. In all that time I never heard her say a sentence of more than three words.'

'You only have to look at her,' Tom protested. 'She's normal. And she – she's beautiful.' *What's got into Chester*, he wondered. *Why's he trying to break Nicola and me up?*

Chester opened a book covered with children's drawings. Tom showed him the first page; a title had been printed in green: CLASSROOM FRIENDSHIP BOOK.

'We used to do these at the end of the school year,' he explained. 'The teacher told us to swap the books round in class. We'd draw a picture of the owner of the book and write messages. That way everyone in the class would have drawn your picture and written something about you. You know, a memento?' He flicked through the pictures. Lots showed a broad-faced boy that was clearly

supposed to be Chester. 'We did this one when I was eight.' Each
page had a child's drawing of Chester – in one he was playing
football, in another eating gigantic cakes; one even had him being
fired from a canon. One caption ran: *Yo! Fat Neck Kenyon.*

'Fat Neck?' Tom gave him a questioning look.

Chester touched his formidable neck. 'Yeah, the nickname stuck.'

The drawings were typical of those by an eight-year-old. The
girls' pictures tended to be neater and dispensed with the 'Fat Neck'.

'I'm showing you the next page,' Chester said, 'because it backs
up what I've been saying about Nicola.'

Tom's blood drained from his face, leaving him cold inside as
Chester turned the page. In the centre of the white paper was a
dense black scribble. All jagged lines. A frenzy of black pen-marks.
This wasn't so much a picture as a savage attack on the page. An
adult hand had written: *Nicola Bekk says, 'Hi, to my nice friend,
Chester.'*

For a moment, Tom couldn't speak. 'Nicola did that?'

'I didn't bully her like the other kids. Even then I knew it was
wrong to call her names because she couldn't read or write.' He
pointed to the *nice friend* message. 'Miss Kravitz added that.'

The rain hissed against the roof, rising and falling like angry
breathing. A searing flash of blue lightning lit up the workshop.

'Sorry to do this to you, Tom.' Chester closed the book, hiding
that scribble – there was something tormented and desperate about
those bursting lines of ink.

'She's not like that.' Tom shook his head.

'She was. She still is. When Nicola comes into the village she
doesn't speak. If she buys stuff at the store all she does is point.'

'No. You're lying.'

'Come on. There's one more thing to show you.'

He led the way into a back room that had been fitted out as a
rest area. There were ancient saggy armchairs facing a television
complete with a DVD system.

'Wait here, Tom.' Chester spoke in a kindly way. He obviously
didn't want to hurt his friend. There was a sense he did this
reluctantly.

Chester left Tom for only a few moments. He soon returned with
a DVD, which he fed into the player. He then switched on the TV.

'My Grandad filmed this at the Christmas nativity show at school.'
He glanced back at Tom before pressing the play button. 'I'm doing

this because you're my friend, Tom. If the police knew you were
. . . you know, with Nicola, and with her being like she is . . .
there'd be trouble.'

Tom could only shake his head. Thunder crashed around the
building. *That's the sound of my world falling down*, he thought.

The television screen flashed. A Christmas carol sung by children flooded the room. The poignant notes of 'Silent Night' always
had a melancholy air for Tom. The carol celebrated the birth of
the Boy Child, yet the melody hinted at tragedy lying ahead. Tom
watched as children acted out the Nativity story. Seven-year-olds,
wearing towels on their heads, pretended to be Bethlehem's
citizens, and here came the Three Wise Men with cardboard
crowns decorated in gold foil. Tom identified one Wise Man as
a seven-year-old Chester Kenyon, grinning hugely as the crown
kept sliding down to cover his eyes. All the schoolchildren seemed
to be taking part, as angels, shepherds, townsfolk, the apologetic
innkeeper, and Mary and Joseph.

All the children, that is, except one.

In the background, by a door, stood a little girl. A tiny blonde
sprite. She stared at the Nativity play as if the children had
deliberately acted in some way that was inexplicable to her. She
wasn't in costume. Her blue eyes glittered with fear. If anything,
she resembled a wild fawn from the forest that had been caught in
a trap.

Chester's grandfather had been filming the children in long shot,
to get as many on screen as possible. For some reason he zoomed
into close-up on the strange sprite of a girl.

The thin, heart-shaped face filled the television screen. The eyes
looked into the camera lens. Tom felt as if she stared directly at
him. Without a shred of doubt he knew the name of that unearthly
child.

That was a seven-year-old Nicola Bekk.

Her eyes narrowed – the Christian festival seemed to be the cause
of physical pain.

At that moment a teacher's voice rang out as she narrated the
Nativity. 'And, lo, a boy child is born. And His name is Jesus!'

In the video, Nicola Bekk let out a piercing scream. The girl was
terrified. She pushed open the door behind her and ran into a corridor.
There were no lights in the corridor. It looked for all the world that
she raced into a tunnel, which led down into the depths of the earth.

Tom's heart went out to the frightened child that was Nicola Bekk. 'The poor girl.'

'You might think that, Tom. The truth is, nobody likes Nicola Bekk. What's more, the villagers hate her mother. Five years ago, Mrs Bekk tried to set fire to St George's church. She was lucky she didn't end up in prison.'

'There must have been a reason why she did that.'

'Oh, there's a reason alright. Mrs Bekk is crazy.' Chester's expression was grim. 'Dangerously crazy at that. If you'll take some advice, Tom, don't have anything to do with the Bekk family. Don't speak to them. Don't even acknowledge they exist.'

Tom shuddered at the sound of Chester's words. They had the same chilling tones as a sentence of death. *But whose death? Mine? Nicola's?*

Thunder crashed again. Such a forbidding sound – as ominous as the pounding of monstrous fists breaking down the doors of a tomb to set the dead upon the living.

TWENTY

Chester Kenyon's shock warning still rang in Tom's ears: *don't have anything to do with the Bekk family. Don't speak to them. Don't even acknowledge they exist.* As Tom walked from Chester's workshop to his car, the words continued to roll about his skull with the same grim resonance as the thunder rolling across the landscape.

Moments later, he drove away along Main Street. Danby-Mask had radiated charm when he first saw the place. The ancient stone buildings, beneath red tiled roofs, nestled alongside the River Lepping. This could have been a quaint hamlet right out of a Victorian painting.

However, beneath those looming storm clouds, Danby-Mask had been transfigured. It had become a troubling place of dark secrets and spiteful prejudice. He couldn't help but think about Nicola Bekk. Her mother must have warned Nicola from an early age that the village was a dangerous place. For hundreds of years the Bekk family had been despised for being foreign invaders.

The whole situation worried him deeply. He shook his head as he recapped the Bekk family legend. *Over a thousand years ago the Bekk family leave Denmark. They arrive here in northern England, perhaps as part of the invading Viking army. Then the Bekks create their settlement in the valley. Danby-Mask hates the invaders; its people launch a surprise attack and slaughter most of the family. Somehow, the surviving members of the Bekk clan hang on. (In the family legend, they're protected by some monster dreamed up by a Viking god.) OK, there are lots of stories like that in Yorkshire. There are myths about dragons that live in wells, about witches stealing babies, and ghost dogs with fiery eyes. But what makes this story different is that Mrs Bekk told her daughter that it was all true, and that Nicola faces terrible danger from the village.*

Tom switched on the wipers as the storm launched its watery attack on the car. Raindrops hit the roof with the same kind of harsh rattle as stones being thrown at metalwork. Falling rain blurred the houses. Those ancient structures began to resemble phantom dwellings: as if they'd manifested here from a sinister realm.

He couldn't help but picture Nicola attending the village school when she was a child. By then she'd have heard her mother's stories of local people murdering her ancestors. Nicola would undoubtedly hurry by the church, while shooting scared glances up at the huge stone tower. After being brainwashed by her mother into believing that Danby-Mask was an evil place, Nicola Bekk must have seen St George's as nothing less than a demon's lair.

Nicola would have been too young to differentiate her mother's fantasies from reality. Attending school would have been an ordeal. *No, scratch out 'ordeal' and substitute 'torture'. She'd think the other kids were planning to murder her. No wonder she ran screaming out of the Christmas Nativity play.*

At that moment, his anger at Mrs Bekk's treatment of her child blazed furiously. His heart pounded. He wanted to protect Nicola. She'd been through an incredibly cruel upbringing. No child should have to endure that. How she'd remained so sweet-natured was nothing less than a miracle. Mrs Bekk had tried to twist her mind. The twenty-three-year-old Nicola should be dosed to the eyeballs with drugs.

Instead, she'd risen above the madness. She'd survived.

And I want to help her stay that way, he told himself. *Maybe when you're twenty-three you feel it's your duty to be the knight in*

shining armour: to protect the vulnerable maiden from danger. But,
damn it all, I'm not going to let her life be wrecked by that lunatic
mother of hers. I'm going to put things right.

Tom accelerated away from the village, his heart pounding. Wipers
swept water aside, yet he still couldn't see clearly. The road, trees
and fields had been transformed into a ghost world. Lightning added
its own strange magic by splashing the fields with electric blue.

'Shit!' He'd rounded a bend to find a figure standing in the middle
of the road.

He braked. No good: the wheels glided across the slick road.

'Nicola!' He stared through the windscreen as the car hurtled on
a collision course towards her. *What on earth's she doing in the*
road? He wrenched the wheel. The car's tail swung outwards. Its
back wheels struck the turf at the side of the road, gouging mud in
an explosion of black.

At least the car had stopped. He sat there panting. His mouth
turned dry as dust.

'Oh my God! Nicola!' He expected to see her broken body lying
in the road. *Where is she?* He could see nothing through that wall
of grey rain.

Then there came a thump. Someone had opened the door.

Nicola stood there. Rain streamed down her face.

'Thank God.' His heart thundered. 'I thought I'd killed you.'

She stared at him. Was that suspicion in her eye? Did she suspect
him of betraying her in some way?'

'Nicola, what's wrong?'

Her next words were very precise. She must have been thinking
about this question. Perhaps even rehearsing the saying of it. 'Tom.
When you look at me, what do you see?'

'What do I see? I don't understand.'

'What do I mean to you?'

Her face wore an expression of dreadful anxiety. It was as if she
stood before a sheeted figure lying in a morgue, and someone was
just about to drag that sheet away.

'Nicola! I could have killed you. Why were you in the road?'

'Tom,' she hissed. 'What do I mean to you?'

'Get in.' His voice softened. 'Please, get in.'

She climbed into the passenger seat.

He looked her in the eye. 'I'll tell you what you mean to me in
a moment. But there's something important I've got to do.'

'What?'

'This.'

He kissed her. The stiffness in her lips only lasted a second. Then she was kissing him back with the same furious passion. This was wonderful. More wonderful than anything he'd ever done before.

He, Tom Westonby, was kissing a beautiful woman in a thunderstorm. The car was slewed across the road. The back half of the vehicle rested on a bank of earth. *This is madness*, said a voice in the back of his head.

Damn right, he thought. *It's glorious madness. I don't care if anyone sees me, honks their horn, or shakes their fist.*

I'm kissing Nicola. She's kissing me. And that's exactly how it should be.

TWENTY-ONE

After the kiss, everything started to go wrong. Not at first, though.

At first, everything seemed to be going so well.

Tom Westonby reversed the car until he'd freed it from the dirt bank. Nicola sat beside him.

'Is that kiss your answer,' she asked, 'to what I mean to you?'

'I like you.' He smiled back. 'You're intelligent, you've a great sense of humour.'

'Looks?'

'You've got some of those, too. Ears, nose, and mouth, just where they should be.'

'So I'm no Picasso portrait?'

'You mean with a nose on your forehead and ears for lips?' He shook his head. 'Your face is just how I like it.' He grinned. 'It's there right at the front of your head where a face should be.'

'Is that a compliment?' She laughed.

He liked the sound of that pleasant laughter. It felt like a nice tickle inside his heart. 'You are beautiful. Sexy. You know –' he thumped his chest as he drove 'the heart-pumping sexy.'

'Thank you. You can give me compliments like that anytime you want. *I like 'em.*'

Tom drove slowly now the storm had well and truly broken. Nicola chatted away. She seemed in an unusually good mood. He found himself driving even more slowly, because he wanted to stretch out these pleasant moments of them being together.

Even so, the journey was over all too quickly. Tom pulled up outside Mull-Rigg Hall. The moment he switched off the engine, Owen opened the front door.

'Hurry up,' yelled the boy. 'We're going to get you packed off to France!'

'France?' echoed Nicola in surprise.

Owen shouted, 'Can I have that chocolate in the fridge, if you're not taking it with you?' With that, he charged back into the house.

Nicola's happy expression switched to one of fury. 'You're going to France?'

'I've got a job there, working on some industrial units.'

'You're going to France and you didn't think to tell me?'

'There wasn't time . . .'

Nicola face registered utter disappointment. 'A few minutes ago,' she began, 'I asked you what I meant to you.'

'You do mean a lot to me.'

'Actions speak louder than words, don't they? You're going to France without even telling me. So what does that say about how you feel?'

'Nicola, I planned to tell you.'

'What, after you'd got me into bed?'

'Nicola—'

'Thanks for nothing, you bastard.'

'Nicola, I love you.'

Tom said the words to a closed car door. She'd slammed it shut as he'd opened his mouth. She'd not heard the *Nicola, I love you.* Already, she was running away through the pouring rain.

He climbed out of the car. 'Nicola!' Thunder roared. 'I love you!' He slammed his fist down on the car's roof in frustration. The thunderstorm seemed determined to prevent him from conveying those three words that had acquired a blazing importance.

Everything was conspiring against him. Nicola, jumping to conclusions, then racing away before he could tell her he loved her. And now the thunder, drowning out his voice. As he headed down the driveway after her, his father hurried out of the house. The man held a jacket over his head to ward off the deluge.

'Tom, wait!'

'Dad, I won't be a minute.'

'Jack Greensmith's on the phone. He needs to arrange where he'll meet you when you get to France.'

'Tell Jack I'll call him back.'

'I can't do that. He's on his way to Frankfurt. He needs to speak to you now.'

'Damn it!'

'Tom, what's wrong?'

Then Tom made a fateful decision. He decided to face this mega problem head on.

'Tom, hurry up! Jack's at the airport. He's about to board the plane.'

'No.'

His father reacted with surprise. 'Tom, didn't you hear? Jack wants to arrange a pick-up time from the station in Paris.'

'No.'

'You're not making sense, Tom. What's all this "No" nonsense?'

'I'm saying "No" to France.'

'I beg your pardon?'

Thunder muttered angrily in the clouds.

'I'm not going to France.'

'Of course you are, it's all arranged.'

'I'm not going. I'm staying here.' Even as Tom spoke the words he felt such a sinking sensation in his chest. The expression of dismay on his father's face was incredible.

'Tom . . .' His father couldn't even bring himself to keep holding the jacket over his head. He let it drop down. The rain immediately struck his head, slicking down the hair. 'I practically begged Jack to give you that job. I did everything I could to persuade him that you were the best man to do the welding.' His voice dropped to a whisper. 'Don't do this to me, son. Don't tell me I'm going to have to let my friend down. He needs your help to get those buildings ready.'

'I'm sorry, Dad. I'm not going. I need to stay here.'

Tom would have preferred his father to fly into a rage; instead, he stood there looking so wounded. Sheer hurt bled from his eyes.

'You needed the money for the dive school. I thought this is what you wanted?'

'Dad, I'll find the money some other way.'

'So you want me to tell Jack that you're turning his job down?'

'Dad, our family doesn't always have to put everyone else first!' The floodgates had opened. Tom stood there in the pouring rain and those issues that had festered since childhood came gushing out. 'You did amazing work in Africa, digging those wells, piping fresh water to the villages. You saved thousands of lives.'

Tom's words, as much as the anger, baffled the man. 'What's that got to do with working in France?'

'Nothing . . . No! *Everything*. Every damn thing!' Tom wiped the rain from his eyes. 'Don't you see? I grew up hearing people tell me you were a saint. You and my mother put everyone else first. But don't you see? You were putting what strangers wanted before what I needed. Dad, I haven't said this before, but sometimes it was so hard to be your son. I was just a child; I wanted to be selfish sometimes and have you and my mother just to myself. But it reached the stage where I couldn't enjoy my birthday presents, because I thought other people were more deserving. I felt so damn guilty asking for anything. Even your time! My blood would boil with sheer guilt if I asked you to play football with me, because I knew you needed to be out there: finding water, digging wells, saving lives.'

'You resented me doing that work?'

'Not now. I know you did amazing, miraculous things. You brought freshwater to villages where children were dying because they didn't have clean supplies. But back then, when I was eight years old, I couldn't handle it. Inside, my heart was breaking. And I hated myself, because I thought I was being a selfish brat.'

His father spoke softly: 'Is that why you want to hurt me by not honouring this commitment to work for my friend?'

'No.'

'So, why are you staying here?'

Tom took a deep breath. He didn't plan to say what he did. The statement even took him by surprise. 'I'm getting married.'

'*Married?*'

'I'm marrying—'

'I know who you've been seeing.' His dad's voice wasn't so much calm as strangely flat. 'You've been seeing Nicola Bekk. I've heard about her.'

'And that's who I'm marrying.' Now he'd made that astonishing, surprising and spontaneous statement it seemed the most natural thing in the world. As if deep down he'd known all along. 'Nicola Bekk will be my wife.'

'No, she won't, Tom. You might hate me for saying this, but I'm going to do everything in my power to prevent her from becoming your wife.'

Owen appeared at the door. 'Hey! Mr Greensmith is shouting over the phone that he's got to get on the plane.'

Tom's father said nothing more. He turned and walked through the rain to the house. He'd have to tell an old friend that Tom would be breaking his promise to work on the industrial units. *After all the sacrifices I've made for you, Tom. And this is how you repay me.* Tom could all too easily read the man's body language. *You've let me down, son. You've let me down badly.*

Storm winds surged through the trees. From the sky came the angry bark of thunder.

For a moment, Tom Westonby was stunned. His father must be disappointed by his decision not to take up the job offer. *But why the hell has he said that he'll do everything in his power to stop me marrying Nicola?*

And do I really want to marry Nicola? I've not mentioned anything of the sort to her. Was it something I said in the heat of the moment to draw Dad's attention away from the rest of the world for once? And to make him notice me properly?

What had been done in the last ninety seconds couldn't be undone. He sensed his life would change in ways he couldn't even begin to imagine.

Tom started to run. Because he needed to have an important conversation with Nicola Bekk – the kind of conversation which just couldn't wait until tomorrow.

TWENTY-TWO

Water fell from the trees in great splotches. The leaves must have collected the raindrops until there was enough to tip out around a cupful in one go. Tom Westonby ran through the forest. Every so often a dollop of water burst on his head. He didn't even notice. All he wanted was to catch up with Nicola Bekk.

She'd stormed away from the car believing he preferred time in France to her. Now Tom had gone and opened a Pandora's Box. He'd released all kinds of terrible and exciting things that couldn't be put back. Tom had just told his father (who was a kind and loving man) that he'd felt neglected as a child. Tom sensed the man's shock. The words must have hurt so much. The truth was that the young Tom Westonby *had* felt neglected while his parents had devoted their lives to finding fresh drinking water for those people in Africa who were forced to drink, let's face it, filthy slops from the bottom of a muddy hole.

Tom felt terrible at making the confession. Yet he felt relieved, too. The guilt at wanting at least a little of his parents' attention had festered inside him for years. But then how could it be wrong for a young child to want to spend happy times with Mum and Dad?

Then he'd sprung the big surprise on his father. He'd told him he was going to marry Nicola Bekk. And his father had sprung an even bigger surprise. He'd promised to fight the marriage as hard as he possibly could. The man was determined to prevent Nicola becoming Tom's wife. *So has Dad been listening to gossip about Nicola in the village?*

Tom's mind was in turmoil. The last ten minutes had seemed life-changing. He'd always got on well with his father; now he wondered if they'd end up hating each other.

He ran faster along the forest trail. Storm winds clawed at the trees. Leaves were falling even though it was midsummer. Briefly, a flash of lightning pierced the branches. Immediately, there was a savage thump of thunder. *This storm wants blood*, he thought grimly. *People are going to die today.*

When he barrelled around the next bend in the path he nearly collided with Nicola. She stood with her chin raised in defiance. Her blonde hair dripped water down the skin of her bare throat.

'This is how we first met,' she told him in a hard voice. 'Are you going to use your fists this time?'

'No.'

'It wouldn't be the first time that I've been attacked. The month before you moved into Mull-Rigg Hall I was waiting for the post office to open – I get there early to avoid trouble – only, this time I wasn't early enough. One of the men from the village hit me in the mouth. I could taste blood for a week.'

The shock of her confession made his heart lurch. 'Did you report it?'

'To the police? It was the policeman's son that hit me.'

'I'm not here to attack you. I'm here—'

'For what? To say goodbye, because you're going to France?'

'I'm not going anywhere.'

'What do you want from me, then?'

Thunder rolled across the forest as he spoke. 'To tell you that I love you.' Damn it, the thunder had drowned out what he said once more. Was he doomed never to be able to reveal his true feelings?

'I said,' he began again. 'I said—'

'I know what you said.' Her eyes filled with tears. For a long time she said nothing then rested her hand on his chest. 'You know it's impossible, don't you?'

'Everything's possible.'

'You don't know what people are like here. They'll stop you getting close to me. They'll break us up.'

He kissed her. She didn't resist, but there was sadness there: a fatalism that this couldn't last.

Tom whispered, 'Sometimes I'm arrogant. I can do stupid things, too.'

'So you're just playing stupid now, when you say that you love me?'

He shook his head and put his hands on her shoulders. 'What I'm trying to say is that although I can behave like an idiot I'm also determined when I want something. You might say: *unstoppable*. When I was fifteen I decided I'd swim to the bottom of a lake, which everyone said was a hundred feet deep. For some reason it became so hugely important for me to make that dive. I didn't have an aqualung back then. So it would be just me, an old rubber mask, and as much air as I could cram into my lungs. One day, I went for it. I swam out to where it was deepest, took a deep breath, then kicked my way down to the bottom. The lake bed was covered with white stones. I grabbed hold of a pebble – my prize. And when I swam back to the surface I felt so . . . I don't know . . . The feeling was more than being ecstatic. It felt as if I'd achieved something important. Hugely important. A rite of passage. That adventure made me into someone who could do the impossible.'

'Do you see me as a white pebble at the bottom of a lake? If you win me over, will you feel as if you've won a prize?'

'I'll know I've won the most important prize of my life. Does that sound too slushy?'

'It does without a physical action to reinforce the sentiment. Does that sound too highfalutin?'

Tom held her tight, kissed her . . . Her blonde hair cascaded over his arm. He felt the rain-wet strands on his skin. Before he could kiss her again, she caught hold of his face and gently pushed his head back.

'You don't have to do this,' she said.

'I want to. After all –' he smiled – 'I . . . love . . . you.'

'It won't be an easy relationship. My mother will be against us.'

'My father will be, too.' Half-jokingly, he added, 'So what have we got to lose?'

'If we're not careful, we'll lose everything.' Her eyes were deadly serious. 'Absolutely everything.'

TWENTY-THREE

After Tom and Nicola had reluctantly gone their separate ways, he returned home. He approached the house with the distinct feeling that the time had come to face the music. He'd disappointed his father by backing out of the job in France. Russell Westonby had gone to a lot of trouble to get Tom that work.

Tom knew that plenty of frosty silences lay ahead. His parents would make polite small talk. They'd go out of their way to show that they didn't hold a grudge. Even so, you might as well paint 'THIS IS A GRUDGE-FILLED HOUSE' over the front door.

That particular door, however, didn't open. He tried the handle again.

Locked.

Hell, they've kicked me out. So much for saintly parents. They've turned me out on to the street.

As he fished the keys from his pocket he saw himself sleeping in his car tonight. But a quick turn of the key proved him wrong.

They'd not bolted the door to keep out their suddenly troublesome son.

'I'm home.' His voice echoed back coldly. 'Hello? Anybody?'

That echo possessed a sense of emptiness. Even abandonment.

When he saw the note on the hallway table he realized that his parents had left. They'd taken Owen with them, of course.

'Owen, the dutiful son they never had.' Tom bit his lip. That line seemed just too snide. *Owen's a good kid. Don't bring him into the Son v Parents war.*

The message proved that his parents were diplomatic to an unusual degree. They didn't want a repeat of today's upsetting confrontation between father and son. Instead of waiting to talk to him, or even phoning, his mother had written:

> *Dear Tom,*
>
> *We're both so sorry that 'words' were said this morning. We love you. Neither of us want to fall out with you over a girl. Dad asks if you will talk to Chester about Nicola Bekk. He thinks you need to hear from a good friend about some of the problems Nicola's had. Nicola might seem a lovely girl. As you get older, however, you'll realize that people aren't always what they first appear.*

A couple of lines were thickly crossed out, so he couldn't read what had been written. No doubt some vile rumour concerning Nicola had been recorded there before being self-censored by his mother's diplomatic heart. Perhaps it was common knowledge locally that Mrs Bekk suffered from the lunatic delusion that her daughter had been fathered by the Viking god, Thor. No doubt that caused the regulars at the George and Dragon pub to collapse into thigh-slapping bouts of laughter. Mrs Bekk's madness must be a source of boundless hilarity.

Villagers clearly didn't care how much Nicola had suffered because of her mother's mental condition.

Tom's fist tightened in anger until he was scrunching the paper. He took a deep, steadying breath and read the rest of the letter. After the crossed-out lines, his mother had added in a matter-of-fact way that they were returning home for a while to pack up the rest of their things, that the fridge was stocked with plenty of food. They'd even left his wages, which they paid by the week, for his work on the house.

You'll find the money under the blue elephant in the lounge.
Love, Mum, Dad and Owen xxx

Guilt money, he thought. *Just who's the guilty party, though?*

His phone announced a call by hollering, 'Your air tank's run out! You're gonna die!'

He answered. 'Hello, Chris. How's life in Greece?'

'Hot, sunny and totally short of cash.'

'I'm doing what I can to raise the money.'

'So you've enough for the rent? Because I was thinking I could get the dive school signs ready for—'

Tom knew this would be a bad day for letting people down. 'Chris, I'm sorry, I haven't been able to get the money.'

'What! You told me that you'd got a welding job in France? I promised the landlord I'd be handing over a cash deposit in a couple of days.'

'I'm not taking the job. Something came up.'

'Some *thing* came up? What's her name, Tom?'

'It's not that easy to explain over the phone.'

'Yeah, I bet.' Chris sounded so disappointed in Tom he could barely speak. 'Didn't we always promise each other that neither of us would get involved with a girl until the dive school was up and running?'

'You're there with your ex.'

'Yeah, as a prospective business partner! An investor! Not some screw-buddy!'

'Hey—'

'You know what, Tom? Piss off!' Chris broke the connection.

Tom headed upstairs. He towelled his hair dry, changed his rain-sodden clothes, looked in the mirror, then clenched a fist.

I'm not letting this beat me. He was determined to keep the dive school on track. This was his dream since he was a teenager. He and Chris had been planning it for years.

And he was going to fight to keep Nicola, too. *I'm not letting Danby-Mask, Chester Kenyon, Mrs Bekk, or even Dad get in the way.*

In the mirror, he saw a flame burning in his eyes. 'You don't beat down a Westonby. I'm going to come out on top.' He grabbed his phone from the bedside table and called up his friend. 'Chris . . . shut up. Listen.' He took the pause as acceptance of his demand.

'You're letting the landlord push you around. No, listen to me, Chris. This is what you're going to do. Offer him cash payments, OK? I can transfer the money to your bank account right now.'

'But he wants twelve months rent in advance.'

'That's too much. Tell him he can have three months' rent upfront.'

'We still haven't got enough money.'

'I'll raid the boat fund.'

'We *need* a boat.'

'We'll rent one. Greece is full of boats. Boats aren't a problem.'

'The landlord wants a year's rent,' Chris insisted. 'He won't back down.'

'Persuade him, Chris – use guile, cunning, skulduggery. Make him realize that we'll rent somewhere else if he doesn't see sense.'

'Well . . .'

'I trust you, Chris . . . You can make this happen.' Tom's voice became more forceful. *Damn it, I even sound inspirational.* 'Listen, I'll go online now and transfer the money for the bond and three months' rent.' In a flash of inspiration, he added with triumph, 'And tell him that we'll bloody well teach him how to scuba-dive for free. Even if he doesn't use the lessons himself he can give 'em away as a present or sell them. What do you think?'

'I think you're a genius.'

Tom knew they were friends again. 'Close the deal, Chris.'

After he'd finished the call, he switched on the laptop, accessed his bank account and transferred the cash. Within seconds he'd ripped out their savings to zero. At least the money should be appearing in Chris's account in the next few moments. Everything was up to Chris now. They'd be living on bread and water in Greece when they opened up the school, but so what? They'd be ready for business. The students would come . . . so would the money.

What's more, Nicola will be with me. The thought made him grin . . . and it was a huge, excited grin. What a crazy idea! But he knew to the depths of his heart this was what he wanted: a new business. A new bride. Did it get any better than that?

Tom felt so happy he sang at the top of his voice.

Great God in heaven! He'd turned everything round in a matter of minutes. From disaster to victory. He felt so incredibly exhilarated. Right now, he wanted to share the brilliant news with Nicola.

But what's she going to say when I ask her to marry me? This all seemed so crazy! Like a runaway train – like he'd taken off the brakes of his life. Everything was coming good. He felt good. He felt wonderful!

He bounded downstairs.

The door yawned open. A cool breeze carried leaves across the hallway floor.

Did I leave it open?

He turned to see three figures strolling out of the lounge.

'Remember us?'

Tom remembered all right. These were the three thugs that had chased Nicola.

'Get out,' he told them. 'There might be three of you, but I can still rip all of you to pieces.' He was on a high from the decision he'd made to ask Nicola to marry him. Bravado blazed in his veins.

'Three of us?' The big, slow-witted one grinned. 'Even I can count better than that.'

Tom felt a terrific blow in the back of the head. As he went down his last coherent thought was: *I didn't look behind me. There weren't three of them – there were four.*

All four pounced. Boots swung as they started kicking. Then there was an explosion of blood.

TWENTY-FOUR

'*Your air tank's run out! You're gonna die!*'

Tom Westonby opened his eyes.

'*Your air tank's run out! You're gonna die!*' That's typical scuba-diver humour: a joke with its own heart of darkness.

Tom stared at his phone on the hallway floor. The screen radiated a faint blue light into the gloom. Someone was trying to reach him. '*Your air tank's run out! You're—*' Abruptly, the device fell silent. The caller had given up.

He still stared at the phone as it lay there on the wooden floor. A black pool linked his head with the phone. He blinked. *Why am I lying here?* The question was an important one. Yet for a full thirty seconds he struggled to find the answer.

At last, the memory came rushing back. Those three thugs from the village had got into the house. A fourth guy had attacked him from behind. Now the memories came even faster. He'd fallen, and that's when those four heroes had started kicking him in the head.

He dipped his fingers into the dark liquid. When he looked at his fingertips he saw that the goo wasn't actually black. *No, this is the red stuff* . . . For a moment he gazed at the bloody fingers. As he did so, he found himself replaying the time he'd confronted the three thugs that had bullied Nicola. They'd ripped the plastic bag from her hand, spilling flour and eggs into the street, then they'd chased her. He'd cut them off and confronted them. He pictured each in turn: first, the big, slow-witted guy. Then there was the middle-sized one with the wispy tuft on his chin that tried desperately to be a beard. The smallest of the three went by the name of Bolter; the leader of the gang. Blisters covered the guy's face. No doubt as a result of gorging on illicit amphetamines.

The blows had left Tom dazed. He knew that a breeze gusted through the open doorway. He could see clouds scudding across the moon. He understood that his blood had been spilled. Only, his thoughts weren't connecting. *Kissing Nicola. The guys that attacked me. Arguing with Dad. France. The diving school* . . . Thoughts poured easily through his head. Yet he couldn't get his brain working properly . . . *Maybe just sleep here. Probably feel better in the morning.* He closed his eyes.

The woman's shout immediately made him reopen them.

'*Don't touch me!*'

The words slammed into him. He knew *exactly* who'd shouted. 'Nicola.'

'I told you not to touch me. I *warned* you not to touch me.'

That was Nicola's voice alright. Only, it sounded strange. There was a flatness to the tone, which seemed so odd that he started to shiver.

'Get away from me.'

Nicola's demand was met with laughter and mocking calls.

What's happening? What are they doing? Something close to an electric shock snapped through his body. In less than a second he'd scrambled to his feet.

The blast of pain that shot through his head made him stagger back to the wall. He leaned against it, his heart thrashing wildly. There was no strength in his legs. More than anything he wanted to rush outside to defend Nicola from those thugs. Yet all he could physically accomplish was to lean there.

Damn it. I've got to help Nicola. I've got to stop those bastards hurting her. But his motor coordination was a wreck. His vision was screwed. Dear God in heaven, he was a mess.

Then came the howl. The sound appalled him. The howl Nicola made resembled the scream of a siren. The sound rose higher and higher, more and more shrill.

Just what are those men doing to her?

'Come on,' he hissed to himself. 'Come on. Don't stand here like a useless piece of crap. Do something . . . Help her.'

Grabbing a huge lungful of air, he forced himself to straighten his body. *Damn it.* The moment he did so it felt as if a ton of rubble had cascaded on to his head. A roaring filled his ears, and all of creation seemed to pirouette right in front of his eyes. Those kicks had done some damage all right.

The next shout from Nicola overrode everything else. The terrible sound *made* his feet move. He lurched across the hallway to the door and out on to the drive. The breeze blew into his face. Rags of cloud shot across the moon. There he struggled to make sense of what he saw. The scene appalled him. There seemed to be a million things happening at once. His concussed brain tried to identify the brutality of it all.

Nicola Bekk stood in the centre of the drive. His car doors were open. The TV from the lounge leaned against the back seat. Evidently, the thugs were in the process of stealing both the television and his car. Nicola must have interrupted them. Now they circled round her. They were laughing, making jokes, and subjecting her to sneering insults. The big guy grabbed a fistful of hair before yanking her backwards.

Tom blinked. His bruised logic couldn't make sense of what he was seeing. Nicola still made that strange-sounding cry. Rising, falling. Yet, she did not move, unless the force of their shoves caused her to move her feet to regain her balance.

No . . . get this. He shook his head in confusion. Nicola appeared to be calling to someone he couldn't see. And she appeared to be calling in a foreign language. The mysterious words rose and fell on the night air.

Her cries were hilarious to the four guys. They laughed and pushed her even harder. The big guy grabbed her by the hair again; after that, he smacked his mouth on hers to give her a rough kiss. Then he shoved her away as if she disgusted him.

Nicola cried out again. Her face seemed so incredibly strange, as if she was sleepwalking. Her eyes were fixed on the forest.

Tom planned to launch himself on the big guy. He'd punch the bully to hell and back. Only, his balance had been wrecked. He took five steps then slapped face down into the gravel. His head spun so much he couldn't even sit upright. With a sense of cold dread filling him, he knew he'd be forced to lie there. All he could do was watch the thugs torture Nicola. Nobody could stop them now.

Nicola shouted again. Her blue eyes remained fixed on the trees across the road.

The big guy made his move. He grabbed her pale blonde hair before ripping open her blouse. Bolter egged him on to do more; his eyes possessed an eager gleam. Bolter was hungry for something more than food.

Then Nicola said one word. The tone radiated a quiet satisfaction. 'Helsvir.'

Gradually, the bushes at the forest's edge were parted. But parted by what? Tom couldn't tell. Yet a massive shape pushed the bushes aside. Smoothly, it flowed from the vegetation. The thing was as big as a truck, and without any fuss, it seemed to swim through the gloom towards the driveway gates. After passing through those, it approached the four men.

For a moment they didn't notice. Their greedy eyes were locked on to Nicola's bare shoulders.

When the huge, pale body had reached the drive's halfway mark, that's when they finally did see what approached. All four stopped pawing Nicola. And all four turned to stare at the creature.

'Helsvir.' Nicola sounded pleased. 'Helsvir, come.'

Tom tried to stand and failed. The world began to whoosh before his eyes.

Suddenly, the four men screamed in panic. They ran towards him, though they paid no attention to their victim lying there. They were making for the safety of the house.

However, they were nowhere near as fast as the creature. As it breezed past Tom he glimpsed legs. There were lots of them: bare human legs. Bare arms, too.

The big man screamed. The creature had slammed into him, sending him rolling forward across the gravel. When the man screamed again, the white gravel was on his tongue. He still screamed as the beast from the wood passed over his body.

Tom blacked out for a moment. He dreamt he was back at the archway near Nicola's house: the one that bore the carving of a whale-shaped creature with lots of legs. She was saying, 'That's the family dragon. You'll meet him later.'

Tom opened his eyes again. The huge, truck-sized beast swept by him. It dragged the guy with the tuft of a beard on his chin. The man's dead face scraped a furrow in the gravel. The creature swiftly dropped Tufty on to two other male corpses. One was the dim-witted giant. The other corpse belonged to a man he'd never seen before. This must be the thug who'd struck him from behind. He had mass of spiky hair that he'd bleached into a bright, yellow blonde. Now the three were piled up on top of each other. Blood poured from the bodies to soak the white gravel.

So where's Bolter? Bolter's missing.

Nicola stood watching with the blankest of expressions. She appeared to be in a trance.

That's when the creature swept smoothly up the driveway towards Tom.

'My turn,' he uttered in a groggy whisper. 'My turn. It's coming for me.'

The massive shape loomed out of the night. Tom found himself looking into its face.

No . . . that's not correct, he told himself as he felt his wits slipping away. *Not a face.*

Faces.

He found himself gazing at the dozens of heads that studded the bulky body. The skin of each face was bluish-white. The eyes were perfectly white apart from a fierce black pupil. Did he see an expression of warning in that multitude of staring eyes?

'Helsvir.' There was a clear note of command in Nicola's voice. The same note as if she called a dog to heel.

The creature advanced towards Tom; air vented from the nostrils of its many faces. Blackened lips parted to expose glinting teeth.

'*Helsvir.*'

The creature glided even closer. He smelt wet earth. He could hear a growing chorus of hissed words. A dozen men and women seemed to be whispering the same sentence at the same time.

'*Go away. Leave her.*'

That's what the words sounded like. A warning. And hissed with such venom.

'Leave her. Don't come back!'

The faces lunged forwards.

Before they could touch him, however, a dark wave swept over Tom Westonby. He felt nothing more.

TWENTY-FIVE

When he woke, he wasn't alone. A body lay alongside of him.

For a moment Tom Westonby gazed up at the ceiling. The sun hadn't yet risen. Outside the window there was a pale half-light. From the forest came the swelling notes of the dawn chorus as the birds sang in the new day.

To his surprise he felt no pain, although he clearly remembered being attacked by thugs from the village. After the attack, however, everything else was hazy.

Concussion. Has to be. His fingers carefully explored his face. *A swollen eye. Split lip. Sticking plaster above the left eyebrow. Stiff neck. A general sense that his head had expanded to twice its normal size. Though no pain. Not a single sting.* If anything, he felt deliciously comfortable. That sense of well-being, he realized, had much to do with the person who lay next to him.

'How are you feeling, Tom?' Her voice was gentle.

'Surprisingly good.' What surprised him, too, was that his speech was normal. He thought he'd be mumbling through a mouthful of shattered teeth. He hoisted himself up on to one elbow.

In the soft light, he could see Nicola's head on the pillow. She lay there on top of the sheet. Fully clothed, too. She wore a white blouse and blue jeans. Only her feet were bare. She must have climbed on to the bed next to him, so she'd be close if he took a turn for the worse.

Memories roughly shunted other thoughts aside. Suddenly, his head was full of images of last night. The way the four men had brutally shoved her around. The big guy had grabbed her by the hair and kissed her roughly on the mouth.

'Are you alright?' His heart pounded. 'Did those bastards hurt you?'

She smiled. 'I'm fine.'

'Fine? Nicola, they were trying to rip your clothes off.'

'You scared them away.'

'Me? In the state I was in I couldn't have scared a kitten.' He sat up in bed. A move he immediately regretted. A wave of dizziness swept over him so powerfully that he slumped back down. Even though he couldn't sit up, he did grab hold of Nicola's hand. He held it tight. 'Are you sure they didn't do anything to you?' The words burned in his throat. 'I'll get the bastards. I'll rip them apart. Tell me where they live.'

'It's OK,' she soothed. 'Nothing happened . . . At least, not in the way you mean.'

'I watched them attacking you!'

'Just a couple of shoves, and the big one pulled my hair. I'm used to rough treatment.'

'You don't have to get *used* to rough treatment.'

'They're gone now, Tom.'

'But I couldn't have scared them. I couldn't even stand up.'

'You were there, Tom. When you came out of the house you scared them away.'

'I don't remember it like that.' He shook his head; the movement made him woozy. 'I collapsed on to the driveway . . . There was something in the forest. It was big . . . enormous.' He felt himself slipping back into darkness again. Damn it, those guys had kicked with a vengeance. 'An animal came out of the wood . . .'

'Animal?' She lifted herself on to an elbow so she could look directly at him, her eyes full of concern. 'There wasn't any animal, Tom.'

'Huge, it was.' His heart pounded as he struggled to correlate the images from last night: *faces. White eyes. A monster the size of a whale. The way the creature had glided towards the house. Four men screaming in terror.*

'Tom, can you hear me?'

He realized she was gently shaking him. Maybe he'd been slipping into unconsciousness.

'Say something to me, Tom, you're frightening me.'

'Helsvir,' he managed to say. 'Helsvir, the dragon . . . It was here. It saved you.' A whirlpool of light spun faster and faster. 'Helsvir killed the men that attacked you. And then Helsvir warned me to leave here.' He licked his dry lips. *'That's what it said. Leave . . . never come back . . .'*

TWENTY-SIX

'Helsvir . . . I saw Helsvir.'

Tom opened his eyes. He'd been muttering the words over and over as he lay dazed on the bed.

'Helsvir . . .' He knew he should stop repeating the name now, only some impulse kept driving the creature's name from his lips. 'Helsvir . . . It warned me to leave. It's going to kill me if I stay . . .'

As part of his diver's training he'd taken plenty of first-aid courses. He knew the symptoms of concussion featured headaches, dizziness, loss of balance, confusion, seeing flashing lights, double vision . . . Boy-oh-boy, he was having plenty of those symptoms right now. The only element missing after the beating was pain. If anything, he felt unusually comfortable and was content to lie there, gazing at the sunlight flooding the room with gold.

Of course, he found himself repeating the word 'Helsvir'. A symptom of the concussion? The dragon's name from the Bekk family legend seemed to orbit the inside of his head. 'Helsvir . . .'

'What's that?' Nicola entered the room with a plateful of toast and a steaming cup. 'Helsvir?'

'I saw Helsvir last night.' He spoke in the same matter-of-fact tone he'd use to say: *I saw Chester last night.*

Nicola put the toast and cup on the bedside table. 'You gave me a scare a couple of hours ago. Your eyes suddenly went dull, like you couldn't see anything; you started muttering. I couldn't rouse you.'

'Last night I saw the dragon. The one carved on the walls of your house.'

'That's an old legend.'

'I saw it.' The pulse in his neck fluttered. 'The thing was the size of a truck. There are faces embedded in its body. Human faces. Dozens . . . and . . . and I remember your mother saying that a Viking god created the dragon out of human corpses.'

She rested her cool palm against his forehead. 'I'm going to call an ambulance.'

'Helsvir came out of the forest. He killed those men. I heard bones snapping, they were screaming, there's blood in the gravel . . . Blood poured out of them all over the drive.'

'Tom, I was there, remember? Nothing came out of the wood.'

'It did.'

'There's no Helsvir.' She smiled to reassure him. 'I would have seen a big monster, wouldn't I?'

'There'll be blood on the driveway . . . you'll see. Masses of blood.'

'You stay there, try to relax. I'm phoning for the ambulance.'

'No . . . I'll be fine. Just give me time to rest.' His eyelids were so heavy . . . the heaviest things in the world . . .

Nicola walked towards the bedroom door.

'Wait,' he said in sleepy voice. 'There are two facts you should know. Very important facts.'

'Try and rest.'

'Fact number one: I love you.'

She smiled. 'You've told me.'

'Fact number two.' Tom pointed at her. 'I'm going to marry you.'

TWENTY-SEVEN

Bolter had been running for hours. He'd been running so the monster that had slaughtered the low-life turds he called 'friends' wouldn't mangle his bones, too.

Only when he was certain that he'd outrun that horror from the forest did he return home. Quickly, he scrambled upstairs, leaving muddy smears on the carpet.

'Where've you been, babe?' called Grandma from the kitchen. 'I've been worried sick.'

'Stop calling me babe!' Bolter slammed the bedroom door behind him, then ripped his old comics from a drawer so he could reach his stash lickety-split. Bolter needed his 'reality cure' as he called them. His Buzz-Bang pills. *Great for making the brain go BUZZ! and the heart go BANG!*

'Damn it. Only three left . . .' His voice rose from a croak to the whine of an outraged child that had found only three presents under the Christmas tree. *'Only three?'* Even so, he eagerly stuffed those dirty grey pills into his mouth.

He needed 'em; by Christ, he needed 'em! Last night at Mull-Rigg Hall he'd loved kicking freaking Tom Westonby . . . The way his blood had burst out of his skull like a bomb. Ha-ha!

But the nightmare on legs had arrived. A huge ugly thing that was all legs, arms and heads had glided out of the forest. Pug was a big guy, a giant, but the monster had mashed him to death. Bolter had heard the powerful man's bones crackle and snap. Within seconds, the animal had spilled Nix and Crafty's blood on to the driveway. Nicola Bitch-Bekk and Westonby had watched the murders. They'd be smirking right now. The bastards.

The speed ripped through Bolter's arteries to his brain. The dangerous blend of toxic chemicals made his heart race; it also granted him blistering insight into the monster attack last night. He picked up a can of deodorant before rushing to the bedroom mirror.

Straight away he clicked into his fantasy role of TV reporter. 'Breaking news . . .' The ugly red mountain range of spots and blisters on his face seemed to pulsate as he spoke into his pretend microphone – the aerosol can. 'Breaking news . . . It is now widely known that Nicola Bekk and Tom-Ass Westonby are responsible for the murder of three Danby-Mask gentlemen. Their guilt is certain, one zillion per cent certain.' His voice raced faster as the drug accelerated his nervous system. 'The only question now is what kind of punishment Bekk and Westonby will suffer. Because surely there will cometh the divine instrument of revenge.'

Bolter loved those words; they were so clever and true: he even saw them spray out of his mouth in a shining stream of light. He added, in a delighted gurgle: 'Bekk and Westonby will suffer terrible injury and death. *Because, I . . . your hero reporter . . . will be that divine instrument of revenge!'* He burbled with speed-driven laughter.

That's so damn good. That's brilliant. The drug inflamed both his paranoia and the powerful delusion that he was nothing less than superhuman. Oh, yes, he'd enjoy getting back at those two freaks: Westonby and Bekk. 'I'll bloody them adroitly!'

Using the word *adroitly* made Bolter laugh louder. OK, he knew deep down he was losing control, and that these illegal drugs would eventually kill him. *So freaking what!* His death would be glorious!

'Babe,' his grandma nervously called from downstairs. 'Babe, are you alright up there?'

My pills . . . my Buzz-Bang. I need more. They make me strong. They make me indestructible.

'Babe, I'm worried about you.'

'Grandma!' he shouted as he stared at his complexion of ruin in the mirror. 'Lend me some money.' He was broke; he needed to buy more of his magic medicine.

'I'm sorry, I can't.'

'OK. *Give* me some money.' He grinned at his reflection and raised the pretend microphone to his mouth. 'I need cash . . . because this reporter is about to go to war.'

TWENTY-EIGHT

Tom Westonby awoke again at noon. This time he managed to get out of bed. Even so, he was extremely unsteady on his feet. He managed to reach the wall mirror by holding on to the furniture. When he stood at the mirror it was as disconcerting as standing on a boat's deck in rough weather. Only keeping a tight grip on the chest of drawers prevented him from staggering.

The face in the mirror didn't look pretty. His dark, curly hair appeared the same as it had yesterday morning. His face, however, bulged with swellings. A bloody split in the centre of his bottom lip was eye-catching to say the least. A sticking plaster covered one eyebrow. Apart from those two new features, there were plenty of scrapes on his skin with an equal number of bruises. *Those thugs were hell-bent on kicking my head right off my shoulders*, he told himself grimly. *I'm going to make sure they get the same kind of punishment.*

Even as he pictured himself hunting down his attackers, he remembered the events of last night. Hadn't he witnessed how the men were attacked by the creature from the wood? It seemed to glide like a shark out of the darkness. The four men had screamed as it pounced. The sound of breaking bones filled his head again. He remembered the blood: spurts of crimson splashing down on to the driveway.

'Helsvir,' he said, murmuring the name. Helsvir, guardian of the Bekk family down through the ages. *That's mythology*, he told himself. *Even in remote parts of England like this you don't find real dragons.*

Steadying himself, he raised his splayed hand to the mirror. 'How many fingers am I holding up?'

His reflection chuckled. 'Hundreds of fingers.'

'Concussion . . . bad concussion,' he murmured. 'I should go back to bed.'

'Just what the doctor ordered,' his reflection said, laughing.

Yet the image of the men being killed out there on the drive blazed so brightly. OK, he must have hallucinated. No avenging monster had broken those men into little bits. So, if they hadn't been killed, they must have scarpered when Tom appeared; that meant there'd be no sign of a struggle outside . . . no blood, either.

'Nicola?'

He listened. Nobody seemed to be moving around the house. Perhaps after making sure he was alright Nicola had gone home? Another memory surfaced through a confused mess of dazed thoughts. *Didn't I tell her I was going to marry her?* He tottered across the room. *Or did I hallucinate about that, too?*

'Dragons and surprise wedding proposals . . . That's what I call hallucinating.'

The walk downstairs turned out to be something of an expedition. Tom couldn't move properly. What had seemed like the prospect of simple detective-work, to check if bloodstains were present on the drive, became an ordeal. More than once he stumbled down a couple of stairs at a time. He only prevented himself from flying head first by keeping a desperate grip on the bannister.

This isn't a good idea, he told himself. *I should be back in bed.*

No. He had a mission now. *Find the blood. Prove that you saw men die.* The details had been so vivid. The way their bones had cracked so loudly. Come to think of it, wouldn't an animal as big as that have gouged up the driveway? The thing must have weighed a ton at least.

He paused in the doorway. 'Of course, you know what this means,' he whispered to himself. 'You're trying to find evidence that a Viking monster killed people. Go ahead. Report a dragon to the police. They're going to say you're crazy.'

A blustery wind attacked the forest, raising a hiss from those millions of fluttering leaves. Meanwhile, Tom Westonby concentrated on keeping his balance as he stepped outside.

Pools of blood . . . gravel drenched in crimson . . . the gore had been everywhere. *So where's the blood?* He frowned. The stones were a pristine white. Not so much as a single speckle of red – at least, none that he could see. He stopped where he'd seen the big guy being mashed into the ground by the monstrous beast.

Tom found an even expanse of gravel. The stones formed a smooth, flat surface. His car sat outside the garage in its usual place. Doors shut. Drops of water stood in beads on the roof. In the road itself, outside the gates, more pools of water stretched across the tarmac.

There's been rain, he told himself. *Rain washed away the blood.*

But the way that heavy creature had hurtled up the drive? The sheer bulk of the thing would have scuffed up gravel into heaps; its feet would have gouged holes. The men had been roughly dragged across the ground. The weight of their bodies would have torn furrows.

Then he noticed something significant. The driveway wasn't as it should be. Visibly, it was different from before. A change had taken place since yesterday.

He murmured, 'It's too neat. Too level. Someone's raked it smooth.'

His head was spinning like fury. Yet he marvelled at the neatness of the drive. It always possessed clear, if shallow, ruts made by his car's wheels. The ruts were invariably there. He remembered how they led from the gates to the garage. Now they'd gone.

Somebody had carefully raked the gravel. The surface of the driveway was now perfectly smooth.

Then the clincher. He inhaled deeply. 'Disinfectant. I can smell it. Someone's been washing the stones.'

TWENTY-NINE

'Have I been asleep long?' Tom Westonby stood by the bed. His sense of balance functioned. The headache had vanished. He felt a million dollars.

Nicola checked her watch. 'Almost twenty-four hours.'

'I've been asleep all that time?' He was stunned.

'There were times I thought you'd died. I wanted to call an ambulance.'

'I'm glad you didn't. The hospital would know I'd been assaulted; they'd have called in the police.'

'Those thugs deserve to go to prison.'

'What they deserve, Nicola, is a visit from me.'

'Before you go to war, can I tempt you to breakfast?' She smiled. 'I brought some of my mother's home-cured bacon.'

'Thanks. I'm starving.'

'I'm pleased.'

'Pleased that I'm hungry?'

'I'm pleased you're like your old self again.'

'I'm always hungry.' He grinned despite the sore cut on his bottom lip where a boot had broken the skin. 'You'll have to get used to my rampant appetite.'

'And why should I get used to that?' She spoke in a light, playful way, though clearly she wanted to know if a deeper meaning lay behind his suggestion.

'I'm a glutton at heart. Right now, I could stick your family's big old dragon on a slice of bread, squirt on a bottle of mayo, and eat him whole.'

'Don't let my mother hear you saying that. She loves Helsvir.' This was only a pretend scold. They were enjoying good-natured banter like friends do.

Tom had dressed before Nicola had come into the room. A glance in the mirror revealed that the swelling had gone from his face, though his jaw still had an interesting mottle of yellow and green bruising. As Nicola headed to the door, he called to her.

'Nicola?'

'Yes?'

'Thanks for looking after me.'

'I wanted to help.'

'That first night after I was attacked, you slept on the bed with me?'

'Fully clothed.' She smiled. 'I couldn't leave you alone after what happened. You were covered in blood. I was scared to death that you were seriously hurt.'

'Did I say anything . . . you know . . . when I was knocked stupid?' He was referring to the promise he'd made to marry her.

She laughed. 'You told me a monster had rushed out of the woods to get those guys.'

'I was convinced it was Helsvir. It looked just like the carvings at your cottage.'

'Helsvir only exists in my mother's head.' Nicola's smile vanished. 'I wish she wasn't so obsessed.'

'She wants to protect you from the outside world.'

'But I don't need protecting. I'm an adult. I want to go out there and see what the world's got to offer me.'

'Come with me to Greece.'

'What? Me work at a diving school? I don't know one end of a snorkel from the other.'

'I'll teach you.'

'Thank you.'

'I mean it. Come with me to Greece.'

Her eyes told him that she suspected he'd start laughing and admit the invitation was a joke and never in a million years would he *really* want her to go with him. *She expects me to hurt her.* The realization shocked Tom. *She's so used to people lying to her, or even openly insulting her, that she daren't believe for even a second that I genuinely like her.*

He rose to the challenge. He'd prove his feelings towards her were genuine. 'Nicola?'

'What?' She seemed wary of what he'd say next.

'Would you like to spend the day here?'

'Doing what?'

'Just being together.'

She nodded at the bed. 'You mean in there? With you?

He shook his head. 'I was thinking of having a barbecue.'

'I don't know . . .'

'Call it a thank you for looking after me.'

'You stopped those men hurting me,' she said.

'Hardly. The moment I staggered out of the house I fell over.'

'Right.' She grinned. 'Helsvir saved the day. Guardian beastie of the Bekk family.'

'When I hallucinate, I hallucinate big time.'

'You can say that again.'

'So shall I start on the steak marinade?'

'What about breakfast?'

He laughed. 'I still want breakfast. I'm keen to try that home-cured bacon.'

'Breakfast then a barbecue?' The smile had fully returned. 'You really are a glutton.'

He did a Tarzan style beat of his chest. 'Fuel me up! I feel a party coming on!'

THIRTY

They had an unspoken agreement: neither of them would mention the incident two nights ago when Tom was attacked by the four Neanderthals from the village. The sun shone down on Mull-Rigg Hall. Skies were blue. They were enjoying each other's company too much to spoil the mood by dwelling on that ugly outbreak of violence.

Tom had eaten a large breakfast of home-cured bacon. Mrs Bekk might be eccentric (even the south-side of batty); her bacon, however, was amazingly good.

'Most bacon I buy just ends up oozing water when it's fried,' he told her as they cleared away the breakfast plates. 'Your mother's bacon sizzles like bacon should sizzle.'

'Are you sure you can eat steaks?' Nicola shared his cheerful spirits. 'That breakfast you put away was colossal.'

'Of course I can. Besides, it'll be hours before the steaks have soaked up the wine and all that herb stuff.'

As he brewed up more coffee she lightly rested her hand on his shoulder. 'I'm going to paddle in your pool again.'

'You go paddle the life out of the thing. Enjoy yourself.' He grinned. 'Party time!'

'Thank you, Tom, I'm really loving this.'

'We're going to enjoy today like it's the last day of our lives.'

'That sounds grim. The last day of our lives?'

'Ah . . . I know a diver who's had one near-death experience too many.'

'Scuba-diving sounds dangerous.'

'It's not, as long as you don't get careless. Anyway, whenever we went for a night out with this guy, Dave Grice was his name, he'd be enjoying himself, laughing, having a brilliant time, then

suddenly Dave'd shake his head like this.' Adopting a mournful,
hangdog expression, Tom sadly shook his head in imitation of the
fatalistic diver. 'Then he'd always say these words: *it's like I'm*
being given one last good time before I die. One last party spree
before they nail down my coffin lid.'

'My God.' She laughed with a quirky mixture of shyness and
glee that appealed to Tom. He liked it when she did that. Pretty –
amazingly pretty. 'What a mournful thing to say! Is he still working
as a diver?'

Tom sighed. 'I find it hard to put into words what happened to
Dave Grice.'

'What *did* happen?'

'Well, we were diving on a wreck . . . when all of a sudden Dave
screamed out that his air valve was stuck. But that's not the worst
part . . . I still can't believe what I saw next.'

'He wasn't hurt?'

'Hurt? No, far worse. The aqualung valve stuck open, and air
kept gushing into his mouthpiece, he couldn't shut it off. I watched
as he . . . No, it's too terrible to describe.'

'Oh . . .'

'But as I've started telling you, I'll finish.'

'You don't have to, Tom.'

'Poor Dave. Anyway, the valve stuck open. The air from the
aqualung kept gushing into his lungs. Of course, he got bigger and
bigger until something went pop and . . .' Tom made a colossal
farting sound with his lips while pretending to watch an object
zipping crazily round the kitchen.

'Tom Westonby!' she squealed. 'You pig. You had me believing
you!'

He doubled up with laughter.

Nicola splashed water at him from the sink. 'You'll suffer for
that,' she cried, laughing all the time.

'You'll suffer right back.' He scooped up a cup full of dishwater.

She fled shrieking from the house. Her blonde hair fluttered in
the warm summer breeze. He loved to hear her laughter. This was
fun – sheer, carefree fun.

Nicola darted for the pond, flicking off her sandals, before wading
out until almost knee deep. There in the crystal-clear pool she kicked
her feet. Drops of spring water glittered like crystals in the sunlight.
He didn't avoid the spray.

In fact, he advanced right into the deluge, laughing all the time. This was glorious. He loved the drenching she gave him. What better way to get joyously soaked.

She stopped kicking and stood there panting. 'You didn't tell me what happened to Dave Grice.'

'Oh, he's still out there somewhere, making a living as a pro diver.'

'Idiot.' Playfully, she kicked more droplets over Tom. 'You really had me believing that he'd blown up like a balloon. I'd decided to persuade you to get a job in an office where you'd be safe.'

'An office? I'm not going into an office without a fight. I'll be a diver until they stick me in the ground.'

'I can believe it.' She gave him a knowing smile. 'You always get what you want, don't you?'

'I do. I most definitely do.'

THIRTY-ONE

Tom asked himself: *did I get my own way? Or did Nicola get hers?*

Both of them were dripping wet in the garden when she kissed him on the mouth. That particular type of kiss: one that's deep, hungry; almost a feeding movement of the mouth; one with pressure. Urgency. Need. Tom was no innocent boy. He knew what that kind of kiss signposted.

He lightly slid his fingers into the blonde hair that had been transformed into soft ringlets by the spring water. Her face was so close that he saw her smooth skin in close-up. A tiny freckle, then a glint of pale blue eye, the flash of white teeth as she broke the kiss for a moment so she could gently press the side of her face against the side of his.

'I think it's time that you should . . .' She kissed him again. 'That we should . . . OK?'

Communication had moved beyond the realm of verbal language. He understood what the kisses, gestures and those few wonderfully precious words of hers meant.

From the garden to the bedroom took no time at all. There they undressed each other.

The soft curves of her naked body made his heart pound. The excitement electrified him. Yet he didn't rush. A full summer's day stretched ahead in all its glory, all its warmth, all its promise of wonderful love-making.

He gently stroked her breasts and was astonished by the darkness of her nipples. He noticed a small pink scar on her forearm – an old wound inflicted by a sadistic bully from Danby-Mask? When he lightly touched the scar she took his hand and guided it downwards over the smooth skin of her stomach.

She whispered, 'There's nothing for you to worry about.'

'The scar?'

'That's nothing. It's in the past. I want you to enjoy being here with me now.'

Nicola rested her head back on the pillow. She smiled up at him. This time she waited for him to make the next significant move. As he embraced her she sighed with pleasure. If there ever was a time to preserve a sensation of physical pleasure forever this was it. Tom Westonby felt as if he'd stolen a piece of heaven all for himself.

Tom Westonby couldn't remember having such a wonderful day equal to this one. The barbecue was perfect. The steaks sizzled to perfection. Salad added a refreshingly crisp accompaniment. He didn't even feel the bruises on his face, or the V-cut on his lip. The attack on him by the four thugs didn't feature at all in the conversations, or even in his own memory.

What made the day so wonderful was Nicola Bekk. Lovely, blonde-haired, blue-eyed Nicola Bekk. They'd spent the morning laughing and splashing about in the clear spring-water pond; it had more than a passing resemblance to chilled white wine.

Then, oh glory of glories, they'd spent the afternoon in bed. He couldn't erase those images of her naked body from his mind – not that he'd want to – or those warm sensations of physical intimacy. The feel of her smooth skin, the silken parts that he loved to caress softly.

That evening, when they'd left the bedroom, they'd glided about the house as if they were floating on air. After the meal, they arranged comfortably padded loungers side-by-side beneath the apple trees and lazed an hour or so away. The sun shone through the branches. Birds wheeled round and around in a blue sky. Honeybees hummed gently and soothingly amongst sprays of bright yellow flowers.

This isn't a bad way to spend a day, Tom told himself. *In fact, it's a brilliant way to spend a day. Great food, great weather, great company. Fantastic love-making.*

Casually, he rolled his head to one side as he reclined there. Nicola lay with her eyes lightly closed. He found himself examining the profile of her face. When a red ladybird landed on a strand of hair he carefully removed the insect without her even noticing. Gently, he opened his hand, allowing the ladybird to fly away. *Nothing must break this magic spell of happiness.*

Later in the evening they returned the barbecue to the garage, where Nicola noticed a large box full of certificates and framed photos.

'You might want to move this box,' she told Tom. 'Rainwater's leaked under the garage door; the cardboard's wet.'

'Ah, my parents' Modesty Box.'

'Pardon?'

He pulled out a framed photograph. 'These were given to my parents as thank yous from people in Africa.'

'When they worked for the water charity?'

'That's right. They dug wells and piped in clean, bug-free water.'

'These are amazing.' She picked out an inscribed parchment from a grateful tribal leader. 'Why don't they keep them in the house?'

He shook his head. 'This is the Modesty Box. That's what I call it, anyway. They won't even put these photographs on the walls.'

'Why ever not?'

'Because it would be showing off. Dad doesn't like any fuss about the fantastic stuff he does.'

'I like the sound of him. He's a good man.'

'He is.'

'So learn to be proud of him.'

'I am proud. It's just sometimes I wish he'd boast about what he and my mother have done. They've dug two hundred wells in Africa. They've replaced dirty, baby-killing scum with clean, life-saving water. They saved thousands of lives. That's a brilliant achievement. It's amazing. And here's evidence of all that brilliant work in a box, dumped in some grubby corner of a garage.'

'Tom, I don't understand why your father's modesty makes you so angry.'

'He doesn't brag like some guys I meet, who boast about any

bit of crap that they've achieved, like winning three games of pool in a row, or brown-nosing their boss into giving them a two-bit nameplate for their desk. Get this: my father saves entire townships and he'd prefer not to even mention it. He's awarded medals and certificates from presidents and kings, and he rams them away into this box like they're a guilty secret.'

'Try and understand him, then.'

'I do try, but I can't find the motor inside his head that drives him.'

'You're just like your father.' Her blue eyes held his. 'But instead of saving people in Africa you've a compulsion to save me.'

Tom couldn't have been more shocked if she'd slapped him. 'I *love* you, Nicola. I'm not trying to prove to my dad, or to myself, that I'm better at rescuing people than he is.'

'Then slacken down.' She smiled to defuse the tension. 'Let's not spoil the best day of my life.'

'You can't say that – it's my line. I was thinking this is the best day of *my* life.'

'Come on, there's strawberries in the fridge. We'll finish those off.'

'OK – but "slacken down"?' He grinned. 'Where do you get these phrases?'

'Ah, that's local lingo. Slacken down. Meaning relax, don't blow a wire.'

'Then I'll slacken down.' He moved the treasure chest of photographs and prestigious awards on to a shelf where they'd be safe from the damp. 'Maybe Dad will even let me put some of these in the house – unobtrusively, of course.'

She laughed. 'I'll find a cover for the Modesty Box. You grab those strawberries.'

His spirits rose again as he headed out of the garage. He'd no sooner walked on to the drive when he heard a voice call to him: 'Tom . . . hey, Tom!'

He turned to see Chester Kenyon ambling up the driveway. 'Hi, Tom. I thought I'd drop by.' The big man let out a whistle. 'What the heck's happened to your face!'

'Some idiots from the village don't like my choice of friends.'

'They made a mess of you, Tom. Have you reported it to the police?'

'No, I'm going to settle this myself.'

'Don't go starting wars. These vendettas have a way of getting out of hand.'

'Great to see you, Chester. Is there anything special you want, or . . .?'

'Nah, just checking you're OK. When you didn't show up for quiz night at the pub I thought . . .' Chester's voice drained away. So did the smile on his face.

Tom saw what Chester had just noticed: Nicola stepping out from the garage.

'Aw, *Tom.*' Chester's expression was one of total shock. 'I warned you, didn't I? If you keep seeing Nicola Bekk, you're going to be in so much trouble. Man, you're heading for disaster!'

Tom saw a brilliant opportunity. 'Chester, talk to Nicola.'

'No way.'

'Do it. You'll find out for yourself that she's perfectly normal.'

Chester stared at her; he didn't say a word. So Tom turned to Nicola.

'Nicola. Talk to Chester. Prove that you're just like us.'

With her eyes locked on Chester, as if afraid he'd suddenly attack her, she backed away a few paces, then she turned and fled into the house.

'Trust me, Chester, Nicola can speak like anyone else. She's perfect; she—'

Tom was talking to himself, because Chester had run to where he'd parked his van. Soon it roared away in the direction of Danby-Mask. Now he was alone with Nicola again. It was as if they lived in their own self-contained universe, while the rest of humanity shunned them.

Then something strange happened: Tom Westonby realized he did not mind one bit. Being alone with Nicola was wonderful. He loved it. While they were together like this it seemed impossible that a disaster could ever befall them. They were safe from any danger the world could throw at them. Weren't they?

THIRTY-TWO

After Nicola went home, Tom strolled through the orchard at Mull-Rigg Hall with a big smile on his face. He even ran his thumb over his lips to feel the size of that huge, carefree grin. Nicola made him happy.

For no real reason Dave Grice's words popped into this head. He even imagined the hangdog face, and droopy eyes, as Dave shook his head at some joyous social gathering and intoned the mournful words: *it's like I'm being given one last good time before I die. One last party spree before they nail down the coffin lid.*

Even at that moment, Tom Westonby wondered if those lines ghosting through his head were a kind of prophecy. A whisper from the dark side: to beware of coming danger. Maybe there are times when future events can be so full of horror and terror that they send vibrations back into the past – and those ominous vibrations touch the nerves of those people who will experience the terrors first hand.

He switched on the radio and played the music loud, determined not to allow such morbid thoughts to poison a wonderful day. After that, he treated himself to a late-evening snack from the fridge, and he wondered what the future would bring with Nicola Bekk.

On the far side of midnight he heard the pounding. A fist on wood. Still in an unearthly mixture of deep sleep and suddenly springing awake he found himself halfway across the bedroom before he'd fully come to his senses. The thump of fists on the door continued. They possessed a frenzied urgency.

'I can hear you!' he shouted as he dragged on jeans and a T-shirt.

The pounding grew louder; even more frantic. The noise pulsated with anxiety.

Tom ran down the steps, thinking: *there's been an accident. This is the police. They're here with bad news. This is about my family . . . . Bad news about my family.*

A pain lanced through his head. The staircase writhed like the back of a snake. He realized he wasn't completely over the concussion yet. Those thugs had pounded his skull with a passion. Lights flickered behind his eyes again, while a headache raged. The pain made him clench his fists.

Whoever beat their fists against the woodwork renewed their assault. Dear God, the noise was like thunder. He crossed the hallway, unlocked the door and hauled it open.

Mrs Bekk stood there. Her white hair glinted in the darkness. Her eyes were shockingly huge as she stared at him.

Gulping in the night air, he tried to steady his heart, which pounded like fury. 'Mrs Bekk? What's wrong? Is it Nicola?'

'Yes,' she hissed.

'What's happened to her?'

'You best come and find out for yourself. Although I'll give you this warning: you won't like what you see. *Because you're going to have the shock of your life!*'

THIRTY-THREE

She asked: 'Can't you walk faster?'

'Mrs Bekk, where are you taking me?

'Stay close. If you don't, I can't promise to keep you safe.'

'Keep me safe? We're only walking through the wood.'

Five minutes ago, Tom had answered the pounding on the front door of Mull-Rigg Hall. He'd found Mrs Bekk there, a wild look in her eye. Then she'd told him to follow her.

All he knew was that this involved Nicola in some way. That's the reason why he followed Mrs Bekk through the forest after midnight. The moon shone through breaks in the cloud. That lunar glow made the leaves glitter as if they were cast from silver. When the cloud obscured the moon the trees became black.

'Mrs Bekk, what's happened to Nicola?'

'You'll see for yourself.'

'Has she been hurt?'

'Once you see with your own eyes, you'll believe everything I've told you. Everything!'

'Mrs Bekk—'

'Stay close, Mr Westonby, otherwise you'll be in danger.'

What could he do, other than follow the woman?

*What if she's attacked Nicola? She was so dead against us seeing
one another that she might have hurt her.* Tom found himself
picturing a horrific scenario: Mrs Bekk and Nicola argue. Nicola
tells her mother that she loves Tom. A flash of a knife. Then screams
– there's blood on the floor.

Tom Westonby felt sick. He realized that he hadn't yet recovered
from the beating. He displayed renewed symptoms of concussion.
His vision became blurred again. Glittering sparks danced behind
his eyes. Every so often, he needed to pause to hold on to a tree
so he wouldn't fall over. On top of all that, he suffered a monster
headache. The intensity of the pain made it easy to imagine that a
madman was slowly sawing his skull in half.

'Keep up, Mr Westonby.'

'Don't worry about me.' Troubling thoughts of Nicola lying in
a pool of blood drove him forward. 'I'll be fine.'

'Nearly there. We just need to get to the top of this hill.'

In Tom's state, the hill that rose out of the valley seemed as big
as a mountain. Nevertheless, he clenched his fists and steadfastly
pushed forward. The landscape kept switching between being awash
with moonlight to being plunged into blackness. Huge, threatening
clouds repeatedly covered the moon.

'We're here.' Her voice held a quiet fatalism. As if she'd brought
him to the scene of a terrible crime. 'Keep close by my side. It's
important you don't move away from me. You'll be in danger if
you do.'

'Danger? In danger from what?' The forest stretched out below
Tom: a mysterious sea of black.

'He'll be here soon. I want you to see him.'

'Who?'

'Who? Can't you guess?'

'This isn't the time for games, Mrs Bekk. What have you done
to Nicola?'

Even in the gloom, he saw the flash of her teeth as she smiled.
'It's not what I've done to Nicola, it's what she is capable of doing
to you.'

'I don't understand.'

'Mr Westonby, remember when you visited me at home? I
explained that my ancestors were Danish Vikings – they settled here
in this valley over a thousand years ago.'

'What has that got to do with Nicola?'

'Because I spoke the truth. When my ancestors were murdered, the god Thor gathered up their corpses into a mound; he breathed life into them. All those bodies fused together to become Helsvir, the dragon that would protect the Bekks for eternity.'

'Mrs Bekk, stop this. You're not well. My God, you're not even sane. Just take me to Nicola.'

'But my daughter is coming to you . . . She'll soon be here.'

'I'm going home, then I'm telephoning the police.'

'Shh . . .' As she shushed him she gripped his arm. 'The cloud's thinning. Soon you'll be able to see them.'

Tom watched a tide of moonlight spread over the forest. Trees turned from black to silver. A moment later he was engulfed as the moon poured its radiance down on the hilltop. Every detail of Mrs Bekk's face became visible. Her blue eyes were fixed on an area of woodland. There was such an expression of wonder. She expected to see something marvellous. Or something terrifying. Her fingers tightened around his forearm.

When she spoke she breathed the words in awe. 'See what stands all around you. Can you see my children?'

Her question was so bizarre that for a moment all he could do was stare at her in astonishment. Then he turned his head left and right.

Figures stood on the hillside. They were completely still. Almost like guards standing outside an important building: all facing the same direction. Their gaze locked on the same area of forest that had caught Mrs Bekk's attention. Tom counted eight figures. They were male and female. At first glance, these people could have been in their twenties.

Tom took a step closer so he could examine the faces. Something wasn't right about those figures. God knows what it was about them . . . Their body language? Their strange profiles?

He moved towards a female with pale blonde hair. From this angle she resembled Nicola; in fact, resembled her to an uncanny degree: fair hair, the delicate build. The defiant way she raised her chin.

Oh my God, what's happened to Nicola? Quickly, he approached the figure. Then stopped dead. *This isn't Nicola. This isn't even human.*

That's when the moon did the cruellest thing: it grew brighter.

And he found himself confronted with an abomination.

She did not move. She did not acknowledge him. She remained standing there like some evil-looking statue. Guardian of the hill. Demon of the forest. Shivers danced their way down his spine with ice cold feet.

Tom stared at the woman. No, not *woman* – this corpse thing could no longer be described as a woman. Beneath waves of yellow hair gleamed a bone-white face. Black lines snaked up her neck and over her jaw. At first, he thought they were black tattoos. However, he realized that the lines formed ridges. No . . . these were thick, black arteries that pushed upward against the skin.

And, dear God in heaven, those eyes . . .

The eyes were wide open. And they were perfectly white: a bright, glistening white. Each eye contained a black pupil in the centre. That tiny dot of blackness made the eyes fierce. As if they glared rage at the world.

The other figures, whether male or female, resembled each other – same blonde hair; same bone-white skin; the same hating eyes.

The clothes they wore – the shirts, jeans, dresses – appeared modern. Though there was something faded about them. As if they'd been left in an attic to gather dust.

A hand grabbed his arm. He spun round, expecting one of the statue people to be attacking him.

Instead, Mrs Bekk thrust her face nearer. 'I told you to stay close,' she hissed. 'If you don't, you won't see daylight as you are now. Do you understand, Mr Westonby? You are in danger.'

'What are these things?' Tom gazed at those figures, and he felt that he drifted in a cold, blue haze of absolute dread.

'Those *things* are my sons and daughters.'

'They're not alive. They can't be.'

'I warned you that you wouldn't like what you saw tonight.'

'There's one that looks like Nicola.'

'That's my Annie. The youngest before Nicola.'

'What on earth happened to her?'

'The same fate befell Annie as befell all my sons and daughters. They thought I was insane. These children of mine turned their backs on their family heritage. As soon as they could, they left home for the cities. They mated with people on the outside. People like you.' She spoke with disgust. 'Within a few months they found themselves back here in the forest. And they turned into what you're looking at now.'

'Are they ill?'

'They are cursed by the gods. They'll stay like this forever.' Mrs Bekk spoke in such a matter-of-fact way she might have been describing an ordinary domestic situation. 'Some might even call them as vampires.'

THIRTY-FOUR

Tom Westonby stood on the hillside with Mrs Bekk. The eerie figures that were her children remained absolutely still. Somehow that stillness made them even more menacing.

Mrs Bekk smiled. 'I know my sons and daughters are so much more than vampires. They are the warriors of the gods. Now they're waiting to be called to the final battle.'

He'd have stepped away from her, if it wasn't for her grip on his arm. Her blue eyes gazed adoringly at her sons and daughters.

'You've made them,' he told her. 'These are statues or mannequins.'

'No, they're real. They hear what you say, even though they appear to be ignoring you.' She let go of his arm. 'The truth of the matter is this: Nicola will become a vampire, just the same as these, if you take her away.'

'No . . .'

'Oh, but she will. If you – an outsider – coax her away from her home, this will be her fate: to roam out here in the forest forever. And it will all be your fault, Mr Westonby. You must tell Nicola you will never ever see her again.'

What Tom had decided were statues suddenly let out low moans. Each one shivered. Their eyes opened wider. They seemed to be reacting to something they'd seen down in the valley.

'Ah, here she comes, Mr Westonby.' The woman gripped his arm again. 'Stay close. I'll do my best to stop you being hurt.'

The forest resembled an enchanted silvery realm as the moonlight became brighter. Mrs Bekk pointed at a dense mass of oaks. 'There,' she whispered in awe, as if she saw angels. 'Don't you see what's happening?'

Tom noticed that the trees were moving. A giant must be walking through the forest, he thought, pushing against trees as if they were stalks of grass, making the branches wave from side to side. A loud hissing came in surges. Was this the leaves being disturbed by a breeze, or a large body brushing against the vegetation?

The figures standing on the hilltop opened their mouths. '*Ahh* . . .' they sighed, as if anticipating the arrival of a special visitor.

'Here she comes.' The woman spoke in excited whispers. 'Here she comes. You'll see her for yourself.'

The object suddenly broke clear of the forest.

Tom had seen this monstrosity before. Back then, he'd believed it to be a hallucination. But surely he must still be hallucinating, wasn't he? Or was he still in bed back at Mull-Rigg Hall and dreaming? He tried so hard to DISBELIEVE what he now saw. Yet all his senses focused on this creature that surged through the long grass. He could hear the hiss grow louder as it approached: this was the sound of people talking in furious whispers. He smelt the tang of some exotic animal. He could feel the rush of air that enormous bulk displaced as it sped towards him.

What he saw nearly overwhelmed him. Tom Westonby didn't know whether to laugh or cry.

The body of the creature must have been ten feet high and twenty feet long. Human limbs protruded from the bottom of the body. Like a centipede, it scurried smoothly on an array of limbs, and although these were a mixture of arms and legs, it moved with controlled precision.

The body itself bulged with human heads. Dozens of them. Then came the moment when Tom believed he'd gone mad. Because he saw faces he recognized. There, in that monstrous body, were the three transplanted heads of the young men he'd encountered so violently at Mull-Rigg Hall. He saw the large skull of the big man. Next to that, the face of the guy with the poor excuse for a beard that barely covered his chin. And next to him was the one with the spiky mass of bleached hair. Part of his face was missing. This was a result of the bald head that poked from the flesh beside him, which eagerly gnawed at his cheek, ripping away strands of skin.

The three men locked their eyes on to Tom. Those eyes were pure white, apart from the black pupils, and they held a screaming quality. They seemed to be pleading for help. When they opened their mouths, however, all that came out was the same reptile hiss that issued from the other heads embedded in the creature's flanks.

'You've met Helsvir before, haven't you?' Mrs Bekk gloated. 'He saved you from the men that attacked you.' She pointed at the three heads. 'Of course, you see what happened to them. Helsvir doesn't just eat his victims. He weaves them into the flesh of his own body.'

'I am dreaming,' Tom told her with a desperate certainty. 'This isn't happening.'

'You aren't dreaming, Mr Westonby – and this REALLY IS HAPPENING.'

He tried to break free of the mad woman's grip.

'If I let go of you, boy, Helsvir would take you, too. You'd become joined with him. Your head would be part of that fine flesh.' She laughed. 'Can you imagine looking out at the world from this magnificent creature? The power you'd feel. The strength you'd possess!'

Tom struggled harder. 'Let go of me.'

'If I did, she would tell Helsvir to claim you.'

She? His eyes roamed over the vast body, up over the dozens of heads that stared at him with wild hunger. His heart gave an explosive lurch, because suddenly he saw Nicola. She rode Helsvir as if she rode an elephant. Her legs were at either side of the part of the creature that narrowed and could be safely described as its neck.

'Nicola!'

'She can't hear you, Mr Westonby. She rides Helsvir in her sleep. Nicola will have no memory of this in the mornin*g. In fact, she doesn't know that Helsvir exists!'*

'Get her away from that thing!'

'Nicola won't be harmed. My daughter is amazing, Mr Westonby. She controls Helsvir. She rides this miracle as if she's tamed him. None of our family has ever taken charge of Helsvir like this before.'

Tom finally understood. 'So this brute really did attack those men on the driveway the other night?'

'He saved your life. Be grateful.'

'There was so much blood . . . I'd have found it the next morning. But you washed it away, then raked the gravel flat. Those men were killed, and you hid the evidence.'

'They haven't been killed. No, they've been . . . what's the word? Incorporated. That's it. They've been incorporated into Helsvir. As I told you, the god Thor created Helsvir out of the corpses of my ancestors.' With deep satisfaction she added, 'And now Helsvir adds to his body. He incorporates more people into him. He knows how to make himself grow stronger.'

Tom stared at the faces that gleamed in the moonlight. They bulged like white polyps from that hulking monster. The three thugs screamed for help with their eyes. The one with the yellow hair tried to keep his own head clear of the biter next to him. His neck wasn't long enough. The biter sank his teeth into the soft flesh of the man's eyelid before tearing a strip of skin away. The wound exposed meat that was blood-red and wet.

The victim's expression was the essence of agony and despair.

Then Tom gazed up at Nicola. Her eyes were dreamy, far away. The sleep-rider didn't recognize that her steed was a fusion of reanimated corpses. She didn't hear the hiss of heads. Nor did she realize that the man she loved stood gazing at her in horror.

Just hours ago Tom had made love to Nicola. But after seeing her astride that abomination could he even bring himself to touch her ever again?

THIRTY-FIVE

A t seven the following morning, Tom Westonby walked along the pathway towards Skanderberg. This strange little dwelling of stone beneath a red roof existed alone in the middle of the vast forest. Dark cloud lumbered overhead. Tom approached the monumental archway, which formed the entrance to the Bekk property. Twelve hundred years ago, Nicola's Viking ancestors had sailed across the ocean from Denmark to this remote part of England. They'd settled here, and this is where they'd been victimized by the local population: English Christian v Pagan Viking. Like so many conflicts between people with different faiths, it had given birth to entire mythologies of war, murder and miracles.

Tom gazed up at the carving on the stone arch. Nicola told him this was Helsvir. The dragon created by Thor to faithfully protect the Bekk family and their descendants. *To faithfully protect the family, that is, as long as they remained loyal to the old pagan religion.* He reached up to run his fingers over the weathered engraving. The moment he touched the image of the creature he shivered. A blast of energy seemed to leap from the stonework into his fingers. His diver's instinct for self-preservation sounded the alarms: *get away from here. Leave Mull-Rigg Hall. Grab a flight to Greece. Join up with Chris. Forget you ever met Nicola Bekk.*

Nevertheless, he pressed his hand against the carving of Helsvir. A jolt ran through his wrist. Was his mind playing tricks? Or was there a form of energy in this masonry after all? Some vital force? Maybe ancient stonework could soak up power like a battery? Tom gazed up at the representation of Helsvir. Snow, ice and rain had eroded it badly, though he recognized the elements of the creature now. *There's the body*, he told himself. *It resembles the shape of a whale. Elongated. Symmetrical. A teardrop shape lying on its side. Here are the legs that support it. And here, the faces.*

But surely you dreamt that you saw Nicola riding the monster last night!

He'd suffered a textbook case of concussion from the beating. Hallucinations and nightmares after a head injury were only to be expected. Yet memories of what he saw – what he half-believed he saw – waged a battle with the rational part of his mind. That part of the mind that had no truck with Nordic dragons or vampires or curses. Tom strenuously tried not to believe what he'd witnessed in the company of Mrs Bekk on the hillside. *Play the Doubting Thomas*, he told himself. *Keep doubting what you saw last night was real otherwise people will think you're insane.* Yet it wasn't that easy. What was frighteningly easy, however, was recalling the mass of faces peering out from the brute. The mental images made his throat tighten: those three thugs were locked into the body. Prisoners of its flesh. They were part of the fabric of the creature now.

Mrs Bekk (whether in reality or in his nightmare) had called Helsvir a dragon. Although it was like no dragon that Tom had ever seen before in books or in films. This monstrosity, which had been built out of human corpses, was a machine designed for vengeance. A Frankenstein beast. It absorbed its victims into itself somehow. This dragon didn't breathe fire and smoke, it breathed violence and destruction.

Even as he drew his hand away from the carving, he recalled the white figures on the hill. Mrs Bekk had told him that they were her sons and daughters; they'd been cursed, because they turned their back on their family's heritage. Mrs Bekk described them as blood-drinkers. Vampires, for want of a better description.

She claimed that the same fate awaited Nicola if she left Skanderberg for the outside world.

Low cloud made the place gloomy. He felt a sense of oppression. As if some terrible disaster approached.

Tom wanted to talk to Nicola. Her mother claimed that she rode Helsvir in her sleep, that she'd remember nothing of what happened there on the hilltop. However, he needed to find out for himself. Because right now he couldn't untangle reality from nightmare. The notion that he'd been hallucinating about supernatural beings made him feel hot and panicky, and it was impossible to dislodge either the headache or those terrifying images of Helsvir.

When Tom approached the house he saw the curtains were resolutely shut. Skanderberg was keeping the outside world at bay. Everything suggested that Mrs Bekk and Nicola were still asleep. Although it was tempting to go knock on the door, he had a sudden change of heart: after all, the figures he'd seen had seemed so real. Helsvir had been MORE than real. And what terrified him now was that if he pounded on the door Mrs Bekk might appear and coolly insist that what Tom had seen had actually been there.

If she did so, what did that mean? That Helsvir and the vampire curse were real? Or would it demonstrate that madness is contagious? And somehow Tom Westonby had caught the insanity bug from that deranged woman? If that was the case, Nicola would surely have nothing more to do with him.

Tom decided to return home to try and get rid of the troubling thoughts and this nagging headache. What's more, he needed time to convince himself that those memories of vampires and a giant creature bristling with human heads were a by-product of concussion – not the creation of the Viking warrior god, Thor.

THIRTY-SIX

'**Y**our air tank's run out! You're gonna die!'
Tom had been walking back home along the riverbank, and the sound of the phone broke his fixation on Helsvir. The caller was his mother; something about her tone made his heart sink.

'Tom, hello. I'm sorry to call you so early.'

'Hello, Mum.'

'I didn't wake you?'

'No. How is everyone?'

'Oh, everyone's fine here.' His mother's lack of relaxed chat hinted that she had important news. 'Listen, Tom. I phoned early, because I thought you should know as soon as possible.'

'Go on.' He felt his heartbeat quicken. *Bad news. This has to be bad news . . .*

'It's Mull-Rigg Hall. We'll have to allocate most of the repair budget to a new roof.'

'It doesn't need a new roof.'

'We've just got the structural engineer's report. The roof timbers have rotted through.'

'OK. But why did you need to call me about the roof so early? You could . . .' His voice tailed off as he realized this wasn't about the roof at all. 'I get it. You want me to move out of the house, don't you?'

'No.'

'I can still stay there?'

'Of course. It's just that the new roof will cost so much that we won't be able to continue paying you.' His mother sounded businesslike now. 'Your father and I spent all yesterday discussing this. By all means, stay at the house.' After a pause, she drove home the important point that she wanted to make. 'But next week will be your last wage payment.'

'Didn't Dad want to tell me this himself?' Tom was angry now. 'Is he still mad at me for turning down the job in France?'

'This is nothing to do with the job in France.'

'No, it's all to do with the girl I'm seeing, isn't it?'

'Tom, calm down.'

'The pair of you have cooked up a scheme that forces me to move away to find work. Because you both know that I've had to spend every last penny on the dive school. And you both know that I still need to send part of my wages to Chris in Greece.'

'Tom, we didn't plan this. The roof—'

'The roof! Those rotten timbers are a godsend, aren't they? You've got the perfect excuse to stop my wages, which forces me to leave, therefore I stop seeing Nicola.'

'Your father told me that you plan to marry the girl.' How cold his mother's voice had become. A voice like that could turn fire to ice.

'Yes. I will marry Nicola Bekk.'

'You know she has psychological difficulties? So does her mother. We heard that Mrs Bekk tried to burn down the village church.'

'Nicola Bekk is not insane. Nor does she hatch vindictive plots against her own family.'

He heard a gasp. *Ouch.* That line about 'vindictive plots' had hit his mother hard.

'Tom! How *dare* you?'

'So now you've put me in a position where I have to choose between continuing to raise money for the dive school, which means leaving the area to look for work, or staying here so I can keep seeing Nicola. You and Dad think you've beaten me, don't you?'

'Tom. We love you.' Strangely, her tone was so brutal when she uttered those words. In fact, the tone was more suited to: *Tom. We hate you.*

'What you *have* done is fired me.'

'Tom—'

'That's an incredible thing to do, Mother. The purpose of this call is to fire your own son from his job, isn't it?'

An urge to throw the phone into the river boiled up inside. Though he recognized childish tantrums wouldn't make his own plans work. *And, boy, do I have plans. Wedding plans. I can't wait to see their faces when Nicola shows them that ring on her finger.* A sudden savage glee caught hold of him as he pictured himself saying, '*Mother. Father. I'd like to introduce you to your daughter-in-law.*'

His mother had still been speaking; however, he'd been so caught up with his own thoughts (of retaliation?) that he'd only been half-listening. She was saying that she was sure everything would be OK between them and Tom. That soon the three of them would go out to dinner and have a nice time. Then she quickly made an excuse about Owen needing her and ended the call.

Tom sat down on a boulder at the water's edge.

He wondered if those blows to his head had caused permanent brain damage when he suddenly called out across the water: 'Helsvir! Listen to me. I've got a job for you. I want you to give some people a hell of scare. Their names are Mr and Mrs Westonby!'

He laughed. There was a vicious pleasure in that sound. He knew he should stop.

But he'd trusted his parents never to hurt him. And just like all grown-up children he'd never expected his own mother and father to try and trap him in a situation where they were controlling his life again. He did feel hurt. He felt betrayed.

And he knew that he would prove in the most spectacular way possible that he could seize back control of his life.

'OK, Helsvir,' he shouted at the wilderness. 'Just you see what I do next. *You won't believe your eyes!*'

THIRTY-SEVEN

Nicola Bekk walked along the riverside path. Tom Westonby didn't know whether she was making her way to his house, or going to catch the bus into the village, or even planning to summon Helsvir, the multi-headed dragon, so they could pick wild strawberries together in the forest.

OK, a flippant thought, yet Tom didn't try to guess what her plan entailed. He didn't care. He had a plan of his own. A breathtakingly audacious plan: the kind of plan that would shock his parents to the core.

He watched Nicola approach. She wore a loose-fitting white blouse, with a white calf-length skirt. The breeze that sent black clouds racing across the sky tugged at her blonde hair.

God, she's beautiful . . . *and she makes me catch fire inside.*

The hallucinations of last night – when he'd imagined that she rode a monster made out of dead men's heads and their naked limbs – just withered away to nothing before her amazing presence. They didn't seem important right now. Even his headache faded into insignificance, because here was that crucial moment when he had to ask the most important question of his life.

If you could see me now, Helsvir . . .

If you could see me now, Chester . . .

Dear parents of mine, if you could see me now . . .

His heart pounded. What he intended to do next seemed so dangerous, reckless and downright impetuous. *But the fact of the matter is*, he told himself, *it feels so absolutely right.*

Nicola beamed warmly; that pleased-to-see-you smile boosted his confidence. Deep down he suspected it fuelled his ego, too.

'Tom,' she began. 'I wasn't expecting to see you so—'

He put his finger to her lips, then held out his hand. Smiling, she consented to be led to a large boulder at the water's edge. She started to speak again. He put his finger to his own lips this time. A little crease formed between her eyebrows as she shot him a glance that asked: *what are you doing?*

He gestured to her to sit on the boulder, which she did, though now she seemed worried. Tom allowed himself to inhabit this special moment. Here the two of them were, on the bank of the River Lepping, which flowed through the forest. He listened to the bird-song. Sunlight pierced the cloud; its heat warmed his face. Briefly, he closed his eyes, making a conscious effort to backup this memory inside his head. Birdsong. The forest. The gentle music the water made as it flowed.

He opened his eyes. Nicola's face shone in the sunlight. Her blue eyes fixed on his. Clearly, she wondered if he had bad news to tell her.

'I've thought of different ways to ask this question,' he began. 'I've decided that the oldest way is the best.' He gently tightened his fingers around her hand. 'Nicola. Will you marry me?'

Her eyes shot a lightning bolt of meaning. Surprise. Hope. Excitement. The sheer intensity of expression made his heart pound. She was moved by the question: *will you marry me?* Yet there was something else: her eyelids narrowed a fraction. As if she'd experienced a sudden stab of doubt. *Can I trust him? Is this for real? We've only known each other for a few days, so why is he asking me to marry him so soon?*

He squeezed her hand and smiled. River water danced with the rocks. Happiness flowed through him. Today was a day for the impossible to come true.

'What do you say?' he asked.

'Nobody has ever asked me to marry them before.'

'Do you need time to think about it?'

'Yes.'

'Take as much time as you need.'

'OK.' Her face had become serious.

The pulse in his neck thudded. Blood roared through his head. The breeze tugged strands of her hair across her face, making her eyes seem smoky and somehow far away.

Nicola's fingers increased their pressure on his hand. 'I have thought about it, Tom. The answer is *yes*. I will marry you.'

'It's a terrible sign. It means we're in for our Five Year Sop.'

'Five Year Sop?'

'Local name for a big flood that follows a five-year cycle. Five Year Sop means that Danby-Mask is going to get sopping wet.' She held out her hand. 'I'm Carol Jenner.'

'Pleased to meet you, Carol. I'm Tom.' Her handshake was surprisingly strong. 'So . . . any prediction when this rain will stop?'

'Bizarrely, it'll get lovely and sunny when the village is underwater. We're prone to flooding.' She brushed raindrops from her fleece. Then she noticed something amiss with her jeans at the knee. 'Damn. Gone and done it again.'

'Anything wrong?'

'Just ripped a perfectly good pair of jeans. Always happening. Bane of my life.' She tapped her knee.

To Tom's astonishment he heard a sharp clicking sound.

'I lost the God-given leg out in Afghanistan.' There was nothing self-pitying about the way she spoke. It was as if she mentioned some routine part of her life. 'The mechanism on this prosthetic keeps tearing the fabric. I get through jeans like folk get through tea bags.'

'I'm sorry.'

'Oh, just one of those things.' She smiled. 'Nobody forced me into the army. I'll stitch this when I get home. I'm just waiting here until my husband picks me up. I'd planned to take a walk by the river.' She shot him a friendly smile. 'I hadn't planned for bloody rain.'

Tom tried not to stare, but this felt so humbling. Carol Jenner might have been even younger than him. Twenty-two, twenty-three at the most. Already, she was a war veteran. A wounded one at that, having lost a leg in an Afghan war-zone.

Carol turned her attention from the ripped denim back to the river. Her green eyes assessed the rapid flow of water. Tree trunks were being swept along by the current. She tilted her head to one side. 'Just listen to that.'

He heard the pitter-patter of rain. 'I think it's starting to ease off.'

'No, that deeper sound.'

'Yes, I can hear something . . . a sort of rumble?'

'It's one of those sounds that's felt, rather than heard, isn't it?'

'Thunder?'

Carol shook her head. 'Boulders. After heavy rain, the force of the current rolls boulders along the river bed.'

Tom remembered Nicola had told him that the sound of rocks being tumbled along by the Lepping made her think of men grumbling angrily. 'There must be some force in that water.'

'You're dead right, and it's destructive, too.' She pointed at the stone bridge. 'See those arches? The current piles boulders between the gaps. Soon it acts like a dam. It won't be long before the water starts coming over the banks into the streets.'

'The Five Year Sop?'

'And it's dangerous, too. People have been drowned in their beds before now.' The woman limped out of the shelter to gaze at the Lepping. 'See? The levels are rising fast.'

'The sound of the boulders is louder, too.' He felt the vibrations through his feet.

'There'll be rocks the size of cars running through those deep, underwater channels. They'll be slamming into the bridge supports like giant bowling balls.'

Tom watched an entire tree go speeding past. The willow must have been uprooted by the flood.

A Volvo pulled up at the shelter. 'Ah, the husband,' Carol said. 'Cheerio.' As she limped towards the car, she suddenly paused. 'Tom, soon the police will shut roads to the village. My advice is to keep away from here until the water levels drop. Danby-Mask is a dangerous place when the floods come. Lives can be lost. Anyway, cheerio again. Take care.'

'Bye.'

After Carol Jenner had gone, Tom stood listening to the sound the boulders made. He couldn't see them in the swollen river, of course – but the rocks were down there: tons of them relentlessly pushed downstream. He heard the thud of huge boulders being slammed into the bridge.

Local people must have had an intense relationship with the river over the centuries. They'd have needed the Lepping in order to survive – they'd have caught fish to eat, drunk its water, and even used its strength to power the water mills. If the river possessed a mind, would it feel snubbed now that they'd turned their backs on it? The thought, though it was an odd one, seemed to have a potent significance. The river wouldn't let people ignore it. Every five years it rose angrily out of its channel and flooded the village.

Tom couldn't help but compare the river to the pagan gods. Once, both were needed by the people of the valley. Both served a vital purpose. And now both the river and the primeval deities were rejected as being useless to modern human beings. Yet what if gods such as Thor did continue to exist – just as this river existed? And although the Viking god didn't exist in the actual landscape, what if he continued to flow through *our emotional landscape*? That was to say, Thor lived inside us, yet hidden from view. It was easy to imagine that being scorned, and then ignored by successive generations, he would be angered to the point of insanity. Wouldn't he brood over his rejection? Wouldn't he draw up his plans for revenge against humanity?

Tom took a deep breath. Perhaps that deep, bass rumble of boulders in the river had prompted those strange thoughts. To prevent himself falling back into that disquieting mindset, he started walking.

Tom needed to visit Chester Kenyon in order to have a conversation that was as important as it was overdue. Then he decided he would heed the war veteran's warning about getting out of Danby-Mask – river levels were rising fast. And all the time the angry rumbling continued. It sounded like an argument of the gods.

Tom headed in the direction of the Kenyon workshop. Already, the floodwaters followed along the pavement. So far the water was only an inch deep. But he knew full well the worst was yet to come.

THIRTY-NINE

Chester Kenyon boiled the kettle for coffee. Tom produced the cherry pie. Meanwhile, raindrops hit the workshop's roof with a hard clatter.

Tom liked Chester. He didn't want to fall out with him over Nicola Bekk. He suspected that Chester felt the same way. The man kept his lips pressed together as he poured boiling water into the mugs. He looked like someone who really wanted to speak, only he knew whatever he did say would come out all wrong and make the situation worse.

So what is the situation? Tom asked himself as he put the pie on a plate. *Chester's known Nicola since childhood. He believes she's mentally retarded and can't speak more than two words in a row, and that she lives with her deranged mother in the forest. Chester worries about me. He thinks I'm going to be in trouble with the police because I'm seeing Nicola. That could be the case if Nicola really was mentally ill. But she isn't. Nicola is perfectly normal. Hell, she's perfect. Totally perfect.*

Neither had spoken more than a dozen words to each other since Tom walked into the workshop. Chester had continued work on a farmer's tractor, and after several minutes of that he'd gone to make the coffee. Tom would have left if it wasn't for the fact that Chester had put two mugs by the kettle.

Chester set the coffees down on the workbench, stared Tom in the eye for a moment, then sighed. 'Tom. Can we talk without you blowing a valve?'

'Are you saying I've got a temper?'

He sighed again. 'Temper times ten.'

'I hadn't noticed. I always thought I was one of the mild-mannered types.'

'In your dreams, Tom. Sometimes you make erupting volcanoes look tame.'

'Only when people are deliberately not listening to what I'm telling them.'

'You've got a temper, bud. A ten-megaton temper.' He examined the cherry pie. 'You should take that back to the baker's. A rat or something's taken a bite.'

'That something was me.'

Chester smiled. 'Yeah, likewise. I can resist anything but temptation.'

'Wilde?'

'No, I've just got a bloody monster of an appetite.'

'No, I meant Wilde . . . Oscar Wilde. The "resist anything but temptation" line?'

Chester shrugged a beefy shoulder. 'Oscar Wilde? Does he come from Leppington? They're a strange lot from there; I never have anything to do with folk from Leppington. Neither should you.'

This was Chester's jokey way of breaking the ice. 'Now that we're talking properly,' Tom said, 'we need dishes for the pie.'

'Half each?'

'Absolutely.'

'I get the half that hasn't had the bite out of it?'

'Naturally.'

'Alright.' Chester's eyes gleamed at the big cherry pie with its tempting golden crust. 'You know what'll go with this?'

'Some cream?'

'Clotted cream. Ma's got some in the fridge. I'll be right back.'

Chester headed for the Kenyon family's house, which stood behind the workshop.

Tom had been working on a plan. He'd ask the big man to come along to Mull-Rigg Hall. The rotten weather was a pain, because he'd decided to hold a barbecue. But never mind. He'd persuade Chester to meet up with Nicola over a couple of beers. Chester would find out that she was perfectly normal. Eventually, he'd learn that Mrs Bekk was to blame. She'd terrified Nicola with stories about the villagers being child-killers and so on when she was a young girl. No wonder Nicola Bekk had been unable to speak at school. Nicola had been terrified to the point of being struck speechless. That had led to her growing increasingly isolated from the other children.

Tom sipped his coffee. He was enthusiastic about his plan. No obstacles stood in his way now. He'd persuade Chester that Nicola was one hundred per cent normal.

Chester jogged in through the door, shaking the rain from his hair. 'Cats and dogs.' He laughed.

'Aren't you worried about the flood?'

'Oh, the Five Year Sop? That's what they call it round here.'

'So I heard.'

'Nah. We've never been flooded here at the workshop. The water gets into the bottom half of the graveyard and no further.' He clinked the dishes down on to the workbench. 'Though it makes you wonder what those graves are like when the ground's waterlogged. All those coffins filling up with water. All those bones and body parts getting all juicy. Masses of wet skulls. It'd look like the cherries in that pie.'

'Thank you for that image.' Tom smiled. 'I've a good mind to give you the half with my bite out of it.'

'No way. There's the cream, help yourself.'

'Cheers.'

Chester grunted, 'Uh, there's an old blanket in the store room. Will you do me a favour and get it? I've been working on that tractor, and I've got oil all over my backside for some reason. Dad'll go krang if I sit on these chairs and get them clarted with oil.' He grinned. 'Clarted. A Yorkshire word for getting coated or covered.' He dipped his finger into cherry syrup oozing from the pie. 'Ooops . . . . just got myself clarted with cherry.'

'In the store room, you said?' Tom asked.

'Yeah, through the door in the corner.' He grinned. 'I'll cut the pie. That way I avoid the bit you've gnawed on.'

Tom opened the door and clicked on the light. 'Where did you say the blanket was?'

'In a box . . . Back of the store.'

Tom stepped inside. 'Are you sure? There's only bits of old engine in here.'

The door slammed shut behind him.

'Hey!' Tom laughed, thinking that Chester was playing a joke. 'You're not getting that pie all to yourself.'

A key turned in the lock at the other side.

'Sorry, Tom,' Chester said through the panels. 'You're staying here until you promise me you're never going to see Nicola Bekk ever again.'

FORTY

H*e's actually locked me in here. Chester's supposed to be my friend, and he's gone and locked me up in this stinking room.*

Tom Westonby stared in disbelief at the thick wooden door. Surely, there'd be the click of the lock, the door would swing open, and there'd be Chester's broad smiling face. After that, they'd laugh, Tom would playfully thump Chester on the arm, then they'd get back to that cherry pie topped with delicious clotted cream.

Only, the door stayed locked.

Tom rattled the handle. The thing was covered in rust and cobwebs. Spiders scurried over the door panels. They weren't used to human visitors in their fusty-smelling domain.

'Hey, Chester. A joke's a joke, OK? Time to let me out.'

A muffled voice came back: 'I'm serious about this, Tom. You're my friend. OK, it sounds soft and dopey, but I care about you.'

'So unlock this damn door.'

'You can come out when you promise you'll break this thing off with Nicola Bekk—'

'Hey, that's nothing to do with you!'

'—and you swear on your mother's life that you'll never see Nicola again.'

'You're insane.'

'Nicola Bekk isn't right in the head. I'm sorry for her. I saw the hell she went through at school, but she's trouble. You must tell her it's over.'

'It's her mother that has the problems. Talk to Nicola, and you'll see for yourself that she's a lovely, warm-hearted person.'

'No, Tom. Ask anyone. They'll back me up. Nicola can't even string more than a couple of words together, and—'

'Let me *out*!'

'—the police will arrest you. It's against the law to have sex with someone who's mentally defective.'

'Mentally defective? Chester, when I get out of here I'm going to beat the crap out of you! Do you hear? I love Nicola!'

There was a pause. Tom could hear the crackle of rain on the iron roof. The smell of water even reached him here in this fusty little cell at the back of Chester's workshop.

'Chester,' he shouted, 'are you still there?'

'Of course I am. I'm your friend, Tom.'

'Then let me out.'

'No.'

'Chester. You damn idiot.' Tom smashed a wooden crate with a single, furious kick. 'Damn, damn, damn!'

'I'm going to leave you to slacken down.'

'I don't need to *slacken down*. I need to get out of here!'

'Try to relax, Tom. We'll talk about your infatuation with Nicola.'

'Infatuation? Didn't you hear? I love her.'

'She's got a hold over you.'

'When I get out of here I'm going to punch you in the mouth!'

'That's another reason why I locked you in there. You might not realize it, Tom, but you've got an evil temper. I don't want to end up in an ambulance.'

'I'd never hurt you . . .' His voice trailed away. *Haven't I just threatened to punch him in the mouth?* He realized he'd been striding to and fro with his fists clenched. *Calm down . . . just get your*

*temper under control. When Chester knows you're not going to rip
his head off, he'll let you out.*

Easier said than done. An inferno had broken out inside his
stomach. *And the insulting description of Nicola?* That did it.
Before he could stop himself he kicked the door. Not just once,
either. At the fifth savage, full-blooded kick he forced himself to
stop. Besides, the solid woodwork had suffered no more damage
than a few scuff marks.

He tried to calm himself as he prowled the room. As he did
so, he calculated his chances of getting out, other than through
the door. He saw a window at one end, but that had iron bars
over it. The room itself contained engine parts and a child's red
bike that leaned against one wall.

Tom intended to be perfectly reasonable. But the moment he
opened his mouth sheer rage took over. He felt wronged, he felt
betrayed. *Why does everyone want to interfere with my life? I've
done nothing to hurt them. This isn't fair. In fact, it's cruel.* The
sense of injustice infuriated him.

'You can't stop this!' he shouted. 'Do you hear? I'm getting
married to Nicola Bekk! Nobody's going to stop me. Not you! Not
my parents! No one!'

FORTY-ONE

In the storeroom, Tom Westonby's anger gradually subsided. *OK,
he told himself, Chester shouldn't have locked me in here. But
he thinks he's trying to help. He's convinced that he can persuade
me to break up with Nicola. All I have to do is get Chester to meet
her; he'll realize she's not crazy. Then everything will be alright.*
Tom took a deep breath. He'd be scrupulously diplomatic now. *So
no more yelling or kicking the door, OK?*

'Nice and easy does it,' he murmured to himself.

A wise move right now would be to give Chester some space to
cool down. *Soon Chester will see the absurdity of keeping his friend
prisoner, won't he? After all, he can't keep me locked up in a
workshop forever. DIY jails are the kind of thing neighbours notice
before long.* Tom smiled. He felt his sense of humour trickling back.

'We'll be laughing about this in a few days,' he said softly to himself. 'Everything's going to turn out fine.'

A rumble of thunder suggested that something disagreed.

For the next ten minutes he amused himself by exploring his cell. The door consisted of big old timbers that were hard as iron. The lock was a formidable piece of rustic steelwork, too, so no point in trying to break that. The fact that this place had been used as a strongroom in the past was forcibly reinforced when Tom found an old safe behind a heap of car doors. For a moment, he expected to see the glint of the Kenyon family treasure. What he did find in the unlocked safe were dozens of glass jars containing screws of all different sizes.

On top of the safe sat a huge jack. This monster of a device must have been used to raise trucks so the wheels could be changed. Tom wondered if he could use this big lump of steel to batter down the door. Tom worked out – he was proud of his biceps – but when he tried lifting the jack he could hardly budge the thing.

As he returned to the locked door he heard the rising wail of a siren.

Keeping his tone light, he called out, 'Chester? What's happening? Are we under missile attack, or something?'

Chester answered, in relaxed tones: 'That's the flood warning. The River Lepping must be breaking its banks.'

'That's a worrying sound, Chester. I mean, sirens aren't things you associate with everything being OK, are they?'

'It'll be fine.'

Tom decided to bring a bit more pressure to bear. 'Chester, I want to confess something right now – being locked in here while a flood siren's screaming its guts out is making me concerned.'

'I told you. It's fine.'

'If I'm locked in here and the river levels keep rising, I'm going to drown, aren't I?'

'Floods never reach the workshop.'

'There's always a first time.'

'Don't worry.'

'You're not the one incarcerated in Prison Kenyon.'

At the other side of the door Chester laughed. 'I'm right here. The key's in my hand.'

'Then let me out.'

'No.'

'When, then?'

'Soon. I've called up some old school friends. You'll hear from them what Nicola is like. That she's . . . you know . . . mentally impaired.'

Tom sighed with frustration, but he managed to keep his cool. For a while, he listened to the siren, screaming out its message of warning: *the river's broken its banks. The flood is coming. Beware, beware, beware!* Then Tom had a sudden flash of inspiration. 'Chester, I need a whiz.'

'No, you don't.'

'I do. I'm busting.'

'There's plastic bowl in there. Use that.'

Tom slammed his hand against the door. *Damn it.* He took a deep breath and forced his voice to be conversational. 'OK. I promise to sit quietly here in my cell and listen to what your old pals have to say. That's on the strict understanding you talk to Nicola. Do we have a deal?'

Chester didn't reply. The warning scream of the siren grew even more piercing. There was sense of urgency in the sound – a sense of danger, too.

'Chester?'

Again, no reply.

'Chester, are you there?'

Nothing. Only the scream of the siren.

'*Chester!*'

Just then came the sound of a bullhorn. He couldn't make out individual words. Yet the tone said it all. The voice was full of anxiety. There were major complications brewing out there.

Chester! Where are you?

After what seemed minutes rather than seconds, Chester returned to the door. He was breathless and excited sounding. *Or is that worried sounding?*

'Tom, listen, there's a problem.'

'What kind of problem?'

'Can you hear the loudspeaker? That's coming from a police car. The flood's reached houses down by the river. They're having to evacuate.'

'OK, then evacuate me, Chester. I want out.'

'Just another five minutes. My friends will be here by then. They'll tell you about Nicola.'

'My God. This is insane. Unlock the door!'

'You'll be safe here.'

'Chester—'

'We're friends, Tom. I don't want bad things happening to you. And bad things will happen, if you continue having this weird relationship with Nicola Bekk.'

'In five minutes the village could be underwater.'

'The floods never touch this street.'

'Sez you.'

'Trust me. Now, don't blow your top, but I've got something to say that you won't like.' His voice tailed away; he'd got bad news.

'What is it?'

'My grandad lives down by the river. I have to drive him up to his friend's house.'

'Chester, you can't leave me locked up here.'

'I'll only be five minutes.'

'Chester—'

'Don't worry. I'll be right back.'

Tom glanced up at the bulb that was the only source of light in his improvised prison cell. 'Does the flood get into the substation? Hey? Won't there be a power failure? Listen! I'll be left here in the dark if the electric fails. Chester . . . Chester!'

This time there was no reply. Chester had gone.

FORTY-TWO

'Do it! Bust out of there! Smash this dump up for good!' Bolter quivered on the bridge. The brown waters of the Lepping roared through the arches beneath him.

God, this is great! Feel the power of the river. Feel it shake the bridge. This has the raw energy of sex! Bolter loved to watch the river when it became so fat and swollen it turned into a roaring, violent monster.

The rain had almost stopped. Not that it mattered. Bolter knew that thousands of tons of water had been dumped on to the hills. All that liquid power would cascade into the valley, and then into the Lepping. The Lepping was his vengeance monster. His destroyer

of all these useless bastards' homes. The Lepping was going to
wreck Danby-Mask. And he was going to love watching it. Bolter
slapped his hands down on the stone wall that ran along the edge
of the bridge.

'Do it!' he screamed at the water. 'Wipe those shitheads out!'

Bolter dragged a handful of pills from his pocket and stuffed
them into the mouth. He gulped down those nuggets of power in
pill form. Amphetamines were igniting his veins. His heart roared
with the ferocity of a jet engine. The drug made him feel like he
could fly.

Of course, drug abuse had turned his face into deep-fried pizza.
Red blisters popped through the ratty stubble on his face. A line of
yellow-headed pimples followed the line of his eyebrow like he was
some kind of mutant. But he loved, just loved, the nuclear blast of
energy through his body.

And, man-oh-man, if he took enough of those pills, he stopped
screaming inside. They distracted him from obsessing about how
that animal had sped out of the forest to rip his friends to pieces.
The way their blood squirted over the driveway at Mull-Rigg Hall
no longer freaked him. Amphetamines were power. They gave him
the power to forget the horror. They filled him with the strength to
do whatever he wanted.

Right now he wanted to watch the river. Already, it burst its
banks into the road. The idiots in the houses down there had piled
up their stupid sandbags. They hoped to stop the river smashing
into their houses. 'Morons!' The Lepping had its own kind of
power: thousands of tons of rainwater.

If the flood was anything as bad – as good! – as last time, then
some of these shitheads would be swept away never to be seen
again.

'Ha-freaking-ha!'

He loved this. The energy: the speed: the force. *Nothing's going
to stop this animal! Animal river's got the claws to scrape houses
from the face of the planet, and it's got the claws to scrape the
smug, self-satisfied grins from everyone's faces.*

Bolter watched trees being swept downriver. Huge willows, with
masses of green leaves, were zipping along like they were nothing
heavier than shitty little blades of grass.

'Cool.' This was turning out to be the best day of Bolter's sorry,
drug-fuelled life.

River water now gushed along the street, a regular tsunami. Already, a guy was knee-deep as he tried to reach his car. The shithead wouldn't get that pile of crap to safety; no way. Within moments, the force of the inundation pushed the vehicle backwards along the road. There was nobody in the car. Pity; it would have been lovely to have seen screaming faces at the window. They'd howl that they were going to drown. *Yeah, that'd be absolutely amazing!*

The car's owner nearly lost his balance as the force of the current became more intense. He was forced to grab hold of some iron railings and haul himself clear. If he hadn't, the river would take him. Probably not hand him back, either. His bones would lie rotting in the mud forever and a day.

With enormous excitement, Bolter watched the car drift off the road into the river. The Lepping swallowed it. *Gulp! And gone!* Bolter's hands were wet with perspiration. Drugs and adrenalin were pushing him higher than he'd ever been before. His heart was a shrieking jet motor caged by human ribs.

A voice yelled, 'Hey, you! Get off the bridge!'

He turned to see a cop calling to him from the other side. Bolter laughed.

'Come off there,' shouted the cop. 'It's starting to collapse!'

The cop daren't come on to the bridge, Bolter thought. *Just look at the big scared eyes!*

The structure shuddered under Bolter's feet. Cracks appeared in the road. He'd love to stay and watch. The river would cause mayhem. It would kill people today.

But it was high time Bolter caused some mayhem of his own.

'*Mayhem! Mayhem! Mayhem!*'

Bolter raced away into the maze of village streets as the bridge began to collapse. He laughed as loud as he could while punching the air. *This is the best time in the world. And just you wait and see what happens next. It's going to be amazing. Absolutely AMAZING!*

FORTY-THREE

The warning howl of the siren filled the room. Tom Westonby panted as he stared at the locked door. He'd tried kicking the thing down. No luck. The hinges and lock had been designed for a strongroom. It didn't help matters that his phone was in his jacket pocket, and that jacket hung over a chair out in the workshop.

'Let's face it,' he hissed, 'I'm locked in here. I'm not going anywhere.'

Chester had been gone ten minutes. He'd promised to be back in five. Meanwhile, the flood siren continued its desperate wail, warning everyone to get out while they still could. Every so often, an amplified voice from a megaphone – a voice that sounded taut with anxiety – would drift into his makeshift prison cell.

Tom could almost reach out and touch the menace that pulsated in the room; every instinct warned him to escape this death trap.

The amplified voice suddenly became much louder and clearer. The police car must be passing right outside the workshop. '. . . *situation is serious. The bridge has collapsed. Floodwaters are rising fast. Residents must leave their homes.*'

Tom pounded on the door. 'Hey! I'm in here!'

'*Make your way to higher ground. The river has burst its banks. Leave your homes . . . I repeat: leave your homes now. You are in danger. Do not collect possessions. Do not wait for neighbours. Focus on your own safety . . .*'

'I'm in here! I can't get out!'

'*You must leave your homes immediately. There is danger of . . .*'

The megaphone voice faded as the police car headed along the street to warn the people of Danby-Mask to flee for their lives. Tom knew only too well that the volume of the megaphone, coupled with the scream of the siren, had drowned out his voice.

Here comes the flood, he thought grimly as he stared down at the gap between the bottom of the door and the floor. *Any moment now, I'm going to see water trickling in. What then?*

When he woke this morning the River Lepping flowed along its channel as it had always done. Now the river had broken out and was invading the village. People who normally lived peacefully alongside the Lepping were running away as it swirled through the streets to their houses. The river seemed to be committing an act of betrayal on its human neighbours.

Tom found himself listing other betrayals that weighed heavily on his mind: his mother and father had fired him, their own son, from a job that would provide vital funds for the dive school. Previously, they'd always welcomed the girlfriends he brought home. Now they were busily scheming to part him from Nicola. Just minutes ago, the man who he considered to be his friend, Chester Kenyon, had locked him in this storeroom. He even found himself half-believing that those embittered, vengeful deities of the Vikings were behind this. Mrs Bekk would certainly claim this was the case: that, in short, he was being punished, because he'd fallen in love with someone from the chosen bloodline of the gods.

He thought: *what day is today? Wednesday. The name means 'day of Woden'. Woden, sometimes called Odin, is chief of the Viking gods and the father of Thor. So it's Woden's day. The day of disaster.*

He kicked the door again. 'Let me out!'

Who was left to hear his yells? The police were evacuating the village. Even the dead in the graveyard would hear the damn siren. His head ached like fury. He pressed his hands against his temples – and that's when he started to laugh. In fact, he didn't know whether to laugh or cry. *Well, laughing's a good start.* After that, he'd cry. Ultimately, he'd start screaming. He could feel madness creeping up the spinal column towards his brain.

He laughed so loud that the noise shook dust from the rafters.

The door abruptly swung open. 'What's so funny?' Chester stared as if he was afraid that Tom really had lost his mind. 'Are you alright?'

'I'm starting to go stir crazy.' However, the sight of his friend – and that open door – made him feel normal again. 'Where the *hell* have you been?'

'I had to get my grandad to his friend's house. They're saying that the flooding's the worst it's been in a hundred years. The water's already reached the churchyard across the street.'

'So, are you going to let me out?'

'Sure. Sorry about keeping you here. I just wanted to . . . you know? Help you.'

Then the gods, if angry, vengeful gods were behind this, decided to inflict three more savage blows.

First: the light went out.

Second: Chester grunted. Someone had shoved him from behind, sending him crashing forward into Tom.

Third: the door slammed shut.

Even though the siren still howled its warning, Tom clearly heard the key turn with a solid metallic *clunk*. Now both men were locked in the room. This time they were plunged into darkness. And the floodwaters were relentlessly moving closer and closer.

FORTY-FOUR

Tom Westonby stood there in the dark. Just seconds ago, someone had pushed Chester into the room. The door had slammed shut again. Now here they were: locked in the storeroom at the back of Chester's workshop. Tom could see nothing – nothing apart from blackness, that was. He did, however, hear the click of a switch.

Chester hissed, 'Damn it, there's no power. The flood must have got into the substation.' Even as he finished the sentence, the siren died away with a feeble croaking sound.

'And it's put the siren out of action, too,' Tom told him. 'So who the hell's locked us in here?'

Chester found the door in the dark. After giving it a good kick he yelled, 'You better let us out of here. I'm warning you!'

Tom tried to be optimistic. 'Might be one of your friends? Playing a joke on us?'

'No, it isn't. I got a call from a pal that was driving over here. The cops are stopping people from coming into the village. The flood's brought down the bridge.'

'Use your phone . . . Call someone to get us out of here.'

'Sorry, Tom. I left the phone with my grandad in case he needed it.'

'Great. Just great. And mine's out there in the workshop.'

Chester pounded the door. 'Let us out or I'll rip your bloody head off!'

A voice came back at him – all fast and breathy, as if the guy was so excited that he'd burst wide open. 'Yeah, yeah! Try it, Chester Shitting Kenyon. My head's right here. Go on, reach through this bit of wood, rip it off . . . rip off my head and wear it like a hat on *your* stupid head!' The laughter that came through the door sounded more like a high-pitched screech.

Chester growled back, 'Bolter. I know it's you.'

'That's intelligent. OK, you know it's me, so what?'

'Bolter, let me out.'

'Nope.'

'I'll break your neck.'

'Still nopey nope.' Bolter squealed with laughter.

Tom whispered, 'He's high on something.'

'Yeah,' Chester whispered back. 'Speed. Amphetamines. He lives on that junk.'

'He's the one that attacked me. There were three other guys there, too.'

'*I heard that!*' Bolter switched from laughter to rage. 'Yeah, we were up at Mull-Rigg. We pounded your face to crap. Then you did something . . .' His voice adopted a hollow quality, as if he remembered something traumatic. 'Now my friends are dead. All that blood on the ground, man – all that blood.'

'Jesus,' hissed Chester. 'Those pills have sent him crazy.'

Bolter snarled. 'My friends are dead . . . It's all your fault, Westonby.'

'Open the door,' Tom said. 'We can talk about this.'

'Talking's for shitheads. I'm going up there. This is something I can sort out myself.'

'Bolter—'

'I know that bitch Nicola Bekk's got something to do with my friends being murdered. She's going to get a visit from me, Westonby. Do you hear? She's going to a get a real visit. She's going to get my ace, number-one calling card! Do you follow?'

Tom continued to speak softly: 'Open the door. We'll discuss this calmly.'

'Do you think I'm calm after what happened to me? After what I saw!'

Tom Westonby stood there in the dark and shuddered. He had the dreadful feeling that Bolter was on the verge of admitting that there *really* had been a creature, which had emerged from the forest the night he was attacked. After Tom had been beaten senseless by those thugs he'd either dreamt or hallucinated that a monster had ripped Bolter's friends apart. So could it be some bizarre coincidence that Bolter'd had a drug-fuelled fantasy about his friends being murdered? Or had there really been a . . .? Tom suddenly felt uneasy about even finishing the thought. *Helsvir isn't real*, he told himself, *so don't fall into the trap of believing it is, or you'll end up as insane as Mrs Bekk.*

Bolter made strange sounds at the other side of the door: crying and laughing at the same time.

The sound both sickened and shocked Tom. That was a human being sliding into total psychological breakdown. A man in such a state could do anything his sick brain told him to do. That was the kind of mental state where people committed murder.

Chester grabbed Tom's arm. 'What's all this about people being killed? What really happened at your house the other night, Tom?'

Tom realized he needed to play this shrewdly. Chester must stay focused on the problem that they faced now: being locked in a room by Bolter, a man close to meltdown.

Chester shook Tom's arm again. 'Tom, what did he see?'

'Humour him,' Tom whispered. 'We've got to persuade him to open the door.'

'I'll persuade him . . . *with my fist!*'

Tom's heart sank. Chester's anger was understandable, but this would only provoke Bolter.

Tom was right. 'Yeah,' Bolter sneered. 'Your fist's going to persuade nothing, you shithead. I'm going to pay Nicola Bekk a visit right now . . . *I just know I can make her talk.*' His voice got all oozy and gloating. 'Pillow talk, Westonby. A little bit of pillow talk . . . she'll fess up about everything.' The voice faded as he moved away. 'Bye-bye. I'll tell you all the exciting details when I get back.' His high-pitched laughter reached them. 'I'll even have some gory souvenirs . . . ha-ha. Gory, gory, gory!'

'He's crazy,' Chester muttered. 'Totally crazy.'

Tom shuddered as he pictured what Bolter might do to the woman he loved. 'He's going to hurt Nicola. We've got to get out of here right now.'

'We need some light. Stand back.'

Tom heard shuffling in the dark. Then clanks of metal as if Chester searched through the mess of engine parts on the shelves.

After Chester blundered into him a couple of times, Tom stood back to give the man space to work.

'What are you looking for, Chester?'

'Something long enough to reach through the window bars. There's only boards over the opening. If I can knock those out, we'll be able to see again.'

Tom took another step back. There was something about the way his foot sounded that made him pause. He lightly tapped his foot twice.

Plish-plash.

'Oh no.' Quickly, he bent down. The darkness made it impossible to see what was there on the floor – he felt it, though.

'Chester. Hurry up. There's water coming under the door.'

'I don't understand it . . . The floods have never reached the workshop before.'

'Maybe the gods are angry with us.'

'Yeah, and I'm getting angry with them.' He'd responded as if Tom had made a flippant comment. 'Ah, this should do it.'

Tom heard a series of loud bangs. After the fifth *BANG*, daylight jetted in through a gap in the boards that covered the barred window. He screwed his eyes up at the sudden glare. When his eyes functioned again he checked the floor and found that a brownish pool was spreading around his feet.

Chester's eyes bulged. 'This's really bad, Tom. At this rate, the whole village is going to be underwater.'

'Then we're going to have to get out before we drown.'

'How?'

Tom tugged at the iron bars covering the window.

'You'll never shift those. My dad cemented them there ten years ago when he planned to use this as the cash room. That's why we put in the safe.' He gave a shrug. 'But Ma persuaded him the bank was the best place for the money after all.'

Tom remembered the truck jack that stood on the safe. 'Give me a hand with this.'

'What you going to do with that?'

'Rest the jack on its side between the bars, then pump the handle.'

'Ah, like the jaws of life! You're a genius, Tom.'

'Call me a genius once we're out of here.'

The heavy-duty jack was a formidable chunk of steel. Even with both of them lifting together, it was still tough to manoeuvre the mechanism so it rested on its side between the vertical bars. As soon as it was in place, Chester pumped the handle.

Slowly, the formidable steel brace, which would normally raise a truck off the ground so one of its wheels could be changed, moved outwards. Chester used all his strength to keep pumping.

'Keep going,' Tom shouted. 'The bar's bending.'

'Stand back.' Chester really put some beef into the job. He pumped the jack handle until sweat bled from his face. A moment later there was a terrific bang.

'Damn it,' Chester yelled. 'I've bust the jack!'

'No, you haven't. That's the bar breaking. Look!' He tugged at one of the window bars. It came free in his hand.

'Reckon you can get through that gap?' Chester panted.

'Try me.'

Tom quickly wriggled through into the workshop. After a struggle, Chester managed to squeeze his muscular body through, too. When the big man dropped feet first on to the floor he sent a wave running across the flood water that was about an inch deep.

Tom asked, 'Have you any sandbags to stop it getting in?'

'I'll worry about sandbags. You go find Nicola Bekk. She needs you more than I do.'

'Thanks, Chester.'

'Don't forget your phone.'

Tom saw that his jacket had vanished from the chair. 'Bolter must have taken it.'

'I've more bad news. It's not all he's taken.' Chester pointed at an empty steel cage in the corner. 'There should be a big can of diesel there. Bolter's taken that, too. He must be planning on starting a fire.'

FORTY-FIVE

Water gently rippled through the open doors of the workshop – so far, no more than an inch deep. Yet there was more to come, that much was for sure. The moment Tom Westonby splashed through that glistening pool and out on to the street he saw the flood pouring into the graveyard of St George's church. The ancient stone building stood on a mound, so it now occupied its own small island. Graves were being relentlessly inundated. Black stone crosses, statues of weeping angels, the vertical slabs of granite that served as tombstones: they all jutted out of the new lake that was forming in the village.

Fortunately, Tom's car remained clear of the water. That state of affairs wouldn't last for long, however. A scummy tide crept up the road. In a matter of seconds the first waves would be lapping at the wheels.

Find Nicola. Make sure she's safe. Bring her to Mull-Rigg Hall where you can look after her. That was the beat of Tom's thoughts as he ran towards his car. *Once you've got her home don't let her out of your sight.* Tom clearly remembered Bolter's threat: *'I know that bitch Nicola Bekk's got something to do with my friends being murdered. She's going to get a visit from me, Westonby. Do you hear? She's going to get a real visit. She's going to get my ace, number-one calling card! Do you follow?'*

Tom did follow. He knew exactly what that thug Bolter intended. The man would do everything he could to hurt her. Bolter had also taken the can of fuel; no doubt he planned to do some fire-starting.

He'd got halfway to his car when he heard a shout. 'Tom! Tom, wait!'

Chester had run from the workshop into the street. 'My van was parked out here. Bolter's stolen it.'

So that's how he's transporting his arson kit, thought Tom. 'I'll get the van back for you.'

'I'm not worried about the van, Tom. I'm worried about you. That lunatic will kill you if he gets the chance!'

'I can take care of myself.' Chester's concern touched Tom. 'Thanks, though, mate. I'll be careful.'

'You do that. Come back in one piece. Remember, you're going to be the best man at my wedding!'

Tom nodded, waved, and then made it to his car as the water touched its front wheels.

A moment later, he dropped into the driver's seat. That's when the river seized his attention. The Lepping had become massive. Yesterday, it had been no more than fifty yards wide. Now it must be almost a mile from shore to shore. Its waters possessed the same cold gleam as a knife blade. Shafts of sunlight pierced the cloud to roam across the surface like searchlights.

The immensity of what he witnessed took his breath away. Where the banks were highest and narrowest, the bridge had once spanned the channel. Now that the bridge had collapsed, the rubble formed a dam, resulting in water building up behind the pile of masonry. This in turn allowed the river to spill over banks of earth to engulf the houses.

There was nothing gentle or placid about the water down there. The flood rampaged through the streets. Muscular currents carried a bus (fortunately empty of people) by the post office before slamming it into the mini-supermarket. Seconds later, a huge whirlpool sucked the bus down.

This is the fury of the gods. This is heaven's vengeance. The notion that this was an attack on humanity was easy to believe. The Lepping had been unleashed to attack the village – smashing in doors, ripping through walls. Waves contemptuously slapped the faces of houses in bursts of silver spray. The river would claim lives today.

Tom glanced down at the road. Damn. The water had already reached the back wheels. Even here on higher ground, the flood must be six inches deep; alarmingly, he could feel the car vibrate as the flow grew faster, more powerful, building up to the moment when it could whirl Tom's car away to destruction.

Tom started the motor and reversed uphill. As soon as he was clear, he pulled a screeching U-turn that left black streaks of rubber on the road, then roared away.

His mission: to find Nicola.

And find her before Bolter got his hands on her.

FORTY-SIX

The flood hadn't finished with him yet. As Tom drove out of Danby-Mask, the road took him uphill. In the rear-view mirror, he saw water gushing into the streets. OK, so he'd escaped those particular battalions of the invading flood. The trouble was, every so often the road would dip downwards again. Then he'd be faced with a brown tide spilling across the tarmac. Nevertheless, Nicola was on his mind. He dreaded what Bolter would do if that psycho got his hands on her. So he put his foot down.

The motor screamed as it hauled the vehicle through the growing lake that threatened to drown an entire village. People were desperately loading possessions into cars. A young woman, with tears making her face glitter, carried an armful of puppies through floodwaters that were waist deep. A man, possibly her husband or boyfriend, beckoned her towards a truck where armchairs, rugs, clothes and treasured possessions had been hurriedly piled. The anguish on their faces was almost unbearable to see.

Villagers were being forced to run from their homes. The River Lepping had turned its population into refugees.

Tom Westonby focused on the road. He didn't want to hit a deep pocket of water at speed. If he did, he'd lose control of the car. He wasn't scared about hurting himself. No, what terrified him was the prospect of Nicola and her mother having to confront Bolter. The man was high on drugs. In all likelihood, he had deep-seated psychiatric problems, too. Tom knew only too well that Bolter enjoyed inflicting bodily harm.

Danby-Mask receded behind him. Ahead, trees arched over the roadway. Thick banks of cloud were turning the day into a strange-looking realm that lingered between light and darkness. His mouth was so dry it felt like he'd eaten a handful of dust.

He murmured: 'Nicola . . . I'm coming for you. Hang on.'

Driving to Skanderberg, Nicola's home, wouldn't be possible. No roads led to the house. Instead, he decided to follow the forest tracks. He knew of one which would take him within a quarter of a mile of the house. The rest of the way could be done quickly enough on foot. Very quickly. Because he knew that he'd run like a hare to reach the place.

Tom turned off the main road on to the forest track. Wet mud sprayed from the tyres as he accelerated. The entire car wiggled from side to side. The slimy gloop that passed for a road surface wouldn't allow the rubber treads a proper grip. Nevertheless, he continued to push uphill through the trees. Here, the forest was a dark place. Roe deer flitted through the gloom. Every so often, he caught a glimpse of their startled dark eyes as they watched the noisy mechanical intruder roar past.

At the top of the hill there was a small clearing in the forest.

'No. I don't believe it. No, no!' Tom braked hard, bringing the car to a sliding stop.

In seconds, he'd scrambled out of the seat. He didn't believe the

sight that met his eyes. From up here he could see the curve of the
swollen river. He should also have been able to see the red tiles of
Nicola's cottage.

He didn't see the roof. He didn't see the strange, ancient walls
of the building. No, what he saw, rising forbiddingly into the sky,
was a tower of black.

I'm too late. He stared in horror at a pyramid of fire that occupied
the clearing where Skanderberg should have sat.

Suddenly, Tom pictured Nicola and her mother lying dead in the
place. *Bolter killed them. Then he set fire to the house. He threatened
to hurt Nicola, didn't he?*

Emotional shock hit Tom so powerfully that he stumbled backwards until he struck the car. He stood there, panting, his eyes
locked on the inferno. In his mind's eye, he could see a sorrowful
scatter of bones across a bedroom floor; a fleshless skull, flames
jetting from its empty sockets.

An explosion detonated inside Tom's own head. Somehow he
found himself in the car. He was driving again. He didn't know
where, and he was screaming at the top of his voice. 'I'll kill you!
You're dead! You're dead! I'm going to RIP YOU APART!'

The car roared downhill, back towards the main road. *This is war.
I'm going to kill Bolter. I'm going to rip him apart bit by bit . . .*

He entered a dark tunnel formed by trees that completely arched
over the dirt track. Tom's screams of fury fused with that of the
engine. The trees blurred, he was travelling so fast.

Then – *BANG!* A white disk slammed into the side window next
to his shoulder. An impression of staring eyes, a wild mass of hair,
an open mouth locked into a desperate scream.

Tom braked so hard he nearly flipped the car end over end.

Jesus, what was that?

He twisted back in the seat, looking through the rear window,
convinced he'd just run down a human being.

Nothing there . . . just furrows where wheels had churned the
mud.

BANG!

He turned forwards again to see a fist smashing against the
window.

Bolter . . . if that's Bolter I'll kill him! Before he could even
reach the handle, the figure on the other side of the door had
wrenched it open.

The next second he was looking into a pair of wide eyes.

'Mrs Bekk?' He stared at the woman.

She was more like a wild, elemental apparition than a flesh and blood human being. Her white hair stuck out from her head in long spikes, almost like the spokes of a wheel. Her clothes were rumpled, flecked with leaves. Her feet were covered with mud. She must have been running through the forest as if demons had been chasing her.

'Mrs Bekk, are you alright?'

'There was a man from the village,' she panted. 'I know him. I know his family. Bolter. Our families have been enemies for hundreds of years.

'Mrs Bekk—'

'It was a Bolter that killed my grandfather in 1932.'

'He set fire to your house, didn't he?'

She nodded. 'Skanderberg will be rebuilt. Those devils from Danby-Mask have burned it down before.'

Tom scrambled out of the car. 'Where's Nicola? What's happened to her?'

'This is your fault. If you hadn't been pawing after her, this would never have happened.'

He grabbed her by her shoulders. He felt thin bones under her skin. 'Where is she, Mrs Bekk?'

The blue eyes that were uncanny duplicates of Nicola's gazed out from beneath the heavy eyelids. She'd stiffened. He'd even felt her muscles harden under the skin of her shoulders. This wiry creature could be a fighter when she wanted to be.

He took his hands away. 'Please, Mrs Bekk,' he begged. 'Tell me what happened to Nicola.'

The woman pressed her lips together. She slowly shook her head.

'I love your daughter. I really do love her.'

When she spoke, her voice was surprisingly tender. 'You can't, son. You can't love her. She can never be your bride.'

He glanced at the black smoke rolling over the trees. 'Is she hurt?' His heart lurched and his blood ran cold. 'Is she still alive?'

Mrs Bekk lifted her blue eyes to meet his. She held his gaze for a moment. The woman seemed to be reading the real thoughts inside his head. Mrs Bekk sighed as she seemed to realize he genuinely cared for her daughter. 'Yes, son. She's still alive. But you can't grasp what will become of her if you continue this courtship, can you?'

'All I want right now is to make sure she's safe.'

'When Nicola realized the flood was coming she went to your house to warn you.'

'I haven't been there all day! I was in the village when the river burst its banks.'

Mrs Bekk spoke softly: 'Then if she's not at Mull-Rigg Hall, she'll be trying to find you. Because I can tell: Nicola does love you.' She suddenly gripped his wrist. 'There's another fact you should know: *you're the first boy she's ever loved.*'

Tom nodded at the car. 'Get in. We'll find her together.'

Within seconds, he thundered down the track towards Mull-Rigg Hall. He thought about Nicola desperately searching for him. And he thought about Bolter on his mission to hurt Nicola.

Tom couldn't help but wonder what he'd find when he finally reached home.

FORTY-SEVEN

After hurtling through the driveway gates, Tom skidded to a stop outside the front door. Within seconds, he'd run round the back of Mull-Rigg Hall. Tom had been seized by the wild notion that he'd find Nicola paddling in the spring-water pool again, wearing a broad, happy smile. Instead, he found the back lawn to be deserted. There wasn't a soul in the orchard – just those apple trees, which forlornly dripped rainwater. Tom raced back to the driveway to find Mrs Bekk climbing out of the car; she gazed up at the bedroom windows as if expecting to see her daughter's face there.

Quickly, he unlocked the door and ran inside. Mrs Bekk followed. She moved slowly, the expression on her face said all too starkly: *I knew this would happen. You've brought calamity on yourself. You should have kept away from my daughter. Now you're going to suffer.*

What was uppermost in Tom's mind was this: *find Nicola. Bolter might know where she is. He could be following her. Then again, he might already have her.*

'Nicola!' he shouted, though he knew she couldn't possibly

be in the house. The doors were all locked when he left that morning.

Then he almost threw himself at the telephone. If Nicola couldn't reach him on his phone – after all, it had been stolen by Bolter – she might have used the landline. He hit the play button of the answer machine. The message played over the speaker so Mrs Bekk heard every word. And every word made Tom sick to the stomach.

'Hello, Tom.' The voice belonged to his mother. 'Tom. We've just heard from the builder; he's told us that it's best if no one's living in the house when he strips off the roof tiles. So Dad and I have decided that you should come home and live here with us until the job's finished; we still have plenty of time before the lease expires and we have to move out. We'll pick you up tomorrow morning at ten. We're sorry to spring this on you at short notice. But you'll realize it's for the best if—'

Tom stabbed the off button, killing the voice dead. Then he stared at the telephone with nothing less than fury. His parents had fired him from working here. Now they'd schemed up a nice little way to force him out of the house and back to their home, which lay over a hundred miles away.

Mrs Bekk read the expression on his face. 'Your parents don't want you to have anything to do with Nicola either, do they?'

'If Nicola and me want to see each other . . . if we want to get married . . . then it's entirely up to us. You're not going to stop us. My parents can't stop us. Nobody will stop us! OK?'

Mrs Bekk wore an expression of gentle sympathy. 'But something will stop you from spending your life with Nicola.'

'No, they won't. I'll fight anyone over this. Just send them to me.' Rage boiled in his veins. 'I won't let them beat me.'

'There are greater powers than you can imagine at work on Nicola . . . Tom, I need to explain some things to you.'

He stubbornly shook his head. 'I'm going to find Nicola.'

'She might have gone to the village to find you. I'll come along and tell you what you need to know. Then you'll realize that there never can be a wedding.'

FORTY-EIGHT

ind Nicola. Find her now. The consequences of not finding
Nicola filled him with dread.

Tom Westonby pushed the car hard. Huge oak trees stretched
their branches across the road, giving the impression the car plunged
through a gloomy tunnel as he headed back to Danby-Mask.

In the space of thirty minutes, he'd discovered that Bolter had
torched the ancient cottage, and now he drove with Mrs Bekk by
his side. The woman appeared remarkably calm. Her house had
gone up in flames. All those impossible-to-replace treasures would
be destroyed – family photographs, and the important souvenirs
which mothers collect as their children grow: that lock of silky-fine
baby hair, the first drawing brought back from school, Mother's
Day cards – all gone. Maybe she had more substantial problems on
her mind? Ones far, far bigger than the loss of her home.

Tom left the vast forest behind, with its thousands of trees, which
created such a mysterious wilderness. Here, meadows flanked the
road. A lone black and white cow watched him hurtle past.

He glanced at Mrs Bekk as she calmly gazed ahead. To his
surprise, he realized how much Nicola resembled her mother.
Yes, Mrs Bekk's hair was white now, rather than the pale
blonde of Nicola's, yet she had the same clear blue eyes and
delicate features.

When Mrs Bekk spoke she was perfectly in control of her
emotions. Again, a voice like Nicola's: so pleasant on his ear. There
was a kindness there. A thoughtfulness – as if she'd decided the
time had come to be both open and honest with her daughter's
boyfriend. 'What I told you of our family history is true, you know?
My ancestors were Vikings. They travelled by longship from
Denmark to this part of England over a thousand years ago. They
weren't like the Vikings in films. They didn't have horned helmets;
they never rampaged through the countryside, burning down monasteries. The fact is, they loved their families, and because there was
famine in Denmark they were driven here to Yorkshire to start a
new life. See how fertile it is? How green those fields are? My

ancestors made the dangerous journey across the North Sea in an open boat, because this place was their last hope to save their children from starvation.'

Tom said, 'I grew up in parts of Africa where children die because they don't have clean water. There are still millions of parents today who struggle to keep their children from starving.'

Mrs Bekk nodded. 'I believe you have a good heart, Tom.'

'So you'll appreciate I want to make Nicola happy?'

'Yes, but you're also headstrong.'

'How come?'

'You don't realize that as you try to give Nicola a good life you'll be destroying her.'

He turned a bend in the road to see Danby-Mask in the valley below. Or, rather, what remained of it. The scene was strangely beautiful. There was a sense of peace – even if it was the deathly peace after the life had gone out of something, whether it be a human body, or in this case a community. Sunlight transformed the floodwaters into a smooth sheet of gold that glowed so brightly that Tom was dazzled. Set in that vast, shining lake were roofs covered with dark red tiles. The effect was of rubies studding a gigantic slab of gold.

The sight was so amazing that it nearly cost Tom and his passenger their lives. A line of tractors straddled the narrow road. With no room to pass, he had to crush down on the brake pedal. Then hope for the best. With a piercing shriek of rubber grazing the tarmac, the car slid to a stop. Even when it seemed likely he'd slam into the back end of the slow-moving convoy, Mrs Bekk remained uncannily calm.

Tom had to make a real physical effort to uncurl his fingers from the steering wheel after the car had stopped. 'Where the hell is that convoy going?'

'When there's a flood the local farmers help the people in the village. Families load their possessions – and then themselves – on to the back of the trailers. After that, the tractors take them out of the flood to high ground.'

'Which means we're now stuck.'

'That means I have a proper chance to talk to you.'

'But I need to get to the village! I must find Nicola.'

'We'll still get there,' she said. 'Believe me, Tom, we really do need to talk. This is important.'

Tom eased the car forwards at ten miles an hour. Tractors, hauling flatbed trailers, snaked along the highway. He couldn't overtake them, and he knew he couldn't honk the farmers to the side. If he did so, as they executed their mission of mercy, they'd simply give what they took to be an impatient idiot a cold, pitying glance, then ignore his frenzied honking. So he'd have to muster his patience, then follow the dignified procession.

'OK, Mrs Bekk. Tell me what you've got to say.'

Mrs Bekk talked in that calm way of hers. The gentle rhythm of her words eased the clamour in his chest. He desperately wanted to find Nicola, but these were important words he was hearing. His instinct for survival hinted that they warned him of the danger to come. *Forewarned is forearmed.*

Firstly, she explained how Nicola had grown up in the remote cottage. 'My parents died before Nicola was born. I had her late, so by then there was just the two of us. I did my very best to protect her from the outside world.'

'Did she need protecting from the outside world?'

'She was a normal child. But I knew if she lived life in a normal way she'd suffer the same fate as her brothers and sisters. They became "blood takers" – that's what people so cursed are called in the Viking legends.'

'Vampires?'

'People today would describe them as such. They avoid daylight. They feed on the blood of sheep up on the moor.'

Tom remembered his nightmare – the one where Mrs Bekk had guided him through the forest to the hilltop. It was there – in the dream – that he'd seen the strange white figures that Mrs Bekk described as vampires . . . those benighted children of hers . . . and then there was Helsvir: the creature that consisted of corpses and dozens of heads. According to myth, Helsvir was the supernatural guardian created by Thor to protect the Bekk clan.

But how can she talk about my dreams as if they were real? Come to that, how does she know what I've been dreaming about? Then came the dazzling revelation.

'Mrs Bekk, I thought I'd dreamt about what happened the other night when you came to the house and I followed you up the hill. You were really there, weren't you?'

'Of course. I knew you'd try and convince yourself it was all a nightmare. But you actually went with me into the forest. You saw my children that had been transformed by the curse. And you saw Nicola riding Helsvir.'

'OK, you came to the house, and, yes, I followed you. You have to remember that I was still suffering from concussion.'

'You were well enough, Tom. You saw what you saw.'

He shook his head. 'You told me what to see. My mind was all screwed up from the beating. Somehow you tricked me into believing I saw vampires and the dragon and Nicola. That wasn't real, Mrs Bekk, that was hypnosis.'

'You're saying I hypnotized you?' She gave a sad smile. 'No, you really did see Helsvir. And you really did see my poor sons and daughters. They were transformed into those vampire creatures because they turned their backs on their old way of life. The same will happen to Nicola if she rejects her heritage and leaves to go to live with you in the outside world.'

'I only saw those things because you put those ideas into my head.'

'Did I? I thought you were brave, Tom, but you aren't brave enough to accept the evidence of your own eyes.'

'So you really are serious about some old Viking curse turning Nicola into a vampire if we get married?'

'Yes.'

'This is the modern world, Mrs Bekk. We don't hide under the blankets from ghosts any more. We don't believe in gods that punish us, if we don't worship them.'

'You don't, Tom – millions, on the other hand, do.'

At that moment it crossed his mind to stop the car, open the door, and simply push the crazy woman out, but could he do that? *She's Nicola's mother. She still might be useful in helping me find Nicola.* His hands tightened around the steering wheel as a gateway opened in his head – it was being forced open by those vivid images of white-faced vampires on the hill. He remembered the black veins under the skin, the fierce pupils in their strange white eyes. Then came Helsvir. Monstrous Helsvir. Bristling with hissing human heads. And Nicola in a trance, riding the thing . . .

'No, it's not real,' he hissed. 'There's no such thing as vampires or dragons.' He hated the tone of his voice. For he'd lost his sense of conviction. No longer was it so easy to disbelieve. *You must stay being the Doubting Thomas*, he told himself. *Don't start believing in curses and monsters, otherwise you'll end up like Mrs Bekk – a crazy loner. A number-one nut-job.*

'I've told you the truth,' she said gently. 'I know it's going to take some time for you to accept it fully. You will believe eventually. You'll have to for Nicola's sake.'

'Hypnotism. Hallucinations. Nightmares.' He tried to inject some force into the words, as if they would become a mantra that would dispel even the remotest possibility that he had witnessed Helsvir tearing those three men apart, or that he actually witnessed the vampires standing there on the hill as they watched their youngest sister ride the beast.

Mrs Bekk continued in that matter-of-fact way of hers (perhaps trying to wear down his resistance by chatting about extraordinary things as if they were profoundly commonplace): 'When Nicola was twelve I could tell that the books she read and the lessons she'd been taught made her doubt what I told her was true: that she must never marry a man from the outside world. So I took her away from school.'

'Didn't you think that was cruel?' *Play the woman at her own game. Keep the conversation going, then she might not succeed in pulling that hypnosis trick again, or whatever it was. So stay focused. Stay alert. Don't let her do all the talking.* 'Imagine the harm you might have caused by taking her out of school.'

'What else could I do? I love Nicola. I'd do anything to keep her as the sweet *human* being she is now.'

'Parents want to protect their children; they're afraid of them being bullied at school, or being hurt by a car, but it's impossible to keep them at home forever.' *That's it, keep the conversation flowing.*

'It's true. Mothers and fathers want to see smiles on their children's faces, not tears. Nicola's situation is different. If I didn't keep her away from the outside world, the consequences would be terrible.'

'Yet the more you try to protect Nicola by keeping her a hermit, the more you'll damage her.'

'I don't claim that isolating my daughter is the ideal solution. I'm just doing the best I can to protect her.'

'And you really believe that this vendetta between your family and the village is continuing after all this time?'

'I know what you're suggesting.' She still spoke calmly, although her words became more precise, and her eyes became even more focused as she watched him. She was reading his expression. 'You think that the Bekk war with Danby-Mask is a paranoid fantasy?'

'Perhaps they see your family as being different. But do you really believe that the villagers would deliberately hurt you and Nicola?'

'The Bolter youth set fire to my house.'

'He's acting alone.'

'I want to show you something.' She undid the top three buttons of her blouse.

'Mrs Bekk! What are you doing?'

'The young man who burnt my home had an uncle by the name of Jack Bolter. Forty years ago he did this to me.' She rested her fingertip on soft flesh just above her cleavage.

The shock of what he saw made him flinch. There, on the pale skin, was a pink scar.

'Jack Bolter stabbed me. You see, my mother forced me to break off our engagement. When I told him, he lost his mind. He grabbed a knife from the kitchen table and stabbed me.'

'So you were going to marry into the Bolter family?'

'He loved me very much. He couldn't understand why I broke off the engagement for no apparent reason. Maybe it was a mistake on my part, but I decided I couldn't tell him that if I got married in a Christian church I'd invoke the curse. That would mean he'd lose his bride anyway.' She fastened up her blouse. 'So you see . . . whatever my family do we are always drawn back to our ancient faith. We are the last of the believers; the Viking gods will never let us join the modern world.'

Those words made Tom's head spin. He now felt his sympathy growing for Mrs Bekk, because here was a woman living in a state of desperation. OK, she had an entire heap of peculiar beliefs, yet she'd once attempted to escape that strange and lonely life in the forest. She'd fallen in love with a man from the village. That had ended in near-tragedy when he'd stabbed her. *Love is wonderful when it goes right*, he thought. *When love goes wrong, though, it's a calamity. Lives are easily lost.*

Even though his feelings softened somewhat towards her, he realized he must still humour the woman. That would mean humouring her in a calculating way. After all, there was a chance he'd need her help to find Nicola when they reached the village. With this in mind he casually asked, 'Why don't you fight against this curse? You can't be held prisoner by your own heritage.'

'Don't you think I tried? I wanted to marry Jack Bolter. But *they* wouldn't let me.' She pointed into the sky.

'Can't you say "enough is enough", and then lead the kind of life you want?'

'The same thing's happened to you, Tom, hasn't it?'

'What do you mean?'

'Nicola told me that your father's done such wonderful work in Africa that he's even been described as a saint, hasn't he?'

'What's that got to do with you breaking away from what happened in the past?'

'Because you need to break away, too.'

'I don't see what you're driving at.'

'People praise your father as a saint. You feel as if you've got to match the good things he does.'

'You're telling me that I only want to marry Nicola as some kind of good deed? That it's my special project to show my father how saintly I can be?'

'Tom, you only met Nicola a few days ago.'

'I love her. I know she's the woman I want to marry.'

Mrs Bekk eyed him shrewdly. 'So what happened when you were young that still troubles you?'

'Nothing happened.'

'I can see it written on your face.' Her eyes became even keener. 'Everyone tells you that your father is a living saint. But he's done something that shocked you. You've seen another side of him, haven't you? What did he do, Tom?'

Tom gently braked to stop the car. The question amazed him. He'd never told anyone about what happened in Africa when he was ten years old. *Somehow she's looked at my face and read that I have a secret.* Right then, he decided to tell this woman, the mother of the girl he loved, everything. True, he wanted to find Nicola, but this was an opportunity to get Nicola's mother on his side.

'My father's mission was to provide safe drinking water for people who'd otherwise die, because they didn't have access to clean wells. His personal quest was, and still is, to save lives.'

'It's easy to see why people regard him as a saint.'

Tom's heart pounded; he realized he was about to reveal the truth behind an incident that he'd promised to keep secret. This was a terrifying moment. 'I was ten years old. We were living in this remote African village where my parents were working. The new well had been dug, and I went with my father to collect the diesel generator that would power the pump. That, in turn, would deliver fresh water to the village. The families really did need it. The old well was alive with parasites and dangerous bugs. One in three of their children died before their fifth birthday.' Tom watched the tractors rumble forward on their own mission of mercy. Down in the village, the floodwater possessed the houses like an evil spirit. 'Anyway. We were returning with the generator. Dad had bought a bottle of champagne to celebrate his and my mother's wedding anniversary. The dirt track we were following went through a really thick wooded area. Dad and I were by ourselves. We'd done this journey before, which took no more than a couple of hours. There seemed nothing unusual about it.' His scalp began to prickle, as if insects with cold, pointed feet marched through his hair. 'Then some men burst out of the trees to flag us down. My father, true to form, stopped to help. He thought they were in some kind of trouble. As I started to open the passenger door he said, "Stay in the cab, Tom. I don't know what's happening here." He'd climbed halfway out of the truck when all hell broke loose. The men started yelling . . . They took out machetes, and they were waving them at my father. As they pulled him down from the cab he turned and gave me this look. You know the kind; it's so full on . . . so full of emotion that you feel as if you'll freeze up inside.'

Mrs Bekk spoke with gentle sympathy: 'You must have been terrified.'

'And me? A ten-year-old? What could I do? What upset me most . . . what nearly breaks my heart today . . . was that expression on Dad's face. He was picturing what the gang might do to me – there'd be nothing he could do to stop them.'

'Your father must have been well known. Would people attack someone that was helping the community?'

'I guess those guys were drifters from outside the area. This was probably an opportunist robbery. You know, they see a new truck, and there's a packing case on the back that might be full of all kinds of good stuff.' Tom shrugged. 'We didn't have a gun, so we were in deep, deep trouble. One guy just kept yanking at Dad's arm to pull him further away from me. The other men climbed on to the back of the truck and began hacking at the crate. My dad starts yelling, "Stop that! You'll damage it! We need the generator!" What happened next caught everyone by surprise. Dad pulled free of the robber that was pulling him away. He ran back to the cab and grabbed the bottle of champagne that was in a compartment in the door. Dad then charged at the guy that had been pulling him. The man lost his balance and fell flat on his back. I remember that he fell so hard it splashed up this big cloud of dust. Dad called back at me, "Tom! Stay in the cab! Keep down! Don't look out. Whatever happens, *don't look out*, OK?"'

'You saw something that's haunted you?'

Tom nodded. 'Like any kid of ten, when they're told not to look, that's exactly what they do.' He took a deep breath. 'Dad ignored the guy on the ground. Instead, he shouted at the guys on the back of the truck that were hacking away at the packing case. My father knew that if the generator was damaged or stolen, then there wouldn't be a replacement for weeks. Without the generator there'd be no way of pumping clean water out of the new borehole. Lots more children would die, because they'd have to use the old well, which was contaminated. So when my father confronted the robbers he knew this was a matter of life and death. The generator would save lives. "Get down from there," he was yelling. "Stop that, you'll damage it." One of the robbers jumped down from the truck. I can picture him right now. He had yellow shorts that came down to his knees. He was wearing a white T-shirt with a picture of a tennis racquet on the front, and it was frayed and wispy at the collar. You could tell the guy was getting fired up. His eyes seemed to bulge right out of his head; he was pointing the machete into Dad's face.

'Then I saw the champagne bottle in Dad's hand. Of course, I was a kid back then. I thought he'd planned to give the bottle to the men as gift. You know, to make them realize he was a nice person and didn't want any trouble. Anyway, the robber in the tennis T-shirt carried on shouting. He jabbed the machete at my father's face. Then he turned to the other guys on the truck and made a pushing gesture with his hands. He was telling them to push the generator off the back. That's when my father killed him.'

'He killed him? How?'

'He . . .' Tom's words caught in his throat. Emotion made his larynx tighten so much he thought his voice might wither away completely. He swallowed, then said hoarsely, 'He struck him here with the bottle.' He touched the side of his head. 'This teenager just slowly sank down to his knees, like he was going to say a prayer or something. The machete fell out of his hand. Then my dad looked at the robber's head. I realize now he was carefully deciding where to hit him next. I remember how cold and calculating he was about it. Then he gave him a full-blooded swipe right in the back of the skull. The guy just flopped into the dust.' Tom turned to Mrs Bekk. He tried to smile but he felt more like crying. 'You know, Mrs Bekk, it's not like in films. If you hit someone with a bottle, it doesn't always smash into little bits. That bottle must have been as hard as iron, because it didn't shatter. So . . . I watched the man lying there. We all did. Nobody moved.'

'Are you sure he was dead?'

'If you'd seen his skull, you'd have known he was dead. The back of his head didn't bulge out any more, it bulged in.' Tom wiped his knuckles across his mouth. His tongue was so dry it felt as if it had acquired a coating of that parched African dust. 'The dead man's friends ran away as fast as they could. My father had saved the generator. And that meant he could save lives.' Tom shook his head. 'I've never told anyone that my father killed a man.'

'You were being robbed.'

'We were, but that didn't stop the nightmares I had for years afterwards. If anything, what happened later was even harder to understand. Dad grabbed hold of the dead boy by the feet and dragged him into the forest. I remember the tennis racquet T-shirt got all rucked up. Even back then, I knew my dad was leaving the body for the leopards to get rid of.' He managed a dry croak of a laugh. He heard the sound of a scared little boy in there. One who'd bottled up the truth for too long. 'Before we drove off my father turned to me and said: "Tom we won't mention what happened today to your mother, will we? We don't want to scare her." Then he held out his hand for me to shake. "In fact, don't tell anyone. We have to keep this a secret." After we'd shaken hands, and I'd promised not to tell, he drove the generator to the village. By nightfall the pump was bringing in clean water. Lives would be saved. And do you know what he did next?' He looked at Mrs Bekk. 'Later that evening, Dad took that same bottle of champagne out of the fridge, opened it, and my parents celebrated their anniversary.'

Mrs Bekk squeezed his hand; a gesture of reassurance.

'So there you are,' he said bluntly. 'Everyone tells me Dad's a saint. I saw him kill a man, then leave the body to be eaten by animals. Hardly saintly, is it?'

'You've got two conflicting images of your father. You've seen him do so much good in the world. You also saw him kill another human being in order to protect the generator.'

'And I know the generator saved lives. Even so, my father's got blood on his hands.'

'I'll tell you what I believe, Tom. You saw what your father did to the man. Since then you've kept asking yourself if there are times when it's necessary to do something bad in order to make good things happen.'

'So you think I should be mature enough to reconcile what happened when I was ten? That my father was justified in taking one life in order to save dozens of lives?'

'No. This isn't really about your father, Tom – this is about you. Soon you're going to have to do something similar. You will have to act in a way that seems terrible. You will be forced to be cruel. You will act in a way that is so contrary to what you believe is right. But you *will* commit that terrible act, because you know that the end result will be good. You will do the unthinkable in order to save someone.'

'Who? Nicola?'

She nodded. 'And the only way you can save the woman you love is by rejecting her.'

He wasn't angry; instead, he spoke softly and directly from the heart. 'Mrs Bekk, I'm going to break whatever it is that has a hold over Nicola. I don't know if it's you, or if there really are Viking gods that inflict curses. But Nicola will be set free. And I'm going to marry her.'

Would Mrs Bekk fly into a rage at such a statement? He expected her to begin screaming.

No, it wasn't like that at all. She gave a sad, sweet smile. 'You might be like your father yet. Just for a moment, wasn't he the brave knight with the sword of righteousness? Killing the enemy that threatened the lives of the children? You might become the St George of this valley that slays the dragon. Or you might be forced to kill the one you love in order to save the lives of people you don't even know.'

He felt as if he occupied a realm that wasn't part of the world he'd always known. He'd crossed over a threshold now, where strange and dangerous events weren't just possible – they were inevitable. Frightening times lay ahead.

Tom put his foot on the accelerator. A moment later he was

heading towards the flooded village of Danby-Mask. They were just moments away from the flooded streets. Night wasn't far away either. Already, the sunlight turned the waters that flooded the valley as red as blood.

Tom found himself picturing Helsvir swimming in those blood waters. The monster would be at home there. The gruesome faces of the dead would be smiling from the monstrous body.

Maybe Mrs Bekk had somehow pulled the hypnosis trick on him again . . . How else had she made him entertain such a strange notion? *OK*, he thought. *Get your head together. Focus on what's important. First, you must find Nicola. Then you can deal with Bolter. Payback time.*

FORTY-NINE

B olter loved what he saw. Bloody loved it! Danby-Mask had been wrecked by the flood. *Just look at the mess. See all those smashed-up houses.* Bolter pushed another amphetamine on to his tongue. He crunched up the bitter pill, swallowed it, and felt his heart speeding up. He'd never taken so much speed before. He'd never set fire to a house before. (*Have now! Ha! Ha! Nicola Bekk's got a charcoal bed and ashes for clothes!*)

His heart did not beat inside his chest – his heart *whirred!*

Bolter stood on a wall and stared at the village, loving every moment of the most glorious day of his life. Floodwater had gathered at either side of the wall, which would normally be ten feet tall. Now the dark, swirling liquid had risen within a couple of feet of the top of the brickwork. The wall itself ran out through the water like a causeway.

Bolter danced along the top of the wall. 'I love you, River Lepping! You awesome, beautiful river! You showed those idiots who's boss. Lovely, lovely Lepping's biggest smash up . . . ever!' His amphetamine saturated body shot the words from his mouth at a million miles an hour – or so it seemed to him.

Even though it was dusk, the drug had mangled his senses so comprehensively that the water seemed to glow, as if made from light. Red roof tiles became slices of raw sirloin. Sweat poured from his face as he danced. His heart now screamed in his chest – he was sure it screamed an awesome jet-engine scream.

He pranced along the wall. The glittering waters were dancing along at either side of him. Cars floated by. Then the body of a cow, its legs comically (to him) sticking up in the air. He laughed a high, screaming laugh that mated its sound with the jet-engine scream of his heart.

'Wow! This is the best day of my life,' he yelled. 'Today I'm going to work miracles. From this moment on, this will be known as Bolter Day!' Bolter pointed at houses near the river. 'Look at them bastards. They're completely underwater. Even the chimneys!'

There was nobody to hear him. The houses had been abandoned hours ago. Even so, he still continued to give a commentary, as if he'd become a TV reporter breaking exciting, just-happening news to an audience that hung on his every word.

'Ladies and gentlemen, here I am, on top of a wall that runs the full length of Netherton Lane. See how the water laps the rooftops. Perhaps you can just make out St George's, the church dedicated to some bloke who killed a bloody dragon. I'm going to ask our brave camera-operator to get a close-up of the graveyard. The grave-stones are sticking up out of the water like stiff little fingers. Ha! The church is dry, though. Praise the Almighty. The church is spared. See, ladies and gentlemen, boys and girls, the church stands on its own teeny-weeny island.'

He started to giggle. 'Not like the houses down the hill. They are so underwater. They are so inundated. They are so engulfed.' He shoved his knuckles against his teeth as laughter roared from his throat. 'Fish are swimming through kitchens. Be careful of crabs in the lavatories. And there goes a brand-new sofa.' He pointed at a leather sofa floating serenely in eight feet of water. A duck had perched on the backrest.

'I'm now walking along the wall. This is incredibly dangerous. I might fall in and be swept away. You know, when these floods hit the village, people vanish. Never to be seen again. But it is a fear-less reporter's duty to show you the extent of the devastation here today.' Bolter suddenly pretended to be horrified. He gave a piercing scream that morphed into laughter. 'Oh no! Ladies and gentlemen, our brave camera person has fallen in. She has been sucked down by vicious currents. How quickly death strikes in the drowned village of Danby-Mask!'

The thought of his imaginary camera operator drowning struck him as so hilarious that he had to fight to keep his balance on the wall. Yet even though he laughed so much that tears filled his eyes, he realized he was no longer alone. Still blubbing with laughter he scraped the back of his hand across his eyes. So there was somebody else in the village? All the other cowardly crap-heads had stupidly run away when they could be here enjoying this lovely destruction . . .

'Whoa, there goes another house. The roof's just caved into the water with a tremendous splash . . .' Bolter liked pretending to be on television, reporting dramatic incidents just-as-they-happen-ladies-and-gentlemen. He was reluctant to quit his imaginary role just yet, even if he had company. (*It makes me feel important!*) His eyes were filled with shit. Maybe the drugs, maybe the excitement: only, it was really, really difficult to get his eyes to focus.

Bolter eventually managed to make out a figure that stood on high ground in a part of the village that was still dry. The figure watched him cavorting on the wall.

'Thank you for tuning in,' he shouted as his heart raced like crazy. 'Keep right there for the latest events coming live from what is rapidly becoming an underwater village. People have died today . . . We will show you pictures of those dead faces in glorious pin-sharp close-up as soon as we get them.'

'Bolter,' called the figure, 'it's not safe there. Come over here on to dry land.'

'I'm just doing my job, miss. Bringing you live-action news as it happens. Hey . . .' He dropped out of character. He was Bolter again: the sky-high drugster dressed in ripped jeans. 'Hey . . . it's you!' His eyes finally identified the figure. 'Nicola Bitch-Bekk. Hey, I burnt your house down today. I destroyed everything you own.' He laughed. 'What d'ya say to that, Bekk?'

FIFTY

Bolter danced on top of the ten foot high wall that ran through the flood. The waters of the new lake that had engulfed the village flowed at either side of him, just two feet below the soles of his muddy shoes. *And here's Nicola Bekk. She stands there like a dummy when I boast about torching her house. All her possessions – boof!*

Abruptly, he stopped dancing. Because he finally realized he'd seen something, or rather *heard* something that he'd never heard before. *Today really is MIRACLE DAY. Nicola Bekk speaks!* For a while he stood and stared at her in astonishment. He'd never heard her speak properly before. *Yet here she is TALKING. USING WORDS.*

'You're not really dumb after all,' he shouted in surprise. 'You can talk – I mean, like human talk.'

'Of course I can talk. You people never gave me a chance.'

'So didn't you hear me, Bekk? I burned your house.'

His astonishment at discovering she could speak like a normal adult quickly gave way to disappointment. The bitch didn't get angry when he gleefully confessed to destroying her home; instead, she called in a calm voice, 'Bolter. If you stay out there you'll drown.'

'Drown? It's not me who's drowning.' Right now he wanted to provoke a reaction. Her calmness irritated him. 'I know something you don't know!'

'Bolter. Come over here on to dry ground.'

'I know where your boyfriend is.'

'Pardon?'

'You heard me . . . Tom Westonby. I know where he is.'

'*Where?*'

'Oh, so I've got your attention, have I?' *The river smashed the village. I'm going to smash her heart.* He loved having this power over her. 'I know where Tom is – you don't.'

'I've been looking for him. I'm starting to get worried.'

'You better be.' Bolter's heart went beyond a jet-engine scream. 'Because I know what happened to him.'

'What do you mean, you know what happened to him?'

'Me . . . *I* happened to him. D'ya understand? I made things happen to lover boy!'

'You aren't making any sense.'

'Tom Westonby's reached an extremely important stage in his life. A crucial stage. I'll explain in a moment.' He enjoyed the moment of suspense. This was like putting a gun to someone's head and making them so scared that their eyes bulged out of their stupid face. 'In fact, he's reached such a vital stage in his life I don't know if I can put what happened into words.'

'Bolter, please don't say these things. You're making me worried.'

'Wait.' His voice rose as excitement blazed through him. 'I actually *can* explain that crucial stage in crappy Tom Westonby's life. That stage is called the *Death Stage!*'

'What's happened?'

'Oooh, you sound frightened now, you bitch.' He pointed across the floodwater. 'Do you see Chester Kenyon's workshop? Well, you can only see the roof because the rest is underwater.'

'What of it?'

Even from here he could see dread in her eyes. The woman knew she was going to hear terrible news. Bolter rubbed his belly with happiness.

'Bolter, *what is it about the workshop?*'

'I locked Chester and Tom into a room there. Look, it's all flooded up to the roof.' His voice soared into a shriek. 'They've both drowned, you bitch! Tom's floating there . . . and he's all like this.' Bolter opened his mouth and eyes wide, pretending to be a floating corpse.

Nicola Bekk stood there. She'd gone stiff as a timber post.

He laughed at her. 'Don't you get it? I've got more brains than they have. I trapped them in a little room. Then the flood came and, hey presto, they both drowned. Can you imagine how scared they were? Water's coming in. They're panicking. "Oh! Who will save us? Will I ever see Nicola Bekk again?" Then . . . glug, glug, glug. Tom Westonby is dead. I had the balls to kill him!'

Bolter wanted tears, screams and grief. Then he'd go across there . . . console her in his own full-on, man-on-bitch kinda way.

But no.

She stood there – stiff as a post planted in concrete. Her face didn't have a shred of emotion. Her eyes stared, though they didn't really stare at him. Or at anything. Unless you really can stare at literally nothing.

Then something happened. Something strange enough to make even the drug-hyper Bolter clear-headed.

Just for a second, the colour went out of his surroundings. The yellow glitter fled from the floodwaters. The red roofs of the houses faded to brown. The deep blue of the sky turned a deathly grey. Just for that extraordinary second, all the colours seemed to fly towards Nicola Bekk. They flowed into her. She sucked all the vibrant hues of the world into her body, leaving a bleached ghost of a village.

The transformation only did last for a second. Because suddenly the colours were back – the red roofs; the golden shimmer of water at twilight; the deep blue sky.

That's when all hell broke loose.

The water exploded in front of Bolter. He was so startled that he very nearly toppled backwards off the wall.

Because he'd seen what surged up from the floodwaters. This was the same creature that had attacked him and his pals at Mull-Rigg Hall: the ugly animal that consisted of human heads and limbs; a nightmare weave of corpses.

He stared into the mass of heads with their open mouths and white, staring eyes. He recognized the faces of Pug, Grafty and Nix. They glared at him, their expressions combining horror and a frantic hunger. They wanted him. They wanted him to be part of this thing.

The creature's limbs acted like dozens of flippers, propelling its massive body towards the wall.

The creature wanted him. Bolter was its target – no doubting that.

As soon as the beast reached the wall, hands were suddenly reaching out in order to drag him into the water. He heard the hissing sound the thing made. Each mouth whispered its hungry need for him. Droplets splashed his face.

The cold shock snapped him out of that paralysis of horror. Bolter ran. There was deep water to the right and to the left of him. The creature sped along the submerged street to his left. The thing swam with only its uppermost part exposed to the air. The bulk of it lay underwater. The churning and thrashing of its limbs created waves that slammed against the brickwork – and it moved FAST.

Bolter screamed to Nicola Bekk, 'Call it off! Call it off!' Deep down, he absolutely knew she controlled it. He also knew that she demanded vengeance. He'd left her boyfriend to drown in the work-shop. Now she'd unleashed the beast.

He charged along the wall that ran like a causeway through the flood. The top of the wall was barely a foot wide – a brick tightrope of a thing: so one misstep; one momentary loss of balance; one slippery patch of moss . . . Then he'd plunge into the water.

He wouldn't be able to outswim the monster. The sound of his pals' snapping bones came back to him. He remembered their screams of pain. Now the heads of Pug, Grafty and Nix adorned the monster. They were part of it. They'd become living components of that nightmare beast.

Bolter relied on the drugs he'd been gulping down to make him run faster. *They don't call this stuff SPEED for nothing.* Even so, the rushing sound of that thing cutting through the water grew louder. He shot a glance back at Nicola. She stared at him with a trance stare. No emotion. No recognition. Just an eerie blankness as she watched the thug that had killed Tom Westonby being hunted down by the monster.

Bolter had reached a cluster of outbuildings in a flooded yard. These lay on the other side of the wall from the monster. Spray from its thrashing limbs drenched him as it closed in. Another second and it would drag him from the wall. After that, it would hold him down underwater where it could really start to work on him.

When Bolter glimpsed a domestic garage through the spray, he did not hesitate. He leapt from the wall. Seconds later, he crashed through its brittle roof.

And he really did hope, with all his amphetamine-driven heart, that the monster wouldn't find him there.

FIFTY-ONE

Tom Westonby parked the car in an area of high ground. The last bit of daylight was dying. Darkness swept down the valley: a second flood that slowly began to hide what remained of the village.

For a moment, he sat there beside Nicola's mother in the car. She calmly watched the village that she both feared and despised lying there in the grip of the River Lepping. Houses had become little individual islands. Probably, at least half the homes in the village were up to their roofs in those dark waters. The river had done a thorough job of invading the place. Streets resembled canals. Even in this gloom, he could make out the oblong shapes of cars that floated on the current like the bodies of dead whales.

Mrs Bekk spoke with a clear sense of purpose: 'We'll split up

to look for Nicola. You head down there by the water's edge while
I search the high ground. Nicola was worried about you. She knows
how dangerous the floods can be, so she'll be determined to make
sure that you're safe. Nicola won't give up until she finds you.'

'That thug, Bolter, will be looking for her, too.'

'You can take care of him, can't you?'

'He doesn't scare me. But what happens if you meet him? The
power's out. There are no street lights working.'

'That young man doesn't frighten me, Tom. I'm only frightened
of what he might do to my daughter.'

'I've got a flashlight. You best take that.'

The white-haired woman shook her head. 'I've lived out there in
the forest since I was born. Starlight's ample for me. You take it.'

So, that's how it went. Tom pulled the flashlight from the back
of the car as they prepared to go their separate ways.

Mrs Bekk had something to tell Tom first. The note of warning
in her voice made his blood run cold.

'Tom,' she began, 'I've told you that you must break off this
relationship with my daughter.'

'And I've told you I will never do that.'

'Then I'm going to give you a warning.' Her voice was calm; she
obviously wanted him to understand some important facts. 'Even
though you deny that you've seen Nicola's brothers and sisters that
doesn't alter the truth. They did go into the outside world, Tom.
They thought they could turn their backs on their family's heritage.'

'Somehow you hypnotized me. There's no such thing as vampires.'

'You might not believe the evidence of your own eyes. But it's
Nicola's fate to become a vampire if you don't stop seeing her.'

'You'll have to do better than that to stop us getting married.'

'We both want to find Nicola as soon as possible. She's in danger
out there.' The woman nodded towards the drowned village. 'So
I'm not going to waste time trying to persuade you to believe in
my family's gods or the curse that's made us prisoners of this valley.
However, you need to watch my daughter for signs of the change.'

'What signs?' He tried to sound contemptuous of her suggestion
that Nicola would transform in some way. Even so, shivers cascaded
down his back. 'What do you mean?'

'Watch her closely for symptoms. What you'll notice first is that
Nicola's personality will gradually change. Then the colour will go
from her skin. Keep watching her eyes. The blue will fade from

them. As her skin turns completely white . . . as white as milk . . . her veins will become black, especially on the neck. They'll look like black tattoos.'

Her pale blue eyes fixed on his. There was sadness there and a certainty of the tragedy to come. She could have been telling him that someone he loved had just been diagnosed with a terminal illness . . . and – *hush* – the village was so silent: he could hear the morbid thud . . . thud . . . thud of his own heart.

Being in the presence of this eerie woman had the power to separate him from the real world. Once again he felt that he had entered a realm where not only the impossible might just happen *but also that it would become inevitable.*

He took a deep breath. Was it some form of hypnosis, or had his brain suffered actual damage when he was attacked by Bolter and his crew? Tom's unease grew as he found himself starting to believe Mrs Bekk's strange story. He tried to find a flaw in what she'd told him. 'Your other sons and daughters . . . Why hasn't Nicola mentioned them to me?'

'She doesn't even know they exist. They transformed before she was born. I keep their existence a secret from her. As with Helsvir, she only encounters them when she's in a state of trance.'

'So why don't they harm her?'

'They understand that she is of the same blood. Her brothers and sisters wouldn't hurt her.' All of a sudden she fiercely gripped his arm and jutted her face forward to within six inches of his. 'Remember what I told you,' she hissed. 'Watch for the symptoms. The colour will leave Nicola's skin. Her eyes will turn white . . . completely white, apart from the pupils. I'm warning you, Tom. It will be terrible to watch the change taking place. There'll be nothing you can do to stop it happening. *It's like watching a death.*' With that, she quickly walked away into the dark.

After taking a dozen steps or so, he realized that they'd not arranged any way of signalling to each other. How would they communicate if they did find Nicola? Maybe, however, Mrs Bekk had already reached a conclusion in that delusional mind of hers: that Nicola faced the grim transformation whatever the outcome of the search.

It's like watching a death. The woman's phrase echoed in his ears as he headed towards the flooded village. He'd never felt so alone in his life.

* * *

Tom didn't switch on the flashlight. If Bolter saw the light, it would warn him that someone else had entered an otherwise deserted village. Right now, Tom's survival instinct whispered *danger . . . danger.* His safety might depend on Bolter not knowing his whereabouts.

A village engulfed by a river that had broken through its levee was a threatening place to begin with. Right now, he sensed more dangers lurking down there. Bolter for sure. And maybe something from his nightmares – something monstrous with those strange dead-alive faces. Even though he could rationally disbelieve in the existence of monsters, a far less rational aspect of his mind whispered just the opposite: *when you're alone in the dark, ghosts and primordial creatures of the night start to seem utterly real.*

The smell of wetness filled his nostrils. A cold breeze played on his face – the breath from dead lungs . . . or lungs that *should* have died long ago.

Already, the very fact of being here alone at night, in a village that had its heart drowned by the river, started to act on his imagination. So easy now to picture a rotting hand bursting out of the pavement to grab hold of his ankle, or ghostly figures gliding out from the alleyways.

Tom glanced up at the sky. Black. An oppressive black. Dense cloud had come rolling in to block out the stars. His thumb found the raised switch of the flashlight. *No, don't use it yet. Conserve the batteries. And, more importantly, don't let anyone . . . or anything . . . know that you're here.* He walked down a steeply sloping lane with cottages at either side. They appeared as blocks of shadow in the darkness. Of course, there were no lights behind the windows. The electricity supply had failed when the river gushed into the substation. What added to the sense of abandonment was that residents on the higher ground had been evacuated, too. Perhaps the authorities feared that the flood would creep even higher?

Tom soon reached the edge of the flood. Small waves lapped just inches from his toes as he looked along a street. The liquid acted like a mirror, catching phantom reflections of the fronts of houses. That was the moment it struck him how difficult his search for Nicola would be. *How am I going to find her in this maze of flooded roads? What if Bolter found her and is holding her somewhere? After all, he locked Chester and me in the storeroom.*

'Nicola?' he called gently into the dark, yawning mouth of an alleyway. 'Nicola?'

The only reply, the faint lapping of floodwaters. Strangely, a sound like someone blowing kisses.

Tom took a deep breath. *Come on. Use your head. Plan this like a diving expedition. Figure out what you're going to do. Then do it!* After all, he couldn't simply wander aimlessly in the hope of bumping into her.

Nicola had striking blonde hair. He remembered how it resembled a flame in the gloom. So he should be able to see her even in this small amount of light. Above him, a glow filtered through the cloud.

Good. At least the moon was there, even if it was partly obscured. That meant some light would be falling on to his surroundings. His eyes would soon adapt, allowing him to see more. Now for that plan of action. He decided to make for the centre of the village. At first glance this seemed an impossible undertaking, because the floodwaters rendered the streets unusable. Then he noticed the ancient walls that divided the garden plots. Each wall stood around ten feet high. They formed a well-ordered criss-cross pattern. As far as he could tell, most of the walls were slightly higher than the flood waters. He could walk along them as if he walked along a causeway.

Or like walking the pirate's plank. His imagination was quick to conjure scenarios of the wall collapsing under his feet, dropping him into deep water.

Panic is the killer, if you let it take control . . . so stay focused on finding Nicola. Keep thinking about Nicola . . .

He sucked in another lungful of that cold air that smelt so strongly of the river. Then he quickly hauled himself up one of the ivy covered walls. Once he was on the flat coping stone he felt more confident. The height gave him a sense of safety: a sense that nobody, and *no THING*, could creep up behind.

He set out along the line of ten-foot-high walls. The brickwork had been capped with white stone blocks, so he followed a gleaming, white path set against black waters. At first, the water swilled along the base of the wall, but the further he walked, the nearer it rose to the top. If the water did come over the top, though, he realized he could climb up on to the roofs of the houses. They were so densely packed together he could probably work his way from roof to roof, as if they were the stepping stones of the gods.

Tom Westonby moved deeper towards the heart of the village. In turn, the water grew deeper. He saw furniture jumbled up with tree branches float by. He glimpsed the upturned belly of a car. Then came a heart-stopping, terrifying sight as the water churned beside the wall.

He expected a vast object to rise up and sweep him away to his death. He couldn't take his eyes from the bubbles fizzing up to the surface: a patch of gleaming white in the blackness of the flood. A moment later came a wonderful sense of relief as he realized what was causing the churning and the fizzing. A gas main must have fractured under the road, probably due to hundreds of tons of flood-water exerting a crushing downward force. The area of bubbling water here must be a result of gas furiously blasting from the ruptured pipe. Now he caught the stink of inflammable gas.

What that spectacular churning had done was divert his attention from what else was happening around him: mainly that the water now lay just a few inches below the top of the ten foot high wall. Flood levels were rising fast. If Nicola was in Danby-Mask, he needed to find her quickly. Or there was a real danger he never would.

FIFTY-TWO

The journey into the drowned village of Danby-Mask required sticking to the top of the walls. Even in this meagre light, Tom Westonby could see that the walls, which enclosed the backyards, formed a white grid pattern. The stone slabs, laid end-to-end on top of the brickwork, possessed the same creamy hues as the locally produced cheese.

As he walked, with the floodwater at either side of his narrow causeway, he constantly scanned the buildings for Nicola. Surely, she had to be here somewhere. By now, his eyes had adjusted well enough to the gloom. Yet he still kept a tight grip on the flashlight. He'd need it if he entered one of the flooded houses.

'Nicola?' From time to time he called her name. 'Nicola?'

Each time he listened carefully, hoping to hear her reply. The only sound, however, was the liquid sucking noises coming from the buildings. By now, the Lepping had reached the upper stories. Small waves lapped at bedroom windows. Everywhere, armchairs, wheelie bins, oil drums, dog kennels, you name it, floated in the yards.

Tom knew these walls were around ten feet high. They were a distinctive feature of the village, and they'd been built two hundred years ago when the community became so prosperous from the wool trade that they'd had to build defences to keep out the thieves and vagabonds. Now those walls were the only dry highway into Danby-Mask.

'Nicola?' He so desperately wanted to see her face that his heart ached. *Where is she? Has she been trapped in one of the houses? Or swept away?* A sudden mental image came so sharply that he felt sick. In his mind's eye, he saw Nicola drifting through that black water, her blonde hair rippling outwards, her eyes staring.

'*Nicola!*' His voice echoed back from those drowned houses. The silence, the lack of electric lights – they all contributed to the sense that this had become a graveyard for peoples' homes.

Nothing less than a burning anxiety gripped him now. He decided to speed up his search. Already, he'd convinced himself that she was in danger. Either trapped in a flooded cottage, or held prisoner by Bolter. What's more, Bolter had proved he would commit criminal acts. He'd burnt down Nicola's house. So hurting Nicola wouldn't be too extreme for him.

'Nicola . . . it's Tom.' The words died out there on this new monster of a lake. 'Nicola!'

Where is she? I just want to hold on to her. Keep her safe. I want her with me.

He turned a sharp right, following that precise white line of stonework. Water that was nigh on ten feet deep lay at either side of the wall.

'Nicola!'

Then came the sound of water being disturbed. He paused, thinking that another gas main had given way under the colossal weight of this inundation. True, there was a white mass of churning foam. Yet this time it was different.

The swirling storm of bubbles didn't stay in one place. Instead, a blaze of white sped along the flooded street. A second later, the bubbles vanished. Even so, he could still see a black wave racing towards him. Years of diving experience told him that wave was produced by a large, fast-moving object just beneath the surface.

Tom held his breath. Whatever headed so purposefully towards him remained invisible. But he had to see it.

Had to.

Not being able to see what raced ever closer, with the speed of a torpedo, became unbearable.

Quickly, he raised the flashlight, hit the switch, then shielded his eyes against the glare of the powerful bulb. He saw a black mass of water being pushed upward into a rounded bulge.

A pale shape raced towards him. He could just make out a huge, bulky body. The water wasn't clear enough to identify much in the way of detail. But he knew what this thing was.

Helsvir.

FIFTY-THREE

The creature sliced through the water. This thing called Helsvir radiated a brutal life-force; the essence of savage power.

There he was, balanced precariously on top of a wall. At either side of him, deep water. *And here comes the instrument of my death.*

Tom Westonby kept the light on the creature, desperately hoping its dazzling brilliance would keep it at bay. The light did no such thing. The creature rose to the surface as it hammered through the water, tearing it apart in foaming sheets.

That barrier of disbelief that Tom had built inside his mind to protect his sanity was blasted into oblivion. He could no longer insist to himself that Mrs Bekk had induced some hypnotic state, or that he suffered hallucinations due to concussion. *No. Absolutely and totally no!* Tom could not play the role of Doubting Thomas any more.

Helsvir was real.

Dear God. Helsvir was MORE than real somehow. The creature was a powerful example of brutally vivid actuality. When it surged towards him, with its hissing once-human faces, the thing seemed more substantial than the brickwork he stood upon. Whatever had created the monster had embedded it so deeply into this world that it had become the essence of solidity. The Bekk family's protector exuded a presence that wouldn't allow you to dismiss it as a dream.

He thought: *Helsvir is real. Helsvir is here to stay. Helsvir will be solid muscle when I'm dead and gone.*

The enormity of this revelation stunned him. All he could do was stand and stare at the brute as it powered through the flood. Fear exerted a paralysis – he couldn't move.

Forty paces away . . . thirty . . . twenty . . .

Tom sensed its eagerness. Helsvir wanted him. Helsvir knew its prey was vulnerable. Helsvir would sweep him from the wall.

Ten paces away.

A shout that combined anger and sheer dismay at being torn from this life exploded from his lips: '*No!*'

'Helsvir. Come.' The female voice had such clarity. What's more, there was a silvery quality in the way it rang out through the darkness. 'Helsvir. Come.'

The creature swung away at the last moment; the flurry of bubbles vanished. Helsvir had submerged itself into deeper waters.

Tom stood there, panting. Perspiration rolled down his face.

'Helsvir, come away.'

He aimed the flashlight in the direction of the voice. This was a voice he knew and had been longing to hear. 'Nicola!'

As he stood there, he witnessed an apparition. A beautiful apparition, at that. But one so unearthly, and so eerie, that shivers danced across the sensitive skin of his neck.

The woman he'd searched for stood on a cottage roof not thirty yards away. She remained perfectly still. Her blonde hair shone in the light of the lamp. The blue fire that was her eyes gazed out over the flooded village.

She is beautiful. She really is.

Tom knew that a vital change took place inside of him at that moment. This was such an uncanny setting. Yet Helsvir, the drowned homes, and the oppressive darkness amounted to nothing in comparison to what he experienced now. He'd found Nicola. And he'd found a shining truth. He realized his love for her was so powerful, so real, so immense that nothing must stop them from being together.

He thought: *I love you. We're going to spend the rest of our lives under the same roof.* That certainty was indestructible.

'Stay there,' he called. 'I'm coming over to you.'

He ran along the wall, following that gleaming route of white stones. Within thirty seconds the wall had taken him to the house where Nicola waited. Deep water still lapped against windows and gurgled around walls, but he hardly noticed the flood now, because he'd spotted a grouping of outhouse roofs that formed a series of steps, allowing him to reach the cottage. Soon Tom was bounding up thick red tiles to Nicola.

Sheer exhilaration carried him up the slope. Seconds later he put his arms round her. 'Thank God.' His heart pounded like fury. 'Are you alright? You've not been hurt?' He crushed her against him. He could feel her ribs, the cool wash of hair against his face; her subtle perfume filled his nose. This was a sweet moment . . . an incredibly sweet moment. Emotion blasted through him, and all he wanted was to stand here on this roof and hold her hard against his chest.

Only after a few moments did he realize that she wasn't responding. She didn't even seem to know he was there.

'Nicola? What's wrong?'

'Helsvir,' she breathed. 'Helsvir. Be gone. Don't hurt him . . .'

He looked into her face. The blue eyes gazed across the rooftops.

'Helsvir, be gone.'

'Nicola. It's me – Tom.'

She stood there without moving. There was something strangely stiff about her body. As if an electric current ran through her muscles, turning them rigid. Her eyes didn't even glance in his direction once. They remained fixed, unblinking. A gaze that remained locked on the heart of a great darkness.

'I'm here, Nicola.' Gently, he hugged her. 'I'm here. I'm staying with you. Listen, I love you. We're going to get married. And I'm going to fix all the problems. Everything's going to be alright.'

She gave a slow blink. 'Tom.'

He smiled. 'That's me: Tom through and through. The Tom-shaped boy.' He knew he was talking nonsense. That didn't matter one little bit. The words were a tender stream of reassuring sounds. He wanted her to feel safe. 'We'll go to my house. There's food, clean clothes. Everything will be good. We'll lock the doors and keep the world out for as long as we want.'

'Tom?' Nicola seemed to be waking up from a deep sleep. Only, she wasn't fully there yet. A dreamy quality possessed her. 'I've had such strange dreams . . . Helsvir.'

'You called him off at the last minute. Otherwise I'd be . . .' He shrugged. No need to finish that particular sentence.

'Helsvir. Yes . . . but how can you know what I was dreaming about?' She sounded so sleepy. 'You wouldn't know about my dream. Helsvir swam down the river. Into the village . . . Then I saw you.' She smiled. 'And here you are.'

Nicola's head rested against his chest, her eyes half closed. She seemed deflated somehow. All the strength had been drained right out of her. Gently, he eased her down until she sat on the roof tiles, her legs resting on the downward slope. He sat beside her with his arm around her shoulders.

For a little while she spoke in a sleepy voice: 'Helsvir isn't real, you know? My ancestors made him up hundreds of years ago . . .' She snuggled against him in such a wonderfully relaxed way. 'They invented stories about how Helsvir was created by the gods to protect them. They told the story to their children . . . to reassure them . . . so they'd sleep all cosy in their beds. I feel cosy now. It's lovely being with you, Tom.'

She lifted her head, kissed him softly on the cheek before allowing her head to sink down against his chest again, as she drifted in and out of sleep. And there they sat: side-by-side on the roof.

When Helsvir had swum towards him just a few moments ago the terror had overwhelmed his senses. He'd frozen up. His body seemed to set solid. He couldn't move his legs; his heart had pounded furiously against his ribs. Now, after the emotional storm, there was a sort of calm. Maybe psychological overload had caused a partial shutdown of his mind to protect his sanity. The panic had left him. His heart resumed its normal rhythm. In the circumstances, it would be entirely understandable if he screamed about creatures built from human body parts; however, he had no inclination to rage or yell. Instead, he accepted that this must be part of the human instinct for self-preservation. *When faced with the extraordinary, deal with it in a practical, level-headed way, otherwise you really will end up losing your mind.* During his training as a diver, he'd been told often enough that panic is a killer. And that whatever dangers you do face underwater, you must always keep your nerve.

Perhaps that training had imposed a calming influence. Yes, he now knew that Helsvir was real. So he hadn't been hallucinating after all when he'd seen the brute attack Bolter's gang at Mull-Rigg

Hall. What's more, he really had seen those stark, white figures on
the hill that Mrs Bekk had declared were her vampiric children.

Then, in a day of bizarre events, came an equally bizarre moment.
It could have been a symptom of the enormity of what he'd experienced tonight screwing up his emotions, but Tom felt almost happy.
*Maybe love really is a type of madness. Here I am with Nicola, and
everything feels alright with the world, even though it clearly isn't.
There's the flood, and there's a monster out there – and I don't
care. I don't care one bit. It's like I've been searching all my life
for something that's incredibly important, only I never knew what
it was. But I've found it now. And it's Nicola Bekk.*

A sense of tranquillity settled over the flooded homes. He
wondered if the shock of nearly being killed had driven him insane
after all, yet it felt so beautifully peaceful to be sat here with his
arm around Nicola. A warm bubble of security enfolded them.

They remained like that for almost an hour, Nicola resting against
him in a drowsy state that seemed closer to sleep than being awake.
Then something changed. The sounds of the water were different.
Instead of random lapping sounds, or the soft gurgle of liquid
swirling around walls, there came a rhythmic splashing.

Tom instantly recognized the sound. *Oars. Definitely oars.
Somebody rowing a boat.*

What he saw quickly bore this out. For, coming round the corner
of the flooded road, was a small boat. A figure sat there; the head
rose and fell as the figure steadily rowed by street lights and the
tops of road signs. A lantern hung from the boat's prow, creating
the effect of a vessel drifting along in its own pool of amber light.

Without any fuss or sense of urgency, the boat drew closer to the
building.

Then a man Tom had never seen before turned to look up at him.
His skin was a smooth ebony black. He wore white-rimmed glasses.
There was the white collar of a priest around his neck, and both the
bone-white glasses and priest's collar shone brilliantly in the dark.

He gazed at Tom for a moment. 'I am collecting lost souls,' the
man declared. 'I will collect the pair of you.'

'We're OK here.' For Tom, sitting with his arm around Nicola,
even in this bizarre setting, was a slice of pure heaven. 'We'll wait
for the waters to go down.'

'The flood is getting higher,' announced the man. 'Even though
the rain has stopped, water is still decanting from the hills. Therefore,

I invite you to step into my little ship. I have a place of safety for lost souls such as you . . . and I.' He smiled. 'Please come along. Otherwise I cannot guarantee your safety. In other words, you and your friend will die, sir. You will die.'

FIFTY-FOUR

Ancient Greeks believed that after they died a ferryman took them across the River Styx to the afterlife. Tom Westonby sat in the back of the small boat with his arm around Nicola; she rested her head against his chest as she slept. Without much of a mental stretch, he could imagine that this dark-skinned man was that ferryman – and they were crossing over to meet the Greek god of death.

The priest applied the oars to the water with a slow, rhythmic action. The village that had been drowned by the Lepping looked so tranquil in the moonlight. The upper parts of houses were mirrored by the floodwater. As the boat drifted through a surreal, half-submerged landscape this could have been the final journey from the world of the living to the realm of the dead.

The priest regarded Tom through those white-rimmed glasses. 'You keep looking at my head.' His deep voice was as relaxed as his work with the oars. 'You know, when I started shaving off all my hair my wife said to me, "Joshua, your head now looks like a bowling ball. If your head should ever fall off those shoulders of yours, someone could stick a finger up each nostril, then pick up your head, and roll it at a set of bowling pins."'

That was an extraordinary statement to make to a stranger. Tom found himself staring at the dark, round head of the priest.

'So I am the man with the bowling ball head,' declared the man. 'I am also the parish priest for Danby-Mask. That makes me the Reverend Joshua Gordon Squires, though I'd like you to call me Joshua. Not Josh, however. Josh is the local dialect word for "joke". For example, "Dear God in Heaven, is this a josh? You have flooded the village that I love. If you are joshing then I don't think it is very funny."' He shot Tom a sharp-eyed glance. 'So, stranger, what's your name?'

'I'm Tom. Tom Westonby.'

'Ah, the famous Westonby family from Mull-Rigg Hall?'

Tom nodded, then asked the question he should have asked before boarding this little craft on its night-time voyage, 'Joshua, where are you taking us?'

'To safety. I don't know what you were doing with the lady on the cottage roof, but this is a dangerous place tonight.'

Tom thought about Helsvir. Instead of raising spectres about a monster that might be lurking under the boat at this very moment, he said, 'This is Nicola Bekk. I came into the village to find her.'

'Ah, the equally famous Bekk family. Yes, I've heard a lot about them.'

'Any of it good?'

'You challenge me, Tom. I respect that. Because you suspect I believe any toxic gossip that comes my way. However, my job, and my nature, demands that I see good in people – until they prove otherwise. I am also open-minded. Absolutely open-minded.'

'So where are you taking us?'

'It's the river that's doing the taking. I can't row against such a powerful current, so we'll head for the parish church.'

'It's surrounded by water. We'll be trapped.'

'Think of it as a safe island. A sanctuary. What's happened to your girlfriend?'

'She's exhausted. She might be in shock, too. Her house is gone.'

'Ah, the demon flood.'

'No, some lunatic burnt it down this morning.'

'Flood *and* fire. Dare I say it? We have disasters of a Biblical nature.'

Nicola stirred sleepily. 'Tom? Have we just made love?'

Joshua diplomatically glanced back over his shoulder as he rowed, as if to be sure of the way.

Tom gently tightened his arm around her. 'Joshua is taking us to where we'll be safe.' Even as he spoke, he remembered what Nicola had told him. That as a little girl she'd been terrified of the Christian church. She'd even believed that the carving of Christ being cruci-fied on the Cross was a warning of what the villagers would inflict on her. That she'd be nailed to the wood, too. Tom wondered what her reaction would be when she entered the building that had been the seat of Christian power in the village for the last thousand years: the Church of St George – the slayer of the dragon.

Just a hundred yards away stood the church. Its white stonework evoked a ghostly aura in the moonlight. Tom saw that the floodwater had stopped just a dozen feet from its walls. The church had been spared because it had been built on a mound of earth. However, the churchyard hadn't been so lucky; that had become part of the new lake.

Joshua sat facing Tom and Nicola as he worked the oars. 'You could help by guiding me in,' Joshua said. 'The water only just covers the gravestones. Some are pretty sharp – I don't want any of those blessed things puncturing the bottom of our little ship.'

Tom gently laid Nicola down on the seat plank in the stern, then carefully made his way forward to the prow.

'You move well on a boat, my friend.' Joshua's large, round head nodded in approval. 'You are a seasoned boatman?'

'I'm used to working on small dive boats.' He found himself smiling at the man. 'The first thing you learn is not to tip the thing over.'

'Ah, then we will work well together . . . we lost souls of Danby-Mask.'

Tom found himself liking this quirky character with the deep, rumbling voice. Now that he'd moved to the front, where an old-style lantern was giving off its soft, amber light, he could see Joshua better. He judged the man to be anywhere between forty and seventy. The round, smiling face didn't have any lines. No wrinkles at all. While the dark eyes behind the white-rimmed glasses suggested that here was someone of gentle wisdom. Yes, he liked the Reverend Joshua Gordon Squires. Tom decided he could trust the man.

Tom said, 'Take her in slowly over the churchyard wall. It's only a few inches under the surface.'

'Ah, take *her* in. All boats are female, aren't they?' Joshua grinned, displaying an astonishing set of teeth. 'If we treat her well, she might be kind to us.' His hand patted the woodwork. 'But, like a woman, we must never take her for granted.' He laughed softly. 'OK, Tom Westonby. Be my guide.'

Tom leaned out over the boat's prow. Just a couple of feet below him was the floodwater. Beneath its surface were submerged grave-stones. And beneath those lay hundreds of the Danby-Mask dead. They'd been collected into this hallowed ground for centuries.

'Keep moving forward, Joshua. Slowly does it.'

The priest dipped the oars, gently propelling the boat towards dry ground.

'Just pull with your left oar.' Tom had spotted the stone hand of an angel, thrusting upwards above the surface. 'Now straight ahead.'

Lamplight filtered down through the water, turning it pale yellow. As he gazed down into the murk he found himself expecting to see Helsvir suddenly looming into view. The boat seemed breathtakingly fragile – a little wooden box of a thing floating on this vast lake. The monster could smash it to pieces in a second.

A stark, white face stared up at him. His heart lurched. Then he sighed with relief. This was the marble face of a statue that adorned one of the big old tombs.

To his surprise, his voice remained calm as he talked the priest in closer to the new island that lay in the centre of the village. 'I can see the footpath now. Just keep on this line. That's it, nice and easy with the strokes. Nearly there . . . nearly there. OK.'

As the boat's prow scrunched up on to the grassy slope that rose towards the church, Tom jumped clear. After that, he hauled the boat further up on to dry ground.

'Here we are,' declared Joshua, sounding pleased. 'We are on *higher ground* in more senses than one.'

After the priest had climbed from the boat, Tom tied the line to a tombstone, then he collected Nicola. For now, he didn't need to worry about her reaction to entering the Church of St George, the dragon killer. She was deeply asleep. As he carried Nicola towards the church door, Joshua walked alongside, carrying the oil lamp.

Joshua paused at the doorway to look back along a street that now resembled a canal. 'I am expecting another boat soon with more lost souls. You see, some people are reluctant to leave their homes when the flood comes . . . understandably so. They want to fight nature in order to protect their property.' He regarded Tom with those wise eyes of his. 'I can tell you are a man who will fight for what he loves, too.' His gaze settled on Nicola.

'You're right. And I'm never going to stop fighting.'

'I wholeheartedly approve.' Then the man's smile was replaced by a deadly serious expression. 'You know, Tom. There is something else out there in the water: something other than that boat with more of our stranded friends. I've seen a leviathan in our village. I don't know his name . . . but if I chose his name I would call him Death.' Joshua's shrewd eyes read Tom's expression. 'You know him too, don't you? You've seen Death roaming this place.'

Tom held Joshua's steady gaze. 'Yes, I've met him. He isn't

Death, though. His name is Helsvir, and he's worse than Death. Much worse. What's more, I don't know if there's anything on earth that can stop him.' He glanced down at Nicola's sleeping face. 'But, as you rightly say, Joshua, I am a fighter. So I'm going to kill that thing out there. Or die trying.'

He carried Nicola into the church. The moon shone through a striking image on a huge stained-glass window. The significance of the scene depicted wasn't lost on Tom, because there was St George in golden armour. He was driving the point of his lance into the heart of the dragon.

FIFTY-FIVE

The interior of the church captured the essence of tranquillity. Although Tom Westonby suspected this peaceful interlude would be brief. The final battle was coming. Soon there would be blood.

Whenever Tom entered an English church, which might have stood for over a thousand years, he felt as if he was walking into a storehouse that had gathered a quiet power into itself. This feeling of his didn't flow from any particular religious faith. For Tom, it seemed as if the ancient stone walls had soaked up the emotions of the people that had worshipped and married under a roof that had weathered many centuries of brutal storms.

Tom watched over Nicola as she slept on a long bench at the back of the church. Meanwhile, Joshua, in his gleaming priest's collar and white spectacles, quietly lit the candles. These were tall columns of cream-coloured wax that stood in brass-candlesticks as high as his shoulder. He also lit a pair of candles that stood at each end of the altar. Soon a pleasantly soft glow filled the church.

Although Tom hadn't been inside St George's before, it still had a familiar air. The building followed the pattern of many a traditional rural church. A central aisle led through bench-style pews to the altar beneath the main stained-glass window. The roof was supported by huge archways of stone. Lining one wall were the medieval tombs; these took the form of oblong sarcophagi, with carvings of their occupants lying on top: lords and ladies in pale marble. The figures lay on their backs, hands pressed together on their chests in prayer.

Tom watched the Reverend Joshua Gordon Squires glide through the church. He lit yet more candles that flanked the aisle. Their light gleamed on the dark skin of his shaved head. The man resembled an ebony angel: one that radiated an aura of protection.

This was a likeable man. A trustworthy and dependable one, too.

'What you saw out there in the floodwater was Helsvir.' Tom spoke softly. 'Nicola's family believe Helsvir is a Viking dragon created out of the bodies of human corpses. The god Thor ordered it to become the guardian of the Bekk family.' Tom waited for Joshua's reaction.

Joshua beckoned Tom to sit beside him on a bench near the wall. Above their heads was the stained-glass window of St George fighting the dragon. A halo shone around the knight's head as he drove the lance into the monster's body.

Joshua plaited his thick, muscular fingers together then spoke in that deep voice of his: 'You thought I'd dash ridicule all over that statement of yours, didn't you?'

'Viking gods. Dragons made from dead men. It takes some digesting.'

'And I will digest it – I will. Why should I ridicule the gods of ancient Europeans when I believe that my Saviour is born of a Virgin? That He died on the Cross, and that three days later He rose from the dead.' He pointed at the image of St George. 'I am the parish priest of a church dedicated to the patron saint of England. St George killed the devil dragon. If I was to doubt what you tell me, then I would poison my belief in the goodness of that man.' He touched his white collar. 'Tom, it is my life's work to believe in remarkable events, miraculous individuals, and I believe that pure evil can manifest itself in our world as a living creature.'

'Like Helsvir?'

'Yes, my friend, just like Helsvir.'

'Then God help me. I don't know if I'll have the courage to fight it.'

'Let me tell you about courage. It's not about doing some flash-bang heroic act. Courage is about steadfastly holding on to what you love and what you believe in.'

'But when it actually comes to fighting that thing . . .'

Joshua spoke softly; his words had a mesmerizing power. 'When

I was a teenager I did crazily bad things. I thought I was brave stealing booze from supermarkets, throwing punches at policemen. Then, when I was seventeen, my mother died. After the funeral I came home and found my mother sitting on the sofa . . . and the ghost of my mother asked me this question: "Joshua, when are you going to have a change of heart?" After that, I did the bravest thing I've ever done. I went to church. I listened to hymns and to prayers . . . and that's when I got even braver. Me, big bad Joshua Gordon Squires cried and cried until I couldn't shed another tear. After that, I found my real courage – and that was the courage to have a change of heart.' He fixed Tom with a stern gaze. 'If you tell me, Thomas Westonby, that you don't believe I saw the ghost of my dear, beloved mother, I'll smack your head right over that altar.' He smiled warmly. 'Now, you tell me what's been happening to you.'

Tom told him everything. How he'd seen Nicola dipping her feet in the spring-water pool in the garden, and how after that first sight of her he'd followed her into the wood, where he now realized he must have had the first bruising encounter with Helsvir. Yet, for some reason the monster had spared his life. Joshua listened patiently as Tom described Chester Kenyon's reaction to his relationship with Nicola, and that Chester claimed she had deep-rooted mental problems. What's more, the village as a whole believed she was insane. In fact, they didn't even believe she was capable of speaking. He went on to describe Nicola's torment at school. That her own mother had convinced her that Danby-Mask hated the Bekk family, and that its population were only biding their time before they killed the last of the Bekk line. That as a child, Nicola even found it terrifying to walk by the church.

'Tom, you'll recall that I confessed that I am open-minded. I want you to know that I believe you.'

'Thank you. Most people wouldn't – and I'm sure that would include priests, too.'

'Ah, I am not your typical parish priest. My bishop often exclaims: "Joshua. You're a maverick. You run your parish in such a way that would make other priests fall down in shock. But I like you, Joshua. Yours is difficult work, but you win success after success." So yes, Tom, I am a strange priest and an indisputably eccentric fellow, as my bishop and my wife would both verify. Yet with all my heart I strive to do what is right. Even if I do achieve that rightness in unorthodox ways. Do you follow?'

'You're saying the ends justify the means?'

'Exactly, my friend. Take Mrs Bekk. I know the lady tried to burn down this beautiful church. All that happened before I moved here, yet I know she resorted to such desperate action through some misplaced sense of revenge against the village. Even so, it took me a long time to get to the bottom of this vendetta. The people of Danby-Mask are very secretive. That secrecy is a result of their shame at the spiteful ways they try to harm family Bekk.'

'They don't show much shame when they shout abuse at Nicola, or beat me up for being with her.'

'Which is very wrong of them. However, I have been quietly plotting in a most benevolent fashion. I am endeavouring to heal the rift between family Bekk and Danby-Mask. Slowly, but surely, I have won most of the villagers round. I'm persuading them to stop bullying the family. Nevertheless, there are still a few violent and stupid men who continue to behave badly. But, eventually I will succeed. I have absolute faith in bringing the villagers and this lady and her mother together as friends.' He solemnly nodded in the direction of Nicola as she lay fast asleep on the bench.

They continued their conversation in the candlelit church. Joshua's dark eyes never left Tom's face. Tom felt good talking to the priest; as if he was at last able to release secrets that had troubled him. And as he put into words what Nicola meant to him, he really began to feel the depth of his emotion for her. He explained that he'd fallen in love with Nicola. That he'd never met anyone who could match her personality. And that he was determined to marry her.

Joshua glanced at where Nicola lay sleeping on the bench. 'Does the lady want to marry you?'

'Yes.'

'Then who can stop you being married?'

'Everyone.'

'Everyone?'

'My friend Chester's against it. My parents are against it, because they believe the lies they've heard about Nicola being mentally impaired in some way. Mrs Bekk warned me there'll be terrible consequences if I marry her daughter.'

'Do you believe there will be?'

'Before I marry her I think Helsvir will hunt me down.'

'It really is so dangerous?'

Tom sighed. 'I've seen what Helsvir can do. That thing rips

people to pieces then adds them to its own body. With everyone it kills it grows bigger. Stronger.'

'Does this lady's mother control the animal?'

'No. Nicola does. Or at least she's in control for part of the time.'

Joshua gave a faint smile. 'Problem solved. Wake Nicola; ask her to send Helsvir away forever.'

'I wish the solution was that simple.'

'Oh? Isn't it?'

'Nicola takes control of Helsvir when she's in a trance. That's the twist here, Joshua. She doesn't even believe it's real. She thinks the monster's just a family legend. But she's the one who commands it, even though she's commanding it when she's asleep.'

'I see. Then you have to find a way to slay the beast. Just like our St George.'

'If I do, there's another line of defence stopping me from making Nicola my bride.'

'So the pagan forces that both protect and entrap the Bekk family have been very cleverly devised.'

Tom gave a grim nod. 'Should I somehow find a way to get rid of Helsvir and leave the valley with Nicola, then it triggers a curse. Nicola will undergo a transformation. Mrs Bekk warned me that Nicola would become inhuman. In fact, she'll become what amounts to be a vampire.'

'A vampire?'

'I've seen her brothers and sisters. They suffer from the same condition. They've turned into these strange white figures that . . .' He gave a helpless shrug. 'That, for the want of a better word, *haunt* the forest. They only appear at night, and they drink the blood of animals.'

'And no doubt people, if they get the opportunity.'

Tom ran his fingers through his hair. A feeling of utter desperation gripped him. 'You see, Joshua, there's nothing I can do to save Nicola. She's trapped.'

Joshua put a hand on Tom's shoulder; a gesture of reassurance. 'Human beings have clever minds . . . We are far cleverer than we suppose. We must use our minds like we've never used them before. We need to outsmart this pagan magic.'

'How?'

'First of all, let us sum up the situation. One: you love Nicola. You intend to marry and leave this place.'

'If that's what she wants.'

'OK. But, item two: there is an obstacle. This creature called Helsvir is programmed to prevent that happening. If it kills you, Nicola will lose the love of her life and will stay here with her mother. Item three: there is an additional obstacle. If you escape with Nicola, and so put yourselves beyond the reach of Helsvir, the curse of being transformed into a vampire is activated. Nicola will become this undead creature and will return to the valley, just as those ancient gods wish.'

'Which means I can never win. Even if I destroy Helsvir, the vampire curse claims Nicola anyway.'

'You're a fighter, Tom. So fight!'

'But I've seen the kind of creature she'd turn into. A walking corpse. A lump of bone and meat that doesn't have thoughts and feelings. It would be better if I left without her.'

'Tom. Fight for the woman you love – *and who loves you.*'

'How?'

'Remember what I told you, Tom. Human beings are smart. If you want to be with this woman for the rest of your life, you must figure out a way to beat Helsvir *and* beat the vampire curse.'

The silence after Joshua had spoken lasted for only a second. Then there was a piercing scream.

Nicola had woken up. Her wild, terror-struck eyes gulped in her surroundings. Then she saw the huge stained-glass window of St George slaughtering the dragon.

Before Tom could reach her, she'd raced through the church door and out into the dangerous night.

FIFTY-SIX

Outside the church there was the flood, moonlight and madness.

Tom followed Nicola when she fled in panic. The church had frightened her as a child. So when she woke to find herself in St George's beneath the looming image of the knight impaling the dragon she must have felt as if her mind would explode in sheer terror.

There weren't many places she could run. The church stood on an island created by the flood. A fringe of dry earth perhaps ten feet wide ran around the building. Nine tenths of the graveyard had been drowned. Moonlight revealed the uppermost tips of tombstones, sticking up above the surface. Beyond the graveyard were the village roads, resembling canals – flanking those, the flooded houses.

As for Nicola, she was nowhere in sight. The nightmare scene of the flooded landscape must have pushed her even deeper into panic. He only hoped she hadn't blundered into the water. Fierce currents whirled cars and whole trees along the street. If she'd gone into that torrent, she wouldn't stand a chance.

'Nicola? It's alright. It's me – Tom!' He ran round the church, following the strip of dry land that hugged the walls. 'Nicola!'

Bright moonlight illuminated the way ahead. But he still couldn't see her. When he sped round the end of the church what he did see immediately was the second boat that Joshua had mentioned earlier. A dozen people were crammed on to a small dinghy; Chester Kenyon worked the oars; Mrs Bekk sat in the prow.

Then all hell broke loose. Suddenly, a plume of white sprayed into the air fifty yards behind the boat. The explosion of water looked like a bomb going off, churning up a mass of bubbles, and from those bubbles a pale object surged towards the boat.

Chester saw it, too. He began rowing as hard as he could in the direction of the church island. Tom couldn't stand there, waiting to see what the outcome would be. Though images of what Helsvir could do to that fragile boat, and its occupants, burned with a monstrous brightness in his head.

I've got to find Nicola, he told himself. *If she goes into the water she'll drown.*

The strip of land took him to the far side of the church. That's when he saw her. As she ran, she desperately searched for a way off the island. What's more, she was scared out of her wits.

'Nicola!'

Either she didn't hear, or she was so panicked she couldn't stop, because she ran a full circuit of the church. When she reached the main door at the base of the tower that's when she did stop. In stunned horror, as if incapable of deciding whether this was reality or nightmare, she stared at the boat, heading towards her in the moonlight.

Nicola had also seen the creature that sped through the water – a purposeful torpedo of a thing, aimed directly at the craft. The creature radiated a predatory menace. This was the savage hunter in pursuit of its prey.

In a daze, she turned to Tom. 'What is that thing?' she breathed. 'Helsvir.'

She gave a startled laugh. 'Helsvir? Tom, that's just a family legend. It's not real.'

'Helsvir is real,' he told her. 'And you're wide awake . . . This isn't a dream.'

Nicola's blue eyes went incredibly wide. Her mouth gaped in astonishment. But here was the evidence in front of her: *Helsvir.* The creature was real. It was a muscular mass of arms, legs, torsos – all fused together into a weapon of vengeance, fury and destruction.

Nicola reached out to Tom. She clung to him fiercely as she watched the horror unfold.

A tall man grabbed a pole from inside the boat. At that precise moment the creature began to submerge itself beneath the liquid blackness. However, its position was marked by the churn of white bubbles as it swam. Now it only occasionally broke the surface, allowing a glimpse of a naked arm, or the flash of a stark, white face in the spray.

The people on board were screaming. Chester rowed as hard he could, driving the tiny vessel in the direction of the graveyard. Abruptly, the boat lurched. For a moment it looked as if it would roll over, then the little vessel righted itself.

A line of white foam revealed where Helsvir circled round for another attack.

The tall man used the pole to strike at where he hoped the creature would be underwater. The tip of the shaft sent up glittering splashes as he tried to land blows on the attacker. All of a sudden, the man was struggling to tug the pole free. A dozen hands had erupted from the water to grab hold of it. Helsvir was fighting back.

The next second, the tall man toppled off the boat into the water. Bobbing there, he shouted for Chester to come back for him. Suddenly, his shouts became screams. The expression of agony on his face was clear at this distance. Beneath the surface those deadly hands would be breaking the man's legs. He yelled in agony once more, then vanished – pulled down into the nightmarishly dark waters.

Chester did not stop. His head rose and fell as he pumped those shafts of wood. The boat shot over the submerged cemetery wall.

Meanwhile, a crimson stain briefly appeared on the water's surface. Tom knew that Helsvir would be breaking its victim apart before performing that secret rite of weaving the dead man's body parts into its own body. With every victim it grew more powerful.

And there were plenty of potential victims tonight.

Chester made good progress. The loss of one of his passengers had at least given them vital moments to escape. The problem was that he couldn't see the reef of gravestones just beneath the surface. Almost immediately, the boat became caught on a stone cross.

Nicola clung to Tom. He felt her tears soak through his shirt to his chest.

'They're going to be killed, Tom. Help them!'

He saw a series of slab-like tombs that lay level with the surface of the water. 'Go back into the church,' he told her.

She shook her head. 'No. *Never!*' The place obviously filled her with dread.

'OK, stay here. But don't follow me.' With that, he bounded across the stone slabs as if they were stepping stones.

The people in the boat fought to free it. And just behind them, Helsvir arrived. It could be clearly seen as it hauled itself over the cemetery wall: a massive body of corpse flesh, a whale-sized creature studded with human heads. From each head there were wide eyes that stared with cold hunger in the direction of the boat. *New victims. Fresh meat.*

Tom leapt from the slab to slab – each one larger than a desktop. Some were just below the surface, and he gambled they weren't so slippery that they'd dump him off their backs into the water. Though it wasn't deep here, he knew that the vicious creature wanted him dead. Being in that new lake wasn't a safe place to be. Tom felt the beat of danger in the air.

When he was ten feet from the boat he shouted, 'Mrs Bekk! Throw me the line!'

The woman stared at him. *She's not going to do as I say.* The reason why was obvious: the moment Helsvir destroyed Tom was the moment that Nicola would be compelled to return to her old way of life: because there'd be no Tom. No fiancé. No prospect of marriage, forever and ever, amen.

'Mrs Bekk, please!' Tom held out his hands for the line.

Helsvir entered the flooded cemetery. In fury, it slammed into gravestones, the hated symbols of Christian burial. At least that outburst of violence against the tombs slowed its progress. However, the moment the monster had vented its anger it would attack the boat once more.

'Mrs Bekk? Are you going to let these people be slaughtered? Are you going to sit there and watch them become part of that bastard?'

Her eyes fixed on Tom; there was such a grave light of despair in them, as if she knew whatever she did would ultimately lead to tragedy. Then, at last, with a deep sigh, she threw the line that was tied to the prow. Straight away, he began to haul at the craft. Chester was helping, too. He used the oar to try to push them clear of the stone cross.

Nicola screamed as she watched Helsvir violently thrashing its way through the water. Ever closer. Ever more threatening. Danger pounded through Tom's body. Any second now . . . Helsvir would rip people from the boat. A woman clung to a baby. A child wept.

The multi-headed creature that was Helsvir rose above them. A menacing tower of dripping flesh.

'*Yes!*'

Tom managed to pull the craft free. Using the flat-topped tombs as his return route, he hauled the boat full of people towards the strip of dry land. Meanwhile, Chester did his best to fend the creature off with the oar. He attacked the multitude of heads – the man had become a born-again warrior – clubbing, stabbing, slashing. Then Chester struck one of the faces with such force that blood exploded from the nose. And, as one, all the mouths opened to howl in pain.

Seconds later, Helsvir came back with renewed fury. A forest of arms reached out, and dozens of hands tugged the oar from Chester's grasp – in no time at all they'd torn it to pieces.

Tom dragged the boat up on to the grass. Nobody needed to be told what to do next: they all dashed for the church doorway. Nicola helped the woman with the baby. Tom picked up the child. That done, he raced across the strip of dry earth to the building.

A dark-haired woman of around thirty didn't make it.

Helsvir caught her up in that bristling mass of arms. They heard her screams. The crack of her breaking bones was shockingly loud. As her yells dropped to a low gurgling sound, Helsvir threw her aside. This time the creature wouldn't postpone its next attack.

Tom stood in the doorway of the church. He was ready to face the monstrosity down until everyone was inside.

Of course, the creature wouldn't be faced down; it lunged forward. A mass of faces filled his field of vision. Eyes fixed on him. Mouths yawned open. He saw jagged teeth. Before he felt the force of its impact, a dark hand gripped his arm, dragged him into the church. Then the door crashed shut.

The humans were inside, the monster was on the outside, but Tom Westonby couldn't guarantee how long that state of affairs would last. Helsvir had tasted blood. It would be hell-bent on tasting more before the night was out.

FIFTY-SEVEN

After the second boat arrived everything descended into chaos. One of its passengers, a white-haired man of around sixty, ran up the centre aisle of the church. He yelled, pointed back at the door, armed himself with a brass candlestick from the lectern; then he tried to hide behind one of the tapestries that hung from a stone pillar. The baby and the child were screaming. The mother tried to calm them without any success.

Another couple of guys were aggressively yelling at their parish priest. They demanded to know what the hell that demon was out there that had pursued them through the flooded village before killing two of their friends. Mrs Bekk sat on a pew bench. She muttered to herself in a low voice, while repeatedly shaking her head.

Nicola stared at the locked doors of the church. She seemed to be in a state of shock.

Chester pounced on Tom, slapping him repeatedly on the back while shouting, 'You're safe. Thank God you're safe. I thought you were a dead man!'

In that whirlwind of yelling people, Tom tried to assess how many had made it into the church. He counted seven men. A baby and a little girl. Four women, including Mrs Bekk and Nicola.

Wait! He took a closer look at one of the men, who sat on the

stone floor with his back to the huge timber doors. He had his arms
tightly folded; he rocked, while muttering to himself, and he was
dripping wet. What's more, his face was bloody from a dozen deep
scratches.

'Bolter!' Tom grabbed the man by the front of his denim jacket
and hauled him to his feet. 'Bolter! Have you any idea what you've
done?'

Bolter's head rolled. 'I killed you. I locked you in the room, Mr
Crappy Westonby. You drowned in there.'

Tom shook the guy like he'd shake dirt from a blanket. 'You torched
Nicola's home. I've a good mind to throw you back out there!'

Bolter grinned. His eyes had a strange shining quality – they
were so glossy that they looked as if they'd been plucked out and
dipped in olive oil, before being rammed into his blistery head again.

Tom slapped Bolter's face. 'You're going to tell me why you
attacked Nicola's house.' That slap felt so satisfying that Tom raised
his hand again.

Chester grabbed his friend's wrist to stop him hitting the thug.
'That won't help. The idiot's out of it.'

'I'll beat him sober.'

'While we were in the boat, he was cramming pills into his
mouth. He's high as a kite.'

Bolter gave a screeching laugh. 'I made sure you drowned,
Westonby. Why are you standing in front of my face?' The guy
suddenly stood up straight and held his fist in front of his mouth.
'Stay with us, ladies and gentlemen. We have breaking news. The
survivors, gathered here in St George's Church, Danby-Mask, have
been attacked by a monster. Earlier this evening it tried to kill me
– I managed to escape by bravely jumping through the roof of a
garage . . . Cut me up pretty bad . . . But I made it here to relative
safety on this new island created by the flood . . .'

Tom was amazed. The guy was actually pretending to be reporting
this live on a news channel. Maybe he really did believe that his
fist was a microphone. Even his speech became clearer as the drug-
induced delusion that he spoke to viewers took hold.

Bolter dribbled. 'There are a handful of us trapped in the church.
While the monster is out there, we cannot leave. We are under siege.
I repeat, we are besieged by the creature. To leave this building
invites instant attack. We'll be back after this short commercial
break . . .' He started to laugh. However, the laughter quickly turned

to snotty weeping. He rubbed his sleeve over the sloppy mess at the bottom of his nose.

Tom shoved him back against the door. The man slithered down on to the stone slabs; there he curled himself into a ball as he blubbered softly to himself.

Meanwhile, the din continued. This was bedlam. The mother of the children had joined the two men to harangue the priest. The white-haired man peeped out from behind the tapestry where he began to shout incomprehensible comments.

Joshua did his best to soothe them. 'Please calm yourselves. We must discuss—'

'Discuss be damned,' yelled a big, red-faced man of around fifty. He had scraggles of black hair that hung down at either side of his balding head. 'What's out there? What attacked us?'

'Phil,' Joshua said, 'Take a seat, please, we—'

'I'll be damned if I sit there jawing while there's some animal out there. What is it?'

Tom grabbed the hefty man by the elbow. 'That's Helsvir.'

'Helsvir? What the hell is Helsvir?' The man's anger made his face even redder. 'And if you don't get your hands off me, I'll rip your bloody head off.'

'Helsvir is a creature made from human corpses.'

'You expect me to believe that?'

'You saw it with your own eyes.'

'Phil,' began Joshua. 'That is a real creature.'

'No!' bellowed Phil. 'Monsters don't exist.'

Joshua spoke in a calm voice, driving the truth home. 'You saw what it did to Marjorie and to Mr Green. Whatever brought it here doesn't matter for the moment. What you need to know is that Helsvir is dangerous . . . very, very dangerous.'

Bolter sat up straight. An idiot grin slashed across his face. 'Now we're fortunate enough to have Joshua Squires, priest of this crappy parish, with an explanation of what the creature is, and what harm it can do to the human anatomy.'

Tom would have liked to kick Bolter. He resisted the temptation. Just.

Nicola gripped Tom's hand. 'Why is that thing here?'

'To stop us being together.' Tom's face was grim. 'Helsvir is the ultimate weapon that will prevent us from being a couple. Isn't that right, Mrs Bekk?'

Before Mrs Bekk could answer, a tremendous crash echoed through the church. Instantly, everyone stopped shouting. And everyone turned to the big, main door. A huge object had just slammed into it from the other side. The impact sounded like thunder.

Bolter's eyes bulged as he stared at the door. The wood slowly began to curve inwards as a huge force was exerted from the other side. Planks creaked. The huge iron bolts that locked the door shut were starting to bend.

Even Bolter's voice became hushed. 'Ladies and gentlemen – *breaking* news. The monster is *breaking* down the door. We might only have moments to live.'

Then the door suddenly jolted again. The creature must have hurled itself at the barrier. Its fury stunned the people there. They now realized that Helsvir was brutally real. What's more, they knew that if the door gave way they would suffer an agonizing death.

But Tom knew that death wouldn't be the end . . . Death would be only be the start of their nightmare.

FIFTY-EIGHT

The church door had kept out the unwanted for centuries. Now that door shuddered as the creature charged again and again. Everyone in the church watched. Even Joshua, the parish priest, gasped as one of the timbers splintered under the onslaught.

But the fact of the matter was this: even that massive door couldn't stand up to Helsvir for long. Each blow from outside sounded like thunder inside. The ancient building shook. White dust swirled from the rafters. The light from the candles became hazy.

'Do something,' shouted the woman with the baby. 'Stop it!'

The burly, red-faced man, by the name of Phil, turned on her. 'What can we do? You saw the size of the thing, you stupid bitch!'

The baby began to cry. The woman hugged the child and gently rocked it back and forth – while all the time she stared in contempt at the man who'd yelled at her.

Bolter pointed at Nicola. 'She controls it. She tells that monster what to do.'

The woman with the child stared at Nicola. 'That's Nicola Bekk, isn't it? The strange girl that never speaks.'

'Oh, she speaks alright.' Bolter had dropped the news reporter act. He advanced on Nicola, jabbing his finger in her direction. 'She tells that monster to do stuff. The bitch will have ordered it to attack the boat.'

'I didn't,' Nicola protested.

The woman with the baby stood up. 'My God, she must be the one that's making it smash down the door.'

Her point got thunderous emphasis when Helsvir slammed into the other side.

'If you control that thing, make it go away,' demanded Phil.

'I can't . . . I don't know how.'

'You better,' screeched Bolter. 'Otherwise, we'll open the door and chuck you right out there. You better be able to control it then, or it's gonna rip you—'

'Shut up.' Tom had heard enough. He put his arm round Nicola's shoulders. 'Nicola doesn't know when she's controlling it. Until tonight she didn't even believe it was real.'

'Liar!' snapped Bolter.

Mrs Bekk rose to her feet. 'It's true. Ever since Nicola was twelve she's had a kind of rapport . . . a bond of some sort with Helsvir. But it's like she's sleepwalking when she controls it. Nicola doesn't know she's giving it orders.'

The door crashed again.

Phil grunted. 'Another couple of those, and it's going to blow the door wide open.'

Tom couldn't disagree. One of the iron hinges had snapped clean through.

A deathly silence followed. The air of tension tightened everyone's nerves to the point Tom felt sure they'd soon start screaming in panic.

'Here he comes,' sang Bolter. 'Here he comes . . .'

Another crash tore through the building. The massive door buckled. The force of that blow knocked the key from the lock, sending it clattering across the stone floor.

Everyone stared at the door; they expected it to give way at any moment. Of course, that's when Helsvir would storm into the church. People clamped their hands over their ears as the furious thunder of what appeared to be fists beating at the timber grew louder and louder . . .

Nicola ran to the door; she pressed both palms against its wood-work. In a loud, clear voice she called out: 'Go away. Stop that. Stop attacking the door. My name's Nicola Bekk. I order you to stop.'

The abrupt silence that followed seemed like a physical presence. Everyone rubbed their ears, wondering if the sheer cacophony of clattering had damaged their hearing.

'See,' said the woman with the baby. 'Nicola Bekk can make it stop. She only had to tell it.' Her eyes narrowed as she stared at Nicola. 'But you never really wanted it to stop, did you? You want to watch us being torn apart by your pet!'

'You've always treated my family like vermin!' Nicola's blue eyes flashed with anger. 'You turned us into outcasts. For years, people have done their utmost to hurt our family.'

Chester shook his head in astonishment. 'Nicola Bekk can actually speak. I'm sorry I doubted you, Tom.'

However, before Tom could utter a heartfelt *I told you so*, Phil turned on Nicola. 'Even as a child you were insane. You were always running out of school in the middle of lessons. Yes, we heard what you were like. Your damn mother was just the same.'

Nicola glared at the man. 'Is it any wonder I seemed strange as a child? Every day I went to school I was bullied. Even the teachers treated me as if I wasn't human. They decided I was the peculiar little creature from the backwoods; something to be tolerated, not educated. So is it really surprising that I was too frightened to speak to other children? Or that every day I'd run home with my head down?' She raked her finger at the people there. 'Because your children threw stones at me. They chased me out of your precious village and back into the forest. Sometimes they caught me, then they pulled my hair, punched me – they made me feel that I didn't deserve to breathe the same air as them.'

In the silence that followed, the men and women stared down at the floor, too ashamed to meet her gaze. Tom realized that Nicola had made them see an important truth that they'd hidden from themselves: that the population of Danby-Mask had bullied the Bekk family for generations. The bullying and the violence had been so routine, and so deeply entrenched, that the villagers didn't even seem to realize that this habitual abuse was wrong.

Joshua spoke up: 'Nicola Bekk speaks the truth, doesn't she? You mistreated this woman and her family.'

Nobody could look the priest in the eye; they kept their gaze downward.

'If you examine your conscience, and you recognize that it would be right to ask forgiveness from this woman, then I invite you to do just that.'

Before anyone could speak, Nicola hissed, 'Don't bother. I've got better things to do than listen to their self-pity. I'm going to stop Helsvir doing what he was created to do. And that is ripping you sorry bastards apart.'

Nicola suddenly ran. At first Tom was afraid that she'd open the door, which would, of course, allow the creature to storm the building and rip its occupants to bloody pieces. However, she dashed through an archway at the end of the church. He grabbed a flashlight from the table and followed.

What was she planning to do? After witnessing her in action today, he couldn't begin to guess.

Other than it would be unexpected, dramatic, and undoubtedly dangerous.

FIFTY-NINE

Nicola must have realized that access to the church tower lay behind the archway. Tom quickly found himself following her up the spiral staircase towards the roof. *What's she going to do?* he asked himself with a growing sense of alarm. *She's not going to throw herself off the tower, is she?* An icy blast of fear ran down his spine. *Because anything seems possible tonight . . . absolutely anything. The village lies underwater. A monster has trapped us in the church . . .*

Thoughts of what might happen to those children downstairs made his blood run cold. If Helsvir attacked them? If they became part of its grotesque body? A young child's head, and a baby's head, among those heads of men and women that budded from its grey flesh? He shuddered.

Nicola paused as she climbed the steps. 'I was harsh with those people down there, wasn't I? When I told them that they'd made my life hell.'

'They needed to know the truth. You were the victim, not them.'
He stretched out his hand.

She reached back and gently squeezed Tom's fingers. He could
tell she was pleased to have him here.

'You're not thinking of doing anything too extreme up there, are
you?'

She gave a grim smile. 'When I told Helsvir to back off from
the door, it obeyed. I'm going to put my powers of command to
the ultimate test.'

'Whatever you do, don't put yourself in danger.'

She shook her head. 'That's why I'm going to do my commanding
from the top of the tower.'

'What are you going to do?'

'Tell it to disappear for good.'

'That might not work. When you've given it orders before, you've
always been in a trance.'

'You've seen me do that before, Tom?'

Quickly, he told her about the night he was attacked by Bolter
and his pals at Mull-Rigg Hall. He described how Helsvir had rushed
out of the wood to protect her. He also told her that he believed the
first time he encountered Helsvir was the night he first met Nicola.
Helsvir had flung him away into the trees as easily as if he was a
child's doll.

'All of which means,' he told her, 'is that you've got an extremely
loyal bodyguard. Helsvir has been trying his hardest to protect you
and your family.'

'You're not trying to protect *him*, are you?'

'No. But that ugly ball of hate and dead people genuinely cares
for you.'

He could tell from her expression that she was thinking about
what he'd said as she turned away to continue climbing the spiral
staircase. He followed, shining the light for her, although neither
of them could see for more than five or six feet ahead at any one
time. The spiral was incredibly tight. Anyone coming down in the
other direction would have a hell of a job passing.

Just pray we don't meet Helsvir, was Tom's ominous thought.
*Nicola might be safe, but he doesn't like me one little bit. He? Why
am I thinking of that monster as He? I need to focus on the thing
being an 'it' – an 'it' that should be destroyed.*

They climbed past the workings of the church clock. No 'tick' or 'tock' came from the mechanism. The clock's motor was dead now the power supply had failed. He could see the silhouette of the hands through the opaque glass. They'd stopped at three thirty. He checked his own watch. The time fast approached midnight. Thoughts of midnight – the witching hour – made him uneasy. Danger floated on the air. He could almost reach out and touch that sense of dread. And DANGER was getting closer by the moment.

Moments later, they passed the church bells that hung inside the tower. They were ancient pieces of cast bronze as large as a domestic fridge. The bells hung silently in the void. There was something uncanny about them – as if they wanted to shout that evil had been released into the world. For the moment, however, they were stifled. Silent. They weren't permitted to peal out their warning.

Tom shook his head. 'Damn it, this place starts to work on your imagination, doesn't it?'

'It used to work on mine,' she said. 'When I was a girl, I was convinced this church would be the place where I'd die.' With that, she pushed open the hatchway to the roof.

Tom moved quickly. He didn't want her outside by herself. What he saw made him catch his breath. The landscape had been transformed into an extraordinary realm. He stared at his surroundings in wonder.

Tom and Nicola stood on top of the tower, a full seventy feet above the ground. The lake formed by the flood stretched out for miles along the valley. A layer of thick, white mist floated above the water; the low-lying vapour was decidedly eerie as it gleamed in the moonlight. There was even less of the village to see now that the mist had joined forces with the water to engulf the buildings. Just here and there, chimneys poked up above the phantom blanket of white.

'It's beautiful,' she breathed. 'Beautiful and frightening at the same time.'

He put his arm around her delicate shoulders as she trembled. 'Helsvir's gone,' he told her.

'You think so?'

'I don't see him, do you?'

'You're calling Helsvir "him" again.'

'Force of habit.'

Her eyes were serious. 'When we refer to Helsvir by name, or call it "him", or talk about what *he's* done . . . don't you think that helps *it* embed itself in our world? I mean, the more we treat the thing as being real, the more *real* it becomes.'

'Do you think if we ignore him – it – it'll stop being real?'

'I don't know, Tom. Maybe I'm just trying to find a way – any kind of way – to make him disappear for good.' She clicked her tongue. 'There I go, calling a knotted up bunch of dead people "him".'

Embracing her, he kissed her forehead. 'Despite all this *madness*, kissing you makes me feel so warm . . . and so great inside. I want to be able to kiss you every day.'

'I want you to kiss me every day.' She gave a sad, sweet smile. 'Only, there's so much out there trying to stop that from happening.'

'We'll find a way.'

'You really want to?'

'What's that supposed to mean?' He spoke softly, but her: *You really want to?* hurt as much as sharp teeth ripping away at some sensitive part of him inside.

'What I mean,' she whispered, 'is if you left here, and went to Greece to start your diving school, then everything would be like it was before you came to Mull-Rigg Hall. You'd be safe. I'd go back to living my life with my mother.'

'Is that what you want?'

She didn't answer. Tom thought she was going to tell him it was over: that they were finished. No more kisses. No wedding. He could picture her saying: *'So goodbye and get lost.'*

Then, as he stood there with his arms round her, he felt her head go suddenly heavy. 'Helsvir . . .' she breathed. 'Helsvir. He burnt our house down . . .'

'Nicola?' Gently, he raised her head. Straight away, he knew she was slipping into that trance again. Her eyes were only part open.

'Helsvir. Come.'

Tom looked out across the mist-covered waters.

Oh . . . he's coming alright. Tom saw a shadowy object moving just beneath the mist. Like a torpedo, it sped along the flooded street. Even from up here he heard the swirl of water.

Nearer . . . nearer . . .

Nicola had summoned this supernatural bodyguard of the Bekk family. She'd told it in her own way that Bolter had destroyed her home. *There's unfinished business at the church. A crime that must be avenged . . .*

Tom knew the church door couldn't take any more punishment. Two or three full-blooded hits from the thing would smash it down. Then that ugly body of dead flesh would squeeze through the doorway in order to rip everyone apart. Chester. The adults. The children.

Gently, he shook her. 'Nicola. Wake up.'

No response. Her eyes possessed a strange dullness.

'Nicola, Helsvir's on its way!'

The monster swam closer. Tom caught glimpses of dreadful faces that bulged from its body. The eyes were wide and staring at the church.

'*Nicola?*'

The trance gripped her. 'Helsvir . . . Helsvir . . .'

'Nicola, don't let it attack the door – it won't hold out this time!'

Helsvir continued to speed beneath the white mist. The churchyard wall lay just a few inches below the surface of the water. This forced the creature to haul itself over the stonework into the graveyard. Briefly, he glimpsed the truck-sized body that was studded with dozens of human heads. A moment later, Helsvir flopped down into the deeper water that covered the path.

A second after that it hammered through the water towards the door.

'Hey! Up here! It's me you want, you ugly bastard!' Tom yelled at the creature. He waved his free hand as he supported Nicola with the other. 'Come and get me. Come on!'

He gambled on the height of the church tower saving him.

He gambled wrong.

The creature plunged towards the base of the tower. Soon it hauled itself from the water. Then it began to climb. Its dozens of human arms still possessed dexterous fingers – they dug into holes that had been weathered in the stone blocks.

Smoothly, quickly, and remorselessly, the creature scaled the tower. Tom looked down into the faces. He saw slack mouths tighten into something like grins of malicious pleasure. A myriad of white eyes glared up at him.

'Come on then,' he yelled. 'See if you can take me!' He knew this was wild bravado. He'd got nothing to fight this creature with. Helsvir would break his bones. He would become part of that gross body. Helsvir: the grim recycler. The cadaver weaver.

'What is it? Why are we . . .?' Nicola emerged from the trance. When she saw Helsvir, she stiffened.

For the first time, she saw Helsvir in all his morbid glory. The thing comprised of dozens of human bodies that had been fused together. Arms and legs had been woven like the interlocking weave of a wicker basket. Yet more arms and legs served as its limbs. And just as the carvings revealed on the walls of her house, the thing was covered in human heads – almost as scales cover a snake.

When she recognized the faces of Pug, Grafty and Nix, she screamed.

Helsvir suddenly stopped its climb. All heads turned to Nicola. The brute had heard its mistress cry out.

Then something bizarre happened. Tom realized what he witnessed now would be seared into his mind forever. Because, in a shocking moment of revelation, he knew what Helsvir reminded him of. This creature resembled a pack of dogs that looked expectantly at their mistress, waiting for a command.

If the multitude of heads could have pricked up their ears they would have done so. All faces turned to her. Every eye focused on Nicola's face. Obediently, Helsvir paused there as it clung to the wall. *He's waiting for orders.* Then the killing would start.

The order it expected didn't come. Instead, Nicola yelled, 'Go away! Never come back! Go on, make yourself scarce. Don't come back here again!'

The faces were blank – a moment of bafflement. Then all the mouths snarled at once. The body rippled as its muscles tensed.

Nicola whispered, 'It doesn't obey me when I'm awake.'

She was right. Helsvir clawed its way up the stonework towards them, hissing from its many mouths – snarling, a creature of utter rage. The sheer menace of the thing made them both flinch backwards.

The weathered stone blocks provided great handholds. Helsvir found the climb easy. Tom knew he was just seconds away from the beast launching itself on him. Nicola should be safe . . . *should be* . . . but as for him? He knew he couldn't fight this monster.

Helsvir's profusion of hands grabbed the face of the church clock in order to scale the last few feet.

That was a mistake. Its weight was way too much for the glass dial, which shattered into a thousand fragments.

Dozens of hands clawed at the tower. They tried to find handholds. However, the creature didn't move quickly enough. Tom watched as the huge body swung out from the wall. It turned end over end as it fell – then smashed into the flooded graveyard, tombstones exploded under the impact, and a ton or so of water blasted upwards into the night air. Tom didn't expect the fall to have killed Helsvir, or even to have bruised its pallid flesh. *Helsvir will be extremely difficult to kill: maybe impossible to kill.*

'Come on!' Nicola seized him by the hand.

Together they ran back into the tower. Quickly, he slammed the door shut before driving the bolts across.

'What now?' he panted.

'We do something that Helsvir and the all the Viking gods don't expect.'

'And that is?'

'We're going to get married!'

He stared. 'Married?'

'You still want to?'

'Of course. I'll move heaven and earth to marry you.'

'Then we'll get married.'

'When?'

'Now.'

'How on earth can we . . .? I mean . . .' The words died on his lips.

'We're in a church, aren't we?' Her grin was amazing – wild and beautiful and outrageous all at the same time. 'We have a priest. We even have my mother here. There's no time like the present. What do you say?'

He grinned right back. 'I say: let's go get married.'

SIXTY

The response to the news that there would be a wedding was extreme, to say the least.

The people huddled in the church were exhausted; they were terrified of being torn apart by Helsvir. This announcement stirred most of them into nothing less than fury. Mrs Bekk, however, stayed perfectly motionless where she sat on a pew. Her eyes, however, were wide with shock. That shock was more than a result of suddenly finding out she was to become a mother-in-law. Tom knew that she feared that the marriage would unleash the vengeful anger of pagan gods. Those ancient beings had protected the Bekk family on the understanding that the Bekks would stick with the old Viking religion, and have nothing to do with what the gods saw as the plague of Christianity that had wickedly destroyed the old pagan way of life.

Phil stormed up to Tom. 'Is this a joke? Have the pair of you gone mad?'

Even Chester looked riled. 'Can't you see the danger we're in? And you're talking about marriage?'

Bolter giggled. 'We have breaking news for you. The wedding of the century has just been announced.' The drugs made his movements twitchy as he paced the central aisle of the church. 'We'll be bringing you all the action as it happens.'

Joshua's grave eyes regarded the couple. 'I take it you've discovered that Nicola cannot fully control the beast?'

'Not when she's awake,' Tom said, and he told them what had happened on top of the church tower.

Joshua nodded. 'So you have both decided you should be married before it's too late . . . because, Tom, I take it that you don't believe you will survive the night.'

Phil's face turned an even darker red. 'I'm not going to watch these two play stupid little wedding games. Not while we're in danger.'

Chester shook his head. 'I agree with Phil. Whatever happens here tonight, Tom, you're not marrying that woman.'

Mrs Bekk spoke up. 'And if you do, everyone here will die.'

'None of you can stop us,' Tom told them. 'Helsvir can't stop us. We're getting married. OK?'

Phil tried a different approach. 'There's almost a dozen able-bodied people here. See all those iron light-fittings and heavy candlesticks? If we arm ourselves with those, we can take the fight to that animal. All of us attacking it together will overwhelm it.'

'You'll never overwhelm Helsvir.' Mrs Bekk shook her head. 'It will consume you all.'

Phil snarled. 'Fighting back is a damn sight better than watching these two lunatics parade about, pretending to get married. Look at 'em, they're just a pair of stupid kids.'

'They're not.' Rachel spoke with conviction as she sat with her arms protectively around the two children. They had silently watched the arguments with big frightened eyes. 'You've decided to get married now in order to save us, haven't you?'

Nicola nodded. 'A marriage is the joining of two individuals. In effect, a transformation takes place. Two people become one. They're bonded. A single unit.'

'How does that help us stay alive?' Phil's eyes narrowed with suspicion. He suspected a trick was being played on him. 'Or is marrying her, Westonby, just a way of you saving your skin?'

Tom said, 'If we swear a bond between ourselves, it must change the relationship between Nicola and Helsvir.'

'How?'

'Think about it. Part of Nicola's mind is linked to Helsvir. When she goes into a trance she can control it. I genuinely love Nicola, and planned to marry her anyway. If I marry her now, then it changes the dynamic between Nicola and the creature.'

And even if I can't control it once we're married, Tom thought, *there's a small chance that by replacing Helsvir as Nicola's protector, the cursed creature will think itself unnecessary and leave of its own free will* . . . However small a chance it was, it was one worth taking.

Chester frowned. 'How do you know this'll work?'

'We don't. It's a gamble.'

Phil snorted. 'Too much of a gamble, if you ask me.'

Tom turned on the man. 'Have you got a better idea to save our lives?'

Joshua moved into the middle of the group; the man's presence made everyone turn their attention to him. They were waiting to see what the priest said . . . clearly hoping that he had figured out a way to save their necks.

Joshua thought for a moment, then spoke in that gentle way of his: 'It seems to me that we have very few choices. After all, how do we escape from here? Our phones do not work. All the streets are flooded. We would be forced to use the boats. One thing for sure: we can't outrun the monster in those flimsy, little craft. If the beast attacks the door again, it will quickly break through. We have no weapons other than fists and candlesticks. Ladies and gentlemen, we would not stand a chance.'

Rachel hugged her children close. 'So let Tom and Nicola get married, if that's the only chance we have to make that thing go away.'

Phil's expression was sour. 'What the result will be, is that Mrs Bekk and her daughter will continue to be safe from that animal attacking them. After all, it's supposed to be their protector, isn't it? And Tom Westonby will probably be safe as well, because he'll be part of the stinking Bekk clan.'

Tom said, 'There are no guarantees this will work. But there's just the slimmest of chances that Helsvir will change its mind about attacking the church. Think about it: don't weddings bring people together who are at the ceremony? We might be creating a good relationship between all of us. If we all become friends here tonight, Helsvir might decide there's no need to kill anyone. Helsvir only exists to protect Nicola; once it knows she's protected by us all, it might simply go away.'

'Or you might just make it even angrier.' Phil's expression was grim. 'I'm still against any mock wedding.'

'It won't be a mock wedding,' Nicola protested. 'Tom and I love each other. This is what we really want.'

Joshua rubbed his jaw as he worked through some weighty problems. 'Of course, it won't be a marriage ceremony that will be valid in the eyes of the law.'

Nicola's voice rose. She sounded excited. 'What does it matter if it's not valid according to the letter of the law? We want it be valid in the eyes of those gods, ghosts – whatever they are! – that have made my family prisoners. I'm going to break this curse on my flesh and blood. I'm going to smash it into a million pieces!'

Mrs Bekk groaned. 'You will trigger the curse, Nicola. This is where you face the greatest danger.'

Joshua's gaze roamed across everyone there. 'It will be an extremely unconventional ceremony, and that's the opinion of this *extremely* unconventional priest, but I say the marriage goes ahead. I believe in taking bold risks. There is a chance that these two people being wed might spare us from that creature. Therefore, I am prepared to conduct the ceremony.'

'I say it goes ahead, too.' Rachel nodded. 'I'm for anything that saves my children.'

'You don't have a ring,' Chester pointed out.

'Here.' Rachel pulled a ring from her right hand. 'This was my grandmother's wedding ring. I only wear it because it looks nice. I want you to use this ring for what it was made for.'

'Something borrowed.' Nicola smiled. 'Thank you.'

'If this wedding gets my children out of here alive, then keep the ring with my blessing.' She smiled back. 'Consider that to be your first wedding present.'

Tom and Nicola nodded their thanks. Then Nicola handed the ring to Chester. 'Usually, it's the groom who invites someone to be the best man. But would you do us the honour, Chester?'

'Maybe it's time I started making amends.' He sighed as he took the plain gold band. 'And maybe we've deserve what's coming to us.'

Nicola took hold of his hand. 'Chester. You were always kind to me at school. You didn't join in with the others when they were being cruel.'

He smiled. 'I'll be honoured to be best man. Thank you for asking me.'

Joshua beckoned them towards the altar at the far end of the church. 'These are going to be the fastest preparations ever for a wedding. So, if the bride and groom would kindly follow me? Everyone else fall in behind.' Clearly, the priest felt happier now that he could actually perform some useful task. The man became energized; his eyes sparkled behind the white-rimmed glasses. Show time. 'Mrs Bekk, you come along, too. It's not every day that a mother sees her daughter getting married.'

The procession might have been dishevelled, exhausted, and still frightened, but it was a procession nonetheless. Burning candles cast a soft golden light on the scene. Joshua went first, leading his party along the central aisle of the ancient church. Tom and Nicola went next, walking side-by-side. After them, there was Chester Kenyon. Following him, Phil, Rachel and her children, and then the rest of the survivors, including the white-haired man who'd taken refuge behind the tapestry earlier.

Mrs Bekk followed, too. Her expression was unreadable. Tom thought he'd seen a glimmer of hope in her eye – that maybe the ancient magic, which was both the Bekks' curse and protection, could be broken.

Even Bolter tottered forwards, too – the last member of the procession.

All of a sudden, there was a piercing scream. Rachel pointed at one of the windows and shouted in panic.

Tom now realized that Helsvir hadn't left them alone, after all. Because there, pressed against a stained-glass window that depicted a sun rising over a green hill, were dozens of heads. The centuries' old panes distorted and blurred the faces. But the staring eyes were plain to see.

Helsvir had climbed up the side of the church. The protective steel mesh over the windows prevented it breaking in straightaway. Even so, it could still push itself forward against the stained glass.

'It must have been there all along!' shouted Rachel. 'That thing's been listening to what we've been saying!'

Joshua's eyes remained so solemn and wise as he said, 'Then Helsvir knows what we are intending to do. So this won't come as a shock to him.' Joshua went to stand before the altar, and as he turned to face the group he lightly touched his priest's white collar. He seemed to find reassurance in its presence around his neck. With that small ritual of his accomplished, he took a deep breath, and when he spoke, his words rang out with absolute clarity and strength: *'My friends, we are gathered here tonight . . .'*

On the other side of the window Helsvir, the monstrous protector of the Bekk bloodline, began to hiss. The same kind of menace-filled sound that a venomous serpent makes just before it attacks.

SIXTY-ONE

Joshua Gordon Squire's voice possessed such power and resonance that even time itself seemed to stop and listen: 'My friends, we are gathered here tonight to witness and to celebrate the joining together of this man and woman in matrimony. I'm not going to use the traditional Christian marriage ceremony, because this isn't a traditional marriage. I will not presume to know the religious beliefs of these two people. However, the willing and voluntary union of two people in heart, body and mind is a universal institution of human beings since the dawn of time . . .'

Tom Westonby stood before the priest, and maybe even before the Lord of Creation, and he listened to that wonderful voice say those beautiful words. Nicola stood beside Tom, the candlelight falling on to her face and shining on the pale blonde hair. He loved her more than he had ever done before. His heart beat with a measured rhythm that was strong and true.

Meanwhile, Helsvir pressed its loathsome body against the stained-glass window. Its many faces were pushed right up to the coloured glass as it stared in; the eyes were entirely white apart from their fiercely black pupils. Helsvir appeared spellbound by what it witnessed, because the creature had the stillness of death.

Joshua's melodic voice soared on the tranquil air. 'Into this union, Tom Westonby and Nicola Bekk now freely and joyously consent to be joined. And we, who are gathered here, witness the joining of this couple in marriage. Do you, Tom, take Nicola to be your wife?'

'I do.'

'Do you, Nicola, take Tom to be your husband?'

'I do.'

'Best man, hand the ring to the bridegroom, please. Tom, place the ring on Nicola's finger.'

Tom slipped the gold band on to the slender finger. He felt her hand tremble as if a numinous power had suddenly blazed through her flesh.

The creature hissed, and its faces became even more distorted as they were forced harder against the glass, as if they wanted a clearer view of what was happening inside.

Joshua's voice sang out: 'Then I declare before God, and before all these present . . .'

Helsvir's limbs suddenly struck the steelwork covering the window. The blow was so ferocious that the entire building trembled. Dust spiralled down from the roof, glittering like tiny falling stars in the candlelight.

Helsvir punched the grid again. Reverberations from the blow even made the bells tremble in the tower, producing a sustained chime that only faded away after several seconds.

Taking a deep breath, Joshua surged on; the huge boom of his voice even defeated the clatter of Helsvir striking the mesh: 'Then I declare before God, and before all these present, that you are husband and wife.' He wouldn't let Helsvir's fury deflect him from his mission. The priest smiled at the couple. 'Tom Westonby, you may now kiss your beautiful bride.'

Tom kissed her.

An absolute silence fell.

Nicola put her hands at either side of Tom's face, pulled him down towards her, and pressed her lips against his.

At the sight of the kisses, and the gold ring on her finger, Helsvir went berserk. A flurry of hands tore at the steel mesh as it screamed and bellowed.

Despite the noise, Nicola turned to the people behind her; she smiled and showed them the ring. Then she shot Tom an *OK-here-goes* look as she faced Mrs Bekk. 'Are you happy for us, Mother?'

'I wish I could be.' Mrs Bekk spoke sadly. 'I wish you could break the curse and be happy. But I know for you . . . for both of you . . . the worst is still to come tonight.'

One of Helsvir's fists punched through the window, right in the centre of the yellow rising sun in the stained glass.

'You haven't stopped it,' Phil cried. 'It's got through the mesh!'

'Breaking news.' Bolter stared in horrified fascination as a naked arm wormed through the hole in the pane. 'Breaking news! The monster is smashing its way into the church. Men, women and children are in imminent danger of death.'

Nicola spoke to Tom. 'We're married now. I'm finally your bride. We're going out there together, and we're going to face Helsvir.'

They walked quickly to the church's main entrance, pulled back the bolts, swung open the door, and went out into the moonlight.

Tom called to Chester, 'Lock this door shut. Don't open it until we come back.'

If we come back . . .

Tom, however, didn't speak the thought aloud. He was with Nicola now. They both trusted each other.

The flood hadn't risen any higher. The band of dry earth still remained around the church. As islands go, it was a small one, but at least it wasn't shrinking any further. They quickly circled the church to the other side.

There they found Helsvir ripping at the mesh. Every so often one of its forest of arms would punch another hole in the glass.

'Helsvir.' There wasn't a trace of fear in Nicola's voice. 'Helsvir. Stop this now.'

'It's time to go, Helsvir.' Tom stood side-by-side with Nicola. 'We both want you to go away forever.'

The monster had been pulsating with fury as it attacked the church window. Now it abruptly stopped. The thing even seemed to freeze as if afraid to turn round. Then the heads that budded from its pale back suddenly twisted a full one hundred and eighty degrees to face Tom and Nicola. The movement was a smooth ripple effect, almost like when a bird fluffs out the feathers on its body. Dozens of eyes locked on Tom, then they fixed on Nicola.

'I don't need you now, Helsvir.' Nicola took hold of Tom's hand and raised it so those glaring eyes could see their fingers were knitted together. 'I have a new protector.'

The beast dropped down from the window. The ground shuddered from the impact.

Helsvir advanced on them. A menacing hiss filled the air. The heads bristled from the body. Those eyes were sizing Tom up. The creature was getting ready to attack.

'No, Helsvir.' Then Nicola made such an intelligent statement of fact that the words took Tom's breath away. 'This man is Tom Westonby. He is going to be the father of my children. If you kill him, those children won't be born. And that will be your fault. I will blame you for his death. And I will blame you for ending my family's bloodline.' That's when she did something that terrified Tom to the core. Because she walked forward and rested her hand on the creature's expanse of damp, grey skin.

'Careful, Nicola. Stay away from it.'

She shot a smile back at him, which said: *it's OK, I know what I'm doing.* Softly, she continued speaking to Helsvir: 'I used to think I saw you in my dreams. Now I know you were real. And I know that we were friends. Whenever you could, you protected me. But even you couldn't follow me into school.' She gently rubbed the wet flesh as if rubbing the neck of a much-loved dog. 'I've grown up now, Helsvir. I'm no longer the little girl that needs you to keep her safe. And I've married the man I love. So I want you to take a good look at him. In a way, Tom's part of me now – just as I'm part of him. If you hurt Tom, you hurt me.'

Helsvir kept the faces locked in the direction of Tom. There was bewilderment duplicated in those dozens of eyes. Even hurt . . . Definitely sadness.

'Tom and I are going to live together . . . We'll look after each other. And we'll take care of the children we have, and we will love them with all our hearts.'

A sound came from the lips on all those faces. A pained gasp as it finally understood.

Tom finally understood too; he found himself echoing the same gasp as he realized the truth. 'Helsvir didn't just guard you, Nicola. He loved you, too.'

At that moment, Tom saw Helsvir as the faithful dog that loved his mistress and would die to save her life. But now that role had gone.

Each eye changed in the animal. Each one was shot through with pain.

'I'm sorry, Helsvir.' She stepped forward to touch it again.

This time it shrank back. An aura of absolute horror radiated from the animal. It knew its relationship with her was over. The body seemed to become smaller as it continued to shrink away from her. Helsvir soon reached the water where it continued to move backwards until the water covered it.

Tom knew it was leaving. Even when the entire body had become submerged, he could see the waves the creature made as it headed back into the flooded street. In seconds, those flurries of ripples were retreating to where the river was deepest. Then the ripples themselves faded away.

Hand in hand they walked back to the church door. Chester swung it open so they could walk inside.

'Helsvir's gone,' Tom said.

'For good,' Nicola added.

Joshua clapped his hands together. 'I knew you could do it. Indeed, love does conquer all.'

'Breaking news.' Bolter's druggie eyes gleamed. Even he was happy. 'The monster's vamoosed.'

The others clustered round. The men slapped Tom on the back. Rachel kissed Nicola on the cheek and thanked her. As Tom held on to Nicola's hand her grip suddenly tightened. He thought this was due to the powerful emotion she must be feeling right now.

But then came the dreadful moment of truth.

Bolter pointed at her face. 'Look at her eyes! What's happening to her?'

'The curse is happening to her.' Mrs Bekk's voice held such depths of sadness. 'Tom, didn't I warn you there would be consequences if you married Nicola? Now you'll have to watch your bride as she leaves this life behind.'

SIXTY-TWO

Even though the church was silent – nobody moving; everyone staring at Nicola – Tom heard thunder. This was the blood pounding in his ears as pangs of dread ran through him. *Because Nicola is changing.*

His memory summoned vivid images of Nicola's brothers and sisters in the forest. Mrs Bekk had told him that her children had been transformed into those still, silent creatures, because they'd dared turn their backs on the family legends. They'd chosen a modern life of careers, nights out with friends, and they wanted lovers that no longer believed that Viking gods were the masters of the universe.

So they'd left their ancestral home beside the River Lepping. What Nicola's brothers and sisters had not succeeded in leaving behind, however, was the ancient curse. They'd changed. Just as Nicola now changed. Into something inhuman. Into a creature that Mrs Bekk had called a vampire.

Chester, Joshua, Rachel, and the others in the church, couldn't take their eyes from Nicola. They watched in horror at what was happening to her face.

'I warned you,' hissed Mrs Bekk. 'I told you to watch out for the first symptoms of the change. This is your fault, Tom. You used that silver tongue of yours to persuade her to marry you.'

'We love each other.' Tom's eyes were locked on to Nicola's face. 'Nicola wanted to marry me as much as I wanted to marry her.'

'Well . . . you got what you wished for. Now you can witness the consequences of defying her heritage. I've seen this happen to all my sons and daughters. Remember what I told you, Tom? *It's like watching a death.*'

Bolter stared, too, with a mixture of glee and bug-eyed terror. 'Breaking news . . .' The idiot still revelled in the drug-induced delusion that he was a television reporter. 'Breaking news . . . We stand here tonight, watching Miss Nicola Bekk turn into a blood-sucking monster. You'll notice how pale her face is becoming . . . how her eyes are now being transformed. Nicola Bekk is—'

'*Shut up.*' Tom had never been so angry before. 'I don't want to hear Nicola's name coming out of your damn mouth.'

'Viewers might want to look away now. Because Nicola Bekk is turning into a monster.'

That did it. Tom threw a vicious punch. Its sheer power lifted Bolter off his feet, sending him crashing backwards to the floor.

Still nobody else moved. They hardly seemed aware that Tom had knocked the thug down. Everyone watched, with horrified fascination, as Nicola Bekk stopped being Nicola Bekk. They felt themselves compelled to see what she became.

Bolter lay there with blood spewing from his mouth. Tom didn't give a damn what happened to that piece of crap. Instead, he focused his senses on Nicola. Because his new bride changed by the second.

Bolter had been right about her skin colour. Her face paled until it became absolutely white . . . Somehow the whiteness was shocking: a strange, luminous white that didn't even seem like human skin any more. Meanwhile, the blue leeched away from her eyes.

By the light of the candles, Tom saw the pupils of her eyes contract into fierce, black points. The veins in her neck darkened, too. Within moments, a swirling pattern had formed on her throat; something like black tattooed lines. An eerie map that traced the route of her transformation from a beautiful, lively woman to this dead-alive statue.

Nicola didn't move. She didn't even seem to breathe. Even though she'd done nothing and said nothing since this began, Tom could tell that her personality was undergoing a transformation, too. A mind profoundly different to the one he'd known, and grown to love, slowly and relentlessly took control of her slender body.

As Bolter hauled himself to his feet, he started chuckling. 'Breaking news . . . Mr Tom Westonby is just moments away from death.'

SIXTY-THREE

'Run, Tom. Go away. Don't come back. You've got to go now.' Nicola oh-so-gently whispered the words. Her eyes were completely white apart from a black dot in the centre of each one. Those fierce pupils fixed on him. 'You must go while I can still stop myself.'

'Stop yourself from what?'

'You know what, Tom. Hurting you . . . *hurting you.*'

Nicola stood near the church door. Her skin had become alabaster – a whiteness that was eerily luminous. While her veins were now the blackest of black.

He gripped hold of her hands. 'You can still fight this. The Viking gods are finished. They aren't worshipped any more, their temples have gone. They're nothing. Please, Nicola. Don't let them do this to you.'

'I . . .' She gasped with pain. 'I don't think I can stop this happening to me, Tom.'

Mrs Bekk's eyes filled with tears as she witnessed her daughter's transformation. This was agony for her. 'I told you it would be like watching the death of someone you love.'

'Mrs Bekk. We both love Nicola. Help me stop this happening to her.'

'I can't, Tom. There's nothing we can do. Your bride is becoming a vampire.'

Chester watched in horror. He was flanked by the others in the church – Joshua, Phil, Rachel, and the rest. They were appalled. Bolter, on the other hand, rubbed his blistered face in glee. He could have been a man who'd just realized he'd won the lottery jackpot.

'Get her out of the church,' Bolter shrieked happily. 'Get *it* out of here!' He pulled open the big timber door. 'Get that bastard monster off holy ground. That's right, isn't it, priest?'

'We've got to help her.' However, even Joshua sounded doubtful as he stared at those egg-like eyes of Nicola's.

'She's a vampire. Get her out!'

Tom raised a clenched fist.

'Go on,' screeched Bolter. 'Hit me again. *Keep* hitting me. But you can't stop her becoming a vampire by beating me up, can you?'

'He's right,' Chester said. 'She's changing by the minute.'

Bolter shoved his blood-smeared face towards Tom. 'Everyone's going to find out what the Bekk family really are. They're a pack of dirty, disease-filthy vampires.' His voice became gloating. 'These two bitches are going to be locked away in some big laboratory. There'll be iron bars, electric fences—'

'Shut up.' Tom got ready to punch that grinning face.

'Scientists are going to sweat themselves into a frenzy when they get their hands on your wife, Tom . . . aren't they just?'

'I'm warning you!'

'I'm only saying what these people are thinking – even the God-loving priest there. Scientists are going to autopsy that bitch of yours while she's still alive.'

Bolter's words stung Tom. He wanted to beat the brains right out of the man's ugly head. However, Tom's big problem was this: *I know that Bolter is right.*

Meanwhile, Bolter poured on the torture. The sadist enjoyed his moment of glory: 'Listen, Westonby. The scientists and the doctors are going to carve up your pretty girl bit by bit. They'll cut away her skin. They'll pop out her eyes. They're going to yank out her guts. Then they're going to formaldehyde them, and they're going to get all those bits of flesh that you love so much, slice 'em nice and thin, then whack 'em under a microscope.' He laughed in Tom's face. 'And then they'll make television documentaries about your beautiful vampire wife.'

'No!' Tom grabbed hold of Bolter and hurled him through the door.

Straight away, Tom went to Nicola, holding out his arms so he could protectively embrace her.

'Don't touch me.' She flinched away from him. 'You can never touch me again. It's impossible.'

Bolter squealed as he stumbled back into the church: 'Good news! The rescue team's here. We're getting off our poxy island. And the vampire bitch will be going straight to autopsy hell.' He beckoned with a furious, hyper intensity. 'Come-see! Come-see!'

Tom strode to the door where he flung Bolter aside. His heart pounded as all kinds of ideas stormed through his head: *I can help Nicola. There must be a way to stop her turning into a vampire. We could stay in the church. Maybe sacred ground's the antidote. Perhaps the vampire curse will burn itself out here. And Nicola will be my Nicola again . . . She'll be OK . . . She'll be saved . . .*

The arrival of a rescue team would spoil everything. Yet if he could hide her away in the church, he might find the means to smash the Viking curse. Joshua would help him. Wouldn't he?

Tom snuffed out the candles next to the door.

Chester was bewildered. 'What are you doing, Tom?'

'We can't be rescued yet.'

'Can't be rescued? We want to be rescued!'

Joshua agreed. 'Son, these people need warm food and sleep.'

Rachel hugged her children close. 'Why not give Tom a little more time? He and Nicola saved us from that animal. We owe them the—'

'No way in hell.' Bolter was enjoying this. He finally had power over these people. 'That vampire bitch's got to be locked up.' He smirked. 'Won't anyone think of the children?'

Tom looked out over the floodwater. Bright moonlight clearly revealed a rescue team dressed in orange survival suits. They carried inflatable boats downhill to the water's edge. Soon they'd reach the church here on its island.

Maybe there's still time to help Nicola before they arrive? After all, they're bound to search the flooded houses before they come here. With that thought in mind, he gently closed the door – not wanting the bang of timbers to alert the rescuers.

'What are you doing?' Chester must have wondered if his friend had gone mad. 'This isn't a safe place, Tom.' He shot a glance in Nicola's direction that packed a hell of a lot of meaning. Meanwhile, her eyes acquired a hungry gleam as she watched the baby in Rachel's arms. 'We've got to signal those people with the boats.'

'No.' Tom shook his head. 'Please wait a while. I really believe I can help Nicola beat this.'

'Tom, are you crazy?'

'You heard what Bolter said. He's right. The government will lock Nicola away; they'll do experiments on her. They'll want to find out why she's turned into . . .' He sighed as words failed him. 'Don't you see? The military will cut her to pieces just on the off-chance they can find some way of making a weapon out of her.'

Chester said, 'What if Nicola attacks the children? Can you live with that on your conscience?'

Tom pleaded with them, 'Don't draw the rescue team here yet.' He snuffed out more candles, so the light wouldn't be seen. 'We can hold out until the morning. That gives me a few more hours to find out how to make Nicola human again.'

'Just look at her, Tom.' Joshua was trying to make him see what was obvious to everyone else. 'Look at the skin. Look at her eyes. All the colour has gone. She's already been transformed.'

'I'm begging you. Don't bring the boats here yet. Just give us a few more hours together . . . I don't want to lose her.'

Rachel spoke up: 'I'm frightened. I'm more frightened than I can say. But let Tom stay here until the morning. We must give them a chance.'

'I have an office here in the church.' Joshua was relenting. 'Nicola could remain there. She'd be away from the children.'

Bolter sneered, 'That gives her the chance to kill us all . . . or to turn us into her vampire pals – that's how it works, doesn't it?'

Chester appeared to be struggling with his conscience, then he sighed. 'OK, OK, we don't let the rescue team know we're here. Give Tom and Nicola until morning.'

Bolter grabbed the flashlight from the table. 'You're a bunch of jerks. I'm going to bring those people over here – NOW!' He brandished the flashlight. '*Hey! Does anyone know how to spell SOS?*'

With a screeching peel of laughter he raced towards the entrance to the tower. Seconds later, the clatter of his feet rang out as he ran up the spiral staircase.

Tom knew he had to catch up with Bolter. Whatever it took – the man must be stopped from bringing the rescue team to the church.

SIXTY-FOUR

Tom Westonby climbed through the hatch at the top of the church tower. The powerful stench of the flood hit him – that thick, dark soup of mud, river water, rotting plants and engine oil from the cars it had drowned. Moonlight seemed to blaze as bright as the sun. He knew this was an effect of the adrenalin pounding through his veins to ramp up his senses. Also, he clearly heard the lap of water. Soft clicking sounds, as if dozens of lips were gently kissing the gravestones in the cemetery below.

Bolter stood on the flat roof of the church tower. The roof itself was so small it could be easily crossed in eight paces. Tom's heightened senses captured the scene. Bolter fumbled with the flashlight switch, trying to find the on-button. He was film on fast-forward. His movements were incredibly quick. They were totally uncoordinated, too. The thug must have gulped down a few of his pills on the way up here.

His jerky, high-speed hands suggested that those illegal, home-cooked amphetamines were roaring through his body. Bizarre muscle twitches made his blistered face look like a living creature that was completely separate from him. His mouth chewed the air, while his eyes bulged so far from their sockets they resembled sticky, wet domes.

'*How'd ya make this work?*' Bolter's voice was a motor running out of control. '*How d'ya switch it on!*'

'Give me the flashlight, Bolter.' The moment the thug found how to work the on-switch would be the same moment that the rescue team saw the light at the top of the tower. They'd be here in moments. When they found Nicola they'd take her away. That was, if she didn't attack them first . . . Either way, the consequences would be terrible. Tom would lose his wife of barely an hour. 'Bolter. Don't switch that thing on.'

'I'll do it!' he screeched. 'Those bastards over there won't be able to miss this light when – *whoosh!* – it goes blazing out all over the place. They'll come across . . . They'll take your dirty bitch away . . . Damn it! How do you make this work? Do you press, or slide the switch?' In nothing less than a wild frenzy, he tugged and pressed the switch. Sweat poured down his forehead. The eyes jutted from his face like they were just about to go *pop*.

Tom crossed the roof. He was determined to get the flashlight from him. He wanted to do this calmly, because if Bolter started yelling like crazy then the rescue team would certainly hear. Tom caught glimpses of people in fluorescent orange suits preparing the boats. Soon they'd fire up the powerful outboards.

Tom spoke gently: 'Bolter. Please give Nicola a chance.'

'Why should I?'

'Your family haven't always hated the Bekks.'

'They have.'

'Listen—'

'We've hated them for a thousand years. The Bekk rats are thieves, liars, swindlers.' He battled with the flashlight switch; his fingernails started to bleed. 'Make this bastard work.'

'I'm begging you. Give me this one chance to save Nicola.'

'I know what you're scheming. You want us to give her enough time to make the full change into a vampire. So she can rip out our throats.'

'The Bekk family aren't evil.'

'You freaking idiot, Westonby. They conned you. Nicola Bekk duped you into marrying her, just days after meeting her. Witchcraft, man. They're all evil.'

'Mrs Bekk was engaged to your uncle.'

'*What!*'

'Didn't you know?'

'That's a lie.'

'They were going to get married.'

Bolter froze. The only part of him that moved was his face. Tremors ran through its flesh. Muscles actually vibrated under that blotchy skin, while the red blisters on his jaw seemed to pulsate like a row of strange little hearts.

'Mrs Bekk told me.' Tom spoke calmly, trying to damp down Bolter's anger. 'Your uncle loved her. If they'd been allowed, they'd have got married. Mrs Bekk would have been your aunt.'

'Liar!' Bolter lashed out.

The heavy flashlight slammed into the side of Tom's face. The explosion of pain made him stagger. Even so, he tried to rip the flashlight from Bolter's hands. But he found he couldn't even keep his balance never mind tackle the thug. When the moon started racing around the sky that's when he realized he was spinning.

I won't be able to stop him. He's going to signal the boats. The thought flowed through his head so clearly. He knew he'd failed Nicola. He wouldn't have those precious hours that would have allowed him to find a way to break the curse. To stop her turning vampiric.

'Bolter. Don't . . . . please . . . you don't have to . . .' His voice slurred.

When Bolter grabbed him by the throat he couldn't stop himself from being pushed back against the low wall that enclosed the roof of the tower. Seventy feet below him, the flooded graveyard gleamed in the moonlight. Tomb markers jutted up through the water. Rotting teeth of stone.

The blow had dazed Tom. He felt something wet running from a gash in the side of his face. Although he tried to stop Bolter from pushing him, his strength had gone. His knees were giving way.

Bolter rammed his bulging eyes right up to Tom's. 'Switch on the light for me, or I'm going to let you fall off the top of this bloody tower. Then: pop, pop, pop go Tom's bones. Drip, drip, drip goes Tom's blood. Gone, gone, gone goes poor Tom's life.'

Tom panted; his head was spinning. 'Bolter . . . no light. Give Nicola a chance.'

'Nope. I'm going to watch you fall all the way down there.' He grinned, and his breath had the same revolting stink as old milk. 'After that, I'll enjoy watching you lying there dead for a while. Then I'll make this flashlight work. The light will bring those people across here. They'll take Nicola Bekk away for her living autopsy. Snip here. Cut there. She's going to suffer. Oh, I wish I could watch her there on the dissecting slab. Your wife's gonna scream and writhe . . . Hmmm, lovely image, isn't it?'

Bolter pushed Tom. There was nothing Tom could do to stop him. The blow had mangled his senses. He couldn't make his arms work. His entire body was saggy, as if the life had already gone out of it.

'Bye-bye, you tiny squirt of shit.' Bolter's words came in a slow ooze. He was enjoying this. 'I'm going to watch you fall all the way down. Splat! This is going to be so amazing.'

'Let him go!'

When Bolter heard the voice, he twisted his head back. Tom heard him gasp with shock. The man had seen something terrifying.

'Don't you *dare* hurt him!'

There – emerging from the hatchway and on to the roof – was Nicola. Her white face seemed to blaze in the moonlight. The blue had completely vanished from her eyes. A pair of vicious black pupils had fixed on Bolter.

'You're too late, vampire bitch.' Bolter regained his bravado; or the drugs he'd swallowed regained it for him. 'Tom's taking flying lessons.'

Bolter pushed harder. Tom could feel himself begin to topple over the wall. Seventy feet beneath him lay hard ground that stood clear of the floodwater. His bones would shatter.

Bolter screeched with joy: 'He's going . . . I can feel it! The bastard's going over!'

Nicola pounced. She didn't touch Bolter. Instead, she grabbed hold of Tom. A second later she hauled him to the middle of the roof, well clear of the edge.

'Bitch!' yelled Bolter; then he came at her, swinging the flashlight as if it were a club.

Nicola moved faster. She flung herself at Bolter. He tried to scream, but she had the heel of her hand under his chin, and all he could manage was a feeble croaking sound. She pushed his head back as she forced him to the wall at the roof's edge. She kept pushing until his back arched over the parapet. His feet scuffed and scraped at the roof as he tried to regain his balance.

Tom shook his head, trying to get rid of that dizziness. With a huge effort, he managed to rise to his knees.

Then he watched what his bride did next to the terrified man.

Nicola pushed harder – her hand under Bolter's chin forcing his head right back. His throat rose into a thick, bulging curve of flesh. His veins plumped up. They were raised against the skin, clearly visible, and swollen with blood.

That's when Nicola opened her mouth. Slowly, very slowly, she lowered her lips towards that plump, naked throat, which gleamed in the moonlight. She gazed at the throat in the same way that someone gazes at their lover's face. Noticing the little details. A total adoration of each feature. In this case, Bolter's veins, which stood proud of the skin.

She's going to bite him. Tom stared in absolute shock. *She wants his blood.* The thought filled him with disgust.

'Not Bolter,' he gasped. 'Not his . . . take mine.' He managed to climb to his feet. 'I'm your husband. You can have mine!'

With a snarl, Nicola suddenly stepped back. But only so she could rush forward.

She pushed Bolter.

Tom watched as the man toppled over the low wall. He didn't have time to scream.

By the time Tom reached the edge of the tower Bolter had already slammed into the ground.

No . . . not quite. Tom's eyes absorbed a deeply gruesome scene. The man hung suspended two feet or so above the earth. He'd landed face-down on a set of ancient iron railings that surrounded a group of tombs. Ornamental spikes had pierced his body; their rusty tips protruded from his back along the full length of his spine. Blood poured from his body to the ground where it trickled along one of the cemetery paths to eventually merge with the floodwater.

Bolter wasn't a problem any more.

No. Nicola demanded his full attention now.

How am I going to save her?

SIXTY-FIVE

S *o this is it*, he told himself. *This is my chance to make every-thing alright.*

Bolter lay impaled on the iron fence. The moon shone down on the water, and Tom Westonby stood with his bride on top of the church tower. He now had his golden opportunity. Joshua would help him find a way to break the curse of the Viking gods. A curse that had blighted the lives of the Bekk family for centuries.

Tom turned to Nicola. Her fair hair now seemed almost dark compared with the extreme paleness of her skin. Her eyes were white globes. Each one possessed a sharp black dot that was the pupil. She was still beautiful. Really beautiful. He found himself leaning towards her, aching to feel her body pressed against his.

As Tom drew closer, he saw the way Nicola had fixed that penetrating gaze of hers on the cut on his face. Or, rather, she fixed her gaze on the blood seeping from the wound.

His blood. He felt it trickling down his cheek.

Her mouth parted as if ready to kiss him. She moved closer, too. He could feel the beat of blood pulsing through the arteries in his neck. His wife looked so uncannily beautiful. *I want this . . . I want to hold her . . .*

Abruptly, she froze. 'No, Tom,' she whispered. 'I mustn't let you touch me.'

'Your mother said you'd turn into some kind of monster. But, don't you see? You know what you're doing. You can beat this.'

'I feel different inside. That's where the important change is happening.'

'Fight it. Don't let yourself be controlled by those things that your ancestors worshipped. You are Nicola Westonby. You are strong. *You decide your own actions.*'

'Nicola *Westonby*. I didn't dream it? I really did get married?'

'Yes, you married me. We've got the rest of our lives together. What you must do now is destroy this thing that's attacking your body and making you change.'

Her brow furrowed. Tom sensed that she pushed against some

powerful force. She struggled to resist the evil that had begun to spread through her veins and her flesh.

She gave a sudden cry of pain. 'I'm sorry, Tom . . .'

'Fight it, Nicola.'

'I can't fight it any more. I've tried. I've been trying ever since we got married. I can't, though. It's too strong.'

'Try.'

'I'm so sorry, Tom.'

Then she gave him a look that drove a penetrating coldness through his body. Because Tom had seen that exact look before on another face he'd loved. The same expression of regret was on his grandmother's face as she lay in a hospital bed. She'd been battling cancer for months, and there had always been a fiery spark of defiance in her eye. Not that day, though, when the family gathered at her bedside; her eyes were growing dull and faraway. 'I'm so sorry,' she'd whispered. 'I can't fight the cancer any more. I'm going to have to let it take me . . .' An hour later his grandmother was dead.

Now the same expression poured from those other-worldly eyes of Nicola's. She'd fought and she'd fought. Now she couldn't fight the curse any more.

'Tom, forgive me. This is too strong now. I'm going to keep changing. And then I will hurt you. The worst of it is I'll *know* that I'm hurting you, but I won't be able to stop myself.'

'Nicola, we can make you well again.'

'No, Tom.' There was such deep sadness in the slow shake of her head. 'I know I can't resist it. You must be strong and let me go.'

Earlier that day, he'd watched the river engulf the village; now he felt an overwhelming emotion engulf him. The grief hurt so much that he wanted beat his fists against the stone wall. Broken bones, however, couldn't hurt any more than this sense of desolation and loss.

'Let me go, Tom. This is the only way now.' Her voice became tougher. 'Don't you dare make me suffer by allowing me to hurt you. Because I will – I know I will. The curse is turning me into a vampire. So, when the moment comes for me to leave, say "goodbye" and keep smiling as you say it.

'Nicola, please . . .'

'When all this is over I'll keep remembering your smile. That will be something I can hold onto.'

'Just give me one more hour.'

'No, Tom. I have to go now, while I still have control over what I do.'

He knew she was right. Even so, he felt incredibly bleak inside, and he dreaded what the next few minutes would bring. 'OK, how do we do this?'

'I'll go down and call for Helsvir. He always did his best to protect me in the past. I'm sure he will again.'

'But you'll be condemned to exist like some wild animal.'

'Remember, Tom. When you say "goodbye", smile. Keep smiling until I can't see you any more.'

With a heavy heart Tom followed her down the steps and back into the ancient building. Chester, Joshua, and the others stood at the far end of the church near the altar. Mrs Bekk watched Tom and Nicola. Her expression was clear: she knew what her daughter intended.

Tom thought Nicola might have said her farewells to her mother. However, she moved faster now – an urgency gripped her. Time was running out.

Within seconds, they were outside on the strip of dry ground. Tom could see lights moving along the flooded backstreets. Rescuers were searching the houses there before venturing into the village's centre. Fortunately, Bolter's corpse lay on the far side of the tower; at least they'd be spared his presence, even in death, when they said their goodbyes.

'Helsvir.' Nicola's call sounded so light, and so normal. She could have been gently calling a dog to her. 'Helsvir.'

'We convinced him to leave,' he said. 'Helsvir won't come back.'

She gave a stuttering sigh. Her body stiffened. The changes to her flesh – and to her mind – were accelerating.

'*Helsvir. Come.*'

Tom wished the creature wouldn't come back. These were his last few moments with his wife. Just days ago he'd met Nicola – and they'd been such magical, enchanting days. He'd fallen in love with her; what's more, he'd soon decided she was the person who would be at the centre of his life. He'd fought some bitter battles as well: with his father, with Chester, and with Bolter. And he'd finally won through. He'd married Nicola tonight. Now this bitter twist of fate. They'd finally been defeated by an ancient curse that was intended to safeguard the Bekk family bloodline. Yet that curse had ultimately ended a dynasty. There would be no more Bekk children after Nicola.

How ironic.

And he still loved her so much. *Love conquers all.* But that glib phrase now ripped wounds across his heart. Love hadn't conquered this monstrous change in Nicola.

'Helsvir, come.'

Nicola anxiously scanned the floodwater with those eerie eyes. She wanted so much for Helsvir to surge from the depths.

Don't come, was Tom's desperate thought. *Don't show yourself here.*

Because I'm having one last good time before I die. One last happy moment with Nicola before they nail down the lid . . . That's what it felt like. This was like *his* death. Because he was losing Nicola forever.

She gasped with pain. 'I can't stay here, Tom. I don't even feel like *me* any more.'

'We could go back inside for a while?' *Any excuse to delay the inevitable . . . Just a few more minutes together . . .*

But his wife was having none of it. Nicola firmly shook her head. 'Tom, I'm leaving you tonight. I don't want to, but there's no turning back. The Viking gods might have lost most of their power, but boy-oh-boy do they know how to hold a grudge.' A ghost of a smile had appeared on her lips as she said those words, then she added with grim emphasis, 'If those evil, mean-spirited gods of my ancestors get the chance to make human beings suffer then that's exactly what they're going to do. That is their nature – they demand vengeance at any cost. I rejected them, and their so-called protection, and now they're punishing me.'

Once again, he had to force himself not to reach out and embrace her with a comforting hug.

'Helsvir,' she called. 'Helsvir, come.' The moonlit waters were smooth. No sign of the creature. Then came the moment he'd dreaded. 'I'll leave in the boat,' she told him. 'The current will carry me far enough away so I can't hurt you.'

Tom seized the moment to embed this scene in his memory: *here's the church where I married the woman I love. And this is the final time that I'll stand close enough to kiss her.*

Even so, he was deprived of that intimacy. If he kissed Nicola, then maybe that would break down the last barrier of her resistance and the change to vampire would be complete. No, he wouldn't risk that, because Nicola was so scared of losing control and harming him.

So Tom Westonby did what had to be done.

Quickly, he grabbed the prow of the boat and pulled it up higher on to dry land, so Nicola could step in. As he did so, one of his feet slipped into the water. He felt its wetness against his skin. The trivial accident seemed to anchor the tragedy of what was happening to reality. And seeing his wife step into the boat was even more heartbreakingly real, because he'd done something as mundane as getting his foot wet.

Here goes . . .

Gently, he pushed the boat. At first it scraped across the ground, then everything became fluidly smooth as it glided across the flooded graveyard.

He watched her – so pale and still in the moonlight. A slender figure standing in the prow of the boat. And she watched him. He knew she was locking the scene inside her own memory. What she saw now – her husband standing there – would last her for an eternity.

Tom raised his hand in farewell. 'Nicola – I'm smiling. Can you see? Just like you asked, I'm smiling.' He wished he could sink into the earth to join the dead in their graves and be at peace. But he forced himself to keep smiling. 'Goodbye, Nicola. I love you.'

The boat drifted out over the submerged wall of the graveyard. Currents caught hold; soon they were carrying the little vessel, and Nicola, along the flooded street towards the part of the valley, which lay in shadow. He didn't let the smile die for a moment. With sheer force of will he held that smile on his lips.

Moments later, the water stirred beside the boat as a glistening, rounded hump appeared.

Helsvir . . .

He watched Nicola step from the boat on to the back of her old friend. Slowly, she lowered herself until she sat astride its back. A girl on a steed from a magic dream. Helsvir would protect her now. He would know a safe place.

And so Nicola, his beautiful Nicola, the last child of the Bekk dynasty, rode the magnificent dragon of the Vikings away into the valley. They seemed to be passing out of this world and into a world where ancient gods were as real as a wet foot in a sodden shoe.

Where dreams had the bite of reality. Perhaps to a place where people that we have loved, and who have died, wait patiently for us to cross over that bridge, which we build from love.

He watched until she'd gone – and all that remained on the water was shadow. He stood there and watched until the sun rose.

And then even the shadow was gone.

SIXTY-SIX

Six months later . . .

The flood had gone. So had Nicola Westonby.

Tom mixed up a batch of mortar for the rebuilding of the living-room wall. This was Skanderberg, and this is where he lived now. Or, more accurately, he lived in the timber cabin behind the house. The fire that Bolter had started six months ago, on the same day the flood raged through Danby-Mask, had badly damaged the part of the house that contained the kitchen and living room.

Tom reclaimed masonry from the fallen walls, cleaned it, then used the stone blocks to rebuild the ancient structure. He loved the solitude. A forest in winter has its own serenity. Every morning, when he made breakfast, he'd watch red deer from his cabin window as they nuzzled among the fallen leaves for shoots.

Mrs Bekk lived in the converted barn next door to Mull-Rigg Hall. His parents and Owen had moved into the main house. They were happy there. What's more, they were happy that Tom was friends with his father again. In the summer, Chester Kenyon had married Grace, and Tom had been best man. Now the couple expected their first child. The dive school had opened in Greece, although Tom played no part in the business, which was operated by Chris Markham. Quietly, he and Chris were going their separate ways. After all, friends occasionally drift apart without a trace of envy or bad-feeling – so, no worries. It's OK. That's just the way life flows sometimes.

More than anything, Tom found contentment living out here in the wilderness. He looked forward to rising early every day in order to gradually reassemble the Bekk family home. He sincerely believed Nicola would be proud of him for rebuilding Skanderberg.

Three days ago, he'd collected twenty straight-backed chairs from Mull-Rigg Hall. Then, as if preparing for some quirky woodland concert, he'd set them out amongst the trees that grew just beyond the garden fence.

Today, Tom hoisted a particularly special stone back into place. There it was again: the carving of Helsvir that must have been made by one of Nicola's ancestors a thousand years ago. Unlike the weather-worn image on the archway out there in the garden, the lines that formed the creature in this etching were sharp and crisp. He could clearly see the circles that adorned its flanks and back – those circles were its many heads. An array of limbs bristled from beneath its large body. Tom Westonby had grown to like Helsvir, even though he'd not seen it since that night in the flooded village. After all, the creature was taking care of Nicola now. Wherever she was. Because he'd never seen her with her vampire brothers and sisters, who seemed content to mysteriously reappear from time to time in order stand out in the forest at midnight . . . as still as death, and never speaking.

After the flood, Danby-Mask, and this remote valley, had returned to their ways of age-old seclusion. If anyone should mention rumours of eerie figures glimpsed in the forest, or the day a gigantic creature prowled the village's flooded streets, then such sightings were judiciously dismissed as *that's just the ale talking*, or the result of a practical joke played by mischievous children.

When Tom was satisfied that the carving was level in its wall niche, he applied mortar to the edges of the slab. He worked so diligently, and was so wrapped up in memories of Nicola – especially when she'd told him how she'd played amongst those chairs at Mull-Rigg Hall as a child – that he didn't notice night had fallen.

Winter had pulled darkness into the forest so quickly that he could barely find the path back to the cabin, even though it stood no more than forty paces from the cottage.

On the way he saw her. A lone figure sitting on one of those straight-backed chairs that he'd brought from his parents' house and placed amid the trees. The beautiful woman was as pale as the moon; her blonde hair fell softly over her shoulders; those white eyes of hers carefully watched his face.

Nicola remained in the chair for only a moment. Then she disappeared as fast as a blink of an eye – some malicious force had tugged her back to wherever that enemy of love had banished her.

Yet he knew in his heart of hearts that she was trying to find a way back to him.

And just as she had been transformed into a vampire six months ago, wasn't there a chance that she could change back into that most wonderful of human beings again in the future?

Yes – and YES again.

Of course, this was just the start of Nicola's return journey. This wouldn't be easy. There'd be a host of obstacles, problems and dangers to overcome before he was fully reunited with her. Nevertheless, at the same moment as snowflakes started to fall through the trees to brush against his face, he knew that all-important flame of hope had begun to burn inside of him.

Tom Westonby also knew that he'd never let the precious flame die. Not while he had life in his body and breath to speak the name of his bride.